A KINGDOM OF FROST AND MALICE

THE WINTER COURT SERIES

A CROWNS OF MAGIC UNIVERSE SERIES

ASHLEY MCLEO

MERAKI PRESS

Editing by Enchanted Quill Press

Proofing by Owl Eye Edits

Cover by Sanja Gombar

Chapter art by Anna Spies of Altra Luna Art

Map by Cartographybird Maps

Ebook ISBN: 978-1-947245-81-5

Paperback ISBN: 978-1-947245-88-4

CONTENT WARNINGS

This book contains violence and fighting.

There is a make-out scene in book one. In future books in the series the steam level will increase to sex on the page. This is *not* a young adult series, but rather a slow burn, steamy adult series.

FOREWORD

Dear reader,

At the back of the book there are reference pages.

One details the nine kingdoms of Isila.

The other dives into the greater noble houses of Winter's Realm. If, while you're reading, you want to know more about the Sacred Eight families, that's where you will find the information.

Welcome to Winter's Realm,

Ashley

Want the playlist that inspired A Kingdom of Frost and Malice to listen to while you read? It's on Spotify.

CHAPTER I

I rushed down the vampire-infested streets of Sangrael, my heart thrumming wildly.

Most days, I'd take care to move more slowly, to not draw a predator's attention. But this week my desire to soak away the pain shooting up my fingers and forearms made me act rashly. Even if the relief wouldn't last long.

Tomorrow night, Palais Immortael would host a ball. That meant that the noble vampires of the court required new gowns, tunics, and jackets, and my master would happily accommodate them. As one of his best seamstresses, I'd been working double-time for the past three weeks, and tomorrow would be the longest day of them all.

Working day and night was bad enough, but the noble vampires didn't only require fashionable attire. No, they needed party food too. Earlier the same day, I'd given two full cups of blood destined for the palace. Though I'd eaten a small lunch since then, I continued to feel the effects of the bloodletting, but at least that was all I had to do. I counted my blessings that I wasn't one of the many slaves forced to serve the ball's attendees in person.

I swung a tight corner around a tavern to avoid a group of gossiping vampires hogging the street, only to nearly run into a particularly nasty-looking bloodsucker. He eyed my wings hungrily, making me tense as I side-stepped him and ran on. A few paces later, I glanced behind me and a shiver darted down my spine.

The vampire continued to watch me, his eyes trained on me like I was a mouse and he the cat, but he wasn't pursuing. Clearly, he'd noticed my red collar. The symbol of my oppression sometimes also saved me from lower-ranking vampires attacking in the streets.

Finally, I reached bathhouse 9, one of many slave bathhouses in the city of Sangrael. Only the wealthiest masters spared the expense to send their slaves to number 9, and despite hating my general position in life, I counted myself lucky to get to use this bathhouse in particular. While the front of the bathhouse resembled a regular business, it wasn't one. Natural thermal pools nestled in a vast interconnected cave system awaited inside, making bathing here a more soothing experience than at the lower end houses.

I opened the front door, and immediately the steam and tang of minerals from the natural pools calmed me. I exhaled, relieved to have arrived without incident.

"Your master's name, girl?" asked a red-haired human guard behind a long desk. All day long, he stood in a small business front attached to the mouth of the cave and deemed whether others were good enough to enter the caverns. A second bald man was present today too, rifling through paperwork.

I ignored the condescension in the human's tone when he'd called me '*girl*'. At twenty-three turns of the sun, I was a grown fae female, probably no more than three turns this human's junior. But he had to make himself feel bigger somehow, and the fight wasn't worth it. All I cared for was a bath.

"Lord Aldéric Laurent." I waited for the first man to check the ledger, while the bald one peered up from his papers to look me over. His gaze lingered on my wings for many uncomfortable seconds, and a hard glimmer sparked in his beady eyes as he licked his dry lips. I recoiled.

The humans given the job of regulating the bathhouses and other establishments used by blood slaves were a nasty sort. Because the House of Laurent gave them a uniform and a sliver of authority, they thought of themselves as better than the rest of the slaves. As if they weren't just another bag of flesh to be drained.

"Lord Laurent's account is in good standing," the first guard said. "What's your name?"

"Neve."

"No number?" He looked at another sheet, this one filled with slave names, to make sure I wasn't trying to sneak into the bathhouse more often than I was allowed.

"No." Slaves didn't have surnames, and even if we did, I wouldn't know mine. I had not been born to an enslaved fae, but instead had been found in the snow with my dead mother. If my mother had been a slave though, it was likely that she'd be unable to recall many memories of her past. Or of her family. Vampiric powers of compulsion often wiped much of a slaves' past from their mind.

Though my best friend, Anna, could say otherwise. She'd been born a slave to a mother who managed to recall a little of her past, like the last name she used in the human realm—Anant. Not that Anna could use her ancestral surname. According to our master's ledger she was Anna-101. Still knowing a little about her family gave my friend some comfort.

I wasn't so lucky, but at least I wasn't Neve-35. Numbered. Like a piece of stock fabric or something.

"Alright you're marked down for the week." The guard gestured to the door behind him. "You have an hour to clean your bits."

An exhale parted my lips as I darted through the door, officially entering the cave. One blissful hour of no one telling me what to do, an hour of quiet. Of true rest.

The disrobing area was right before one reached the first cavern dotted with pools and I thanked the stars that it was empty. This time of day was slow, which I preferred.

I threw off my pants, tunic, boots, and, more carefully, removed the red collar. I retrieved my small wedge of soap from my pocket, set the collar on top of the folded pile, and tucked my garments under a bench in a place where they wouldn't get wet. Threadbare towels waited on a table by the door. I plucked the freshest looking out of the bunch and wrapped it around my curves before entering the bathhouse.

In the first of a dozen interconnected caverns the scent of lavender grew stronger. The purple flower was sprinkled throughout the pools, and refreshed every few hours.

One less accustomed to vampires might consider it a kind gesture meant to calm the bathers, but that was certainly not the case. Vampires had sensitive noses, and lavender shrubs grew wild and abundant in the Vampire Kingdom. Not every master provided soap for their slaves, and many slaves worked in physical labor to build the city. The plant provided a cheap and effective way to reduce their workers' stench.

I scanned the first cavern. A witch-light lantern illuminated a single pool, making it particularly inviting. I padded over, weaving carefully between other springs as I went, so as not to slip on the damp ground. When I reached it, I dropped my towel, set the soap on the rocky edge, and slipped into the warm waters.

I sighed and dipped beneath the hot water, allowing it to cover my head and soothe the tension in my shoulders. This one went so deep that I couldn't touch the bottom.

Upon surfacing, I slicked back my long silvery-white hair, draping it over my silver iridescent wings. Stars above, the water melted so much of my tension and eased the ever-present ache in my mutilated wings. I could already feel my strength returning, my body warming from the inside out.

I rarely felt cold, even in the dead of winter. Yvette believed that, because of where I'd been found with my dead mother, I was born a fae of Winter's Realm. The subjects in that kingdom sustained the cold far better than others. Despite my ancestry, after a bloodletting, I grew weaker, just like any human. In those hours, sometimes for days, depending on how much blood the letter took, I became more susceptible to the cold. Partaking in the mineral pools, the heat rising from the ground to warm the water, felt like being reborn.

If only claiming a new life were that simple.

I grabbed the soap and began washing my face, hair, and wings. When I moved on to my body, I scrubbed my pale skin pink, taking more care only on my forearm where the bloodletter's needle had just punctured me, adding another mark to the dozens of faint needle scars on my arms and the backs of my hands.

Unlike the more frugal masters, Lord Aldéric provided us with rose-petal soap. He favored the scent, and soon enough, I smelled like a rose bush in full bloom. I dunked once more, trying to get all the soap out of my long hair. Once completely clean, I could lounge in the water for the remainder of my hour.

The moment I surfaced, however, whimpers filled my ears. I stiffened, but before I could be sure of what I'd heard, the sound fell quiet. The cavern I'd claimed still appeared empty. Had I imagined the noise?

I treaded to the side of the deep pool, content to sit and rest for a while, but I'd just reached the stone bench when the whimpers came again.

They sounded fainter, drifting from deeper inside the bathhouse. Thinking someone might have slipped on the damp stone floor, I hopped out of the pool and wrapped my towel tightly around my body. Following my keen ears, I entered the next cavern. Empty. As was the one beyond. I moved deeper into the cave system, and my blood chilled when the whimpers abruptly turned to sobs.

I stopped, suddenly rethinking what I was doing. Should I leave the person alone? Most people who frequented slave bathhouses were miserable. But a niggling voice inside told me I had to check. The cries weren't morose but verging on frantic. Someone needed help.

When I entered the fifth chamber, my blood froze.

No one had fallen. No one sobbed because the Fates had forsaken them. Actually, the person who had been crying wasn't even conscious any longer, thanks to the vampire drinking from her neck.

Bastard! My fists clenched into hard balls.

I had no idea how the monster had gotten into the bathhouse. The only vampires allowed on the premises were the masters with accounts in good standing, and judging by this male's disheveled attire, he couldn't claim that status. And even if *he could*, drinking from the vein was forbidden in the bathhouse. It was one of the only places in all the city where blood slaves were safe.

No. This vampire had to be a newblood if he dared sneak into the bathhouse and assault someone's property.

He hadn't noticed me either, which all but confirmed his status as a newblood. Once a newblood found a target, their focus didn't waver. Not until the person they drank from was dead, anyway. I shuddered. Newbloods were death personified, and as far as I knew, they had only one downfall. Compared to older vampires, they were clumsy—having not had time to adjust to their super speed and strength yet.

I debated what to do. It would be all too easy to slip through the bathhouse and retrieve the guards at the front door. But would they do anything to help the woman?

I doubted it. Newbloods were always ravenous, and once this vampire finished his meal, he might need another one right away. The guards knew that as well as I, but I also couldn't just leave the woman.

Pivoting, I scanned the area for a weapon, and my attention caught on a rock dislodged from the cavern wall. Moving as light as a feather, I scooped up the rock and tiptoed closer to the vampire. He remained hunched over the woman, oblivious to everything except the slave hanging as heavy as wet silk in his arms. Her legs floated in the pool she'd been bathing in, lifeless.

Terrified I might be too late, I got as close as I dared and pulled back my arm to strike. Using all my strength, I slammed the rock into the back of his head, hoping to knock him out.

The vampire dropped the woman and a loud *crack* resonated through the bathhouse as her skull hit rock. Then the vampire spun my way with a monstrous hiss. His eyes blazed crimson, making my heart stop.

Burning moon! It hadn't worked. He hadn't dropped in pain, nor gone unconscious.

Panicking, I struck again, slamming the rock into his face and knocking him backward a few paces.

"Worthless shrew!" He tripped and barely caught himself. If there'd been any doubt in my mind that he was a newblood, that would have erased it.

"You shouldn't be in here!" I yelled back. "If the masters—"

My words died on my lips as the vampire jumped, arms extended for me. I spun out of the way in time, thankful that the potion Lord Aldéric force-fed me each full moon to extinguish my fae magic could not dim the natural speed and strength of my kind.

"Help!" I screamed, hoping the guards at the front would hear. "Someone fell! They're bleeding out!"

The guards wouldn't help if they knew a vampire had attacked. Actually, in that case, they might even run. But if a blood slave fell and lost what made them valuable, the guards would come.

"Soon, you'll be bleeding too." The vampire darted toward me a second time.

I spun out of his grasp again, and as I did so, I clocked him in the back of the head with the rock. The vampire stumbled again, his own great speed driving him straight into the uneven stone wall.

A roar rang from his throat, and I darted backward as far as I could into the next chamber. The vampire twisted, focusing on me once more.

"You little—"

"Take a step back!" a voice shouted behind me right as a blast sounded, and air blew by my right shoulder.

9

I gasped as a wooden bullet slammed into the rock wall, so far from the vampire. Had the guard even been trying? That had been closer to hitting me than the vampire!

The monster's eyes burned a deeper crimson.

With heat pummeling through me, I twirled and ran toward the red-haired guard standing on the precipice of the room. His eyes widened when he saw the threat behind me and realized what he was really dealing with— a vampire who had lost all sense of logic and law. One that wouldn't be scared off by a poorly aimed wooden bullet.

"Give me that." I ripped the weapon out of his hands. The device had been fashioned after a weapon in the human world. Its official use was to dissuade vampires of lower status from harming a lord's property.

"Bleeding skies!" the guard snarled. "Give it back."

Instead, I took aim at the vampire blurring my way and released a bullet.

The monster shrieked as the bullet buried itself deep in his heart, stopping him in his tracks and dropping him to the ground. He didn't move a muscle.

I sucked in a breath as the weapon fell from my fingers. Wooden bullets were essentially small stakes. Hit a vampire in the arm or leg with one and it caused great pain.

Hit their heart and they'd die.

"Get out," the guard spat, coming up around me and scooping up his weapon.

"What?"

"Leave."

"There's a person in the pool. I need to check on her."

The guard opened his mouth to argue, but now that no one would rip my throat out, nothing could keep me from the woman. I ran back to her, slipping on the slick floor as I went.

Her torso lay on the stones, arms splayed against the ground, keeping her nose and mouth out of the pink-stained pool. Blood seeped from her head from when the vampire had dropped her, but it wasn't too much. Maybe she was actually fine, maybe she was just passed out.

My hope dissolved as I knelt and gripped the female's shoulder. No magical imprint that I'd expect from a witch or other magical order leapt out at me. Nor any warmth. My throat tightened, and with a shaking hand, I searched for her pulse.

I found nothing.

"Are your ears broken, fae?" The guard shouted and stomped a foot. "I said, *get out!*"

"Did you even want to hit him?" I pivoted to the guard and gestured to the vampire on the ground. "Or is your aim really that atrocious?"

"Killing one is against the law."

"That doesn't mean you can't hit their arm or leg!" Had I been thinking more clearly, that's what I would have tried to do, but I hadn't thought at all when I pulled the trigger. And I didn't regret it. Not one bit.

The guard's chin jutted out. "I scared him off. He didn't deserve to die."

What a lying piece of dragon dung. A poorly flung bullet had no chance of scaring off an enraged newblood. It would only piss them off more.

"You're weak," I spat as I pulled the woman away from the pool so that she lay on the rocks. "And a traitor to your own kind. How could you side with that monster? How could you say that he didn't deserve what he got after this?" I thrust a finger at the woman.

"I'm sending a messenger to your master," the guard retorted, his face turning as red as his hair. "And the vampire's sire too. They'll know what happened, and that I had nothing to do with this. That I—"

"Do what you must. And if you can find it in your shriveled heart, take care of her body, too." I marched by him to prepare for the punishment sure to come my way.

CHAPTER 2

I passed the long night wondering if Master Aldéric had received the bathhouse guard's message, and when the sunlight finally broke through my window, I felt like I hadn't slept at all. Dressing and eating breakfast passed in a blur. There was no telling what my master would say, but one thing was certain.

I'd soon find out.

I swallowed as I crossed the threshold into my master's workshop. Blood slaves in uniform—drab gray dresses, tunics, and trousers—worked tirelessly at their tables. They sewed, beaded, and cut luxury materials into gowns and suits fit for royalty, each one a beautiful work of art. As I passed by, my fingers itched to touch one particularly lovely chiffon gown.

Even though I didn't get paid for the work, I had to admit that I *loved* creating elaborate gowns. Often, I'd spend the hours dreaming that one day I'd get to make something beautiful for myself and attend a ball or some

ASHLEY MCLEO

other glorious function. There, I'd meet my soulmate and we'd live happily ever after.

Of course, I kept those dreams to myself. Others would call my flight of fancy foolish, and they were right, but daydreaming passed the time. After all, one had to make the best of their situation.

Anna, my human best friend, appeared at my side and leaned against the wooden cane she used to ease her mobility. Her upturned brown eyes searched me questioningly. "Are you scared?"

Of those in our slave complex, she alone knew of the events at the bathhouse. Being such a good friend, Anna had held my hand until I'd fallen asleep. But when I woke that morning, she had already left.

I bent my head. "Is *he* here?"

"Yes. That's why I arrived early. To gauge his mood."

"And?"

She looked away.

I closed my eyes. A part of me had hoped that my master would call me to his home last night. That way, my humiliation and punishment wouldn't be so public. But vampires rarely rushed. They had eternity to do as they wished, even longer than the fae. I swallowed down that uncomfortable thought. Sometimes, the vast span of time I had ahead of me made me wish I were human.

"Maybe I should—"

"Neve! In my office!" My master bellowed my name over the workshop and many seamstresses and tailors froze, though they didn't look up. Didn't look at me. They didn't dare.

16

"I think the vampire's sire was important." Anna grabbed my hand. Like everything about my friend her hand was small and delicate, so much so that I sometimes felt like a giant next to her.

"Neve," Anna whispered, tears gathered in her eyes as she met my stare. "Be ready."

I squeezed her hand. "I'll see you later."

Dozens of gazes followed as I shuffled through the busy workshop to the back office. When I arrived in his office, I found Master Aldéric in his large leather chair, reviewing his ledger. Today he wore a suit of dark navy and his long black hair was tied back. Color bloomed in his pale cheeks, indicating that he'd fed recently.

"Leave it open," he said as I made to shut the door behind me. "I heard of what transpired in the bathhouse."

"It was self-defense."

In the case of slaves, the law said absolutely nothing about self-defense, but if it saved me lashes, I would use any reasoning possible to penetrate my master's stone-cold heart.

"Are you aware the vampire you killed was Prince Mylan's latest conquest? A lover he turned so as to keep him forever. Or so I'm told."

A cavernous pit opened in my stomach. He'd been a bleeding prince's child! That was worse than I could have imagined.

I cleared my throat softly. "I had no idea. It's difficult to keep up with the ever-growing royal family."

The Laurent dynasty ruled the vampire kingdom.

While the king and his mate were the ultimate authority, the princes and princesses held great sway. Prince Mylan had been born into the royal line, a third-generation natural-born Laurent. His generation became the first one descended from King Vladistrica and Queen Narcissa that did not possess the ability to bear children. Rather, if they wanted offspring, the third generation had to turn another creature, be they human, mage, fae, or other, into vampires.

Some said that made the third-generation princesses and princes all the more savage. Unstable.

"There are two things saving you from my princely nephew's direct wrath." My master, a relation to the royal family, held up a finger. "That my own sire outranks Prince Mylan, and therefore, I'm not forced to hand you over right away. And two, that the offending vampire should not have been anywhere near other lords' property. Not so soon after he was turned." He dropped his hand. "However, I've decided that your offense is more trouble than you are worth."

My lips parted. My great skill as a seamstress aside, as a faerie, they also considered me a prized blood slave. Bloodletters paid more for my blood and could resell it at a higher price point. I'd even heard that Master Aldéric received offers to purchase me weekly.

"What do you mean?" I asked, terrified for the answer, though somehow I kept my voice level.

"I will put you up for auction tomorrow. After all, many masters are in the city for the Blood Ball. I wouldn't want to miss out on potential buyers."

My knees buckled, and I barely caught myself on the door. My master, however, remained calm, cold. He stood and poured himself a goblet of red liquid from a crystal carafe.

He planned to sell me. At auction. The highest bidder would win.

My heart began to thunder.

Masters far worse than my own lived in Sangrael. They drank from their slaves, beat them regularly, kept them chained, and sexually abused them. Master Aldéric was no hero, nor even a person to admire, but he fed his property well, gave us comfortable beds, and kept us clothed. He also didn't physically hurt us and rarely drank directly from the vein.

"You may go, Neve."

I sucked in a breath. "Isn't there another way?"

He froze, goblet partway to his lips. Only his dark brown eyes flashed up to me. "You dare to challenge me?"

"No, but what if the prince purchases me?"

My master glanced away. "You should have thought about that before you killed one of our kind."

"So I should have let that newblood kill me?"

"You have work to do."

A lump formed in my throat. Some slaves could trick themselves into believing that their masters cared for them. I'd never been among those delusional few, and yet, this cut to the core. The work I'd done to build his wealth, the pain he'd inflicted on me by smothering my magic, handicapping my wings, and stealing my very blood—it meant nothing to this vampire.

I meant nothing.

Deep inside me, something sparked. Something I usually kept smothered—defiance. My hands formed fists, and I spun on my heels, storming out of the room.

In the workshop, humans, witches, and even one elf who'd strayed too far from his kingdom stared at me with sad eyes. No doubt they wondered what had transpired. Perhaps the elf had even heard.

He can spread the tale then, I thought as I stomped toward the door.

Master Aldéric was going to sell me! I refused to spend my last day working only to be cast out, no matter what I did. Who knew what sort of situation I'd find myself in next? I swallowed the potent fear rising inside me.

Screaming stars. I could be dead by the end of the week.

Chilled autumnal air blasted me in the face as I hurled open the workshop door and stepped outside. Angry tears came like a waterfall, and I rushed around the corner, desperate to be out of sight. I didn't want anyone to see me break down.

And yet, much to my dread, the door to the workshop opened again. I opened my mouth to tell whoever it was to leave, but the sound of their footsteps stopped me. That distinct footfall pattern told me it was Anna. Out of all the souls in Isila, she was the only one I'd welcome at my side.

"Neve! What happened?" She approached and placed

a soft hand on my shoulder. I couldn't meet her eyes, so I focused on a stray red thread lodged in her raven-wing hair.

"*I'mbeingsold!*"

"What?"

I took a deep breath. "Master Aldéric is putting me up for auction. Tomorrow."

Her hands clapped over her mouth. "No!"

"He doesn't need a slave as troublesome as me."

"He fears his own family," my friend replied, making the connections.

"Yes and I'm scared of who will purchase me," I admitted. Many bloodsuckers would be happy to own me, to drink from me. Magic that I couldn't use filled my blood. They loved that flavor.

"Someone can talk to Master Aldéric." Anna's soft voice fluttered with fear and red splotches of color began appearing on her high golden-brown cheekbones. "Perhaps Rose?"

I snorted. Rose was our master's oldest slave. She worked in his household and traveled to his country home when he did. Occasionally, Rose even spoke to lower-ranking vampires on our master's behalf. Rose wore silk dresses and held her head up high. And yet, she remained a collar-wearing slave; drained like the rest of us. She held no rights of her own, no sway that mattered.

"That won't work. I killed one of their own." My tone rose with the words as my blood boiled hotter.

I couldn't believe that I was being punished for simply

saving my own skin. Skin that my master was now selling! There was no way to win here, and I hated that.

Burning moon!

"And you know what, Anna, I'd do it all again!"

Anna looked about nervously. "Don't say that."

"I would! The newblood tried to kill me. He deserved it! He—"

"Was quite poorly watched," a smooth, deep voice cut me off, and the hair on my arms stood on end. "Even my family will admit to that. My twin should have done better to keep his child on a leash."

Judging by how all the blood had left Anna's face, someone of importance stood behind me. How important, I couldn't have fathomed until I turned.

My mouth dropped open. Of all the bad luck!

Prince Gervais, Prince Mylan's twin, sat before me on horseback. I only knew it was Gervais and not Mylan himself because the latter had a penchant for absurdly flamboyant attire and this vampire was dressed rather plainly. Not that it made him any less terrifying. The wind tousled his dark curls and stained Prince Gervais's pale cheeks pink, but there was a dangerous gleam in his eyes. One that promised pain. Behind him, four others rode, and to try and calm myself, I took them in.

Judging by their style of dress, they hailed not from Isila but from the human world. And as they weren't chained, they clearly weren't being taken as slaves. One, a woman about my age with one blue and one green eye, watched me with particular interest.

"Apologies, my prince." I fell into a deep curtsey. "I allowed my anger to get the better of me."

Gervais's lips pulled up at the corners. "You were loud enough for everyone on this street to hear, which I cannot take lightly. It is treason to speak of any Laurent, newblood or not, in that manner. Considering that my brother turned the human, I might have you drained right here."

The woman with the two-toned eyes let out a strangled sound. As if he'd anticipated her reaction, the male she rode next to, clearly a vampire by how he held himself, placed his hand on her arm. Perhaps he'd hoped to silence her.

It didn't work.

"You wouldn't!" the woman blurted out, and in her indignation, an odd sort of magic pulsed from her. She wasn't human. Was I seeing a free witch? "She said she would have died! That sounds like self-defense."

"*Meredith*." The male let out a low growl. His shoulders tightened as Prince Gervais turned to take them in, his expression one of astonishment. The other male scowled at the prince, but added, "my mate, it is their way."

"Well, it's stupid!" The woman, Meredith, narrowed her eyes. Behind her, one male and one female, respectively, with black and white *feathered* wings that marked them as non-fae, nodded their agreement. They too wore human style clothing, so I assumed that their opinions meant little here. And, yet their combined opinions lent me strength.

"It is!" I spouted, and immediately, I wished I had not as Prince Gervais returned his piercing attention to me.

He studied me with amusement that I did not understand. "You believe that as property, you should be able to take justice into your own hands?"

"When my life is on the line, yes. Or that of any blood slave."

Meredith gasped. "Blood slave. Tobias, I—!"

She said no more, however. Or if she did, I didn't hear, for Prince Gervais urged his horse closer. Behind me, Anna shuffled to press herself into the building.

Shame crashed over me. I could not hold my tongue, and for that, I could be killed. But Anna was innocent. I should have considered her.

"My friend did nothing," I added, hoping that when the prince ended me, he'd spare Anna.

"That mouse? No, I don't expect that she did." He leaned over the neck of his stallion. "But you, you're a bit of a wildcat. I like that, and wouldn't you know it? My two fae recently died." He licked his lips. "I wonder if your master might be persuaded to part with you?"

If a more terrifying notion existed, I couldn't think of it. I was under no illusion that this prince's fae died from natural causes.

"Hey! Back off!" Meredith yelled, and nearly swung off her horse. Again, the vampire she rode next to, Tobias, stopped her from getting too close to the prince. "You're terrifying her."

"What of it?" Gervais asked, not taking his piercing eyes off me.

"Well, don't you have a job to do?" Meredith's chin jutted out. "Like taking us to the palace? Aren't the king and queen just *dying* to meet me?"

This mystery woman was either incredibly brave or incredibly stupid.

"Alas, you're right, witch." Gervais let out a frustrated huff and backed his horse up. Before the prince left, however, he met my eyes once more. "I'll find you later, wildcat."

CHAPTER 3

The rest of my working day was spent in bed, shaking and crying so hard that the day's end bell didn't even register. Nothing did. Not until Anna burst into our room.

"I've been so worried about you." She perched next to me, the ancient straw mattress sinking beneath her slight weight. "Master Aldéric was furious that you didn't stay and finish your garments."

When I stormed out of the workshop, I hadn't been thinking clearly, but of course my master would have been upset. He wanted to squeeze every last bit of sweat and skill from my fingers.

"The only reason he didn't come here is because we were so busy. Important vampires kept stopping by." She paused. "Rose had to finish your dress."

"Well, *that's* why he was mad," I said, only half jesting.

With a needle and thread, Rose wasn't as talented as

me. No one in Master Aldéric's workshop could sew like me, save for Anna, but she had her own dresses to finish for affluent lords and ladies.

"Luckily, the patron came in as she finished and seemed very pleased with your work. Rose's hemming too." Anna added the last bit as though an afterthought and cleared her throat. She was veering off to unimportant side stories, which meant that she wasn't telling me something.

I frowned. "What are you too scared to tell me?"

"Master Aldéric told his clients about the auction, Neve. Many appeared interested in purchasing you."

"He has to recoup what he can," I spat.

"Three who expressed interest are staying at the castle, dining with the king and the royal family."

My blood froze. She spoke subtlety, but the meaning became clear. How could it not be? For hours, I'd been terrified that Prince Gervais would sweep into the slave quarters and kill me as I wept in bed.

"I doubt they'd gossip about a slave auction," I replied.

"Not to buy humans. But you're *fae*."

Outside, the dinner bell sounded. Though I wasn't hungry, Anna surely was, and I was tired of sitting in my room, alone and fearful.

"Let's get dinner."

Anna blinked. "Are you sure?"

"No, but I need to get out of this room."

Together, we left our quarters and ventured down the hall to the common areas of the slave complex. The U-

28

shaped stone building housed over two hundred blood slaves, each with pity in their eyes when they saw me. I knew all of them and this place like I knew every rod of metal stuck in my wings. Somehow, that only made things worse.

When we reached the dining hall, more people stared at me. I kept my head down as I fetched my bowl of pottage, vegetables, roll, and a small portion of meat.

"They gave us more than normal," Anna commented after we'd received our rations.

"Cook pities me," I said.

Normally, I'd delight in the generous portion. As food sources for the vampires, they never exactly starved us, but in the same vein, blood slaves weren't allowed to overindulge. Our overlords aimed to keep us healthy but slightly too thin. *Weakened*, I often thought—not that my body complied with their wishes.

As a fae, I was naturally stronger, faster, and had more endurance than the people—mostly humans—I'd grown up around. My body held more fat than others' frames and my muscular thighs supported me through all the trials of life. In my current situation, that didn't feel like a blessing though. I suspected Master Aldéric would use my strong physique to boost the bids tomorrow.

Side by side, Anna and I ate. In two hours, we'd have to be in bed. In what time we had left, I wanted to converse with my best friend, to relish her company. Come tomorrow, I might not live in the same city as her.

I might not even be alive.

I stiffened and shoved a spoonful of the hot pottage into my mouth.

"Don't think about it," Anna whispered.

"How can I not?"

Our master kept me alive because he recognized I was more valuable alive than drained for his pleasure. He sold my blood bi-weekly, which earned him a great profit. When I'd shown natural skill with a needle and thread, he prized me even more. As the turns wore on, I'd become his best seamstress, which only added to his coffers.

But Master Aldéric wasn't like all vampires, though. It would be asking a lot for my next owner to recognize that I was worth more than my blood. Many vampires were greedy and had more coin than they could ever spend. They might simply want to drain me for their own pleasure.

"Did you hear Simon and Yvette are engaged?" Anna asked, trying to pull my mind from my impending demise.

My heart leapt at the good news. "Since when?"

"Last night."

The pair had been together for as long as I'd been alive. Separately, they'd come from the human world and had to remake their family here. As they were also among the oldest of Master Aldéric's slaves, they often saw the younger generation through troubled times.

Yvette had helped me celebrate every passing turn and sang to me on my namedays. She had also been the one I'd gone to when I'd first bled. Four turns on the wheel of time later, she wiped my tears when a male I'd been so taken with broke my heart. She'd taught me to read in High Vitralic, the ancient language of vampires, Old High Fae, and her native language, English which had also morphed into the common tongue of the nine kingdoms. As far as I was concerned, Yvette was my mother. In any case, she was the only one I'd ever known.

Yvette and Simon deserved nothing but whatever happiness they could seize from this life.

"When's the ceremony?"

"Two weeks." Anna bit into her roll. "Yvette asked Master Aldéric if she can use scraps to create a dress, and he agreed, so she wants time to whip something up." Anna's lips softened into a smile that I felt in my soul. At least, until I remembered that any union between blood slaves only lasted for as long as they had the same owner.

If Yvette and Simon ever pulled something like I had, they'd be sold. Separated.

Bleeding skies, this life is rubbish.

But I wouldn't say that. Not when Anna looked so happy for the older human couple. As slaves, it was hard enough to find someone to trust. To find genuine love and a person who desired a wedding? Most never even tried because we were tied to the whims of our masters.

The clanging of the front doors announced a late arrival. I looked past Anna and gaped. "New humans!"

Whispers shrouded the room as a vampire soldier led a trio of people, two men and one woman, to Cook's station. They wore clothing from the human world and held the dazed expression of the compelled.

They all arrived that way. Human blood slaves were

either born in this court or they showed up with no knowledge of how they got here. I'd often wondered how.

"Your replacements," a soft feminine voice said from behind.

I twisted to find none other than Yvette looking down at me, smiling softly. The corners of her eyes crinkled with age, and though she smiled, I could see the sadness in her body.

"We'll miss you, Neve."

"Thank you." I tried to keep my chin up. I wouldn't ruin her day with the horrors of my own. "So, I hear congratulations are in order?"

A sweet blush crossed her cheeks. "Thank you. Simon and I are quite excited."

I patted the table. "Tell us what you have planned."

Yvette took the seat next to me. Her aura enveloped me and eased my nerves. Our trio devolved into chatting about how Yvette wanted her marriage ceremony to go. It all sounded quite nice, very human with traditions I knew nothing of. All that distracted me for a while. At least, until Anna froze, her eyes widening. I didn't dare turn, but when an icy hand clamped on my shoulder, my stomach sank.

"Neve, stand up," my master commanded. "Prince Gervais wishes to get a better look at you."

I stiffened, hoping I'd hallucinated those words. But one glance at Anna's tense shoulders told me I had not. The prince and our master must have entered through a side door. Prince Gervais was already making good on his word to find me.

Slowly, I turned and rose. My master stood next to the prince, smiling down at me with a serpent's smile. Prince Gervais wore finery I recognized as coming from Master Aldéric's workshop. Anna had done the gold embroidery on the jacket. Clearly, he'd stopped by here before going to the Blood Ball.

As his appearance was even more intriguing than the new humans, everyone watched us.

"That's the one who caught my eye," the prince said, as if he didn't want to pounce at that very moment and stick his fangs into my neck. "You truly are selling her?"

"Due to the events related to your brother's child." My master cleared his throat. "I thought it prudent."

"I'd like to purchase her. Now. I wish to have her waiting in my rooms after the Blood Ball."

Aldéric's eyebrows twitched, the only tell that Prince Gervais had not mentioned this before. "I've already entered her at the auction."

"What's the point? I'll win, Aldéric." The prince smirked.

"Of that, I have no doubt." Light sparkled in my master's eyes. "However, I have spoken to other interested parties. I will keep her entered—see who the most *motivated* buyer is."

Gervais snorted. "A shrewd businessman. Lucky that you're family, too." His eyes traveled over me hungrily. "Fine. A day matters little. And I expect she'll be worth the wait."

"Shall we make our way to the palace?"

"We shall." Prince Gervais gave me a wink before he allowed my master to escort him to the door.

I didn't breathe until they disappeared. At once, the entire room came to life again—slaves whispered over what had transpired and my ill fate.

Tears fell down Anna's cheeks. She, too, had heard the horrid tales of Prince Gervais and his twin, Prince Mylan.

"Perhaps someone will compete with the prince?" Yvette laid a soft hand on my forearm and pulled me back to sit.

"Unless it's another Laurent, that's doubtful," I said.

Yvette frowned, sat up straighter, and looked around. When she faced me again, her expression had hardened. "I have an idea. Something that might help you."

"I'm listening."

Yvette did another scan of the room, and in that time, Anna threw me a look of concern. What did Yvette have to say that required so much discretion?

"The Blood Ball is tonight. Any vampire who is anyone wants to go, including soldiers. Most of the city gates will be closed for the night." Yvette leaned closer. "Only one remains open, and it's being guarded by humans."

"How do you know?" I breathed.

"Simon is friends with one of the bathhouse guards. Not the one that ratted on you, mind. His friend said that five men from the bathhouse are to watch the wall tonight. The vampires want their revelry on their holy night."

I couldn't believe that, nor what she was implying.

Anna shook her head slowly. "Are you saying Neve should . . .?"

"I would try," Yvette whispered. "The humans will be armed, but it's the best chance you're ever going to get. The Winter Court is closest to the east. You could run for that border. Once there, you could travel through the Red Mist Mountains. Go south."

"To the Autumn Court?"

"Or the Dragon Court." Yvette nodded. "It's directly south. If it were me, I'd aim for there, rather than taking the longer route to the Autumn Court. Fae or not."

Stars above. Did I dare? The journey would be very perilous.

I'll find you later, wildcat.

Prince Gervais's face flashed in my mind, and the way his hard eyes promised pain made me recoil. He would not fail to purchase me. I would take my chances with escape and maybe survive, or I faced a fate worse than death.

I met Yvette's eyes. "Please, help me plan."

CHAPTER 4

Moonlight streamed in through the bedroom window. Outside, vampires reveled in the night of the Blood Ball, regardless of if they'd been invited to dance among the elite or not. They ducked into private parties, taverns, and brothels, taking their pleasure where they could.

A few streets to the west, the bell atop the tower tolled eleven times. I swallowed, the signal sending a fresh wave of terror through me as I gripped my threadbare blanket tighter, clinging to the false sense of safety it provided. Perhaps the last security I'd ever feel.

"Oow my stomach!" Anna whined right on cue.

A few beds away, two of our roommates turned their backs to Anna, just as we'd hoped they would. My best friend's stomach pains were a common occurrence. After many turns of being woken at night, those light sleepers in our shared quarters always pretended to not hear. The other five slaves in the room remained snoring, definitely asleep, like usual. Nothing but the clanging of the wakeup bell would rouse them.

"Stars," Anna gasped dramatically, "I can barely move!"

"I can help," I offered, just loud enough to be sure those still awake heard.

"No, no," Anna grunted. "You've had a hard day. I've got it."

"Are you sure?"

Boy, what an act we were putting on for them, but they'd expect it. Nine times out of ten, I escorted Anna to the bathroom.

"Positive. Keep sleeping, I'll be back soon," Anna replied, her voice remarkably strained for someone who was actually just fine.

As quietly as possible, covered by Anna's loud moaning and struggles to get out of her own bed, I slid out of mine, arranged the blankets to resemble a fae-ish shape, and bent to grab my shoes. I wished they had thicker soles, but they were the best I owned, and I'd need to make them work for what came next.

On a rickety side table rested my red collar. The sign that I wasn't really a person, just something to be owned.

The urge to hurl it out the window nearly overcame me, but I just turned my back on the collar. Never again would I wear that hideous thing.

When I turned back to Anna, I found she was watching me expectantly, so I double checked the room. No one so much as blinked in our direction. Stars, our roommates were so predictable.

I waved for Anna to move, and she shuffled loudly to the door while I tiptoed out of the room and to the communal washroom four doors down. Quietly, I scanned the area. Empty.

"Please, come with me," I whispered. "I don't know what I'll do without you."

"I can't. My job is to get you out of the room without notice and make my issues look real for when Yvette arrives." Anna bent over the toilet, shoving her fingers down her throat and forcing herself to vomit. The air filled with the smell of sickness, and I slowed my breathing, trying not to be ill myself.

I looked away. She did everything possible to make sure that my cover was complete. Once the alarm sounded, which would hopefully be in many hours, our roommates would say they heard only Anna leave the room. They would know that Anna had told me to stay behind, to not bother with helping her tonight.

I didn't deserve a friend like her.

Once she finished emptying her stomach, Anna rose, looking pale. Childishly, I stuck out my lower lip, prepared to try one more time.

"Neve, stop. You know I'd slow you down." She gestured to her clubfoot. In normal life, the handicap was minor. Perhaps she walked a touch slower than me, but it didn't impair her any other way.

But when on the run through dangerous woods and over mountains infested with orcs, ogres, trolls, and giants, slowing down could easily spell death.

I exhaled, knowing she would not be dissuaded. And

that she was also right for not coming. Not tonight anyway.

"I'll get you out of here as soon as I can," I promised. "Once I get to the Dragon Court and earn enough coin, I'll hire a dragon to extract you. One who breathes fire! The vampires won't be able to stop them!"

"I know you will." She swallowed. "I love you, Neve, but you need to go. Even if no one raises the alarm before tomorrow morning, you're at a disadvantage. The vampires are so fast."

I closed the distance between us, enveloping her in a hug. "I'll miss you so much. Stay safe and alert for when I send someone."

"Don't worry about me." She pulled back and looked me in the eye. Slowly, her hand rose to touch the crescent moon scar over my right temple, the one she had a twin of just below her collarbone. While I'd had mine for as long as I could recall, I used to dislike it. That was until the day an eleven-year-old Anna carved the same moon into her skin so I wouldn't feel bad about myself. "I'll see you again soon, Neve."

"I promise."

"I believe you." She smiled a teary smile.

Stars and the moon above. Could I really do this?

"Neve, *go*. If you don't leave soon, I can't promise I won't raise the alarm myself to selfishly keep you here." Tears fell down her cheeks now, hard and fast.

"You're a terrible liar." Unable to bear her tears, I wiped the track marks and landed a kiss on the top of her head. "I love you."

"I love you too."

I turned because if I didn't do so then, I might never have gathered the strength. Shoulders shaking from sobs I was forcing deep down, I left the washroom and moved swiftly through the barren, dank-smelling halls. Everyone slept, and because I'd lived in the slave complex since I arrived in Sangrael at two turns of age, I knew exactly where the guards around the complex would be. And tonight, I knew who would distract them.

Yvette stood in position as I stepped out the eastern side door and into the chilly night. The wool pants, tunic, and thick black cloak she'd snatched from the laundry room sat right where she said they'd be. I sniffed and exhaled. The cloak smelled like expensive perfume and the material felt luxurious beneath my fingers. It had to have been owned by a vampire, which meant it also smelled like their kind. Both smells were perfect for smothering my fae scent.

I thanked her resourcefulness as I shimmied into the clothing and swung the cloak over my silver wings, pushing them down to lie flat against my back. Once I'd secured the cloak's clasp, I pulled my hair back and raised the hood to hide the shimmery-white hue. Something in the pockets bumped against my leg, and I peeked inside.

A lump rose in my throat. Not only had Yvette supplied me with a disguise, but she'd also finagled more food from Cook. Three rolls wouldn't last long, but on my journey, they might become the difference between life and death.

As quickly as I dared, I moved through the shadows

until the main gate came into view. Once in position, I lifted my hands to cup my mouth and performed my best impersonation of an aura owl hooting.

At our signal, Yvette slipped from the alcove of the western door. Rushing forward, she entered the small courtyard between the wrought-iron gates that protected us from outsiders and the slave quarters. Throwing up a hand, she waved to the human man on guard duty. "A word, if you please!"

"What are you doing out this late, woman?" The young man on guard scowled and prowled closer to Yvette.

"Don't 'woman' me, Elias!" Yvette scolded. "I changed your soiled nappies!"

"Oh, I—sorry, Yvette." The tone of the first guard shifted into apologetic and a faint snicker from the other, a human named Ted, filled the air. "You caught me off guard. We were told to be extra careful tonight. The vampires are celebrating, and they might take liberties."

"Like that one Neve offed." Ted added his two cents, swaggering over. "I think Master Aldéric is scared one might seek retribution."

"Newbloods don't have friends, stupid." Elias snorted out a derisive laugh. "They can't hold themselves together and its sire can just buy her tomorrow, if they want."

"Be that as it may," Yvette said. "I require help."

"How so?" Elias asked.

"Anna is ill again. She can't walk, and I'm not strong enough to lift her on my own." She lifted a thin arm and shrugged. "Not all the way down the hall anyway."

"I'll help," Elias offered as we'd known he would when Yvette mentioned he was on duty. He'd fancied Anna for many turns.

"I'll keep watch." Ted turned back to the black gate.

"We'll be quick," Yvette assured him, and together she and Elias walked toward the main door.

The moment they disappeared into the complex; I double-checked that Ted's back was still turned. Once I was certain he wouldn't see me coming, I sucked in a breath and made a run for it. As a faerie, I had wings, and if they'd been usable, I would have flown in complete silence. But my wings had been mangled as a precaution to keep Aldéric's property from running away. He didn't bother to injure humans, as they were far slower and weaker than those of other magical orders. Anyone born with magic flowing in their veins, however, wasn't so lucky.

Still, like all faeries, I was fast and very light of foot, so Ted didn't hear me coming. Not even when I launched myself into the air and aimed my elbow at the back of his neck. A soft burst of air left him, and he fell to the ground.

I unsheathed his dagger and cracked the heavy hilt over his head. All the tension left the man's body. I exhaled, and looking down, swallowed. Ted breathed. I hadn't killed him. Thank the stars.

I took Ted's belt and scabbard, upon which the keys to the gate hung. I looped the belt with the blade around my waist and, once armed, opened the gate. I slipped out, shut the gate behind me, and tossed the keys back inside.

Without so much as a second glance back, I took off into the darkness. With each step, my chest heaved harder. I was so glad Yvette had found a thick cloak for me. Hidden beneath it, no one would see my fear.

The cobble streets were bustling, filled with vampires walking to and fro, trailing from tavern to tavern, hoping to find the perfect blood source for the night. Judging by the laughter and other sounds coming from the brothels, those were busy too. The street merchants had even stayed open late to hawk their wares, mostly items of clothing or ornate masks. Wearing those, the common vampires could pretend they held enough importance to attend the Blood Ball.

Nearly every building, new and sleek or rundown with a thatched roof, featured a flag outside. On it, a red serpent poised to strike the onlooker against a field of black; paying the House of Laurent tribute.

I strode through the streets like I owned them, as if I had become one of the same creatures that had enslaved me all my life. All the while, I also took care to maintain a distance between my person and every vampire I passed by. The heavy cloak would mask my fear and my scent, but if I came too near, they still might smell a fae. I could take no chances. The gate Yvette told me about wasn't far, barely a ten-minute walk. But in that time, so much could go wrong.

The moment Elias returned to his post and found Ted, he might sound an alarm. I counted on Anna flirting with Elias to distract him for a bit longer than usual. Yvette would also stall to buy me more time, but they could only do that for so long. The question then became would Ted and Elias want to risk bringing vampires to Master Aldéric's gates and admitting that they'd been ineffective guards? Most wouldn't want to do so.

I shook myself. No use in worrying about that. I just needed to move and find a *proper* weapon.

The dagger I'd stolen would be useful against wolves or other wild animals. Perhaps it would even help against some magical creatures I might come across on my travels. Vampires, however, required something else entirely.

I needed a stake or a sword. Stakes were uncommon in a city filled with vampires, so a sword to decapitate my enemies was my best bet. And that meant stealing one off a vampire soldier having the night of his or her life.

Putting on that air of confidence all vampires possessed, I chanced glances at those in the streets. Reacting to my attention, no matter how brief, more than one male leered at me. In response, I did something I'd never done before; I scowled and hissed. They replied with equal ire and kept moving, thank the fates.

Precious minutes passed, and I'd nearly given up on finding a sword, when *finally*, I spotted a promising sight. Tied to a nearby post, an imposing black horse wore a saddle emblazoned with the red serpent, indicating the soldier who rode him owed loyalty to the Laurents. Saddlebags weighed down the horse and a rucksack leaned up against the post. The owner must have stopped on his way to wherever he headed. Perhaps I'd find a weapon in the bag? I checked the sign on the establishment. A brothel—perfect. The steed's owner would probably be busy and not see me snooping about.

I took two steps toward the horse before an alarm rang out. It sounded faint where I stood, but close enough for me to hear. It had to be coming from Lord Aldéric's slave complex. My heart rate kicked up and blood began thrumming in my ears.

I spun, taking in my surroundings. The vampires in the streets listened intently. A few pointed in the keep's direction. When they ran that way, my timeline halved. Our plan had not bought me nearly enough time . . .

Time to pivot. I forgot all about searching for the weapon and sized up the horse. I'd ridden before. Twice.

In both instances, I'd traveled with two of my master's soldiers to a country estate to design and measure a suit for a noble vampire who did not deign to enter Master Aldéric's shop. During both journeys, my horse had been much smaller, and Master Aldéric's soldiers had helped guide and teach me to ride so I didn't fall off. All in all, both journeys hadn't even taken up a full day, but once I'd gotten the hang of riding, we'd trotted a bit.

Though if I had to gallop . . . and stars, that horse stood so high. It was intimidating, to say the least.

But when one had no other options, they seized those in front of them. Besides, I was far more scared of the vampires catching me than a bleeding horse, no matter how large.

I approached the steed as though I had no fear and

untied it from the post. Shockingly, the horse didn't fight me, though it did seem a little annoyed.

"We're just going for a little ride," I whispered kindly, hoping to soften it toward me, and positioned myself alongside it. Inhaling deeply, I placed my foot in the stirrup. Then, I hoisted myself upward.

I huffed as, despite all my efforts, I barely mounted. Thank the Fates I was tall and strong. A shorter or weaker person would have had much more trouble.

Seated in the saddle, I rearranged my cloak. Vampires rarely had my silver-white colored hair, and none had wings. If I wanted any chance of escape, I needed to remain covered.

"Alright," I whispered, grabbing the reins and quickly going over what I'd learned of riding, before giving it the cues to back up.

Immediately, the seemingly skeptical creature did as I requested. I then turned him and met no resistance. An exhale parted my lips. This creature was well trained, indeed.

"Oh, good boy," I said, and guided the horse forward. It moved slowly, too slowly, so I applied more pressure with my legs and feet.

It took off in a brisk trot, leaving me to grip the reins and swallow a squeal of terror as I pulled back to slow us. Stars, I hadn't been ready for that at all. My heart thudded in my chest, and I felt thankful that all the vampires in the streets ran toward the alarm.

I pulled back a touch, leaned over the horse's neck,

and applied less pressure to its sides. "Listen," I muttered softly, "we don't have time to go slow, but maybe not *so* fast right away?"

It slowed. A bit.

I fought against the urge to slow our progress even more. As I was still settling in, becoming reacquainted with how riding felt, the pace wasn't comfortable. However, the trot did seem to be a natural speed for an experienced rider to travel, and I'd garner no notice. With that knowledge, I continued onward.

When I reached the gate, relief flooded through me to find Yvette had been correct. Humans manned this city gate tonight, not vampires. Even better, the gate, though blocked by five men, lay open.

"My lady?" one asked. "Everything alright?"

The *absolute gall.* As I was unaccompanied, he had to believe I was a vampire. And yet he dared to question me?

Then, a thought struck. Was it because of the alarm? But no, impossible. From here, I couldn't detect the noise, and the fae sense of hearing was far keener than that of humans.

"All is well." I slowed the horse as it approached the gate. Oddly, instead of moving to the side, the humans remained standing in place. "I wish to pass."

"Of course. After payment."

Payment?

"Explain." I used my best *'I'm a master and you're scum,'* tone.

"Our orders come from King Vladistrica, my lady," another guard replied. "We had thought that he would explain the tax at the ball."

"I did not attend."

"Ah, apologies. Allow me to explain then. It's for all vampires coming or going from the city." The man's tone wobbled. "He requires ten golds apiece."

What in the stars? What was the point of this tax?

Actually, it didn't matter because I had no money. I'd never possessed more than a few tin coins in my life. Golds were out of the question. And when I thought about it, these men likely had never touched a gold piece either. Might they be trying to put one over on me?

"Are you trying to steal from me, human?" I barked.

"No! Apologies, my lady. Here's the edict!" A third guard stepped forward with terror in his eyes. "We should have shown you this to begin with." He stretched out his trembling arm and handed me a scroll.

I reached for it when another alarm sounded. This one came louder, closer, and more insistent than the one Master Aldéric had for the slave quarters.

The city siren. No!

The men shared looks and one backed up, his hand going to the lever that would shut the gate.

"What are you doing?" I demanded.

"We have to lock down the city." The guard closest to me extended the scroll for my taking. His hand shook. "We're sorry. When the city siren soun—"

Hard, I kicked my heels into my steed's sides and

hugged my legs against the horse. With astonishing power, he lunged forward. The humans scattered and shouted behind me, but I paid them no mind as I clung to the horse's neck and rode beyond the city wall for the forest.

CHAPTER 5

My horse's hooves did not falter or slow as we raced away from Sangrael. In the forest's darkness, one hour passed, then two. And still, my steed ran, a testament to the horse's training and endurance.

I, on the other hand, grew ever more exhausted. I was not fully recovered from the bloodletting I'd undergone the previous day, and that meant riding was taking a larger toll than it would have normally. Stars, had I been back to normal, the journey still would have been difficult enough.

I needed to walk, to enliven my limbs, or soon enough, I'd fall off the horse. To be sure we weren't being followed, I took one more look behind me. I saw nothing and no one, so I pulled back on the reins.

"Whoa."

The steed snorted loudly and slowed to a stop.

"Good boy." I patted the side of his neck, as soft as

soft velvet and damp. The poor thing needed water and food too.

"I'm sorry I don't have anything for you to drink," I whispered. "Maybe we can find a stream?"

The horse let out a huff, turning the air around his nostrils white. It was the middle of an autumn night and the temperature had plummeted.

"I'm going to get off," I added to the horse. "I need to walk."

The process proved as elegant as mounting the horse had been, and in the end, I nearly face-planted, catching myself seconds before I would have hit the forest floor.

"Burning stars." My hands gripped my aching thighs for support. "This is worse than I thought."

The horse snorted. I chose to believe that he was not laughing at me, but rather, telling me to toughen up.

"You're right. I can't complain. Thanks again for your help."

He looked away, as if to say that he had no choice in the matter. I grabbed the reins. "Let's find a stream."

We'd gone due east, and the Red Mist Mountains loomed large to my right. I knew from books about the history of the Blood Kingdom that a large river flowed from that very mountain range separating the Winter Court and the Vampire Court. It flowed all the way to the sea in the far north. The area had many tributaries too, many of which orc tribes on the fae side of the border lived by.

As I walked, I took in my surroundings. I found it a miracle that no one had come after me. I would put coin on the theory that the city guards were too scared to tell anyone about me. Given how I'd left, it wasn't unfathomable for one of them to suspect that me leaving the city might be related to the siren. Their fear had bought me time, but eventually, tales of an escaped slave would reach them, and the city guard would crack, whether on their own or from compulsion.

One hand went to my dagger that hung off my hip. As a seamstress, I'd never been trained in how to use the weapon, but at the very least I could stick an attacker with the tip. Or slice. Like hacking into meat. Either way, I felt better having the weapon and if I needed to use it, I'd have to learn quickly because the only other option was to perish.

However, as the dagger wasn't large enough to decapitate a vampire it wouldn't save me from them. To be sure of my safety against the bloodsuckers who would come for me, I needed to whittle a stake.

My chin dropped, and I scanned the ground for a stick to carve into a weapon. The waning moon loomed ahead, and Autumn, in all her glory, rioted across the kingdom. Some of the leaves had already fallen, creating a thin blanket of color on the ground.

That would soon change. The closer I came to Winter's Realm, the colder it would get. It would also become more likely I'd encounter deeper snow. The thought of snow was not welcome. Already, I was sure that vampires would hunt me, but snow made that hunt far easier because it left tracks.

All the more reason to get whittling.

With each step, my body loosened a bit more. We walked for another twenty minutes when I spotted a fallen tree limb in the woods that would do nicely for my project.

"Hold up, boy."

The horse blinked at me as if to say *you're lucky that I'm deigning to listen to you*. Black as night, he struck a regal picture.

"I ought to give you a real name."

I ran through a few options as I trudged through the underbrush. The limb didn't match the trees around it, hinting that it had blown away from its origin. Pulling it close, I examined the limb beneath the moonlight.

Back in her world, Yvette had spent a lot of time with plants and many in this realm were the same, or so she said. As a slave, she could no longer indulge in that hobby, but she'd still taken every opportunity to teach Anna and me about trees, flowers, and even herbs in the rare instances when some landed on our plates. The branch I held looked like it could be from an elm, walnut, or hickory tree.

Suddenly, I stilled, realizing that I stood in a wild forest. Yvette claimed that elm, walnut, and hickory were often mistaken for ash. So the branch might even be from an ash tree.

My mouth went dry at the thought.

I'd never seen an ash tree. They weren't planted in Sangrael for a very good reason. That wood was the only type that could be fashioned into stakes that killed the royals. But the vampires didn't scour the forests for ash trees. Why would they when the vampires held complete control in their cities, villages, and estates?

If this *was* ash, the Fates had gifted me a boon indeed.

Of course, the chances were slim, but I decided to take them. I needed a stake anyway, and it was better to begin working on it now.

Finally, I settled on an offshoot about the right diameter and length for a stake. Using my dagger, I sawed off the section I needed and trimmed the thin ends. Eyeing the perfectly sized wood, I smiled. Now, I could work with it.

I made my way back to my horse, who snorted loudly.

"How do you like the name Judge?" I teased, for he appeared even more exasperated with me than before I left him to go hunting for wood.

The horse snorted again, though a bit more softly, which I took as an affirmation. "It's settled then, Judge. I'm Neve."

He looked away, which made me chuckle. At least he remained true to his character.

"Come on, then." I pulled his reins, and despite being generally unimpressed by me, Judge followed. Once we got into a rhythm and I felt certain that he'd walk alongside me, I released him. The horse didn't break step, so I pulled out my dagger to work on the stick.

Used to crafting items and working with my hands, it didn't take me long to transform the stick into a stake. I held it up to the moonlight, examining my work. Not beautiful, but it would do.

Finally, properly armed against vampires as well as

other foes, I listened harder for running water. I needed to make good on my promise to Judge.

Water, however, wasn't what I heard first. A few minutes later, the sounds of hounds baying in the distance, causing my spine to straighten.

"Bleeding skies!" Quickly, I rammed the stake into the interior pocket of my cloak. "Come here, Judge!"

I gripped the reins tighter, and the horse threw his head in protest, but I slid my foot into the stirrup and hauled myself over him anyway. Water and rest would have to wait.

I needed to ride east, toward the Winter Court of the fae and cross that boundary line. I shivered. Master Aldéric claimed that my birth mother died trying to run *from* the Winter Court. It felt ominous to be returning, but no matter her reasons, right now, the border between this court and Winter's Realm meant relative safety. I had to make it there before vampires tore me apart.

Digging my heels into Judge's sides, I spurred him forward. The horse began a slow trot, an obvious protest to not getting what I promised.

"Faster." I dug my heels in harder. The horse responded to the command with an annoyed snort. "I know I said water, but if you value your life, you'll run."

The baying of the hounds grew louder. Fates, how close were they? Were they following my direct path?

My throat dried up. The vampires used hunting dogs for sport. They related to the creatures as hunters and killers. The masters and royals loved their dogs, and they alternated kills with them.

Heart pounding, I leaned over Judge's neck as he trotted slowly through the trees. Soon enough, a dusting of snow appeared on the forest floor. It wasn't cold enough for that, not here anyway, but in Winter's Realm it would be far colder. I had to be close to the border.

"Judge, *please*, go faster!" I said and tried to get the creature to speed up again, but this time, he refused.

Instead, the horse turned south, and I learned why as, through the trees, I caught the glint of moonlight on water. Judge had sensed running water, a wide river from the looks of it. The horse slowed, determined to get the drink he was owed.

"No!" I gasped. "We can't!"

Done taking my orders, the horse cantered straight for the water, paused at the bank, and drank deeply.

My pulse pounded in my ears. Each second that passed, the dogs and the vampires came closer.

"Judge!" I hissed and dug my heels into his sides. "We must go! Now."

The horse lifted his head and gave an indignant whinny.

My throat tightened as the sound of rushing blood filled my ears. This would not be how I went out. I'd done the impossible by escaping Sangrael. I'd come close to the border. I'd not end this night tied up and taken back to my captor.

"Fine!" I swung off Judge's back, and this time managed not to fall as my feet touched down.

Once on the ground, I craned my neck to look out at the river and walked a few paces, trying to assess all the angles. The water ran fast but didn't look too dangerous.

But is it really safe to cross? Burning stars, does it matter? If I don't make it to the border . . . No, I couldn't finish that thought.

In the distance, the baying of hounds sounded once more. Closer, this time. So close that my heart began to beat erratically. At any moment, I felt sure that a hound or a vampire would burst through the trees and tear me limb from limb.

I needed to run, but I'd never be fast enough to outrun a vampire. And crossing would only erase my scent in the water . . . Not beyond. What if I was wrong and the border was still a fair distance away? Or what if they ignored the border and ran through it, even though they shouldn't, because they were so close to catching me?

Judge whinnied, and I turned to the horse as an idea sparked. Unclasping my cloak, I shrugged it off and pulled the stake from the pocket. Then I shifted the cloak under Judge's saddle to keep my scent on him strong.

"You're done with me, boy." Careful to keep to his side, I smacked him as hard as I could on the rump.

He let out another sharp whinny that sent pity through me, but he did as I'd hoped. He bolted straight across the river and into the woods on the other side. When I could no longer see Judge, I gripped my stake tightly and leapt into the cold water.

CHAPTER 6

In the dark, I rode the river currents, never daring to lift my head too high above the water, or to look too closely at the western bank. All the while, I kept my stake clenched in my hand, ready to be attacked.

Time blurred, and I ended up staying in the river until the sun's first rays broke through the trees. Only then did I swim to the eastern shore and pull myself from the current, shivering and sopping wet.

I hadn't heard the hounds for hours, nor anyone else, a fact that, at first, relieved me. But as I walked through the deep snow, I began to worry.

Thanks to my ancestry from the Winter Court, I had a strong tolerance for the cold. However, now that I was fairly sure I was in Winter's Realm, I understood the stories of the place.

I might not be far from the boundary of the Vampire Court, but the temperature had plummeted drastically since arriving in this snow-covered land. It was colder than anything I'd ever experienced. That, coupled with enough time wandering the forest sopping wet and even I could freeze to death. After all that I'd endured, I felt that time approaching. To survive, I needed to find shelter, fire, and food. And I needed to find it fast.

I shivered and ran my hands along my arms. What I wouldn't give to have my cloak back. I wished I hadn't been so hasty and would have attached a sock to Judge instead. Still gripping the stake I'd fashioned tightly, I walked deeper into the stunning white woods. How long would I have to walk to find civilization? Or even a single home?

I didn't know, but I remained alert, trudging through the ever-deepening snow and fighting off the cold that threatened to take me to the afterworld. Even the sun's rays gently warming me weren't enough to stop the shivering that became more violent.

Then, *finally*, after I felt like I'd walked for hours, I stumbled across a boon.

A road appeared through the trees, and I rushed over to it, climbing a drift and sliding down the other side to stand upon the ribbon that cut through the trees. Pivoting from side to side, I gazed up and down its length. In one direction, a bend hid the rest of the road from sight. On the other, a long stretch of snow-packed road stretched on as far as I could see.

I rubbed my arms more vigorously, trying to generate heat. Which way would be best?

A village might exist in either direction, so I tossed up a prayer to the stars, and turned right. On shuffling feet, I began walking to see what lay around the corner. I'd nearly made it to the bend when the clopping sound of horse hooves met my ears. I gasped, terror spiking. Before I could even think to stop myself, I scurried up the snow drift and stumbled behind the nearest tree just as a brawny fae male with a long brown beard appeared, driving a cart pulled by two horses.

My heart rate slowed, and I realized that, though rationally, I didn't actually think the vampires would follow, my body hadn't been certain. All my life they'd been near me, a looming threat, and that wasn't going to be easy to shake.

The question then became was this fae friendly? Winter's Realm had a reputation for cold and tough subjects. To be safe, I remained where I was, and sized him up as he guided the wagon filled with chopped wood.

Nothing about the fae insinuated wealth, a factor I correlated to danger. Nor did he look mean, though looks could be deceiving. Perhaps most important of all, his wings had stunted. If he came after me, he wouldn't be able to fly. We'd both be on foot, and even after hours of walking, I felt confident that I'd be faster than the bulky, muscular fae.

Did I dare announce myself? It was a risk, but wandering the forest for hours longer and freezing to death seemed a far greater one.

The Fates determined my answer for me when the cart stopped close to where I hid, and the fae male turned in my direction. "I can smell ye out there! See your marks in the snow too!"

Bleeding snow! A foul whisper of curses left my lips.

"If you're meanin' to rob me, all I have is wood for the Warden of the West. But if ye mean me no harm, I won't hurt ye either," the faerie added, his tone a little softer.

I took a deep breath. He sounded genuine, and seeing as I was desperate, I decided to take a chance. First, though, I folded my wings down, compacting them so the rods weren't noticeable. Then I stuck the stake in the snow. Though it gave me comfort to hold, it would also be a dead giveaway as to where I'd come from. Once I'd hidden my past as best I could, I stepped out from behind the tree and onto the road.

The fae's eyebrows, as bushy as his beard, rose. His gaze strayed to my hip where my dagger hung. He said nothing of my weapon but opted for the obvious. "Are ye wet?"

"I was, still am a little." My teeth chattered so hard I thought I might break a tooth. "Do you have a spare cloak?"

He studied me and then patted the bench beside him. "Ye won't be usin' that dagger on me, will ye?"

"I have no intention of doing so."

"Then, come 'ere. Ye can borrow me cloak, and I'll take you into town. Can get yer own cloak there."

For the first time in hours, I smiled. It hurt. "Thank you."

Shakily, I climbed onto the cart and scooted next to the faerie. Up close, he seemed even larger than before. Was it normal for faeries to be so big? Was I actually a runt among my kind? I didn't think so, but looking at him, I felt like one. He also looked to be about ten turns older than me, around thirty, which meant he could be any age. Faeries aged, but around thirty, the turns wore on us more slowly than I'd observed with humans. A fae might celebrate thirty-two namedays or ninety and look about the same.

"What's your name, lass?"

"Neve. Yours?"

"Frode. Ye from around here? Certainly not the Western Range of Winter's Realm. Don't sound like it."

"I'm passing through. Heading east."

He eyed me sidelong but said nothing else as he passed over his thick, enormous cloak. I wrapped it around me, sighing as the dense fur teased my cheeks.

"Thank you for this." I clasped the cloak tightly, trying to keep in as much heat as possible. "And for the ride."

"The stars would smite me if I left a freezing lass on the road. In fact," he reached into a bag just behind him and pulled out a metal flask, "take this. 'Tis broth and it's still hot."

With trembling fingers, I took the flask. It was indeed still warm, so I pulled off the cap and sipped. Warmth filled my mouth and ran down my throat as I swallowed. Stars, it was so good. Just what I needed.

"Go slow with it," Frode warned. "Might shock yer system."

I nodded. "I will."

He cracked the reins, and his horses started walking.

Soon enough, the muffled clopping of hooves on packed snow were the only sounds filling my ears. So much had happened; I didn't mind having a minute of peace to focus on warming up, which the cloak was enabling. Those in Winter's Realm really did know how to make insulated clothing.

We continued to ride in silence for a while, though I didn't miss Frode casting me glances. Finally, it apparently became too much, so he broke the silence. "Where were ye comin' from? The Autumn Court? Through the passes in the Ice Tooth Range?"

"Yes," I lied.

Telling anyone where I had really come from was not a smart idea. Thankfully, because the vampires fed anyone with magic a potion to stunt their magic, I was not bound by faerie magical restrictions. Meaning, unlike others of my race, I could lie—until the potion wore off, anyhow. As I'd taken it just yesterday, after my last blood-letting session, I had nearly a full moon cycle to go.

"Yer tough to go through the Ice Tooth Mountains. The orc raids have been blasted 'orrible of late. I heard larger numbers than ever are moving west, into the Red Mist Range—maybe cause of the weather. Haven't seen any though, not when I go for lumber, but I don't usually go too deep into the hills."

I frowned. I still wanted to go south and had always known that orcs often lived in mountains, but this news was troubling. More orcs would only make my journey more difficult.

"So, you sell wood?" I gestured back to his wares,

trying to shift the conversation. As I did so, I noted that my body was already moving better, and my shivering had become less violent. Thanks to fae accelerated healing and Frode's kindness, I'd likely just managed to avoid hypothermia. The Fates were smiling down on me.

"I sell to the Warden of the West himself." His chest puffed with pride. "Few other merchants too, but the castle in Guldtown takes most of my wares."

"I don't know much about the warden or his family," I admitted.

"Just the warden. His father, mother, and brother are dead." His tone dipped when he brought them up. "Right around the time the blight struck our lands hard. 'Bout twenty something turns ago."

My heart sank for the fae I did not know. I had never met my mother, and to hear my old master tell it, my father was nowhere to be found when, twenty-one turns ago, his soldiers had found my mother, dead in the woods near the border of the Winter Court. She'd been dead in a snow drift, a bundled up two-year-old baby—me—in her arms. Lord Aldéric's soldiers had taken me to his estate, and there, he'd claimed me and given me my name. Every so often I thought about my past and of course my loss hurt, but it *had* to be worse to know your family and then lose them.

Then the other part of what Frode said caught my attention. "What do you mean by the blight?"

Frode stretched out his stunted wings. "A sickness that's been sweeping our kingdom for a long time. It's why my wings stopped growin'. Ye don't have it in your court?"

I wracked my brain. Had I read about this affliction? Vampires certainly wouldn't care to gossip about it. Not unless a slave was affected, and I'd never met one that was.

"Not that I've encountered," I settled on.

"Yer a lucky lass."

Not for most of my life, but things seemed to be changing. I hoped luck stayed with me long enough to retrieve Anna.

We chatted about other small matters, mostly pertaining to Frode and his work, until we crested a hill and a city appeared in the valley. Snow covered the roofs of small homes, and a castle rose in the backdrop. It didn't appear as large as the Laurents' castle, but it was nothing to sneeze at either.

"Beautiful," I said as Frode directed the cart down the hill toward a stone wall that surrounded the town.

"Had a fresh snow the other night, we did. Guldtown always looks pretty in white."

She did, and I admired the city as we rode up to the wall. Two male fae stood watch. Their eyes widened at our approach.

"Who's this, Frode?" one asked, studying me more than the product he needed to check.

"Neve. She's from the Autumn Court. I found her lost on the road."

"That's a long way away." The guard grunted. "The warden will want to know."

"It's a good thing I'm goin' to the castle then, eh?" He arched an eyebrow.

The fae gave Frode a look that plainly said that he had better do as he promised and opened the gates.

We drove through. Frode stayed quiet until the gate closed again and then turned to me. "Ye don't mind if I stop at the castle first before I take ye to the shopping district for a cloak? I really was supposed to have this wood here earlier but got delayed."

"Not a problem," I assured him.

How I'd purchase a new cloak, food, and a room was anyone's guess, but I'd figure it out. Perhaps an innkeeper would have garments they needed mended or dishes to do? No matter the task, I'd do whatever it took for a soft bed to sleep in and another layer.

Perhaps I'd get new shoes too. My toes wiggled in my boots. They'd been worn down before, but after walking in the snow, the soles felt as thin as parchment. I had a long way to travel and blisters and sores wouldn't make that easier.

Frode wound through the city, and for the first time, I was surrounded by those of my own magical order. All types of fae bustled in the streets, working, gossiping, generally going about their days. I recognized a dryad with his bark-like skin and vivid green hair, hauling a basket of brooms on his back. A circle of nymphs, all dressed provocatively and giggling, watched a duo of male faeries stride down the street. Pixies zoomed through the air so fast I could barely catch their faces, and a trio of leprechauns fought in front of a building that, judging by its luxurious exterior, I thought must be a coinary.

Many fae were dressed in thick fur cloaks, some of them even embroidered, and everyone appeared clean and healthy. The dominant industry of the city had to have been lucrative for such fine clothing to be common-place. I opened my mouth to ask what the city was known for, when we turned a corner and the castle appeared at the end of a short road. In face of the majesty of the castle, the question flitted away.

While lovely from far away, up close, it became more stunning. The gold-capped towers sprung from white stone, and the red doors and ice roses pictured in stained glass windows made for a beautiful contrast.

"Lovely, isn't she?" Frode asked, catching the awe that I wore clearly on my face.

"Indeed. Is that tower genuine gold? Or painted?"

"'Tis gold. Comes from the mines nearby. The Lisika family is so rich they fill their toilets with gold."

I snorted out a surprised laugh at Frode's indelicacy. "I see."

Well, that explained the well-kept appearance of the rest of the town. A mine of that sort would maintain the area's wealth.

We reached the castle gates and after a brief conver-sation with a castle steward, Frode drove around the building to the area where he needed to drop off his wares. He stopped the cart, jumped into the snow, and offered me a hand.

"Thank you." I took his hand and stepped down. "I—

hey!" The moment my feet touched the ground, the fae pulled the dagger from my sheath, and threw it aside as he scooped me up, and tossed me over his shoulder. "What are you doing?!"

"Ye think I didn't notice your markings?"

My heart stuttered as I stared down at the snow, packed tight from footsteps. "I have no idea what you're talking about."

"Where they took yer blood."

I stiffened. Bloodletters, vampires of inferior status, drew blood from slaves by needle. It was one of the few inventions that King Vladistrica had borrowed from the human world. Even with my fae healing abilities, over time, a letter's needle left marks. Small scars lined my forearms and the backs of my hands. I'd been so careful about my wings, but these scars? I hardly ever noticed them now.

I also wondered how Frode had recognized them for what they were, though? Surely, this fae had never been to the Blood Court.

"I can explain."

"To the warden, ye can." Frode entered the castle through a servant's entrance. "I donno how you did it, but all ye told me was lies, and I won't listen any longer."

The backstabber! I gave him an awkward kick in the stomach, to which he only laughed.

"Lass, I'm as Winterborn and bred as they come. Try as you might, ye won't harm me."

I took that to mean that he was tougher than he looked, which was quite tough indeed. After a few more kicks and punches to his back, which earned only more chuckles and shakes of his head, I decided to save my energy for when I could run.

Aside from being strong, Frode also seemed to know his way around the warden's castle, for the fae stomped down the corridors without asking for directions. Finally, though, he stopped walking. "I'm here to see Warden Lisika."

"Your business?" a sharp female voice asked.

Frode's shoulders tightened. "What's it to ye? These are the hours that he hears his people's concerns."

The guard sighed. "You're not on the list, Frode."

"Bugger yer list! I found an escaped blood slave!"

A pause echoed in my ears before the guard asked, "a new one?"

New one? What did it matter if I was old or new?

"Judgin' by the markings, she's been there a while."

A quill scratched paper, and a door creaked open. "Very well, you may see him but only because he's free now. Next time, get on the list."

Frode grumbled beneath his breath about where she could stick her list and took a few lumbering steps into a room. Immediately, I noticed that the echo of his steps became louder, so I twisted as best I could and looked up.

Above me, gilded buttresses joined in the center of a soaring ceiling. To the sides of the crimson double doors, two large golden leopards leapt toward the middle of the room at the person daring to walk down the aisle to speak with their lord.

I swallowed. This castle might not be as intimidating

or dark as Palais Immortael, but something told me the Warden of the West was not a fae to mess with.

"My good fae, Frode, what brings you in today?" A male voice, smooth and deep, rang through me.

"Found this faerie on the side of the road leadin' into Guldtown, my lord. She was wet, had no cloak, and has markings all over her arms, clearly an escaped blood slave, my lord." Frode yanked me forward by the legs. My hands went back to break my fall as he dumped me on the hard ground.

I groaned, rubbing my rear, trying to erase the shooting pains radiating from it.

"She lied about where she came from, though," Frode added. "Not sure how."

"The Blood use witchcraft to dim the powers of their slaves who possess magic," the lord said with certainty. "They gave you a potion, girl?"

"I'm no girl," I spat back, twisting to take in the warden for the first time.

Copper-red hair flowed past his shoulders, and the bright hue made his emerald-green eyes pop. He was pale, with not a single mark on his skin, and even though he sat, I could tell he was tall and well-muscled. Though his tunic was red, a color I would have thought would not go with his hair, it suited him. Just as he seemed to have been born sprawling in the gold throne he lounged upon.

The warden's wings were his only imperfect features. They curled backward and were shorter than they should have been. Unfortunate. The golden color was exquisite.

"Yes, I see now that you're not a youngling. My apologies." The warden stood, his penetrating green eyes watching me like a hawk watched a mouse. "However, you were given a potion, correct?"

"I was," I admitted. No use in denying it. Clearly, he knew something about the Blood Court.

He came closer, his gait loping and graceful. At the sides of the throne, two male guards shot the warden side-long looks, but he waved for them to stay in place. Clearly, he saw no threat in a bedraggled female. As much as I wished to prove him wrong, I didn't think I could. I hadn't slept in a day and had traveled for hours through the woods. I wasn't exactly in peak physical condition.

"They are quite ingenious in that court, aren't they?" the warden mused.

"They're monsters," I hissed. "I wish a stake of ash to every heart in the Vampire Kingdom."

The warden's lips curled up before he caught himself as he came to stand before me. "I suppose if I were in your position, I'd say the same." He held out his hand.

I recoiled.

His face fell a touch. "I won't hurt you."

"Forgive me if I don't trust in lords or kings."

"After what you've endured, I suspect that's only natural. But I have taken no potion masking my magic. I'm a full-blooded faerie of Winter's Realm. I cannot lie to you."

I swallowed and looked at his hand. Then, surprising myself, I took it. The lord helped me to my feet, and when I stood, he tilted my chin upward.

"Your eyes are astounding."

I blinked. "T-thank you." Whatever I'd been expecting him to say, it wasn't that.

"Even here, where fae have eyes of many colors, that hue is rarer than most," he explained.

I looked at the floor, unsure of what to say. My violet eyes had been very rare in the Blood Court too. Most of the blood slaves had been human.

"I must ask, how did you get that scar?" the warden asked, surprising me again.

The crescent moon scar over my right temple wasn't large, about the length of half my pinkie finger and very thin. That he'd noticed it spoke to his powers of observation.

I lifted my shoulder in a half shrug. "I actually don't know. I've had it since I was very young."

He released my chin. "We all acquire scars as we age. If we're lucky, they tell a worthy story."

My hand went to the scar. How was it that I suddenly felt self-conscious over something I rarely even thought about?

"I apologize for my forwardness. I didn't mean to embarrass you," the warden said, and after a pause, added, "are you hungry?"

"I am," I blurted, unable to act indifferent. The idea of food made my stomach rumble, and all odd interactions with this fae disappeared from my mind.

"Then, you shall eat."

"And what of my prize, my lord?" Frode asked gruffly, coming to the warden's side. "She's a blood slave. She is worth gold if we send her back. I can take—"

A blade pressed against Frode's neck. His eyes went as round as the moon as his lord threatened him with the dagger, his own gaze penetrating the lesser fae.

"There will be no sending her back," the warden commanded in the tone of someone used to being listened to. "You will tell no one that you found this female. You will not speak of her at all. I will have a prize sent to you, and that will be the end of it. If you so much as *whisper* to anyone about her, you will be punished. Do you understand?"

"I-yes, my lord!"

The Warden of the West withdrew his blade. "Leave us, Frode. Guards, too. I'll see no one else from my territory today."

Frode's face hardened as he marched from the throne room. The guards left behind him, closing the door.

When we stood alone, the warden turned to me once again. "I'm Roar Lisika, Warden of the West and head of my noble house. But, please, just call me Roar."

"Um . . . are you sure?" Never had I been asked to address someone above my station with such familiarity. I might have done so in my head, but not to their faces.

"Believe me, the titles grow wearing. I prefer Roar." He smiled. "However, if you must, my lord will do."

Burning skies. This lord was *different*.

"Alright, then," I said slowly. "Well, I'm Neve. No house. No titles. Nothing to my name at all, in fact." I paused. "Thank you for not returning me to the Blood Court."

"Did your mother give you that name?" he asked.

I blinked. "Excuse me?"

"Neve is not a common name in this kingdom, but you're quite obviously one of us," Lord Roar said. "No Summer, Spring, nor even an Autumn fae could survive the cold we've been experiencing. Especially not wet, as Frode said. But, you'll soon learn that the fae of Winter's Realm look out for one another."

"Ah, no. My old master named me. I don't know what I was called before I became a slave," I answered.

"Perhaps one day you'll choose your own name." He smirked. "I have to admit, I like a fae with the tenacity to fight for herself. As you escaped the Vampire Court, you certainly have done so."

Was he genuine? Or was this some twisted form of the truth? I couldn't see how . . .

"As it so happens, you've arrived at a very good time for me. I've had a problem I needed solving and your appearance might be the answer. Should you wish to hear my proposition, that is?"

"Excuse me?"

"Come. I've promised you food." He swept a slender-fingered hand to the door. "And if you're amenable to hear a fae out, I believe we might come to an arrangement that benefits us both."

CHAPTER 7

The Warden of the West led me straight into the kitchens. "What would you like?" he asked as three cloven-foot cooks stopped what they were doing and waited; hands clasped behind them.

"Um, whatever you have?"

"We have anything your heart desires."

My lips parted in shock. All my life, I'd only been able to choose from a few rotating foods on the day's menu.

For a moment, I allowed myself to dream of what I might actually *want* to eat, but the possibilities quickly overwhelmed me. Not to mention, I suspected that the food here differed from in the Blood Court. It certainly had to be different from what I'd been given, which had always been nutritious enough to keep a blood slave healthy but never very tasty. I swallowed loudly, starving but at a complete loss for what to say. Noticing the cooks still waited, my cheeks warmed and I pulled Frode's cloak, which he hadn't bothered to reclaim, tighter around me.

"Might I offer a suggestion?" the high lord asked softly.

"Please."

"Last night I had an excellent roast with freshly picked vegetables from the greenhouses. While I wouldn't normally give a guest leftovers—"

"Actually," I interrupted, as my stomach growled. Roast was something I knew, something I liked better than most foods, particularly after a drawing. The meat here would likely have salt and flavor too. "That sounds great."

His eyes twinkled. "I'm of the opinion that the roast my cooks prepare is often better on the second day anyway. Something about the sauces having time to meld. Or so they tell me." He grinned conspiratorially. As if I would know anything about decadent sauces. "Of course, you'll want wine from the Summer Isles to pair with it. I have a few of the best bottles in all of Isila. How's that?"

"That all sounds wonderful," I replied as my mouth began to water.

"Perfect." He gave the order to the cooks.

They assured their lord that the roast would be ready within minutes. Pleased, the warden took me by the elbow and guided me out of the kitchen into a smaller room down the hall.

A circular table for four sat near a hearth, already lit. Plush crimson rugs looked so inviting that I wanted to sink my cold toes into them, and landscape paintings lined the walls. The large window overlooked the vast expanse of the castle grounds. Greenhouses dotted the lawn, many more than I would have considered practical.

"It's how we supply our own vegetables here," Lord Roar offered when he caught me looking. "It's often too cold to plant them in the soil, and we sometimes import them, but with the use of greenhouses and fae with earth magic, we make it work."

"Does everyone have one?" A palace was one thing, but did the common fae have access to vegetables?

"Every household in Guldtown has some sort of greenhouse either in communal spaces, their own property, or, in the heart of the city, on rooftops. I made sure of that." Pride crossed his face as he pulled out the chair closest to the hearth. A white spotted animal hide was draped over the back of the chair, making it feel cozy. "Please, Lady Neve."

I sat, unable to believe the turn of my luck. Last night, I'd been floating in a freezing river and now I sat at a lord's table, a fire warming my back, about to be fed. I shrugged off Frode's cloak, revealing my filthy shirt and pants and my mutilated wings. I winced, realizing just then how bad I looked. Surely, I stank too.

Roar's eyes took in my attire, his gaze lingering on my wings for a moment before coming to my eyes. "Even if you are Winterborn, you'll be needing something warmer than that in this kingdom. I'll have a servant fetch you clothes from town. Is the fire enough for now?"

"It is," I assured and was about to thank him yet again when a servant entered the room, carrying two red goblets of wine.

"My lady." He handed the first to me. I'd never had wine before and certainly not out of a glass goblet with a gold rim.

"Is that a snow leopard?" I pointed to an etching on the base of the glass.

Roar's finger ran over the animal on his goblet. "They symbolize my noble house. All the Sacred Eight have claimed an animal."

"Sacred Eight?"

"The eight ruling families of Winter's Realm. We preside beneath the Royal House of Aaberg. Each has a sector of the realm or economy to manage."

"You are the Warden of the West," I said, working through the information bit by bit. "In this kingdom that means that you're the high lord who presides over the western part of the realm?"

"Precisely. There is also a Warden of the East, North, and South, as well as other lords and ladies who manage other aspects of diplomacy and economy, such as the Lord of Coin or Lady of Ships." He took a sip of his wine as if he'd said nothing more than his family ran a local tavern. I marveled at the male across from me, wondering how one got to be so self-assured. "Would you prefer white wine to red?"

The glass remained aloft in my hand, forgotten in all the talk of the ruling families of the Winter Realm. I supposed that by not drinking it, I appeared rude to my host, so I brought the goblet to my lips. Slowly, I sipped.

My eyes popped open wide as velvety, warming drink swept across my tongue. It was sweeter than I'd imagined and though I wasn't personally familiar with magic, I could tell that someone had poured their own power into the drink, somehow making the flavor dance in my mouth unlike anything I'd ever eaten.

What would it be like to be that person who made wine and gave a little of themselves to create it? That something so small could open my eyes to parts of the nine kingdoms I'd known nothing about was both exciting and a little terrifying.

"Is it to your taste?" the warden asked when I set the glass down.

"It's lovely."

Warden Roar smiled. "Very good. I don't like my guests to be uncomfortable."

For a person like me, a fae born and raised as property and also considered food, being completely comfortable in a palace was asking quite a lot. I might revel in the luxury, but deep inside, I couldn't help but feel like something was going to happen to put me back in my place. However, that wasn't the warden's fault. "I thank you for your generosity."

"It is my pleasure."

Servants bustled into the room, bringing with them steaming platters of meat and vegetables. The aroma made my mouth water, and when the feast landed before me, I nearly burst into tears.

This looked like no roast I'd ever seen.

Decadence did not describe the platter in front of me. The meat looked tender enough to fall off the bone and the vegetables certainly weren't what I'd been raised on.

Each part of the meal had been cooked to perfection. And the decorative garnish of berries and some sort of greenery around the edges of the platter made it look quite pretty.

I must have held in my awe well, however, because no one noticed. The servants made a plate for me, and Warden Roar insisted I eat, which I could hardly wait to do.

With a trembling fork, I took my first bite, and a moan nearly escaped my lips. The roast tasted excellent; moist and savory, spiced and flavored with herbs I could not name, but they danced on my tongue like perfection. The sauce the warden had mentioned pooled on top of the meat, enhancing the flavor. I gobbled up half the plate before realizing that I resembled a wild orc and set my fork down.

"Don't slow on my account." My benefactor took another sip of wine, as if he hadn't watched a guest act like an animal.

"I should, though," I replied. "This is a lot richer than the food I'm used to. I don't want to make myself sick."

"Excellent point." He set down his goblet and leaned closer. "Perhaps I can distract you for a few minutes with my offer?"

"That would be welcome."

"It has to do with the court in the capital city of Avaldenn."

I thought back to the maps I'd studied whenever a book about the nine kingdoms became available to slaves, thankful for his gentle instruction as I recalled the area.

For some, it could be confusing. Sometimes the kingdoms were referred to as their courts. Other times, the kingdoms had more than one name—like Winter's Realm and the Winter Court.

"I know the general area," I said.

"Very good. Well . . ." He cleared his throat, showing the first signs of nerves. "I try to avoid attending court as often as possible. For a fae in my position, that means attending functions about twice a year. This year, the king has commanded that I come to a third, for a festival I do not wish to attend alone. I wish for you to come with me."

I leaned into the chair, taken aback. "I have to admit, I am not well equipped to become part of one's household staff. In the Blood Court I was a seamstress."

His eyebrows arched. "Handy, that skill. However, you mistake my intentions. I have no need for more fae in my staff. Rather, I hoped you would accompany me as a lady and play the part of my fiancée?"

I barked out a laugh, stopping only when he watched me expectantly. Wait, did he really mean that? He looked like he meant every word, but the idea was preposterous!

"*A fiancée?*" I gestured down at my dress and my general bedraggled state. "But look at me! I'm no lady, Warden Roar. Surely, there are many females dying to be seen on your arm. Ones who are acquainted with this realm and its customs."

"Of course," he replied. "But I've been thinking of this since the Courting Festival summons arrived nearly a month ago. I've played out many scenarios, and believe me when I say, those same ladies have their own agendas.

I do not wish to bring them before the court because I'm not sure their motives are pure. With you, I would not have to worry. Our relationship would be a farce. And I would make it well worth your time."

Oh. I looked down at my plate. Why had I not considered that the moment he'd suggested me being his fiancée? This would be an arrangement, not a true marriage agreement.

"But why bring anyone at all?" I asked, still confused. "Can't you arrive as a bachelor?"

"Usually, I can, but this trip is different." His lips flattened for a moment before he continued. "His Grace has called for a Courting Festival. It's an old tradition, in which the king, or queen if that is the dominant ruler, arranges matches for the lords and ladies of his or her land. They can force alliances or break them at their will. If the ruler does not favor you, things can end badly."

"And you're not favored?" I asked.

"My house is of great importance to Winter's Realm. The soldiers sworn to House Lisika protect against vampires crossing the Red Mist Mountains and attacking border towns, rare as those attacks may be. Not to mention, we supply the kingdom with gold." His gaze dipped to the goblet. "Much of the kingdom's wealth comes from my lands. That being said, I don't agree with most of what the Royal House of Aaberg has done of late, and I do not wish to be forced to marry, especially not into their family. So it would be best to bring someone to avoid the forcing of my marriage. One I have no say in."

"Ah. There is a princess?"

"There is, though she is already spoken for by another noble lord. However, the king has a niece from House Vagle, the queen's blood house. I fear King Magnus would force Lady Calpurnia Vagle upon me to bind our houses. Then he can lay claim to more of my wealth and use my people as he wishes." His eyes flicked briefly to my scar before he locked gazes with me. "But from the moment I set eyes on you, I knew the Fates had brought you here for a reason. And I'll admit that you can lie at court is *quite* a boon."

I found myself at a loss. What Warden Roar suggested seemed so far out of my realm of normal. Not sure what to do with myself, I took two more decadent bites of roast. When I was done, I set down my fork.

"What sort of plan?"

The warden's chin lifted, ever so slightly. "You act as my fiancée at the Winter Court. There will be a contract to sign, of course, since you can lie, and much is at stake for me. It will bind us. Before signing, you name a price, and I will do all that I can to compensate you for your time acting at court."

Part of me was baffled that he'd come up with all this so fast, but it was clear that the warden was clever and a fae of business. He knew how to get what he wanted and if he really had been considering the Courting Festival for some time and an answer was delivered to his doorstep . . . well, who wouldn't be keen to seize it?

And if I agreed, I could set a price, a fact that someone in my position could not ignore.

So, what did I want?

Safety, the word materialized as soon as I asked the question.

"After we're done playing our parts, could you get me far away?" I asked. "To the Spring Court? Or even as far south as Summer? With guards to ensure my safety?"

When I'd first cobbled together an escape plan, I'd only thought to venture as far as the Dragon Court. It lay closest to the Blood's Kingdom, and therefore, I could manage to walk there. But with a lord's wealth and might behind me, it would be possible to travel much farther. That would buy me far more security.

A second thought struck. *Anna!*

"Maybe you can help me save someone else from the Blood Court? A dear friend."

"Arranging armed transport to the Spring or Summer Courts is not an issue." He drew in a deep breath. "The other inquiry, however . . . I assume your friend is a blood slave?"

"She is. A human one."

He pressed his lips together briefly. "I cannot say whether that is achievable. Especially after your escape."

My chest deflated.

"I can put you in contact with those who might be able to extract her, though. People with experience in heists," he said. "Perhaps I can help you with your wings and the other markings, too?"

Instinctively, I tucked my mangled silver wings against my back.

"Those metal rods must be quite painful," Warden

Roar continued. "And I assume you cannot fly with them in?"

"No," I said. The shape of faerie wings was butterfly-like, though the membraneous tissue was stronger, and the color varied with each faerie. Despite the strength of the tissue, however, flight was impossible with metal piercing my wings. "I've had them since I was a small child, so I've never flown."

I'd never considered the option that one day I might fly. But now, he had enticed me.

"Could you really extract the rods?" Even saying the words made my heart rate speed up.

"I have an excellent healer. If anyone can help you, it's her. Would you like to visit her and get them removed once you've eaten?"

"I would. Would this be part of your proposal?"

"No. This is simply what's right."

I swallowed, struck by the kindness. Perhaps I'd heard wrong about the fae of Winter? Frode might have betrayed me but this lord seemed valiant indeed.

"I'd appreciate that," I said finally. "As for your proposal, might I have time to consider playing your fiancée?"

While I appreciated his generous offer, I needed to consider whether it would be the best decision. As someone who had always been under another's thumb, I couldn't help but feel wary.

"Absolutely," the warden replied. "I understand that this matter requires time to consider. Just know that if we're to travel to court together, we have little more than a week until we must leave. In that time, you will be tutored nearly every minute of the day on court etiquette."

My chest tightened. A week was so short and if I were to put on a convincing show, I had much to learn. That put a new level of urgency to the deal, but instead of showing my rising anxiety, I inclined my head. "I understand."

He nodded to my plate, and a lock of red hair covered his eyes before he swept it away with a grace that poured effortlessly out of him. "Your meal is getting cold. Why don't you finish up while I go speak with the healer?" He pushed his chair back and stood. "Will you be alright alone?"

"I will. Thank you." I leaned into my chair, the heat from the fire seeping into my back.

"Enjoy, Neve. I'll return soon." The Warden of the West gave a small bow and left me alone with my meal and a thousand questions spinning in my mind.

CHAPTER 8

Belly full, I trailed a half step behind Warden Roar toward the healer's quarters. My wings tingled with anticipation. I couldn't recall life without the metal rods in my wings. What would it feel like once they were out? In time, would I be able to fly normally? Just the idea sent a jolt of excitement through me.

"Here we are." The warden stopped before a wooden door and opened it. "Healer Althea?"

"I'm here, my lord," a deep female voice called out. "Is she ready?"

"She is," the high lord replied as we walked into the room.

The healer's quarters were larger than I'd imagined. Twenty beds lined the long room and shelves that held vials and bottles filled with either potions or dried ingredients loomed at the far ends of the space. From the ceiling, groups of plants hung too, infusing the room with a floral scent that almost covered up a more astringent stench.

"Morning, miss." A fae at least two heads taller than the towering warden, appeared through a doorway. A bottle of liquid bubbled away in her hands.

My heart rate spiked and I took a step back, eyes widening as I studied the fae. She was, simply, the largest being I'd ever seen and with her fangs and bulging muscles, somewhat terrifying, too.

"I take it you've never seen someone with troll blood?" The healer had no judgment in her tone.

"No. I'm sorry. You're very tall." I paused. "You're a troll *and* a healer?"

The moment I said it, I realized how rude I sounded, but I found it hard to believe. According to the stories, trolls were dim creatures. They survived by brute strength, their skin being impervious to most magic, and they stayed in loyal and protective family groups.

The healer burst out laughing. "I'm actually half troll and half faerie, else I wouldn't be out in the daylight, now would I?"

I nodded, belatedly recalling that fact about trolls. The sun turned them to stone, and they had to wait until night came to turn back.

"And for my troll half, I'm very small." She smiled warmly at me. "They'd consider twelve heads tall a true runt. Most of my family on that side is at least fifteen heads tall. Some up to twenty-two!" The healer set down the bottle she'd been holding. "As for the matter of trolls rarely possessing the intelligence to be a healer." She arched an eyebrow as if daring me to deny that was what I'd thought.

I couldn't, so I waited.

"They aren't all so dimwitted," the healer continued. "My family is intelligent. And then my faerie half is too, of course. I assure you, Lady Neve, you're in excellent hands."

"Oh," I said because not only did her calling me a lady throw me off, but I had no idea what else to say.

Instead, I stood there, feeling stupid and unworldly, a combination I rarely experienced where I came from. The vampires in the Blood Court saw me as the lowest of the low, but there I knew what life had in store for me. I understood how to navigate the hand I'd been dealt—how to survive. Here, everything was different.

"Althea is a gifted healer." The Warden of the West smiled at the healer with appreciation. "Her father taught her and brought her to Guldtown when she was young. She has helped to save the lives of many of my soldiers."

"And I'd do it again." Althea nodded. "It's always a pleasure to serve, my lord. You've always been good to me."

Warden Roar smiled. "So, you can help Neve?"

"Come." Althea motioned me to a bed fitted with white sheets and a downy blanket folded at the bottom. She pulled off the blanket and set it on the next bed before patting the mattress.

I shuffled over and sat. Her hands, gentle despite their large size, explored the contours of my wings, and I held my breath.

"I'm sorry," Althea said, "I may not have them, but I know wings are sensitive for faeries."

She spoke true of course. Others didn't normally touch a faerie's wings for that reason.

"These markings," she pointed to the needle marks on the backs of my hands and arms, "will fade substantially, if not completely disappear with my balms."

"Really?" My heart skipped a beat. This was more than I dared to hope for.

"Yes. They're already quite faded, with time, I suppose, but given a proper course of balms, we can possibly even erase them. Would you like the one on your temple to fade too?"

I paused. That scar was with me before I left my mother's dead arms, before I became a slave. It was mine, even if it wasn't beautiful. "No. Leave that."

She did not seem surprised. "And as for the wings, I *can* excise the rods. Six in each wing, though, is quite a lot," Althea let out a thoughtful hum. "I'm no Master Healer and the wings are complex and fragile, but once the rods are out, I have an elixir that I think can help fade that scarring too. I'd prefer that to the balm you'll use elsewhere, the elixir is more gentle."

I could hardly believe it. "Thank you."

"Of course, I will do what I can. Right now, however, I advise you to take a sedative, Lady Neve. Are you willing?"

"Will I still be awake while you work?"

"You don't have to be. I'd suggest one of my stronger doses so that you pass out. Though, you might do so anyway from the pain."

My mouth dried up. Stars, what had I gotten myself into?

"Her elixirs and balms are effective," the warden said softly, clearly trying to assure me.

"I'm willing." I reminded myself that no matter what, I had to attend to these matters one day. Once I truly became free, I did not want others questioning my scars or wings. "I'd like to take the strongest one that I can stomach."

Althea drifted to the far wall and plucked two vials from her stash. Inside the glass, red liquid sloshed. "Drink these."

I uncorked one and downed it. The elixir wasn't unpleasant but sweet and tangy. I licked my lips. "That was far better than I'd expected."

"I made countless tweaks so that it would taste like raspberries," Althea said with a little laugh. "The recipe my father used was revolting. Unnecessary."

"Much appreciated." I finished the second vial and handed the glassware back to her.

She placed it in a sink and picked up a scalpel and an overly large set of tweezers from a table. "My Lord Warden, now is the time to make yourself scarce."

"Take good care of her, Althea." The high lord turned to me. "I'll see you tomorrow, I expect."

"Thanks for everything," I replied. In the short time that I'd known Warden Roar, he'd done so much for me that a thanks did not seem enough, but I only had it to offer. "I'll have my answer ready soon."

ASHLEY MCLEO

"Very well. I hope the procedure goes smoothly." He let himself out of the healer's quarters, and when I turned back around, Althea wasn't the only one in the room any longer. Two dwarves flanked her, both muscle-bound and bearded, though one had red hair while the other had brown.

"Who are they?" I asked, taking a half-step back.

"Castle laborers. I requested their help in this matter. They didn't mean to startle you," the healer replied. "The red-haired one is Thom, and the other is Regil. They will help hold you down until the elixir kicks in. Is that alright?"

Hold me down. Wonderful.

"Yes," I said even as fear trickled in and circled my ribs.

"Face down on this bed." Althea set a metal bowl on a nearby bedside table. "I'm starting with the wings and will apply the first round of balm elsewhere once the hard bit is done."

I did as she requested, and the dwarves stood on either side of me. "Pardon our touch, miss," Thom, the red-haired one, said. In unison, they pressed one hand each into my shoulders and then the other went to my wings.

I hissed, but they didn't loosen their grip, didn't apologize again, didn't even acknowledge my pain as Althea began to explain where she'd start her work. Hopefully, the elixir would start working soon and they wouldn't have to keep me pinned down for long. It made me feel like a wild beast.

"Steady yourself, Lady Neve," Althea said. "I'm starting."

I braced, but when the knife cut into my wing, I still wasn't at all prepared for the singe of agony that cut through me. A scream tore its way up my throat, and instinctively, I tensed and tried to jerk away, but the dwarves held me down and kept me from moving too much.

"I know it hurts, but try to stay still," Althea murmured. "We don't want to damage your wings more than they already are. Soon, the elixir will overpower you. I promise."

She continued to work, and I screamed at the stars. It seemed like the elixir would not be enough, that I should have taken three, maybe even four, vials.

Thom's and Regil's firm hands kept me still as tears streamed down my face and my fists balled up so tightly that my nails drew blood on my palms.

But when the first *ping* of metal hitting a dish caught my ear, my breath caught. No matter how much it hurt, I had to soldier on; I had to do it for my future. More than that, I had to know what it felt like to be as the Fates intended me to be.

"First one out," Althea announced. "Next, I'll extract the second one in the same wing."

My jaw clenched as I prepared for the second incision, but before she cut into me once more, the elixir took hold like a dragon ripping me off the ground, and I slammed into darkness.

CHAPTER 9

A groan slipped through my lips as my eyelids fluttered open. My body felt like a frost giant had pummeled me into the side of a mountain, particularly my—

My wings!

I attempted to sit up, only for stars to spot my vision and a sharp pain to rip through my shoulders and back.

"Ow," I groaned, but remained undeterred by the discomfort as I reached behind me. My wings were not free as they always had been. Instead, a soft fabric covered them.

"Miss! You must be careful!" a feathery voice shouted. A short fae with a mess of black hair on her head and extremely pointed ears, even more so than mine, rushed through a doorway across from my bed, waving her hands wildly. "No sudden movements. No jostling the wings! Those are Healer Althea's orders!"

"I—who are you?" *What* kind of fae are you, I wanted to add, but didn't. I'd already embarrassed myself with Althea. There was no need to do so here too.

She wiped her hands absentmindedly on her pants, leaving behind wet marks. "My lord sent me to nurse you through the night, though of course, I was here longer than expected."

"How long?" I asked, taking in her expression, which was reluctantly impressed.

"You slept two nights and a whole day! Through it all, I barely left your side."

"What?!" I'd never slept that long in all my life. Even when I became so ill that I could barely walk, my master had forced me to return to work.

Then again, I had also never escaped slavery, nearly frozen to death as I traveled into another kingdom, and had a surgery, all in the course of a very long day and night.

"You must have been right knackered," the fae affirmed. "I've nursed all the wee ones in the palace over the turns and even the adults a time or two. Never have I seen anyone sleep so long!" She held out hands, also covered in a thick carpet of hair. "Let me help you up, nice and slow."

I took them, and she helped me to sit up. This time, no stars swam in my eyes, and no pain came either.

I wasn't in the healer's quarters like I'd assumed. Rather, I lay in a bed in a nice bedroom and wore a nice nightgown. I fingered the ties, astonished by the softness of the material on my skin. I'd worked with silk many times but had never worn it. The material against my stomach, my back, and my thighs felt so soft, even softer than when I'd run it through my fingers.

Then, I remembered that I'd not been wearing the nightgown when I'd seen Althea. I stiffened. Someone had changed me.

"Everything alright, miss?"

I cleared my throat. "Who changed my clothes?"

"I did, though you're a bit large for a brownie like me to manage." She gestured to her size, about half of my height.

Brownie. I committed her appearance to memory; sure I'd meet this sub-order of fae again. I'd read that they often helped in households.

"So Althea helped, of course." She smiled. "My lord wished for you to have nicer chambers and comfortable attire to rest in."

Thank the moon above that Warden Roar had not been around. I was no stranger to being naked around human females and the odd witch. When you shared a room with others and used a communal bathhouse, it was a fact of life. And I wasn't innocent either. Two human men had seen my body in all its glory. Still, the thought of the charming warden helping to undress me would have been too much to bear.

"So, whose room is this?" I gestured to the wider space, three times the size of the quarters I'd shared with seven other blood slaves. Hues of gold and red dominated the room, and a fire blazed in a hearth along a windowed wall. Two chairs were tucked in front of the hearth, one of which an abandoned knitting project rested.

"My Lord Roar says these are to be your quarters."

Did he? I shifted my legs and touched the floor. My eyebrows screwed together. "Is the floor heated? Or is the fire just that hot?"

"'Tis heated by fire magic, miss. Warden Roar is Winterborn and bred, but he does love the finer things."

I thought back to the faerie lord I'd met yesterday. He'd been so well put together and kind. He was also prettier than most females I'd met, with long lashes and a thick red mane. Most of the fairer sex would envy him.

"I should alert the warden that you've awoken," the brownie said. "Will you be alright alone for a few moments?"

I nodded. Being alone with my thoughts would be a blessing.

"Very well, miss." She pointed across the room. "Your wardrobe is in that armoire. Perhaps pick a dress to your liking? The warden had many brought in for you. I'm certain they will fit."

"Sure." As I stood, I became keenly aware that I needed to relieve myself. Sleeping for two nights and a day tested my bladder to its limits. "And a chamber pot? Where might I find one?"

"Ah! Of course! You have a personal toilet and bath, just through there." She gestured to the door by the armoire, the very one she'd entered through, and my lips parted. My own toilet? I'd never had such a luxury, but the Laurents and other vampire nobles did. Apparently, so did Warden Roar.

"Thank you."

The brownie saw herself out, and I hobbled to the toilet. After doing my business, I looked in the mirror. A gossamer fabric I couldn't identify protected my wings. That made me think the fabric was used for healing because, while I wasn't a worldly fae, I knew my fabrics.

The mystery of how my wings looked aside, the rest of me looked better than I ever had. My violet eyes shined bright, color filled my cheeks, and the stress that riddled my face in the Vampire Court had vanished. I pushed a lock of hair behind my ears and gasped when I caught sight of my hand. Pulling it away, I examined it with awe. Just like Althea had said, the marks on my arms and hands where the bloodletters liked to draw from had faded already.

I shook my head, astonished. I'd never seen myself like this. Healing, rest, and a good meal had gone a long way.

Mindful that the warden might arrive at any moment, and I wore only a nightgown, I padded to the free-standing closet that towered over me at twice my height. I pulled open the double doors and once faced with the wardrobe inside, I let out a small shriek of delight.

Warden Roar had not purchased one or two dresses, which would have been sensible and still overly kind. No, he'd bought at least *two dozen* lovely gowns.

Silks hung heavy, beads gleamed, and intricate embroideries lined the gowns, alongside everyday shifts of immaculate quality. Each beautiful garment took my breath away.

As if to reassure me, I caught sight of my old attire in the corner, the baggy gray tunic and pants, now cleaned and shoved on a shelf in the wardrobe's corner. They looked plain and rough-spun next to the finery of the dresses. I fingered the pants thoughtfully just as the door to my room creaked open.

I sucked in a breath and grabbed the pants, placing them before my body as I hid behind the wardrobe door. "Warden?"

"No, Lady Neve," a feminine voice replied. "I'm a lady-in-waiting for you. Lady Clemencia, if you please."

A lady-in-waiting? By the stars, what had happened to me?

Slowly, I peeked out from behind the door and found a tall female faerie standing just inside my room. We locked eyes, and she curtsied. This fae had the longest black hair that I'd ever seen falling all the way to her rear, and her deepset, hooded eyes reminded me of Anna's eyes, though this fae's eyes were a bit larger.

"Is that what you've chosen to wear?" She smiled as she rose and sunlight from the window danced across her flawless porcelain skin and enviably high cheekbones. "Please forgive my forwardness, but the warden hoped that you'd wear a new dress. The best seamstresses in Guldtown made them."

"I—what—no. I grabbed the pants because I thought you were Roar, and I wished to cover myself."

Clemencia's brown eyes brightened. "He asked you to call him by his *given* name?"

He had, quite soon after we'd met, perhaps in an attempt to ease my nerves, though I hadn't used his given name before that very moment. I'd been more careful in front of him.

"It's a good sign," Clemencia added.

"Thank you." I supposed it was. Another feature of my time with Lord Roar rose to the forefront of my mind.

The proposed arrangement—a fake engagement. I'd had little time to consider such a matter, but when faced with the luxury I stood in and what gold could really do, did I actually need much time? I wanted to flee as far from the Vampire Court as possible. Gold and guards would help me. I'd travel comfortably over mountain passes. I'd be safe.

I only had to play at being in love for a period. So easy, especially as the warden seemed very amenable. It was a paltry price really . . .

I was leaning toward saying yes, but was there a downside I wasn't seeing yet?

"This is for you." Clemencia extended a hand in which a vial of green liquid gleamed and walked toward me. "It speeds up healing and will reduce scarring in your wings. Althea will supply you with three vials a day until we leave, and I'm to make sure that you take them."

I accepted the elixir. My wings felt tender but given that a dozen metal rods had been extracted from them, it was a miracle I wasn't writhing in pain. I popped the cork top and downed it. Just like the one I'd taken to make me sleep, it tasted pleasant, a bit like citrus. Althea knew what she was doing.

"I'll take that." Clemencia held out her hand for the vial, which I passed back. "I was present when the others brought the dresses to the castle. Might I make a suggestion for your attire?"

I nodded. "Please do."

"Now that I've laid eyes on you, I believe the indigo would be lovely with your hair and eyes. And it is not too formal, suitable for daily wear."

I turned back to the closet and found the dress she referred to. She was right that out of the bunch, it looked to be on the simpler side, which suited me. The dresses with beading and embroidery, and certainly the silks, needed to be used for any events I would go to at court . . . if I accepted his proposal. I chuckled dryly, already knowing which way I was leaning on the matter.

"Yes." I hung up the shift dress and took down the indigo one. "Good choice."

"Perfect!" Clemencia's eyes twinkled. "The warden also asked me to invite you to breakfast with him. He will be down in just an hour. That gives me time to prepare you."

"What do you mean by prepare?"

She glided over to a vanity and opened a drawer. Inside, powders and tubes rolled about. "You're very pretty, but might I suggest freshening up and doing something with your hair?"

Growing up, I'd never used beauty enhancers even though I'd often wished to. I only knew how to do the most basic plaits and how to pull back my hair with a ribbon. "Do whatever you think looks best. I'm afraid I don't know how to do much with cosmetics or my hair."

"That's where I come in." Clemencia sashayed into the bathroom and called over her shoulder. "I'll draw you a nice hot bath, and after, I'll make sure that you're the most stunning faerie in all of Guldtown."

CHAPTER 10

Clemencia had magic indeed. My lady-in-waiting's ministrations curled my hair to perfection and made me look like a highborn lady fae.

The apples of my cheeks had a rosy hue, my lips shone a perfect shade of pink, and for the first time ever, I didn't see the scar over my right temple because she'd covered it with a powder. All that combined with the dress, which hugged my wide hips and accentuated my ample bosom, and I barely recognized myself. And somehow she'd managed all that just in time for breakfast.

Not knowing the way to breakfast myself, I followed Clemencia down the corridors to find Warden Roar sitting at a table large enough for at least six, reading a sheet of parchment with his eyebrows knitted together. Platters of food were spread across the table, though they looked untouched.

"Good morning." I stepped into the room, taking in

the few paintings on the walls, the only decor besides the heavy crimson drapes hanging to the sides of the windows.

He turned and his lips parted as he folded the page and put it in his pocket. "Neve. You look stunning. How are your wings? Healer Althea told me the procedure went well."

"My wings feel tender, but I'm fine. And thank you for the kind words, though I cannot take credit. Much of my attire was Clemencia's doing." I gestured to my lady-in-waiting.

"Nonsense. She's a natural beauty. I merely enhanced her features," my lady-in-waiting said. "I'll allow you to eat breakfast in peace. When you are done, I'll be in the next room."

I wondered what she would do, but the question proved short-lived as Warden Roar approached and held out his hand to me. "Please, take a seat."

A pleasant flush of heat warmed me through as he focused all his attention on me. It was nice to be looked at like I was something precious, not just a creature to profit from. After pulling out my chair and making sure I was seated, the lord went back to his seat at the opposite end of the table.

"This is quite large." I gestured to the table and the platters of food, meats, cheeses, fruits, and breads of every sort. Pitchers of juice sat on a smaller table to the side. "Are more joining?"

"It's middling. Not as intimate as where you ate the day we met, but not as grand as my formal dining room.

And today it is just us." He paused. "We can move, though, if the size makes you uncomfortable."

"Not if it means leaving this spread." My stomach gave a loud growl.

"Take what you wish," he urged with a dry chuckle. "I instructed others not to interrupt us, so no servants will swoop in. I thought you might like privacy to discuss matters."

Matters. That had to mean the engagement.

"Very well then." I poured a cup of apple juice before piling food onto my plate. Food had to come before our discussion.

The warden watched me. An expression between amusement and astonishment rippling across his face as he picked at a plate of fruit. It appeared I wasn't the only one experiencing many firsts. I suspected that he hadn't seen someone starved of good food in the quantities they desired.

A roll dusted with a fragrant spice I didn't know the name of called to me, and I took a huge bite. A groan escaped me. "What is this?"

"A cinnamon roll," he replied.

"Whoever came up with this is a genius." I devoured the roll, not at all caring that I looked like an animal. Once I finished, my hunger had somewhat dimmed, and I decided it would be kind to put an end to the questions swimming in his eyes. "So you wish to know my answer, my lord?"

The warden took a bite of his own food. "If you're ready to speak it."

I was. In such a short time, my hesitation had vanished because why would I rebuke such an opportunity? Such a gift?

I nodded. "I am. I will do it."

"You'll become my fake fiancée?" He set down his fork.

"I will. For passage to the Summer Court and a sum of gold." Unable to stop myself from pigging out, I took a bite of a wedge of cheese. For a moment, my eyes shuttered closed in ecstasy. Burning stars, everything tasted delicious!

"Money is no issue. You will have whatever you wish and go where you wish." His eyes gleamed. "Thank you, Neve. You have no idea how much this means to me."

"No one wants to be forced into a marriage." I wetted my tongue with the sweet apple juice. Blood slaves were not required to wed, but some were forced to mate and produce more slaves. "The practice is backward, isn't it, Warden Roar?"

He smiled. "When in private or in my castle, please do call me Roar. As my fiancée, that is only natural. And you don't mind me calling you by yours?"

"I don't," I said, though inside I squirmed a little at the thought of being so familiar with a high lord. To calm myself, I took another bite of fruit from a platter.

Though I'd slipped with Clemencia, I'd been careful to stick with formalities around the warden, just as I always did with lords in the Blood Court. Using his given name openly and with him would take some getting used to.

"Wonderful. At court, we will need to be more formal, but it is unnecessary here, in my home and among my people." He winked as if sharing a joke. "Now, as you said, the practice of arranging *is* backwards. Actually, the Courting Festival has been out of fashion for many turns. That King Magnus is bringing it back so suddenly is curious."

"Why do you think he brought it about?"

Roar shook his head. "Since receiving the invitation, I've pondered that many times and still cannot say, though I hope to learn his reasonings when we arrive in Avaldenn."

Upon hearing the name of the capital of the Winter Court, I froze. Soon, I'd be in the company of the king and queen and would stay at the palace! And the Winter Court was rumored to be very cutthroat. I needed to ready myself . . .

"You mentioned a tutor," I said. "I'm afraid that I will require a lot of instruction before we go. Maybe more than you can imagine."

"I've thought that through," the warden said with a nonchalant wave of his hand. "Once we sign the contract, those lessons will begin today, if you're up for it?"

"How long until we must travel again?" I'd slept for so long, I wasn't sure I recalled correctly what he'd said before.

His eyebrows furrowed. "We have five days, including today, before we must set out. We must leave early on the sixth to make it to court on time."

That wasn't much time at all. I shoved another wedge of cheese into my mouth. "Then, I agree, we must not delay. Let's sign the contract and get on with it."

"I had hoped you'd say that, so I took the liberty of drafting one already."

"What if I wish for changes?" I asked, loving the feeling of having this power. It felt intoxicating to even deal with a person of Roar's rank in this manner. A little terrifying too, but mostly intoxicating.

He shrugged. "Then we'll change it. I expected you might and left room for additions. We'll discuss anything you wish to strike from the contract."

"Show me."

We left the table, and Roar led me into a study that was far more decorated than the middling dining room had been. Dark and moody in atmosphere, images of prowling snow leopards graced the walls, and a large gold statue of one loomed behind the dark wooden desk. The statue stood at least three times my height, and that wasn't the only intimidating thing about the work. It had been positioned as a clear call to power; the leopard leapt over the seat of the person at the desk, right at whomever they met. Today, that person was me.

"Take a seat." Roar gestured to my seat, and I lowered into it, eyeing the leopard with both unease and admiration.

The warden took his own chair, a supple brown leather one, and pulled open a drawer. The contract rested on the table's smooth surface a moment later. He'd kept it quite handy.

"Here you are." Roar turned the contract toward me so that I might read it.

I leaned over the thick parchment that felt creamy beneath my fingers. He'd spoken true when he said it was short, and as I read through it, much of the tension in my shoulders released.

"I'll begin training in the ways of a lady right away, and we're to be engaged from this day on until we return to Guldtown after the festival? Why wait until we return here and not when we leave the capital?"

"Spies. I'm certain the Royal House of Aaberg will have people watching our journey back. Once we're safe under my roof, we can plan how to move you south."

That sounded reasonable.

"And the binding?" I pointed to one of the last lines. This wasn't merely a deal one signed for. Magic would be involved. As mine had been stifled, I didn't know how that would work.

"My staret, that's our word for a holy fae," he explained, in case I didn't know, which I had, but I still found the thoughtfulness charming, "will perform the binding. And the binding allows for full trust, which is essential because until the potion quelling your powers wears off, you can lie to others, including me." He gave me a slightly sheepish smile.

I couldn't fault him for that provision. In his place, I'd do the same.

"Neither can betray the other until we fulfill the contract. Else there will be repercussions," he finished. "Do you have any other questions?"

I thought that over.

One idea entered my mind right away. "I want to amend the contract. We are engaged outwardly to others and by contract, but there will be no physicality." I paused because, looking at Roar now, I had to admit that kissing him, especially for the view of others to sell our tale, wouldn't be the worst thing in the world. He *was* handsome. "Not unless both parties consent. If either of us puts up resistance, there will be no touching."

He leaned over the parchment. "Allow me to add that."

"And as payment for fulfilling my part, I'd like a sum of gold for my travels *and* enough to see me south and purchase housing and food for six moons." That might have been overkill, but I had no idea what awaited me in the Summer Court or how I'd make a living. This was my best chance to make a new life.

"Done." With a bright red quill that I suspected might have been plucked from a phoenix, he added both clauses and then looked up. "Anything else?"

I tried but could think of nothing. Both Roar and I would get what we wanted most out of the arrangement, and he would not push me in ways I did not wish to be pushed; nor I him.

"Nothing." I took the quill he offered. It warmed in my hand, hinting that I'd been right about the phoenix.

I signed, and the warden went to get the castle staret, leaving me alone in his study.

I took in the area again. Aside from the leopard statue, which stuck out most to me, this time I noticed that other paintings of faeries lined the wall by the door. A male with red hair and a female with blonde hair stood in the largest portrait. Two male younglings, both copper-haired, joined them. It seemed to portray a family—Roar's, if I wasn't mistaken.

"Thank you, Staret Celi," Roar's voice came from outside. "This will be fast, so you can return to your duties."

"Of course, Warden."

When Roar opened the door, an older male fae wearing a robe that glittered like the night sky joined him. Wrinkles lined the staret's pale face, but his lively blue eyes looked alert. "Miss Neve?" he asked.

"That's me."

"This is High Staret Celi," Roar introduced. "He is the highest ranking holy fae in Guldtown, answering only to the Grand Staret in Avaldenn, and will perform our binding. All fae in his order are sworn to secrecy, so you need not worry about the news getting out."

I hadn't been, but I was glad the warden considered such things.

"A potion has stifled Neve's magic," Roar continued. "Will that affect the binding?"

"No need to worry, my lord." High Staret Celi held up two gold vials. "Magic lives in the blood. I will draw some life-force from both of you, and you two will carry that of the other. Shall you betray one another per your agreement, it will cause crippling pain to the betrayer."

I winced.

"Are you amenable?" Roar asked.

While no one wanted to consider the possibility of crippling pain, I recognized it as a way of protecting both the warden and me. He would seek to avoid pain as much as me. That made us equals.

"Yes," I said.

"Hold out your arms." The staret produced a blade with a ruby encrusted hilt.

Roar and I both did as we had been told. When the staret opened my vein first, I blinked.

"No pain," I said, surprised.

"It's spelled." He placed a vial where my blood poured. "It will also only allow the wound to be open for as long as I need it."

As soon as High Staret Celi said the words, he pressed the flat edge of the blade to my cut, and it closed.

Roar did the same, and when two gold vials of blood no longer than my thumbnail filled, the staret closed his eyes. He said nothing, but silver-white magic filled the air, swirling around the vials.

Jealousy crept over me like an ice spider climbing over mountains. I'd never seen my magic act like that. What would it look like? What color would it be? Would that change when I used it in different ways?

Soon, I told myself, *in less than one moon, I'll learn what lay inside me all along.*

When the staret's magic stopped, the old fae looked between us. "The vials are charmed. You, Neve, will carry Lord Roar's blood. And he will carry yours. Should one betray the other, the slighted person only needs to ingest the blood to cause crippling pain to the other."

High Staret Celi handed over the vials, and I clutched the vial of Roar's blood. As much as I didn't want to consider drinking blood like a vampire would do, this was a safeguard. A contract written on paper, while valuable, could be ignored, but not this.

"That's it?" I asked.

"It is." The staret nodded.

"Very good," Roar said. "Do you have other questions, Neve?"

"I think not."

With the staret's job done, Roar saw the holy fae out, and when he returned, he smiled at me. "Shall we begin?"

CHAPTER 11

After sealing our contract, Roar insisted I needed to be seen around town.

Frode knew the truth of my identity, as did the guards who had heard him proclaim my blood slave status, and Staret Celi—all of whom had been sworn to secrecy. But no one else knew. Not even Althea knew the truth because, as Roar claimed, she didn't ask. She merely agreed to help because that was what her lord had asked.

So, it was time to begin reinventing myself.

"Would the Winter Court really send people here to ask about me, though?" I asked as we walked toward the castle gates. "That's quite a journey from the east."

Above, the bruised sky promised snow, and the temperature was far lower than anything I'd ever experienced in the Vampire Court. Even *I* might truly get cold here around the eleventh or twelfth moon of a turn, those true winter months. But not today.

In lieu of the thin slave garb I'd arrived in, I wore a

dress and a fur-lined cloak that would keep out any wind and hide my bandaged wings from view. Completing the ensemble, comfortable, thick-soled boots protected my feet.

"If, after we arrive at court, the king has even the slightest suspicion that I made a deal with you, then yes, he will send someone to ask around. So we must spread your tale far and wide." Roar blew out a breath, and the air plumed white. "With clear roads, the trip takes eight or nine days in a covered sleigh. But a single knight on a strong horse can make it in five days. Be sure that King Magnus will send a swift rider."

"Alright then," I murmured still somewhat astonished, but ready to do as I must.

My story had already been planned. I was no longer a former blood slave but a commonborn faerie from the northwest part of the kingdom, a desolate area with only a few small villages. Together with my fisherfae father, we had been traveling to purchase a new cart, and got caught in a storm. We veered off course and orcs killed my father while he defended me and allowed me to run. Luckily for me, I stumbled into Warden Roar's territory to be picked up by Frode. The lumberjack brought me to Roar, who fell so deeply in love that my station did not matter.

Of course, I could say all that, but Roar would have to be more careful, claiming to be taken with me right away. He'd be vague and allow people to draw their own conclusions whenever possible. And, most importantly, he'd suggest that people talk to *me* as much as possible. In that way, they'd feel as if their lord wished for them to get to know the new Lady of Guldtown, and I could tell the full tale.

A lot was riding on my shoulders to get the gossip rolling, but slaves talked as well as anyone else, and I knew all I had to do was find a few key people to tell my story to. From there, they'd spread the tale for us.

"Do you really think they'll buy you marrying so below your station, though?" I pulled back a lock of silver-white hair from where it was blowing wildly in my face. "Those in your territory, I mean."

"I like to think I'm a fae of the people. I've entertained a few ladies in my city, and perhaps most notably, I've never courted a noble. So they probably won't think it too odd."

When I thought of how well he'd treated me and how those in the palace loved him, I believed that he was well liked.

"Would you allow me to hold your hand?" Slowly, he extended his.

The question took me by surprise, but only for a moment. He was merely following our agreement and asking before touching me. I extended my hand. "Naturally."

The moment my smaller palm slipped into his, snow began to fall, the flakes so small they looked like sugar dusting my shoulder.

"It makes things pretty." I stuck my tongue out to catch a few flakes.

"That it does." He squeezed my hand and smiled. "Perhaps it's Winter's Realm welcoming you."

Ease settled over me. The warden was kind, influential, and handsome, and although we only held hands for show, I liked the touch of his skin to mine. I found it reassuring to find kindness in this world.

My pleasure would make for better acting, so I did not push it aside. Instead, I stepped closer to Roar. When we reached the gates, we appeared to be the picture of a sweet couple.

A contingent of knights in sleek fighting leathers escorted us into town and down a wide busy street. Almost right away, a fae female, well-dressed in a dark mustard sheath dress lined with fur at the cuffs and neck, caught my eye. I beamed at her, and when she scowled back, I frowned.

Roar chuckled. "Not everyone will be pleased to learn that I'm taken."

Oh. Right. I was sure many females in the city would have tried to enchant him before.

"Don't worry about it," he added, his tone soft as we stepped onto a cobbled street. "She will help spread the gossip, and your expression was perfect. It looked genuine."

"If you say so."

Thus, our time in Guldtown began. Roar traveled through the city like a lord who owned every snow-dusted paved stone. He smiled at all who approached to have a word, which included fae from all walks of life. In each interaction, he introduced me as his fiancée.

"I knew she was special the moment I set eyes on her," he told the baker and his wife.

"May the stars bless the both of you!" The baker's wife took both of my hands in hers, beaming.

We thanked her and moved on to the next fae and the next. Mostly, Roar's people indeed seemed delighted with the news of his engagement. And Roar showed me off so effectively that I was able to tell our story many times, keeping him somewhat in the background.

Two females, however, appeared particularly irate. So much so that when they got up the nerve to approach and asked to speak with me privately, I hesitated. But only for a moment.

"Neve, darling?" Roar eyed me as if he didn't want to let me go, but I knew better. Though the females appeared unwelcoming, they also looked like they'd spread gossip far and wide.

"I'd love to speak with them," I smiled as if nothing would delight me more. "Now that I'll be living here, I'll need to make friends!"

"Very well. I'll leave four knights with you but will be right down this street. I have business to conduct." He gestured to a road that veered off a main thoroughfare. The smell of heated metal wafted from it in waves. I suspected the blacksmiths' forges and their shops were that direction.

He chose four knights, all wearing fighting leathers and minimal metal armor on their torsos. They grinned at me, as if pleased to be protecting me.

The two lady faeries led me to the side of the road while other fae who had approached us, all wanting a word with Roar about one thing or another, walked down the street with their warden. The lady fairies and I stopped beneath an awning on the side of the street, where the pair brushed the fallen snow from their dresses. Just a couple of doors down, the knights Roar had assigned to me huddled together and shared a laugh.

I tried to mimic the knights' happiness as I smiled at the ladies. "Hello, ladies. I'm Neve."

"Lucilia Gladial," said the tallest with long dark hair before pointing to her blonde friend. "This is Valiz Rifiel. Both of us are merchants' daughters. Our fathers are wealthy and powerful. What does your father do?"

The first sour-looking female had prepared me for this, so I did not so much as blink at this odd, and frankly insulting, introduction. Lucilia and Valiz intended this to be a pissing match of who possessed more coin. They wouldn't be pleased to hear my story.

"He's a fisherfae."

"I knew it!" Valiz muttered. "You walk like a commoner."

I balked. The nerve! Though some people had looked upon me skeptically, none had spoken so rudely. Determined to show that they couldn't beat me down, I rolled my shoulders back. "Perhaps. But at least *I* know how to talk to someone who will soon be the Lady of Guldtown." I paused and glanced around. "Which shops did you say your father owns?"

Valiz gasped, but Lucilia placed her hands on her hips and glared at me. "Why?"

I smirked. "If I continue to hear such disrespect, I'll

make sure not to spend any Lisika coin at your establishments once I manage the warden's household."

Valiz gripped her friend's hand. "You can't!"

"Once I've married the high lord, I can."

Stars, I would burn in the afterworld for all of my lies, but I couldn't help myself. These arrogant, rich fae would reap what they sowed, perhaps for the first time in their lives. I would have loved to do this to the stuck-up vampire nobles in Sangrael.

"Please!" Valiz said. "I don't agree with her! Lucilia has always been too quick to judge. Foolish, really. I wish to——"

A blast of a horn cut her off, and both females' faces paled. Without another word, they spun and ran down the street, leaving me standing there as dozens of other fae scattered and fled into buildings.

My heart pounded as the four knights rushed over, swords drawn around me. What was going on?

An answer came when a dozen hideous orcs turned the corner. Their gray-green skin seemed to absorb the sun's light, and gnashing teeth revealed a mouthful of decay and rot. But the most alarming thing about the creatures facing me was their sheer size. Each was at least one and a half times the height of Warden Roar and bulging muscles made them all the more intimidating.

I took a step back, hoping not to draw attention, but at my motion, the one in front spotted me.

He pointed at me with his sword. "Hostage."

Burning moon! For the first time in my life, I wished I

wore unassuming clothes and not the beautiful dress Roar had gotten for me. It made me stand out far too much.

The horde descended but before they made it halfway to me, three of the faerie knights Roar had left with me rushed them. The last knight came up to me and gripped my forearm. "Milady, come with me. We must return to the castle."

I glanced back at the monsters and down the street where Roar had gone. Sounds of clanging metal, grunts, and monstrous roars came from that direction. Some of the orcs rushed that way too. "What about the warden?"

"When they come into the city, my lord helps us handle the hordes."

His wording made it sound like the orcs appeared in Guldtown often. And maybe they did. The fae had been surprised to see the orcs, but none had frozen like me. They knew exactly what to do.

Under the knight's protection, we carved a path through the city toward the castle. The gate stood just in sight when another orc stepped into the road from an alley directly in front of us.

The monster bellowed and lifted in an axe slick with blood. I froze and reared backward, but my protector was not so cowardly. He lunged at the beast.

I held in a scream as the orc's axe came close to the knight's chest, but he dodged just in time and his sword slashed across the monster's arm.

The orc roared, and though such an injury would have taken me out, the creature spun and swung again.

Rooted in place, I watched, both aghast and

impressed as the faerie and the orc battled. Sword swung against axe, the pair grunted and growled, and blood sprayed when one managed to strike. I held my breath until finally a moment came that the faerie dropped the orc to his knees. My fists clenched, ready for the end, ready to run again.

The sword rose, an instant from decapitating the orc, but before the sword came down, the orc pulled a dagger from his boot and slammed the blade upward, under the faerie knight's ribs. My mouth dried up as the knight fell to the snow, where the orc swung his axe again, decapitating my guard.

Blood sprayed; some of it so far that it struck my cheek. I swallowed down the vomit climbing my throat as the head rolled, and I had to bend over to breathe.

Then, the orc roared, and the sound sent shivers down my spine. I straightened, only to find that the creature had lost no time. His beady, black eyes were already latched onto me. He lifted the axe, blood dripping from the blade and charged.

I twisted to run, but I had underestimated the creature's speed. Who would've thought such a lumbering monster could outpace a light and agile faerie?

I didn't even make it a dozen steps before large hands grabbed my cloak and sank into my wings. White-hot pain seared through me as his long claws ripped through the cloak and into the bindings to dig into the sensitive, healing flesh. My knees buckled. He took advantage of the disarmament and yanked me closer so that my back was pressed against his chest.

"Pretty fae." The orc's rancid breath washed over me, turning my stomach. "I take you back."

I didn't know where he planned on taking me, but I definitely didn't want to go. And yet, I felt powerless to fight this monster.

"Come." The creature shifted his hand to my armpit and drew me up, only to stop abruptly. A look of annoyance flashed across the monster's face as he growled and shoved me to the side. I fell but caught myself on a barrel someone had abandoned in the street. I turned to see what had captured his attention.

"My stars!" My hands flew to my mouth.

Roar stood over the orc. The creature now had an arrow straight through the eye, one I assumed Roar had shot, given the quiver full of arrows strapped to his back and the discarded bow laying a few paces away. But the warden wasn't done yet. He held a sword—though where it had come from, I had no idea—and I watched in awe as he arched it high and brought it down to sever the orc's head.

The head rolled, staining the snow with fresh blood, and making my stomach revolt. Quickly, I pressed a hand to my mouth.

"Are you alright?" Roar asked, blood spattered across his face like freckles.

"I am." Slowly, I lowered my hands. "You came so fast. Where did you get the weapons?"

He hadn't had either a bow and arrows or a sword when we'd left the castle.

"I was in the right place at the right time to acquire a

bow and quiver full of arrows. The sword was my knight's blade." Pain filled his eyes as he gestured back to his fallen soldier. "I'm sorry I left you alone. The moment I saw the horde, I just had to get to you."

He sounded so sincere, it made my heart ache a little.

"Well, thank you for saving me. That was terrifying." I exhaled a long breath.

"I'm not sure they're gone yet either. But before I join my men, let me get you to the castle so that you're safe." He dropped the sword and went to scoop the bow he'd dropped as he ran my way.

"I'll have to return this once I'm done, or the bowyer will be furious." He slung his arm through the bow before taking my hand and without asking, swung me into his arms.

I winced, and the warden's eyes landed on my back. He took in the rips in the cloak.

"He got your wings?"

"Yes," I admitted.

"Where else are you hurt?"

"Nowhere. And I don't think the wound is large. But after yesterday, I do worry about my wings."

"The healer will see to you right away." He ran to the gates, which opened for him without hesitation. The moment we stood on the other side of the barrier protecting the castle, the warden waved over a soldier. "Get my lady to Healer Althea. I have to continue to assist my people."

"Of course, my lord."

The warden set me on the ground. "You're safe now. I'll see you soon."

"Be careful," I whispered, leaning into the gate for strength.

He had better means of protecting himself than I, but those orcs had murdered a knight. And they were so large and vicious. It seemed like the fae of Guldtown knew how to act, how to flee quickly, when the orcs arrived, but surely some hadn't been lucky enough to survive. How many had been injured or died?

"I'll take care." Warden Roar's emerald eyes blazed into mine. "I have something to come back to now."

CHAPTER 12

Outside my window, the sun rose over the snow-dusted evergreen treetops, and the warden jumped his stallion over a fence. Claps and whistles followed as the horsemaster and stablefae showed their approval of their lord's prowess. Roar reined in the stallion, dismounted, and patted the creature's neck before the horsemaster accepted the reins.

I shook my head. Roar had been out there for an hour, training and impressing others. Me included. Yesterday, I'd watched him train with sword, bow, and sharpened staff. Seemed to me that the faerie lord was skilled with basically any weapon one put in his hands, and riding seemed as natural to him as breathing.

A knock came at my door.

"Yes?" I turned away from the window and toward the door.

"It's Clemencia, my lady."

"Oh, right."

139

It was time for my lessons—hours and hours of drudgery in which Clemencia taught me how to act like a lady.

I answered the door and smiled at my lady-in-waiting. Though what Clemencia taught often bored me to tears, I had found that I liked my lady-in-waiting very much. She was sweet and kind and in a short time was learning to anticipate my needs before I even knew what I wanted. My acceptance of her help was touch and go, but that was to be expected. She had been trained to attend to a noble lady whereas vampires trained me to be a noble lord's food.

However, I needed to get used to such splendid treatment. As Lord Lisika's fiancée, I might ask the world and others would wish to give it to me.

At least for a while.

After we tricked King Magnus and returned to Guldtown, I'd continue my travels south. In my new home, I wouldn't have a wealthy and powerful fae to supply me with unlimited indulgences. I'd have to make my own way.

The thought was both daunting and exciting.

"Good morning," my lady-in-waiting said. "You've eaten already, yes?"

"They took my breakfast tray away not long ago."

"Good." Clemencia held out a vial of regeneration elixir that I downed without a second thought. On Althea's orders, I'd taken so many elixirs I could no longer count them.

"I thought we might go over the courtly dances

today," my lady-in-waiting said. "We'll start with the most popular ones and move on to the classics from there. Healer Althea cleared your wings, correct?"

"They're still not healed." I gestured to the wraps on my wings. "But she said that today I can leave my room and do just about anything."

Two days ago, the orc attack had opened new wounds, but yesterday afternoon, Althea had reexamined me. She'd beamed when she proclaimed that though the orc had hurt me, the damage was righting itself nicely. She left the bandages on but felt sure that by the time we left for court, they'd be healed.

I'd likely still have to explain the scarring if anyone asked, but orc, ogre, and even giant attacks were not uncommon in the Winter Court. Nor were animal attacks. I planned to use that excuse at court.

"Would you be good with dancing?"

"I suppose." I set the empty vial on a table. I'd only danced a few silly jigs at nameday gatherings for the blood slaves. But how hard could courtly dances be?

"Do you know any already? Perhaps you saw them in your village?" Clemencia cocked her head at me.

I shook my head. "Afraid not."

"That's alright." Clemencia shrugged. She had obviously gotten used to me knowing little about this kingdom. "I'm quite versed in them. Let me show you to the ballroom."

We left my room, the silk skirts of the dress I'd chosen that day swishing and sighing around my legs as Clemencia led me through the castle. Brushing my hands

ASHLEY MCLEO

across the smooth fabric, I smiled. Days ago, I lusted over the gowns I made for others. Today, I wore a dress of similar quality. How quickly life could change.

If only Anna were here, too.

The thought crept up on me, like it so often had these past days. I missed my friend and wished I could have brought her along. But with her foot and the conditions I'd undergone to get here, there would have been no way we'd have made it. Fae were far more resilient than humans. Stronger and faster, too. Anna never would have survived the cold river.

"Here we are!" Clemencia's voice rang out, lovely and lyrical. Though I had yet to hear her sing, I suspected she could carry a tune well.

I entered the ballroom, a grand affair that could fit at least three hundred fae and stood tall enough for a giant to prance around inside. Tapestries and banners in Roar's house colors of crimson and gold lined the walls, many bearing the image of a leaping snow leopard. The wooden floor had been patterned like interlocking diamonds and just like in the room where Roar listened to his subject's complaints, two pure gold snow leopards flanked the entryway, a symbol of the Lisika wealth and prowess.

Clemencia sashayed to the center of the patterned wood floor and held out her hand. "Take my right hand and put the other on my shoulder."

I did as she instructed, faced her, and waited.

"Watch your feet and mirror me." The lesson began as Clemencia stepped forward. "You go back."

She continued the verbal cues as we wound our way through the ballroom. And when she stopped saying the cues, we both learned those had actually been quite necessary and were the only thing protecting her feet.

I stepped on her feet not once, not twice, not thrice, but four mortifying times!

On the last occurrence, I cringed, and poor Clemencia sucked in a breath before her features rearranged themselves into an expression of serene patience once more. "Perhaps we should rest a moment?"

"I'm so sorry," I said. "I *am* trying, but—"

"You need a stronger hand."

We spun to find Roar in the doorway. He leaned against one of the golden snow leopards, his arms crossed over his barrel chest and red cheeks glowing in a way that hinted he'd just returned inside from the cold.

"A stronger hand?" I smirked and arched an eyebrow. While I'd been recovering from the orc attack, we'd taken our meals together in my room and I was feeling far more comfortable around the warden. "And I suppose *you're* here to provide one?"

Roar inclined his head. "If my lady wishes."

"I don't know . . . I've never been fond of others telling me what to do." Though I spoke true, I kept my tone light and playful.

He winked and prowled closer, exhibiting as much feline grace as the leopard of his noble house. "I assure you I'm only speaking of dancing, Lady Neve. And trust that *I* am known for my grace on the dance floor."

I snorted at the dig on my dancing skills. Who could

argue? Surely, as he spied on us, he'd seen me stomp on my lady-in-waiting's feet.

"He is a very good dancer," Clemencia said in a low tone. "My lord throws a ball each Winter Solstice, and all the ladies in Guldtown line up to dance with him."

I grinned when Roar gave a shrug that told me he'd heard every word Clemencia had said and he didn't disagree. "Then I guess I should see what all the fuss is about."

Roar came up to me and Clemencia melted into the corner of the room as Roar took my hand. "Your lady-in-waiting already taught you the steps? I couldn't tell from what I'd witnessed."

I rolled my eyes dramatically. "She did. Don't blame Clemencia, I'm just that poor a pupil."

"All of that is about to change. Follow my lead." He swept me into the same dance Clemencia had shown me, though with no verbal cues. Rather, Roar led with steady hands and confident steps that stole my breath and left me with no room to question where we were going next. I simply followed with surety, and maybe even a little grace. It was in that moment that I realized he was right—I did need a strong hand. As we swung around the ballroom, I didn't stumble or step on his feet once.

No, under Roar's strong hand, I *flew*.

We spun and glided across the dance floor like we'd been dance partners for forever. Like I hadn't massacred Clemencia's feet mere minutes before. Though no music played, I imagined the tunes I'd heard in the Vampire

Court, usually coming from vampire taverns, and somehow, they fit the way we moved.

"Last twirl." Roar sent me into a spin. I whirled away from him and returned, pressing my back against his chest with a smile.

"That was wondrous!" I laughed.

He turned me around and took my hands, continuing to sway gently with a smug look on his face. "See? You just needed the right teacher."

"I suppose I did." I conceded. "Though someone should teach him some *humility*."

Roar barked out a laugh and spun me once more before releasing me and giving a small bow. "Humility was not included in my father's warden lessons. Not even for the spare heir to the western territory."

I paused. The question had been burning in my mind and now seemed like the best opening I would get. "What happened to them? Your family, I mean?"

Frode had told me they died, which came as a shock. Faeries lived quite a long time, some for thousands of turns. The painting of the two younglings in Roar's study came rushing back. They'd been only a few turns apart in age, both so young.

"They're dead." He pulled away. "My older brother, Brogan, as well."

I swallowed as his once joyful face fell, contorted with pain. Roar didn't want to open up about it. "I'm sorry for asking."

"It's alright. Without them, the castle is empty, so your curiosity is only natural. I have had two decades to come to terms with the loss. They perished when I was seven turns, nearly eight. My brother was only ten." His voice broke as he spoke of his brother, and pain flashed in his eyes.

Instead of pressing, I sought to ease the pained lines on his face. "Time heals wounds, but there's no saying how much of it is necessary to do so."

He gave me a soft, knowing smile. "You speak the truth."

I checked that Clemencia stood far away. "Vampires lie, but I've found that the books they gave us ring true. Mostly, anyway."

"You read quite a lot in that court?"

"Books were passed around, and I read them whenever I got the chance. I would have loved to read more, though."

"I see." He paused and let out an exhale charged with a million emotions. "I should let Clemencia continue her lessons."

"You don't wish to continue instructions? Or to show me more of your *prowess*?" I teased, trying to lighten the mood.

"I never said that." His tone lowered, and for a moment his eyes lingered on my lips.

My stomach fluttered. Would he kiss me? If so, what would I do? There was no denying that Roar was attractive and kind and I suspected that any fae would be lucky to have him as a mate, but with our agreement, would such an act be smart?

The question became moot as Roar met my eyes once

again and continued as if he had not been staring at my lips. "I'm late to meet with the Merchant Guild. I hope they'll forgive my tardiness."

"Ah, good luck." I pursed my lips, wondering what exactly the Guild did. It wasn't the first time he'd met with them.

"I'll see you at dinner then?" Roar lifted an eyebrow at me in question. "In the small dining room?"

After the orc attack we'd eaten dinner together, but his question and the hope in his eyes struck me as significant. It made my heart beat harder, confusing me even more. "Wouldn't miss it. After all this dancing, I'll be ravenous."

"When are you *not* hungry?" he teased.

I wrinkled my nose, which made him laugh as he left the room.

The moment Roar shut the door behind him, Clemencia stood there, her eyes wide. "My lady, that was *so sweet*, sensual even."

"Was it?" It had felt fun, natural, and thrilling to me, but not sensual. Had it truly appeared otherwise?

"I think so, yes. And you danced for so long! How romantic!" She fanned herself in a way that made me hold in a laugh.

"No, we didn't. It was barely any time at all."

"It might have felt that way to you, but you danced for the length of two songs, at least!"

It *had* felt like less.

She chuckled lightly at the shock that had to be creeping over me. "But you are engaged, and he clearly adores you. It's nice. I've known him since I was a girl—

seen him at various functions, I mean—I did not know him well. At any rate, he has never looked so light and happy."

That gave me an idea. She had known Roar as a girl, which meant she had to know about his family.

"I made the mistake of asking about his family, but he didn't say much. So I was wondering, could you tell me what exactly happened to his parents and brother?"

Her mouth snapped shut, all joy over the dancing gone in an instant. "Pardon me, my lady?"

"Roar told me they died, but not how. Can you tell me? I want to know but also tread lightly and not re-open any wounds."

She shuffled from side to side and glanced at the floor. "I suppose it isn't a secret, just rarely talked about."

"I won't gossip about it. I merely wish to understand the fae I'm marrying better."

Her gaze lifted to me in earnest. "Of course. Well, it was an accident, you see. Shortly after the White Bear's rebellion, the realm was unstable. Many lords and ladies were recreating alliances. The previous Warden of the West, his lady wife, and eldest son went on a journey. Supposedly, they were traveling to see House Balik in the southlands to propose a marriage contract with Warden of the South." She shrugged as if to say she wasn't sure, but it sounded reasonable to me. "At any rate, they were traveling through a mountain pass when frost giants attacked their traveling party, and all three of them were lost. We never found their bodies, only one of a frost giant laying dead atop a crushed horse. The horse's saddle bore the Lisika emblem."

"That's awful."

Sadness swept across her face. "The only mercy was that my lord had not joined his family on their journey. He'd taken ill a few days earlier. The sickness ended up sacrificing his wings but saving his life."

The blight. Yes, Frode had mentioned it struck around that same time. The illness had taken Roar's golden wings, curled back and inward as if the edges tried to touch his spine. It must have been horrible, but I had to agree that Clemencia spoke true. Misshapen wings were a small price to pay to keep one's life. I would pay much more.

CHAPTER 13

My feet ached as I walked to the smallest dining room.

After the warden left, Clemencia taught me five more dances, stopping only so I could catch my breath and drink another vial of regeneration elixir. Though I was not a natural dancer, the choreography got easier and more fluid as we practiced. At the very least, my lady-in-waiting seemed impressed, and said we'd practice at least once more before we traveled to Avaldenn.

Two more days, I thought. I'd learned a lot in my time in the castle, such as how to use proper tableware, to dance, and how to address and interact with the varying levels of fae from the less powerful jarls and their families to the high lords and ladies of the Sacred Eight and the royal family.

But, of course, there was always more to learn, such as history and current events in Winter's Realm. The names of the most important lords and ladies and their families were high on our list too. Thankfully, much of that could be learned from reading and I'd have plenty of time to do that in the sleigh on our journey east.

I reached the dining hall, and a servant dressed in a crimson uniform with a gold snow leopard above the heart opened the door for me. Roar waited at the small round table lit by six candles in the center. He stood at my approach and gave me a small bow. As I'd been taught, I curtsied.

"A natural," he said, beaming at me. "Come, sit closer to me tonight. I want to hear about the rest of your lessons."

"Clemencia is a strict teacher. I'm sure my feet will never recover." I took my seat, and a servant swept in with wine and bread. I took both, and the servant gave an approving nod before he left the room to get the first course.

The household seemed to love the fact that I never skipped the bread or appetizers, and especially enjoyed it when I requested seconds. I suspected they weren't used to ladies with a healthy appetite. How could I deny them the pleasure of serving one?

"You walked hours through the woods to get here. In piss poor shoes too." Roar arched a brow. "Surely that was harder on your feet."

"Snow and a wooden floor are very different." I grabbed a roll and began to butter it. "How did your meeting with the merchants go?"

He released a long breath. "Well enough. They wish to import more from the Autumn Court. Unfortunately, no resolution was reached as I will need to clear such matters with the king. We might need to bring in more goods from the human world too." He frowned.

"Really? Like what?"

"Foodstuffs." A sigh gusted out of him as he plucked his own roll from the bread basket. "Once, my family did not need to ask the king for anything. We cared for our own people, but if something requires dealings with other kingdoms, now I must grovel."

"That's frustrating," I took a bite of my roll, chewed, and swallowed before asking. "Why did the king become stricter?"

"Pardon?"

"You said that once your family did not need to ask. What changed?"

Not only did I hold interest because it pertained to Roar, but a lady needed to know this when at court.

"Ah, the change was in the past, not in my lifetime. Nor that of my father or grandfathers." He rubbed the back of his neck sheepishly. "But fae have long memories, and it's difficult to let go of one's family's illustrious past."

"Illustrious?"

"Once, we were more than wardens and protectors," he explained. "The Lisikas were kings and queens of the west."

My eyes widened. "That's astounding. Were the other highborn families kings or queens once?"

Roar nodded. "The other high fae families were too. But there was a great war. One that decimated our lands, and only Queen Sassa Falk and her king consort had the power to save us all."

"So, they made the rest bow?"

"And gave us a sliver of the power we once had in exchange for our loyalty. A pittance." He spat the last word out with frustration and tore open the roll as though it had personally wronged him.

To me, it didn't seem so bad. Roar lived in a castle. He had servants and whatever his heart desired. Yet, his family's loss troubled him.

Long memories, indeed.

The first course arrived, a salad with the freshest of vegetables, and our discussion shifted. Roar instructed me in matters of his city or the kingdom, and I soaked it all in. By the time dessert came, sleepiness overcame me, and I considered skipping it. At least until I took my first bite of the dessert. "What is this?"

Roar grinned. "I thought you might like that."

"Oh don't be so smug! Answer me!"

He laughed heartily. The food had done him some good too and his dour mood when he spoke of his family had lifted. "Chocolate with vanilla icing. The Summer and Elven Courts specialize in growing chocolate. Believe it or not, they imported it from the human world and learned to work with the beans themselves."

"By the stars, it's amazing! I'm so glad that they did!"

Roar laughed. "Chocolate cake and stories entice you. I enjoy learning the small things."

I grinned. I really did enjoy making fae friends for the first time, though Roar was not so fast to offer details about himself. I usually discovered what I found most interesting by accident.

"I should actually be careful with the cake. The dresses you bought for me are getting tight." I'd been curvy for a blood slave, but with a more decadent diet, I learned I had been nowhere near as lush as I should have been. Just days in this court and my bust, hips, and belly had swollen.

"We will look for new dresses." Roar replied, his eyebrows knitting together. "You're beautiful, and I will not have any part of you disappearing."

"I'm not used to that sort of talk," I admitted. "Vampires prefer more slender females. They spoke of it openly."

He frowned. "Vampires are fools if they look down on beauty like yours. You'll find most at court will agree with me, I'm sure."

I smiled and continued eating and enjoying the cake, as did Roar.

Once both of our plates were clean, Roar stood and offered his hand.

I rose and looked at him. He had something to say, I could tell.

"I lied by omission today," he said, which was not at all what I'd been expecting.

"About what?" I arched an eyebrow.

"Where I went."

"Oh?"

"As mentioned, I had a meeting with the Merchant's

Guild, but I also went to get this." From his pocket, Roar pulled out a box.

My lips pursed. The green box was so small that it left me wondering what he could have gotten that would fit inside.

"As my fiancée, you should wear it." Roar opened the box to reveal a ring of gold holding the largest ruby I'd ever seen. I sucked in a breath, realizing what he meant.

"You didn't have to." My fingers trembled slightly at the idea of wearing such a ring. Even though we weren't really engaged, the ring had to have cost a fortune.

"I did, and when we're done with all this," a frown marred his face as he spoke the words, "you can keep it. As a gift."

I shook my head at him as my eyes widened. "Roar, it's too much."

"It's not. It's what would be expected for my fiancée, and that's without others knowing that you're putting your life on the line to help me. Should King Magnus find out about our deal, he will be furious, and he is quite a dangerous fae. A ring is nothing to the risk you're taking on." He pulled the ring from the box, and the ruby glittered beautifully in the candlelight. "Try it on?"

Because I couldn't help myself, I held out my right hand.

Roar noticed the trembling and smiled. "No need to fear a piece of jewelry, Neve."

I gasped as he slipped the band on my ring finger, and surprisingly, it fit. "It's so beautiful."

"Just like its owner."

Butterflies fluttered in my stomach. Sometimes Roar became so sweet that it was easy to forget that this was all an arrangement.

"How did you guess the size?" I asked. "Not even I would know what to say to a jeweler."

"I didn't."

"Excuse me?" I was certain I'd know if someone had measured my finger. I was not *that* light a sleeper.

"The ring is dwarf made. They are masters of metal and can infuse magic into it. This band will adjust its size if your finger grows or shrinks."

"How handy!"

"It is." Roar beamed. "And at risk of sounding too much like I'm trying to impress you, I have another thing to show you."

"Roar . . ."

"Let me have my fun."

I sighed, taking in the ring again. It all felt like too much, but he seemed to enjoy giving. How could I say no?

"As long as we're not going to the ballroom to dance." I patted my belly. "I am so full!"

"Then this surprise is perfect. Come with me." He led me through the halls, none of which I'd recognized.

"Where are we going?" I gazed around us, taking in the tapestries and paintings, most of which depicted Winter's Realm of Guldtown.

"You really must work on your patience." He stopped before a set of double doors. "Though not tonight, for this is what I wish to show you." Flinging open the doors, a familiar smell I knew in my heart met me.

Books.

"My library," Roar announced as he ushered me inside. "And yours, while you're here. Find as many books as you'd like and devour them until your heart's content."

"Stars alive!" I exclaimed, rushing deeper into the room lit by floating spherical faelights and candles along the outer walls.

Books climbed from floor to ceiling, sitting on more shelves than I could count. On one side, a map of Isila hung, though this appeared to be a far finer map than I'd ever seen. On the other side hung portraits.

I bit my lip. The same male and female fae with a young boy had been beautifully painted on the portrait. The male had bright red hair, as did the boy, just like in Roar's study. "That's your family, isn't it?"

"It is," Roar admitted. "Those portraits used to hang in the dining hall. I had them moved here because we used to eat together as a family and when they were gone, seeing them was too painful. But I still wanted to honor them with a place of beauty."

He had done just that. Aside from the multicolored books, gold and crimson swathed the library, like the rest of the palace. It struck me as both regal and homey, and also had an unlit fireplace and chairs before it, waiting to be sunk into.

"What are your favorite types of books?" he asked.

I rubbed my hands together. "Tales of adventure. Of

slaying dragons and fighting giants, ogres, and orcs. I like it when they have romance too."

His lips turned up in amusement. "You ought to be a knight!"

In my flights of fancy, I'd often wished for that same thing. But I had been born nothing, and even being Roar's fake fiancée had been more than I could ever imagine. Being a knight was far out of my reach but fun to think about.

"Perhaps I'll study up," I said, playing along. "You can teach me the sword, right?"

"Of course. But first, allow me to show you to the books you might enjoy." Roar pivoted and walked down an aisle, stopping about midway down.

"This was one of my brother's favorite stories." He lifted a book from the shelf. It had an image of a dragon on the front. "It's of the true dragons of the wilds, not the shifters, and an elf that learned to ride one of the wild dragons."

"Scandalous!" Playfully, I covered my mouth with my hand.

"Brogan thought so, too. Imagine the reaction the shifters at the Dragon Court would have if an elf rode a wild dragon?"

"They'd have a fit." I took it and flipped open the pages. After only a few lines, I found myself enjoying the tale too and shut it. "I think I'll enjoy it."

"My brother and I used to pass notes back and forth to one another in our favorite stories." Roar stared down at the book in my hands; the corners of his eyes crinkled with fondness. "He used this one often."

"Are you sure you want me to take it out of here?" After hearing about what happened to them, I figured the book must be one of his prized possessions.

"I'd prefer that someone else got enjoyment from the tale. I already checked each page for a note after his passing. Multiple times, I looked. There was none."

"Thank you." I held the book close to my chest. "Can I borrow a couple more? I'm a fast reader. We had to be because other slaves always wanted the books after us."

"Take as many as you'd like." His hand swept over the space. "I'm afraid that I am not very familiar with this section, preferring histories myself, but I'll wait for you to finish and show you back to your room so you can enjoy them."

I smiled. "Thank you so much. This is the most wondrous surprise."

"Anything to see you smile like that."

My heart fluttered. When he said things like that, I could not help but believe he had taken an interest in me. But that would be ludicrous. We'd known each other only a few short days, and I had little to offer a faerie like him.

Putting aside the odd thoughts, I perused the shelves. This library had more stories than I'd ever thought imaginable, and I ended up with an armful. But one more caught my eye—one about a lady pirate dwarf.

It rested high on the shelves, so I stood on tiptoes and shifted the other books into one arm, trying to reach the book. To no avail, however. I stood too short, and the book rested too high on the shelf.

"Need help?" Roar asked.

"Please." I nodded. "The blue one with the sword on the spine."

He came closer, and I breathed in, appreciating his scent that reminded me of fires lit in a castle and riding a horse in the forest. Roar plucked the book from the shelf and offered it to me.

"A treasure." As they'd done in the ballroom, his eyes dipped to my lips. We were so close that I could count his lush lashes.

"Neve," he whispered, and in that moment, I knew I'd been right before. He *had* wanted to kiss me.

"Yes?" I pressed my back to the the shelf, creating space because I was unsure of what *I* wanted. Roar was attractive, enticing even, but I didn't know him well at all.

As though my position was an invitation, his eyes widened, and he leaned closer, his full lips parting. My heart began to hammer and tingles rushed through me. An instant before his lips would have touched mine, he paused. He was close. So close that I could feel his breath on my skin. And though there was something undeniably sexy about our situation, it just didn't feel right.

In that moment, I chose.

"Roar," I whispered. "I can't."

He stiffened, pulled back. "You're right. This is improper and not part of our deal. I'm so sorry, Neve." He straightened, though not without obvious effort.

"Come, I'll show you to your quarters." Without so much as another glance my way, he took most of the books and walked out of the library.

I followed, in shock and wondering how I would have felt if I'd have made the opposite choice.

CHAPTER 14

When Clemencia arrived at my door the next morning, I was ready and waiting. Actually, in a novel turn of events, I'd already been up for hours. Most of them I'd spent reading, though I'd also spent a lot of time gazing at my ring.

"You always smell wonderful." I inhaled her floral scent as she swept into my room, shutting the door behind her.

"Snow lily perfume." Clemencia's cheeks took on a pleased pink hue at the compliment. "The perfumer in town makes it just for me, but I can get you some, if you like?"

"Only if you have time." I waved my hand and my lady-in-waiting flashed a grin at my ring. I'd shown it to her last night, and she'd nearly died over the gem. "Or perhaps I should make my own signature scent?"

"Every lady needs one," she said in all seriousness.

"I'm sure," I replied, though I'd never thought about

that once in my life. Slowly, I went to the windows, peered outside. Roar wasn't practicing weapons or riding today. I wondered what he was up to. "So, what are our lessons today?"

"First, we must visit Althea. I saw her earlier and she asked that I bring you by."

My heart leapt. Maybe the healer thought today would be the day to remove the bandages. And if so, how soon might I be able to try flying?

"What are we waiting for?" I hastened to the door. "Let's go."

Clemencia gave a little chuckle, but humored me as we left my room. Excitement sailed through me as we traveled the corridors. As my wings felt fine today, I couldn't help but hope for good news.

"I've never seen you walk so fast," Clemencia said when we made the last turn to the healer's quarters.

"I'm excited to see them."

"I would be too." Behind her, her own blue wings rustled. I didn't think she knew she did it, but I suspected she pitied those fae born without wings or those injured by the blight—or, as she believed to be my case, a violent attack prior to my arrival in Guldtown.

When we reached Althea's workshop, she bustled around a cauldron, popping in two sprigs of juniper before grabbing a jar of berries and pouring a few into the pot.

"Healer?" Clemencia piped up. "Lady Neve is here to see you."

"Ah!" The half-troll, half-faerie spun and smiled at

our arrival. "Come here, my lady. Lie down on your stomach."

I did as she requested, giving her access to my wings. The bandages peeled off layer by layer. When cool air touched my silver gossamer wings, I held my breath. What would Althea say?

"Good stars, my lady. You're making a fast recovery!" The healer's tone was pleased, which made me smile. "We can leave the bandages off from here on out and let your wings breathe and move more freely." She paused. "Would you like a looking glass to see them?"

"Has the most recent clawing diminished too?" I asked, sitting up and hanging my legs over the side of the bed.

"Very much." She turned to open a drawer. "You have been taking the elixirs I provided to accelerate healing and reduce scarring?"

"Like clockwork," I assured her.

Clemencia always carried vials of potions and made sure that I took them at the appropriate time. As with everything else she did, my lady-in-waiting had done her job perfectly.

"It's nice to have a responsible patient." Althea rummaged through a second drawer. "Ah! Here it is!"

A mirror appeared in front of me. "Hold it up and look, my lady. I'll hold another at your back."

I swallowed and, with a trembling hand, lifted the mirror. It took some angling, but when my mirror caught Althea's, I gasped.

As we'd suspected, scars marked my wings many times

over, but they were also *whole*. "Thank you so much, Althea."

"It was nothing, my lady."

"It's *everything* to me." I dropped the mirror into my lap and swallowed the lump in my throat. The urge to hug the healer washed over me, though I refrained.

Now that I was engaged to Roar, I was a lady fae, and they did not act that way to their servants, which Althea technically was.

"I wish I had some way to repay you."

"My lord does that." Althea waved her hand. "It's good enough to see you thriving, my lady."

I shifted off the table, still marveling at my wings, stretching them in new ways. Without rods in them, and no bandages covering them, I felt every vein twist, every muscle that supported the membranous tissue move. Before there had only been restrictions, and if I tried to move them too much, pain.

"They feel different," I marveled.

Althea smiled warmly. "Soon, you'll be used to them, and perhaps you'll fly too. Though I can't say when that will be. Much of it depends on how fast they strengthen."

I returned her smile with one of my own. "Let's hope it will be soon."

A knock came at the door, and all three of us turned to find a brownie standing there, holding a letter. The brownie's chest heaved with exertion, though he tried to hide it. "Pardon, my lady, the Warden of the West wishes for me to give you this. It took me a while to find you, so he's been waiting."

"Thank you." I walked over and took the letter, breaking the crimson seal. My eyes scanned the parchment, and I smiled. "My lord wishes for me to meet him at the gates right away."

"Then you shouldn't keep him waiting," the healer said.

"Thanks again, Althea."

If I had been rushing to get to the healing wing before, it paled compared to my pace now. Clemencia had trouble keeping up, and when her breaths became labored, I slowed.

"Sorry," I said.

"You're excited to see your fiancé." She grinned at me in a way that made me think we might be friends one day. "I wish I understood the feeling."

"You have no love interests?" A pretty fae like her should have a dozen suitors waiting for her to call.

She shook her head. "My father is very protective. I still live with him, when I'm not staying at the palace to help you, that is. He does *not* allow suitors."

"How old are you?"

"Twenty-two."

A year younger than me. My eyes widened in surprise. She held herself with such poise and grace, I'd thought she was in her late twenties. "Is that common here?"

"In certain circles of Guldtown, a female will live at home until wed, or until their liege lord calls upon them for a task such as this one. My circle observes such practices." She sighed, which made me think she wished things were different. "In the capital, and some territories, such as Virtoris Island, females of my station have more freedoms. Some even live outside their family home before marriage. My father calls it a life of debauchery."

I thought about that, and about how she was spending so much time with me. My lady-in-waiting only rested when she slept.

"You know, Clemencia, I don't need you to do everything for me. Now that you've gotten a little freedom, if you wanted to go on a date or two, I'd understand. And of course, I wouldn't say a word."

She eyed me sidelong. "You still need a lot of help to learn the ways of the court."

I couldn't deny it. I'd made progress in etiquette these past few days, but I had a long way to go before I became a perfect lady.

"Plus, my father would know if I went out in Guldtown." She shrugged.

"The offer stands," I said. She deserved a life too, and she would not get one under her father's thumb if he had any say. "If a male catches your eye at the Courting Festival, I'd like to know."

Clemencia didn't reply, and remained quiet as we exited the castle. Soft snow fell, but today had warmed compared to most days in Guldtown, and when the clouds broke, the sun shone through. I smiled, delighting in the weather, which I considered perfect.

Roar already stood at the gate, among others in the distance. He caught sight of me, and his face lit up as he waved.

In just a few days, he'd become more relaxed around

me. Laughing and smiling more and even teasing me about my enormous appetite and love of desserts, all the while making sure I was well fed and taken care of.

A part of me thought that he'd grown more relaxed because there was an undercurrent of attraction between us, which I considered only natural. We were both good-looking fae, and we were intentionally playing a couple in love.

For my part, I knew my attraction had to be at least partially down to the fact that Roar was the first male faerie I'd grown close to, and he was really everything a female could want.

And yet, oddly, I felt that *he* was more attracted to me than I was to him. He certainly initiated contact and sought me out more. Like when he showed up at dance lessons or took dinners in my room after the orc attack.

Or when he'd tried to kiss me.

Those actions gave me pause. After all, why would a high lord truly like me? By comparison, I had little to offer, while Roar had much to give.

But then again, perhaps I was just that unused to kindness from those in power. Before coming here, I'd experienced no such thing.

I tried not to think of it too much. If I'd been certain about my feelings for him, things might be different, but I wasn't sure about how I felt. Were my feelings more of an infatuation with someone so unlike myself, a person who truly seemed to like me too? Or could they be real?

For now, all I knew was that I needed to convince the King of Winter we had become a couple and save Roar from an arranged marriage he did not want. *That* was my focus.

As we got closer, it became clear Roar dismissed the other fae and turned to me. "Your wings look much better. And they're finally unbound."

I flexed my wings, reveling again in how different they felt. "Althea said they should have the chance to breathe."

"That's wonderful news."

"So what's going on?" I held up the letter.

"As an orc horde interrupted our first trip into the city, I thought we might try again."

I swallowed, suddenly nervous. Behind the castle gates, I felt safe—safer than I'd ever felt in my life. "Is that a good idea?"

"I've had the surrounding area swept for orc hordes. Don't worry. That will never happen again."

"Alright then," I conceded. It seemed like too large a promise to make, but I trusted him to keep it—for the day, at least.

"Clemencia, you may relax at the palace," Roar said. "I'll take care of Lady Neve for the rest of the day."

Clemencia blinked. "Are you sure, my lord?"

"Absolutely."

She performed an enviable, perfect curtsey. "I'll see you later, Lady Neve."

"Bye."

We left the castle grounds with an escort of three knights. The streets appeared less crowded this time around. Had Roar had his soldiers clear them of fae when they went looking for orcs? Or was it an off day? I was not sure how the markets ran here.

"Neve," Roar said as we turned onto the main road. "I want to apologize again. For last night. I shouldn't have acted so forwardly."

I stopped, halting him with me, and stared into his eyes. All around us, a few fae milled, some throwing us curious glances. How to play this in a way that didn't hurt him, but also did not lead him on?

I cleared my throat. "You don't have to apologize. Even if I'm not sure it's the best idea, given our situation, it's kind of natural to want to kiss." I smiled playfully, hoping to lighten the tension I felt coming off him. I didn't want to make him feel bad as he'd done nothing but act on his feelings. "Or at least, I don't find it odd."

A few seconds of silence passed between us before Roar spoke again. "Good to know. Should I show you around?"

"Um . . ." I wasn't sure what to think of his reply, so I settled for, "Yes, please."

We began walking again, and my head swam. "Good to know"? What in all the nine kingdoms did he mean by that?

Though I wondered what he meant, I stayed silent as Roar led me to a shop door and opened it for me. Stepping over the threshold, a million scents hit me all at once, and I staggered back, overwhelmed.

"You've never been in a tea shop, have you?" he laughed lightly.

"No. It's *very* pungent." I wrinkled my nose. "The only

teas I've had were very weak. Barely more than hot water to warm us in the winter."

The vampires didn't keep wide selections of teas on hand. Why would they? A vampire's preferred drink of choice was blood, followed by wine. Anything else and they turned their noses up.

"That's a crime," Roar said. "I'll buy you a cup of tea here so you can have the real thing. The owner of this shop is a brilliant teamaker as well as the leader of the Merchant's Guild, which is why we're here. I need to speak with him."

We ventured deeper into the empty shop. In the back, someone moved things about.

"Tvali?" Roar called out. "It's the warden. Are you there?"

"Warden Lisika? Just a mo!" A portly fae sprouting deer horns from his head entered the room. "Ah! And you brought your fiancée! The lovely Lady Neve, it's a pleasure to meet you!" A chubby hand gripped my forearm.

I did the same, completing the fae greeting custom. "It is good to meet you too, sir."

"I was hoping to purchase a cup of tea for my fiancée, and speak with you, of course."

"Anything she wants!" The teamaker rubbed his hands together. "What do you like, my lady?"

"I've not had much tea." I gestured to the room. "So I don't really know."

The fae lifted an eyebrow. "You don't say? Well, I have an excellent local brew. Made of pine needles from the mountain forest. Some say that the brews blended with southern ingredients are the best, but I disagree. A good home brew, when made by a practiced teamaker, is very indulgent!"

I nodded. "I'll take your word for it."

He set to work, and Roar caught my eye. "Let me speak with him privately for a moment. You should look around. If any of the teas smell nice to you, I'll get them."

I smiled. "Thanks."

We separated, and I began pursuing the teamaker's wares as Roar and Tvali spoke. Such pretty things lined his shelves. Small strainers one could fill with tea and handmade painted mugs seemed to be the most numerous items beside tea. The brightly colored mugs made me smile.

As for the teas themselves, I sniffed a few, but after the fifth, perfumed with cinnamon and oranges, it became overwhelming. I resigned myself to reading the labels, pausing only when I got to a shelf with eight tins bearing the most interesting names.

Lady of Silks
Lady of Ships
Lord of Tongues
Lord of Coin

The other four honored the Wardens of the East, West, North and South.

"Those blends honor the high lords and ladies of the Sacred Eight. They're some of my best work," a voice came from behind, making me jump. I turned to find

Tvali standing behind me with a steaming cup of tea in his hands. "I didn't mean to startle you, my lady."

"Don't apologize. I was engrossed." I gestured to the tins. "This is a clever idea, to blend teas representing the highest lords and ladies of Winter's Realm"

"They're our leaders, so fae like the idea of drinking a tea attached to their name." He held the steaming cup out to me, and I took it. "This here is the one I created to honor our own Warden of the West. It's popular in Guldtown and sells quickly, but I always keep the blend behind the counter. I hope you like it."

He waited, clearly wanting to see my reaction, so I sipped. My eyes widened. Flavors I could not place rolled over my tongue. The brew tasted spicy but also earthy. It reminded me of the forest that I'd ridden through with Frode to get here.

"Local needles and a hint of spice made from local pinecones." Tvali continued to observe me. "Everything in that blend is from the Western Front, as it should be when it honors the Lisika family."

"It's delicious," I said.

"She likes my tea, doesn't she?" Roar called out from where he waited, leaning against the counter with his arms crossed over his chest. Suggestively, he arched an eyebrow.

"It's good enough." I rearranged my features to be less enthused. "Bit bitter, though. Could use some sweetening up."

Tvali muffled a laugh.

"Please, my lady, I saw the way your eyes lit up. I'm

irresistible, and there's no denying it." Roar ran a hand through his long hair, and I had to admit the effect looked equally devastating and ridiculous, just as he'd wished it to.

Tvali burst out laughing, and I followed suit. The sounds of our laughter filled the room, warming every corner. "That's what we of Guldtown think too, my lord."

"I'll buy any of that tea that you have in stock today, Tvali. Clearly my lady likes it, and I like to please her, so I'll need it on hand." He winked at me.

Heat filled my cheeks, which only made the teamaker grin even broader.

CHAPTER 15

R oar directed me down the street that I'd glimpsed the day the orcs attacked—the one that smelled of burning steel.

"What are we doing now?" I asked. For hours, we'd been stopping into shops, purchasing wares, and just generally allowing me to get to know the fae of Guld-town. Though I'd enjoyed the day out, I had to admit that my feet were beginning to ache.

"This is the last stop," Roar replied. "I need to speak to the Master Smith of the city and see that my order is ready." He shot me a sidelong glance. "I know we've been going a long while, but this is too important to wait to send someone later."

"So, this *is* where all the smiths are! I thought so the other day but wasn't sure." Just as I said it, we passed the first forge, then another, and another. This far down, the street didn't just smell of burning steel but of fire and coal and sweat. Between the fae talking and the clanging of metal, it was the loudest and most boisterous part of the city that I'd seen. "There seem to be an awful lot of forges. Why is that?"

"My army is the largest in Winter's Realm and that means many smiths congregate here." He gestured to two forges set side-by-side, one a rundown shack with a single smithy, another a building with the door and windows open. Inside the latter, at least five smiths worked tirelessly.

"Even larger than the royal army?" My hand brushed the snowy top of a barrel as we passed by.

"Yes, though when they have me send fae to fight for the royal house, mine appears smaller." His lips flattened.

"How often do you send fae?"

He huffed out a breath. "Whenever House Aaberg requests it. With the Warrior Bear being so careless with fae lives, it is more often than I like."

I cocked my head at the odd title. "Who's the Warrior Bear?"

"Prince Vale, spare heir to the throne." Again, his full lips went flat.

"You don't seem to be a fan."

"We have a history—one that cost me many fae." His tone soured as he spoke, and a hard glint formed in his eyes. "I despise the prince, though I must bow to him all the same."

He truly looked furious, even without the prince nearby. I could not help but take his hand. "What happened?"

"I—," he paused. "It was a long time ago, not important anymore, but it still rubs me the wrong way."

"Your face and words say otherwise. If you're still upset, it *is* important." I looked Roar in the eyes and saw the pain there. He'd helped me so much, and I wanted to help him. At the very least, if I couldn't do that, I wanted to understand him. He didn't offer insight into his past often and I couldn't pass up this chance. "Please, Roar."

The warden let out a long breath before pulling me over to the side of the narrow street and motioning for the knights that had been following us and carrying packages to stand watch. "I haven't talked about this for a very long time, and I can't say that I'm happy to relive it."

"I understand. But I want to support you, like you've been doing for me. You can trust me with this."

His lips curled up a touch. "I know. And because you're going to the court for me, I will tell you. But you mustn't tell others."

In the street, someone called out the warden's name, and he broke our stare to wave at them. When he looked at me again, he took my hand and pulled me close.

"I won't say a word," I promised.

"It happened when the prince and I were just twenty turns of age," he started his story. "Back then, orc tribes raided the villages around the Ice Tooth Mountains daily, and the king commanded me to bring my army southeast. I did, and there we joined forces with the prince." He let out a long breath. "Vale and I have never been friends, but back then we put aside our differences and worked together to eradicate the tribes—until one day . . ."

His face hardened, and I swallowed, worried about what he'd say next. "We'd just moved closer to the foothills of the mountains and had battled one of the largest tribes I've ever seen—orc, goblins, and even ogres were united."

"No!" I sucked in a breath. "Ogres?!"

Ogres lived in small groups, and they viewed anyone outside that group as food. Even other ogres. I found it astonishing that they teamed up with other ogres.

"Yes. It was a massacre for our soldiers. I was fighting in a valley and things were going poorly. I sent a rider for the Warrior Bear's help, knowing that he wasn't far away, and I expected him to come, and he did." His tone dropped into a growl. "Almost. I saw Prince Vale and his forces crest the mountain on the western side of the valley. But the minutes passed, and I fought, my soldiers still fought to the death, and Vale's forces didn't help. Instead, they fled back down the hill, the other way, out of sight."

I shook my head. "But why? Those are his people too!"

"I can't say. Soon after, the army dispersed to take on smaller tribes. All I know is he left my forces to fend for themselves. Since that day, I have despised him to my core." His fists clenched.

I stared at his hands, not sure what to make of the story. What kind of ruler left their people to fight and suffer like that? "Did you tell the king?"

"Prince Vale is his son who had already been in many battles and won the hearts of fae in the east. You haven't met them yet, but the Aabergs always stick together, no matter the cost to others. The king would have sided with the Warrior Bear over me." Roar sniffed. "The king cares more for the fae of his city, and his ancestral seat in the midlands, than those in the west. No matter that my territory provides the most soldiers, the most gold too." He paused, hate burning in his eyes. "No, it wouldn't do to complain to the king. I merely had to live with the deaths. The bodies that I sent home."

My mouth fell open. How could someone do that to those of their own kingdom? It was cruel and uncaring. Prince Vale had treated the fae beneath him as though they were disposable, much like the vampires had treated me.

Tears tracked down my cheeks, and before I could wipe them away, Roar's hand lifted and caressed my cheek. I cupped his hand. "I'm so sorry that happened to you. To your people."

"I was too. Still am." Roar swallowed. "The soldiers who survived that day know the story of what happened, but others don't, and it's not a good idea to spread the tale. Vale is a celebrated prince of the realm, Neve. Since then, he's cinched his reputation as a savior of sorts. The royal army is deeply loyal to him."

"I understand. I won't mention it again."

He pulled me into a hug. "I don't want to put you off, and you should feel like you can ask questions, but thank you for understanding. It's for our safety."

When we broke apart, I smiled up at him. Though we hadn't known one another long, at that moment, I understood him a bit better and felt particularly close to the warden.

He pivoted and pointed across the street. "Now, we need to get down to business. We're going just over there. Please be careful when we walk inside. Forges are hot."

"You don't say?" I replied playfully, trying to lighten the mood.

He smirked and shook his head, but as we entered the forge, the warden's mirth left his face and the regal lord of the city appeared.

A faerie lad of about fourteen ran up to us. He wore just a tunic and pants as the forge was so hot that furs and cloaks weren't needed. "My lord! Are you here to see my master?"

Roar nodded. "I am."

"I'll show you to the back."

The faerie boy led us to the back, where a dwarf with a long, braided beard plunged a sword into water. Steam filled the air, making me cough, and the dwarf looked up. "Lord Roar! I have words to say to you! Just a mo'!" He turned to the boy and began to give orders.

My lips parted in shock. Since visiting the teahouse and buying half of Tvali's stock, we'd been by seven other merchant's shops so I could meet them, and Roar could do business. None had spoken to him so gruffly.

"Dwarves," Roar grumbled. "So crass."

"And blasted good at working with Zuprian steel, which is more than I can say for the faerie two doors down. What a bleeding amateur. Wouldn't even pay him to make a spoon!" The dwarf glanced up slightly and

184

seemed to notice me for the first time. "Who's that?" He jerked his head to me and went back to pick up another sword and began sharpening it. Did this dwarf ever stop to breathe?

"My fiancée, Lady Neve."

"A fiancée. Good for you, my lady." He kept working the blade. "You're well protected and won't be meetin' the same end as the other strangers that find themselves in the west. Poor buggers."

What did he mean by that? I opened my mouth to ask when Roar leaned closer. "People traveling through the mountains. They can't always get through the passes, so they end up roaming our territory, looking for safety."

"And they don't get it?"

"The lands surrounding the mountains can be just as harsh as the passes and peaks. Wherever there is no civilization, deadly foes lie in wait. So no, their end is not always kind."

I shuddered. I'd planned to travel the passes too and had been woefully underprepared, especially after I lost my horse. Would I have been one of those people?

"Master Smith," Roar said, trying to gain the smith's attention, but the dwarf remained focused on sharpening the blade. "I've come to make certain that my order will be ready in two days' time?"

"Why do you think I'm still here workin' when I should be at the tavern havin' a pint?" The smith scoffed and, finally, stopped moving. He set the sword he'd been working on down and scowled up at his high lord.

"You'll be able to buy many more pints with the gold bears I'm paying."

The dwarf spat on the ground. "Those blasted bears are the reason I need to keep makin' so many swords! If King Magnus needs more fae on the fronts, he should pull them from his own taverns! Not be askin' for them on such short notice! Why must we give our sons and husbands to the king when his own city is rife with bastards who can surely hold a sword?"

Roar let out a long breath. His face said he agreed, but as he began to speak to the smith, he was the picture of a loyal subject.

I wrapped my arms around my middle and shook my head. So far, what I'd learned of the Royal House of Aaberg had not been flattering, and I had not learned that much at all.

The idea of the Courting Festival and what I would encounter there loomed larger than it had before. What obstacles would I have to overcome? Would the royals believe Roar and I were engaged?

And if they found out that we played the king for a fool, what exactly would they do?

CHAPTER 16

"**L**ady Neve! Stop lusting after all the books in the library. We must *study*." Clemencia rapped loudly on the table. "Now, tell me, who is this?"

I tore my eyes from the shelves and all the stories they held. It was too bad I wouldn't have more time here to devour them. I'd much rather be doing that than the lessons we'd moved on to.

With a groan, I looked down at the parchment Clemencia pointed at of a hand-drawn royal family tree with the name blotted out. Not far away, a fire crackled in the hearth, emitting heat and the faintest smell of smoke. I pulled a shawl around me tighter, buying time as I wracked my brain for the answer my lady-in-waiting sought. But it was no use. After hours of going over the House of Aaberg's history and dabbling in the other families of the Sacred Eight, my mind had turned to mush.

I leaned back and sighed. "I don't know. We ought to

189

have been doing this all along instead of dancing. This is much harder with all the names and titles and then they all intermarry over the centuries! It's just too much."

Clemencia's face softened a touch. "As you're from a village, no one will expect you to be perfect. Why would a village girl know the extended family members of the Lady of Ships and Lord of Tongues? *But* you will not have as much leeway as your father granted you." She shook her head at my ignorance. "What was he thinking?"

I looked away from her. "About catching his next fish and feeding us."

"Of course, you're right. But you didn't answer my question." Clemencia tapped the page again, back to business as usual. "It's the last one, and it's important."

I studied the page. I recalled King Magnus Aaberg, Queen Inga Aaberg née Vagle, Prince Rhistel the heir, and Prince Vale the Warrior Bear, the same faerie who had betrayed Roar. A twin to the heir, born only minutes apart. But who was the other sibling? A female . . . I knew that much.

"Her name is like an epic tale," Clemencia added, likely taking pity on me.

It finally clicked. "Princess Saga!"

"Very good! Sometimes also called Winter's Delight. True to her given name, they say that she is a notable writer."

"What does she write? Maybe I'd like her stories."

"She keeps most of it private. So I don't really know." Clemencia shrugged. "Should we go—oh! My lord!" She stood when she noticed Roar in the library's doorway and curtsied.

I rose as well. "My lord."

"My ladies, I hate to interrupt your lessons, but things have gone awry. We must leave for court today."

My eyebrows screwed together. "But why?"

"It has begun to snow harder than is normal." He gestured to the window at the far end of the room. It was far away, but even so, I could see the falling flurries of white. "Those in other towns along the Queen's Road have reported heavy snowfall too. So to be sure that we arrive on time, leaving now would be wise. We cannot be late to court."

Fae in Winter's Realm were used to snow falling for most of the year. They trained their horses to travel in deep drifts, and depending on the weather, they traveled in both sleigh carriages and wheeled ones. Knowing all that, I feared that we were about to travel through a true blizzard.

Roar turned to Clemencia. "How far have you progressed in her studies?"

Clemencia's teeth dug into her bottom lip. "Today, we were going over the Royal House, my lord."

"And I'm sure Neve is doing well, right?"

"She's improving. Though there is still much to cover if she's to fit in among the lords and ladies."

"You'll still have many days to study while you travel," Roar said encouragingly. "I've had servants begin to pack up both of your things, so I suggest you check your rooms for anything they missed and prepare for the journey. Dress warmly."

"Might I borrow more books for the trip?" I asked.

"You're finished with the first batch already?" Roar's eyebrows arched.

"I still have one left—your brother's favorite," I fessed up in case he asked how I'd liked it. "But I'm a fast reader, and we have a long journey. Then we'll be at court for a while after."

The levity in his expression faded at that. "Hopefully not *too* long."

I agreed. People had few nice things to say about the king and his sons, whom we'd likely be seeing a lot of. Fewer knew anything about the queen, which set me on edge. The princess however, seemed well-liked, so that was a plus. And yet, we hadn't even left for court, and already I wanted to return to Roar's castle, to the cozy, snow-covered Guldtown. Even if I might not have been here long, this place had started to feel safe, almost like a home.

"Take as many books as you'd like. I'll send a servant up here with a small trunk to store them in your sleigh." Roar's voice held only kindness and his eyes softened on me. "Meet me at the main gate when you're ready. That is where the soldiers and sleighs are amassing."

I nodded, and he swept away to continue preparations for the journey. "Do you know how many will travel with us?" I asked Clemencia.

I knew it had to be many. The Master Smith had been working his beard off the day before to fulfill Roar's orders. He'd been so irate over the rush order of weapons and now we planned to leave early. Whoever took that message to the smith had probably received a tongue lashing. And what of the soldiers whose last hours at home were now disrupted?

All this because the king wanted his hand in marriage alliances. I found it to be ridiculous.

"A small army and a few servants are to accompany us during travel, but I don't know exactly how many," my lady-in-waiting replied and turned toward the stacks. "Can I help you select books, my lady?"

"Of course. Pick some for yourself too. There's no way we can study for the entire trip." Clemencia opened her mouth, I assumed to protest that idea, so I quickly changed the subject. "What stories do you like?"

Pink stained the apples of her cheeks. "Romances, mostly."

"I like those too. If they have adventure in them, all the better."

"Then I have one you'd like! It's about a Winter Maiden stolen by the Summer King. I've seen it over here." A wistful expression crossed her face, making me wonder if, like me, Clemencia dreamed of far-away lands.

A flurry of excitement ensued as we plucked book after book from the shelves, exclaiming over the romance or monsters or adventures within. By the time the servant arrived with the trunk for books, I found my arms weighed down with stories. He took them from Clemencia and me with care and began packing them away.

"My wife loves this one." The servant held up a book that Clemencia had hinted was quite risqué.

My lady-in-waiting and I looked at each other and dissolved into giggles, which judging by his furrowed brow, confused the fae.

"Best be finding a thick cloak, my lady." He shrugged. "The temperature is falling fast."

"I'll do that now," I said. "I'll meet you outside, Clemencia."

We separated and rushed to our rooms. When I arrived in my room, maids were just finishing packing up my room.

One pointed to the bed. "There are cloaks for you to choose from to wear during travel. They're the warmest. Once you have the one you want, we'll pack up the others."

"Thank you." I scanned the options.

I chose two crimson cloaks lined with thick brown fur. If I were to arrive at the Winter Court as Roar's fiancée, I needed to make the king believe it. So I would wear House Lisika's colors as often as possible.

"Excellent choice, my lady." The maids scooped up the others and packed them away for me. "They'll be in this gold trunk with black straps." She patted the one she worked on. "In case you need an extra along the way."

"Thank you." I looked about, checking that they had not missed anything.

As I'd arrived with nothing and possessed only the clothing Roar had given me, I came up nearly empty. Aside from extra clothes and books, I only wanted to pack one other thing myself. I went to my bedside table and opened the drawer. Inside, the golden vial of Roar's blood stared back at me.

Since the day we'd made our deal, Roar had given me a chain so that I might wear the vial around my neck, but I noticed that he didn't do so and I followed suit. Truthfully, it felt too weird.

Thankful that my dress had pockets, I slipped the vial into one. This was my safeguard that he would not betray me at court, which, to be honest, I found a preposterous notion. He needed me as much as I needed him. And yet, I would guard the vial until our deal finished.

When I arrived at the main castle door, a thrill of excitement coursed through me. I felt excited to see the lands of Winter's Realm and experience traveling with an entourage and soldiers.

How many soldiers exactly, I had no idea until I stepped outside. At least one hundred fae waited outside on horses, all in armor and heavy cloaks, to shield them from the cold. The warden spoke with them.

Undoubtedly, Roar routinely traveled with a retinue of soldiers, but this many? Surely not. How many had come just to join the king's army?

Three conveyances waited, each one a carriage poised on gleaming planks of wood like sleighs. The nicest one stood between the other two. Painted gold and crimson, the sleigh donned colors of House Lisika. A snow leopard had been carved on both sides of the door, dancing on its back paws. The other two carriages looked plain by comparison, so I assumed Roar would want me in the sleigh meant for a lord or lady. I began walking through the freshly fallen ankle-deep snow for the most ornate sleigh.

"My lady!"

"Yes?" I turned.

Clemencia burst through the castle door. "I need to help you into the sleigh!"

I scoffed. "I'm capable."

"But she's right." Roar rode up to me. He looked quite dashing, wearing a cloak of muted gold with the fat snowflakes falling into his red hair. My core gave a flutter. "She's your lady, and at court she'll assist you in most matters, much like a maid would."

"Not an actual maid?" I frowned.

Roar cleared his throat. "The king has demanded that every lord or lady with children of marriageable age attend. No matter how small or large their estate is, hundreds of nobles will arrive at Frostveil Palace, and that means the castle must house them. It will be too crowded for my servants. Hence, I cut the traveling staff because I will have to put them up at inns while they wait for the journey home."

I found the imposition astonishing.

"And it will force their own servants to work harder," I added.

"Likely." Roar leaned closer. "It's also a way for the king to use his own staff to spy on us."

My lips parted. Of course he would. How frustrating.

"So, how many of these soldiers are being sent to fight the orc hordes?" I asked.

"Eighty of the one hundred and ten we will travel with. The rest will remain in the city, waiting for our trip home." He exhaled. "It is not a total loss. They'll be working during their stay. I like to have eyes and ears in as many places as possible."

He was a cunning fae, my fake fiancée.

"Very well. I'll learn to better accept assistance." I nodded, and with Clemencia, set off for the sleigh.

We didn't even make it there when Roar rode up alongside us. He peered down at me with a devilish glint in his eyes. "Actually, I just had a thought. Would you like to ride part of the way? At my side?"

Clemencia clutched her heart, like she was about to swoon on the spot.

"I've ridden before, but not often." I rubbed my arms. "And last time I was in poor shape afterward."

Roar smiled warmly. "We'll go slow. And you'd only have to do so at the start of our journey. My people would love to see you as you leave for court."

I swallowed. "If you think that's best."

The warden dismounted and waved a soldier holding the reins of two horses over. "Bring Anya over here!"

The male handed over one horse to someone else and approached us. I sized up the horse.

She stood shorter and stouter than Judge and, like all of the horses in the yard, had a far thicker coat to keep out the cold. From the way she trotted, Anya practically vibrated with energy. Spirited, as some horsemasters might say.

"She'll be perfect for you," Roar assured me, and I rearranged my features into a smile.

Though I'd rather be in the sleigh, it *would* be good to get more horseback riding training. What if I had to ride at court? And Roar thought right about having the townsfae see us ride off together. The warden seemed certain the royal house would send spies to Guldtown after we arrived at Frostveil Castle. The more he presented me as a lady who had stolen the heart of the Warden of the West, the better.

"My lady," the soldier said as he neared. "You'll be riding Anya?"

"I will." He brought the horse to me and positioned her so I could mount.

"Allow me to assist." Roar's powerful hands landed on my waist and lifted me onto the horse.

The moment I sat in the saddle, I realized that with my thick skirts, I'd have to travel sidesaddle. I wouldn't be able to grip the sides of the horse with my legs, which was how I'd managed to stay glued to Judge before. The seat was less comfortable this way too. I shifted, not really liking the position and already wanting down.

But Roar watched me with such pride and expectation that I had to try.

"Alright then." I exhaled, taking the reins as Roar stepped back. "I have to admit that this is—*eek*!"

Someone dropped a trunk, creating a loud noise, and Anya jolted forward. As I hadn't been well situated in the first place, I lost my balance. Before I knew it, I had slipped and landed on the soft snow.

It would have been fine if I had fallen alone. But in the castle yard so many fae stared.

Heat filled my cheeks as I stood. "Maybe this won't work."

"Apologies!" Roar came to my side in an instant and extended his hands.

I took them, embarrassed. "I should probably just ride in the sleigh. Sidesaddle might not be my thing."

"Oh, you rode astride before?" His eyebrows rose.

"Yes. I think I have better balance that way."

"I see." Roar cast a glance at where Anya had been stopped some twenty paces away. "Perhaps you could simply ride with me, rather than next to me?"

I stiffened. "With you?"

"If you're comfortable being close to me, that is. You'd still be sidesaddle, but I can keep you on the seat."

Riding with so little space between our bodies would be intimate. But then again, we *were* supposed to be engaged and it *would* make an impression.

"Yes, we can do that," I said before I could back out. "For a bit."

The warden's grin could have melted all the snow in the courtyard. "Then, allow me, my lady."

He called for a soldier to bring steps as he led me to his horse and mounted. Once he got positioned, a soldier brought the stairs closer and helped me up. As Roar could steady me, I felt more secure—even if my rear nestled against his loins. Stars, there had only been a handful of times when I'd been so close to a male and in those moments we hadn't worn clothing.

My chest flushed at the thought, and of replacing one of my lovers with the image of Roar. It was both an intriguing and odd idea that I wasn't sure I liked. I thanked the stars above that he could not see how red my face became as I sorted through the emotions warming me from the core.

"Comfortable?" he breathed, his lips drawing close to my ears in a way that made me shiver.

"Much better."

"Good." Roar called for his soldiers and the sleighs to fall in line, and we trotted to the castle gates, which opened for us. "Now, smile, Neve," he whispered. "Give them a love story to remember."

I beamed and even leaned back so that we'd look like a couple in love. As I did so, Roar's chest and strong arms cradled me and he whispered into my ear, his breath tickling my neck. "Best be careful, my lady. Or I might start to think you're not pretending."

"Apologies," I muttered as, once again, heat climbed my face.

"I did not say I didn't like it."

I was grateful for the fae who approached and waved and demanded our attention as we rode out of Guldtown, because I didn't know what to say to Roar. His hard body behind me was tempting, and he'd made it clear that he wanted me.

And yet, I still wasn't sure it was smart to push our new friendship further, to make the farce a reality. I might be attracted physically, but my heart wasn't convinced, and another part of me still could not fathom why his was.

CHAPTER 17

In the moon's silver light, I descended the sleigh's steps and took in the longhouse two-story inn that had been built partially into the side of a steep, snow-covered hill.

"Well, it's nicer than the last two." Clemencia rubbed her hands over her arms, and ducked her head to avoid a particularly blustery gale. "Perhaps we'll get more than one blanket apiece. Or maybe because it's built into the hill it will be naturally warmer? I'm not used to such a design."

Nor was I, but one could hope that the inside of this inn would be warmer and cozier than the rest. Since we'd left Guldtown three days prior, the snow had only fallen heavier and faster, putting us many hours behind schedule. The wicked winds that blew through the forests and down the ribbon that was the Queen's Road wasn't helping matters either.

In our traveling troop, spirits were down and more

often than not, fae shivered beneath their heavy cloaks as they rode. Truth be told, the persistent chill had even gotten to me, but I tried not to complain. I rode in a covered sleigh, largely safe from the howling wind. Most of the poor soldiers and servants riding along with Roar could not say the same.

"I have a good feeling about this one." I tried to be positive and looked for Roar. Thanks to his flaming red hair, I found him quickly.

The warden was speaking to the captain of his guard, but sensing my gaze, he turned and waved. I pointed to the door, and Roar gestured for us to go inside.

I hooked my arm through my lady-in-waiting's. "Come, Clemencia, my lord will join us later. Let's get an ale and stew to warm our bones."

Her face lit up, and together we shuffled down the narrow, snowy path until we reached the inn. No sounds came from inside.

"Maybe we're the only ones staying here?" I pressed into the door, only to find it quite heavy, probably to keep out the raging wind. Another shove of my shoulder and the door creaked open a crack.

Music blasted, making me gasp as I got a glimpse inside. How wrong I'd been about our group being the only travelers.

We stood frozen upon the threshold, taking in the revelry, the likes of which I hadn't seen in a long while. A tavern filled the lower level of the inn, and inside fae from every race drank, ate, and sang along to a song. A few even danced. Candles flickered on top of the tables, illuminating the area and spilling wax upon the wood. This inn appeared clean, not always a given along the Queen's Road, and also large enough to fit most of our soldiers inside, also, not always a given. I hoped there were ample beds as well so that most of Roar's people wouldn't have to sleep on the floor. Overall, the ambiance was pleasing, and the tavern seemed safe.

"Close the bloody door!" someone shouted, and we scurried inside waving our apologies.

Clemencia exhaled a long breath. "Shall I get us food and drink? There's a table tucked away just over there that you can sit at, my lady."

"I've been sitting all day. I'll join you at the bar."

Together, we walked through the crowd, garnering no notice now that we weren't letting in the wind. I enjoyed the pleasant change of anonymity. Our caravan had left the far reaches of Roar's western territories late this afternoon and ventured into the midlands of Winter's Realm. At every rest stop, local fae stared and whispered about the visiting warden and the female he fancied.

"Good evening, mi' ladies," a towering, muscular barkeep slurred. From the look of him, I was certain that he, unlike Althea, was a pureblooded troll. He had the distinctive small head and upper fangs. "Where are you riding from?"

"Guldtown," Clemencia answered. "With the Warden of the West and over one hundred of his soldiers. A few of his household too. If you do not have a spare pot of stew on the fire, I'd suggest righting that error immediately."

The troll's dark eyes widened. "You don't say?"

"I do."

"Blessed stars," he beamed, exposing a mouth missing at least three teeth in the back, "this is what we need after a string of bad luck."

"What bad luck?" I asked.

"Groups of goblins have been roaming the midlands and stealing everything that they can. They tried to steal a cask of ale. I only just beat them away with the 'elp of me son. Many of my patrons have been divested o' their coin. Some lost their horses too. I've had to pay stable lads to stay on day and night." He shook his head in annoyance.

"Horses?" I balked. "How would goblins take those?"

I hadn't met a goblin yet, but I'd seen images and read stories. In some kingdoms goblins were civilized, but in Winter's Realm the small tribal fae lived in the wild and rode animals like wolves, wild boars, or, in the case of the smallest goblins, bats.

"Many to a steed, mi' lady." The barkeep poured an ale for another patron. "I found it hard to believe, but it's true. Keep your purse close as you travel."

I had no purse, but we traveled with a lot of coin. Roar needed to be informed.

"Thank you for letting us know," I said. "Might we get two ales and two bowls of stew? And start a tab for the warden."

"Right away, mi' lady." He prepared our drinks, handed them over, and said that he'd bring the stew to our table, so Clemencia and I found a spot close to the music and settled in.

Soon after, the food arrived in the massive hands of the barkeep. He set down the bowls, and my stomach rumbled. The stew smelled perfectly meaty and swam with vegetables. My mouth watered, and without a word to one another, we ate.

"Mmmm." I closed my eyes.

Clemencia gobbled down the stew faster than I did, which made me smirk. Eating so quickly was against all that she'd taught me about etiquette, but I understood. It had been hours since we ate, and the cold made the hunger pangs sharper.

By the time Roar joined us, we'd cleaned our bowls. He smiled. "I hope you left some for the rest of us."

"We told the barkeep that there would be hungry soldiers arriving." I sighed as a renewed sense of energy that came with a full belly flowed through me. "He'll make sure there's enough. We also started a tab for you."

"Very good. I'll have my captain get me one." Roar turned and hollered to a soldier, who took his lord's order and strode to the bar.

"The barkeep had news," I said when Roar turned back to us.

"Oh?"

"Bands of goblins have been raiding the countryside." I shook my head at the poor luck of the midlands. "They've stolen horses from those staying at this very inn."

Roar laughed in disbelief. "Goblins? You can't be serious. This far from the mountains?"

"They don't only live in the mountains, my lord,"

Clemencia pointed out. "The Eriking tribe favors the forest."

"The *deep* forest," Roar corrected. "We travel the Queen's Road, which is too close to many civilizations for their liking."

"Unless the harsh weather is pushing them to where they can find food and supplies in greater quantities," I said.

Roar mulled that over until his food arrived. "We'll be safe. With such a large guard, no one will harm us. And I'll be sure that after they eat, some of my men stay in the stables."

I wasn't sure if he said it for our sake or his own, but his next words made it clear that we needed to drop the subject.

"How are your wings, my love?" Roar gazed at me with concern in his eyes.

"Better than ever." I rustled them beneath my cloak.

"How would you like to try flying tonight?"

My breath hitched. Before I'd wanted only a meal, a warm fire, and then a bed, but now . . . "I'd love that."

His lips curled up. "I thought you might. Once I'm done eating, we'll go to the barn."

"Why the barn?"

"If you fly tonight, I doubt it will be far or high," Roar replied. "Your wings likely aren't strong enough yet. But should you catch air, there's hay in the barn to soften a less than graceful landing. I'll try to catch you too, of course. Not to mention, the barn will keep out most of the cold and wind."

It made sense, though it also begged the question of how Roar would teach me. He'd had wings once, but they'd been ravaged by sickness. Did he recall how to use them?

The idea made me sad, and I didn't voice it. That he vanished away his wings when he was out of his castle told me that the warden felt self-conscious over what he'd lost. I could relate to that. Though fae did not use magic for everything, I was constantly aware I did not have that option. Not for a while, anyway.

When my magic would begin showing, and what I would be able to do with it, remained a mystery to me.

So, I sat there, excited and fearful, as Roar ate his stew and sopped it up with a lumpy roll before drinking down his ale. Luckily, the tavern had much to see, and the music was delightful.

The troop of dwarves played drums, a horn, a stringed instrument, and a wooden flute. The effect sounded magical, and though Roar and Clemencia attempted conversation a few times, I was happy to listen to the songs they played.

As one tune died, the dwarf on the drums called out to those in the tavern for requests. A pixie dressed in winter clothes so thick that they looked like nothing but a flying ball, shot into the air.

"The Ballad of Sassa and Tore!"

"Bah! Sing of Sassa and her blade!" a faerie called.

"Or the great Shadow Battle!" A dryad waved his branch-like arms in the air.

"Nah! Sing of the twin bears!"

"Of how the Warrior Bear can cream our soft-handed heir?" A drunken pixie laughed. "The Warrior Bear is alright but please, nothing of that silver-tongued scholar!" He pretended to be the heir reading a book, which was apparently a hilarious jab because others in the crowd laughed.

"Queen Sassa it is!" the dwarf agreed and struck up a tune.

I leaned forward, enraptured, and wondered which the band would choose. When the dwarf began to sing of battles and blood, I thought he'd decided on the Great War that Queen Sassa led. But only a few stanzas in the song twisted to the Unification. The bard sang of how all the great houses bent the knee to Sassa Falk, how she unified them all so that they might fight off a common invader.

Though Clemencia had told me of this period, it sounded so different in song, more chilling and important. And then the bard finished the tune, crooning about blood on the ground of Winter's land, blood on the hands of the Shadow Fae, a now extinct race, and blood on Sassa's legendary blade.

When the last chord rang out, each fae stood and clapped. I did too with tears in my eyes. The song sounded so beautiful, so haunting, that it struck me deeply.

"Ready?" Roar asked, getting to his feet next to me.

I blinked, taken aback by his tone. "I guess so."

"Clemencia, will you ready my lady's room? She'll be tired once we're done."

"Of course, my lord." Clemencia's red eyes had teared up at the song, but she wiped those tears away and rose to do Roar's bidding. Looking about, I found that everyone else in the tavern looked emotional too. Only the warden appeared untouched.

I took his offered hand. "Did you not like the song?"

"Excuse me?" Roar lifted his eyebrows.

"Everyone else seemed moved by the music, but it doesn't appear to have had that effect on you."

"I prefer not to think of the Unification."

"But—wasn't that the only way for the Winter's Realm to stop the invasion?" That's what I'd learned during my short time in Winter's Realm. But Roar had access to the best books and education and insider information from great houses. Perhaps he had learned something different?

"That's what they say, what all the tales, songs, and books tell us, but all those who fought during the time of the Unification are long dead," he replied as we wove toward the front door. "As a descendant of the Lisika who lost their crown, I have other ideas."

I stayed silent. It could be possible Roar was right. It seemed just as possible that he wasn't, but it wasn't my place to debate. The song had been beautiful and moving, and only that mattered.

He led me from the tavern and into the cold night. The barn wasn't far, and I was glad for it because the snow still came down in heavy sheets and the wind still whipped my cheeks fiercely.

Stars, it's awful out here. Will we be able to ride again in the morning?

Roar didn't seem worried, so I kept the question inside. No reason to search for problems that no one could fix. Or try and predict the future. Even if I was a seer, my magic was dead inside me, so I wouldn't know.

The warden pushed open the door to the barn. The scent of musty hay and animals flew at me, and I wrinkled my nose.

Two young stable hands sitting in the hay leapt to their feet.

"Mi' lord!" the taller one spoke up, his body practically vibrating as he took in Roar and his young eyes landed on the gold snow leopard crest that clasped Roar's cloak shut. "We've just finished putting away as many of your horses as we can manage! The rest are—"

"I'm sure they're fine. My soldiers will take care of that," Roar interrupted the lad. "I'm actually here because I wish to teach my lady to fly. Might there be an area where we can have some privacy? A place with a soft landing?"

"Oh, yes. In the far back we keep bales of hay and there's lots on the ground," the older youngling said, eyebrows pulling together at the request. "Some of your soldiers are already sleeping in the stalls, but they aren't close enough to the bales, so they won't be able to see. And we'll stay up here, by the door."

"Good lad." Roar pulled two silvers from his pocket, which made the younglings' eyes go wide. Their eyes went wider still when he retrieved a second one for each stable hand. "Tell no one of this. My lady is quite embarrassed to not be able to fly yet."

The younglings' faces softened. The smaller one had wings, but the other did not. The smallest one came forward. "It took me many weeks, my lady. My older brother teased me for being clumsy and falling a lot, but I think you can do it!"

"Thank you." I smiled. "With your encouragement, I'm sure I'll manage."

The boy beamed, and when Roar handed over the silver coins, they appeared ready to die from happiness. I suspected that it was more money than their entire family might get in a week.

Taking my hand, the warden and I walked to the back of the barn, where hay and other tools lined the wooden walls. The ceiling arched high, so that if I got a few feet off the ground, I'd not hit my head.

Roar turned to me. "Seeing as I've not used my wings since I was a youngling, I can only teach you what I remember. Mostly what my parents taught me."

My heart clenched. He seemed so unaffected by his loss, but I suspected that was only because two decades had passed and he was good at burying things. I wondered if it actually hurt him to think of his lost wings.

"I'll take whatever you can offer," I replied.

"With your scarring, you'll have reason to not fly while at court, but should you need to . . . Say if there is danger, you should be able to do so and not draw attention."

"Do you foresee danger at court?"

His face hardened. "We might act with sophistication and manners, but the courts of Isila are the most dangerous places in the realm. Make no mistake about it, Neve." He took a deep breath. "Now, spread your wings."

I shucked off my cloak and did as he commanded, loving the feel of my extended wings and relishing how far I could stretch them. Before, I'd never been able to do such a thing. The metal rods placed in them would have made such an action painful, so I usually tried to make sure my wings took up as little space as possible. Squished together, they ached less, much like tucking into a ball when one's stomach roiled sometimes helped.

"We'll start easy," he said. "Flap them a few times. Get the sensation of air beneath them and determine how much resistance they can manage. Vary the speeds as you do so."

I fluttered my wings, testing out the motions of flapping. Before today, I'd been hesitant to do too much with my wings. But no pain came, and after a few test flaps, I went faster. Air billowed against the thin but sturdy membranous tissue, and for a brilliant moment, I imagined being lifted from the ground.

"More!" Roar encouraged, perhaps noticing that I loosened up. "Go up on your toes! Trust your wings to catch you."

I did so, pushing up and working my wings harder. Within minutes, they ached.

"I'm already tired," I admitted to Roar.

"You'll have to build the strength. Do you have the feel of it, though? How it'll feel when they catch air?"

"I think so," I said, still beating my wings, determined to give this my all, even if I didn't expect to get off the ground.

"Then, here. One last try." Roar stooped and rushed toward me. Before I knew what he was doing, he grabbed my legs and threw me into the air.

"Stars!" I breathed, not expecting such an action, nor my wings to catch air, but I hovered a few hands above the dirt. "Roar! Look! I—ohhh!"

The air I'd managed to ride gave out beneath me, and I fell to the ground, arms flailing. Thankfully, the warden stood there with me. He caught me at the waist with a smile on his face.

"You did it!" He did not let go and our chests pressed together as I breathed, trying to calm my racing heart.

I laughed, the sound of it somewhere between nervous and elated. "You act as if I soared in the rafters, but I was not that high off the ground. I could probably jump higher." Proud as I might be, I had to admit that it wasn't that impressive.

"It's a start. How do you feel?" His face hovered so close that I could count his lashes, but I tried to ignore this closeness that made my insides twist and confused me. Instead, I tried to focus on the matter at hand.

"Exhausted," I admitted. We'd been at this for only minutes, and already I was not sure I could go much longer.

"That's to be expected. What do you say we give it one more go, and then I'll see you to bed?"

I smiled up at him, tired, but happy that he believed in me. "Yes, once more."

CHAPTER 18

I leaned back into the velvet-covered seat of the sleigh, eyes fluttering closed for a moment of reprieve. My stomach gnawed at me, but I'd learned that interrupting Clemencia when she was trying to do the work her lord had given her was a bad idea. Five days into our journey, she'd grown increasingly more insistent on hours of lessons, and I resigned myself to being a dutiful student. But I couldn't hold out much longer.

And then the squeal of a trunk opening, no doubt the one filled with books, told me that my lady-in-waiting was switching tasks. I opened my eyes, prepared to seize the moment.

"I think I need a break, Clemencia. It's nearly lunchtime, right?"

"We could have an apple, I suppose." Clemencia shut the trunk and looked at the basket of food we kept in the carriage. It got refilled at the inns each night and was supposed to last us during the long days of travel. Aside from heavier fare we were served at supper, we'd only eaten traveling food such as apples, crackers, cheeses, and, if we were lucky, dried meats. I was already tired of them.

In a shockingly short amount of time, I'd gotten used to the heartier dishes, as had my body. For lunch, an apple did not seem appealing. Not on its own, anyway. But then again, we didn't have much choice.

I sighed and leaned forward. "Is there any cheese or meat to go with it today? I—"

The door to the moving sleigh flew open, and before I saw his face, I knew who it would be. Roar was the only person who visited us throughout the day.

"We're coming upon a city." Roar shoved into the sleigh's carriage and took a seat beside me. Since we'd begun traveling, the snow had not stopped falling and it covered his gold traveling cloak lined with reddish-brown fox fur.

He shuddered in the sleigh's relative warmth. "It's cozy in here. I should spend more time with you ladies."

Clemencia beamed, but I was glad Roar didn't join us most of the time. I didn't need the warden looking over my shoulder as my lady-in-waiting tested me.

"Are you ladies hungry?" Roar gazed first to Clemencia and then to me. "I know of a tavern in the city. It's excellent."

"I am," I blurted.

The excitement that came with the prospect of real food must have shown on my face, because Roar's lips twisted with amusement. "We'll stop then. The city is called Traliska, quite a charming place, and the fae are welcoming. It'll be a good place for you to see and be seen. Especially seeing as we're getting close to Avaldenn."

I understood. Upon arriving at court, the royals would know where we'd passed through. If they later sent anyone to check on our story, they'd stop off in the cities, towns, and villages on the Queen's Road, the road that ran from east to west in Winter's Realm. Here, we would need to act the part of a couple in love.

"Perfect," I said, stretching my legs out a little.

Roar eyed my attire, which consisted of pants, a long-sleeved tunic, and a heavy traveling cloak. "Perhaps you should change. You look wonderful as always, but a dress would be best for touring Traliska."

"Very well." My gaze shifted to the small trunk that held clothing, set beneath Clemencia's feet. Most of the clothing trunks that the maids packed stayed outside the sleigh, but a couple of smaller ones traveled inside with us, along with books, study materials, and food.

"I'll leave you to change then." Roar hunched over and shuffled toward the door. He leapt out of the moving sleigh, shutting the door behind him.

I peered out the window in time to watch the soldier who had been guiding the warden's horse while the line plodded forth stop so that Roar could mount. Once astride, Roar sent his horse into a trot to inform the front of the column of his wishes.

"Put this on." Clemencia shoved a dress in my face.

Startled, I turned. "How did you even get it out of the trunk so fast?"

"It is my job to anticipate your needs." Her narrow, almond-shaped eyes crinkled at the corners when she smiled proudly. "Pull the curtain so no one will see you change."

I did as she said and began undoing my boots. Once my feet were bare, the rest of my clothing followed, and Clemencia helped me into the simple dress. The red shift with gold snowflake embellishments around the wrists and neckline wasn't pretentious, but clearly declared that Roar and I were together. It would be perfect for our outing.

"Should I use the same boots?" I asked.

"They'll do for here." Clemencia nodded. "Save your best footwear for court."

I pulled on the brown leather boots and laced them up. By the time I finished, the sleigh had slowed considerably.

I pulled the curtain aside to view the city. "Looks like we're here."

As Roar mentioned, it looked larger than most of the towns we'd passed on the way, but not nearly as large as Sangrael or even Guldtown.

"Does this place have a dominant industry?" I asked.

"It's mixed. About a thousand fae live in Traliska. The sea is not that far away, so many fish, but it's also the home city of a wealthy branch of House Qiren. Do you re—"

"The Head of House Qiren is Lady Nalaea Qiren,

Lady of Silks," I said before she could ask, which made my lady-in-waiting beam.

"Correct. The dominant branch of that great house now lives in Avaldenn, but smaller offshoots live here, where their ancestral seat is located. Of course Lady Qiren, Head of House, visits that seat occasionally, to keep up appearances. And now that she's Lady of Silks their industry is also fabrics."

My face lit up. If I knew one thing it was fabrics—how to work with them, what they should be used for, and how to alter them. Perhaps we could stop in a shop so I could peruse.

"Warden of the West, Roar Lisika!" a booming voice cried out as the sleigh stopped. "And Lady Neve, his betrothed!"

The door to the sleigh opened, and Roar appeared, holding his hand out. Without his wyrm-hide gloves, his hands had chapped from the cold. I took his hand, squeezing it to infuse some warmth into the warden, and emerged from the cabin.

For the last hour, the snow had let up. The sun had even peeked through the gray clouds above, which explained why so many people were out. They had to take advantage of the pleasant weather because, in this kingdom, one never knew when the snow would fall again. Nor how thickly.

"Clemencia, you may do as you please while we're here." Roar motioned for two armed fae to follow as escorts. "Lady Neve, if you would, come with me?"

I batted my lashes, playing my part to perfection. "I'd be delighted."

Roar led me past the line of horses and plunged us into the streets. As we went, fae stopped and bowed or curtsied. Most appeared happy to see us, and so I beamed and waved, putting on a show for the people.

"House Qiren lands are the northern heart of the midlands, right?" I asked, trying to learn more about the area.

"Correct."

From what I recalled of the map Clemencia had shown me a few days ago, that meant we were far from the western territory. "They seem to know you well though."

"The Qiren family's seat is in the midlands, but this village benefits from gold in my city flowing east. So, they like my family." He shrugged. "Gold has a way of swaying people to your side."

Roar turned down a side street that I'd almost missed, and after asking his guards to wait outside, he veered into a clean and comfortable looking tavern. Inside, all heads turned, and many stood to pay their respects, but Roar waved a hand. "Please, sit."

The fae did, and one wearing an apron approached. "Warden. It's good to see you again. Are you here for the usual?"

The usual? Roar had said he'd been here before, but if he had a 'usual' then surely, he visited more often than I'd thought.

"Please, Galfu. And one for my betrothed, Lady Neve."

"Of course, my lord. My lady." The fae wearing an apron turned and disappeared into the back. Judging by the sounds of pots and pans, it had to be the kitchens.

"Over here." Roar led me to a small table tucked in the back near the fire.

"I'm shocked this table was free." I shrugged off my crimson cloak. My wings stretched, and I relished allowing them to breathe and move after being bundled for so long.

"Galfu might have asked someone to move because he heard that I'd stopped in town." Roar leaned back in his chair and took off his cloak too.

I gaped. A vampire would say something like that, and though Roar was a great lord of this kingdom, he never acted as though others owed him. "Are you serious?"

"I am," he replied, not a hint of bother in his tone, though he studied my face with interest. A touch of bewilderment, even. "The common fae will often act that way around the noble houses of the Sacred Eight. It's for their benefit, too."

"How so?" My lips pursed.

Roar shook his head as if I was a child that simply did not understand the way of the world. "Whenever I travel, I pay well, Neve. Galfu is treating a good customer to the best he has to offer. And I so happen to be a lord of the realm too, but that doesn't change the fact that I line his pockets with gold bears and silver stags when others will give him coppers."

I leaned back. It wasn't what I'd expected to hear, nor humble, but it wasn't wrong either. "I see."

"But you don't agree."

My jaw tightened. "I—I don't know."

"Look around."

I turned to take in the tavern. Unlike when we'd entered, no one watched us any longer.

"What's different here?" Roar prompted.

It took only a few moments for me to notice something off. "No one has wings here. Or if they do, they're vanished."

As my magic remained stifled by the potion my old master had forced down my throat, I had not yet learned to vanish my wings into the aether, but vanishing, a basic form of glamouring, was a very common fae ability.

Roar shook his head. "Not glamoured. The blight has hit this village harder than most. Jobs that used to require flying are all but gone and industries have shifted. Now they fish or make fabric, but it's not enough. In that shift, visitors became important in propping up the economy. In fact, the blight here was so bad that some fae here have even had the remains of their wings removed. You're seeing the results of that."

"What does that mean, though?" I asked carefully.

His own wings had been stunted from the illness called the blight, and that had to be hard to bear, but I was so curious. Plus, he'd been the one to bring it up.

Clearly, he seemed open to speaking about it, and as a lord, he'd probably know more than Frode had told me.

I shifted in my seat, crossing my ankles for comfort. "Does anyone have an idea what exactly causes the blight?"

Before he answered, Galfu arrived with two steaming bowls in hand. Behind him, a young, short male brownie carried a basket of rolls. Freshly baked too, by the smell of them. "My lord and my lady, the famous fish stew of Traliska!"

Roar beamed. "It smells as good as ever."

As Galfu set the plates in front of us, I had to agree. Fish and vegetables swam in the creamy stew and an herby delectable aroma had me salivating. I'd had fish before as a blood slave, but never freshly caught.

"And bread right out of the oven." Galfu motioned for the brownie to come forward. He did so on trembling legs and presented us with the basket. "My lord."

"Thank you." Roar smiled. "We can't wait to devour this feast."

"Ale?" Galfu asked, cheeks rosy with pleasure.

"Please. And wine for you, Lady Neve?"

Galfu turned to me.

"That'd be lovely."

Without being asked, the boy darted away, only to return seconds later with our drinks. Once Galfu took care of us, he bowed and left us to our meals.

"Try it." Roar nodded to the stew.

I hadn't forgotten my question, but the soup tempted me more than answers. I dipped a spoon into the bowl and took a bite. My eyes popped open as a heavenly melding of flavors tantalized my tongue. Delectable.

"Stars alive," I breathed.

"Good, right?" Roar took a bite and closed his eyes. "My cooks can't recreate this magic, and believe me, they've tried. It's actually a bit of a sore spot for them."

I reached for the bread, determined to make this meal last as long as possible. "*So*, what about the blight? What causes it?"

Roar's smirk dripped with amusement. "You don't miss a beat, do you?"

Where I came from, anyone who missed a beat ended up dead. "Rarely."

"Well," he glanced about as if to let me in on a secret, "no one *really* knows what caused the blight. But my mother had a theory that she shared before her passing to the afterworld."

"Which is?"

"Since the White Bear's rebellion, the magic of Winter's Realm has been in a terrible flux. Of course, it's always winter here—in varying forms of the season—but not always snow and ice for turns on end."

"Do you *ever* see grass? Or is it just lighter snow?" I gestured out the window where heavy piles of white fluff lined the streets.

"When I was younger, each turn we had a string of moons when the land was bare of snow and it rained heavily. During those times, it was still colder than any other kingdom in Isila, but we managed to grow a few key crops. More recently, the snow is ever-present, which is why we've had to innovate more than ever with green-houses and earth magic. The storms have grown more violent too."

The seasonal courts predominantly experienced their own seasons. So in this court, for most of the year, it would be some form of winter, whether that be doused with rain or snow or merely frigid outside. When the summer sun arrived in the Blood, Dragon, Mage, Wolvea, or Elvish Courts, here it would remain much cooler than any other area in the nine kingdoms. As someone who'd experienced four seasons her whole life, I found it to be an odd concept, but the magic worked that way. It always had.

"Does anyone know *why* the magic is off?" I asked.

Roar cast another look around and resumed his attention on me. "During King Magnus's rebellion against King Harald Falk, a Hallow of our land called the Ice Scepter was stolen. The king doesn't like to talk about it, but most of the Sacred Eight have agreed that was what happened. No one has seen it since the rebellion."

"And that regulates magic?"

"Yes. It might have impacted the blight and the magical prowess of fae born since then. Similar things have happened in other kingdoms before. The Spring Court being one."

"Really? How so?"

"Since the Shadow Fae War, a good number of faeries and other winged fae there have been born without wings. It's said that the Spring Court underwent a flux of magic, and nothing has been the same since. Much like here, when the Ice Scepter went missing."

"So a powerful flux can change us," I murmured, astounded by what I'd just learned.

Roar lifted one shoulder. "Most are only sure that the Hallow's disappearance has affected our weather. Many actually believe the blight to be a separate issue, an illness of some sort."

"Why have they not tried to find the Ice Scepter? That would settle matters, wouldn't it?"

He arched an eyebrow. "I'm sure they have. Magnus would desire it above all else, as he is of royal blood and can wield it."

"That's a requirement? If you sit on the throne, you can wield it?"

"Tales say that Falk blood, specifically, is required. King Magnus is our ruler, yes, but he is also a Falk bastard by birth. The blood is strong in him." Roar let out an unamused laugh. "Of course, he's by no means the only noble who can claim Falk blood. The Sacred Eight have married and joined families for generations. Even my family married into the royal Falk house right before the Unification. Most notably, Tore Lisika wed Sassa Falk, fought in her name too."

"So, there might be lots of fae who could use it." I hummed.

"No one knows if that requirement is true, or if it's rumored that the wielder of the Ice Scepter must have Falk blood in their veins. They've had the Scepter since

Isila was created. Some say that it was a gift from the gods-turned-stars."

My eyes widened. In Isila, it was widely known that all magic came from the stars, gifted to other magical orders by the angels. Additionally, some of the oldest fae, and maybe vampires though they never offered such information to slaves, believed that the stars responsible for magic's creation were once gods. That they now slumbered. Or had died.

I'd never been sure what to think. Never had a chance to talk with a fae who would know the most about such a subject, such as a High Staret. Did Roar believe such a thing?

"Whatever the case," he went on, "the Falks never let anyone else test it out. So it might as well just be a matter of raw power. As the last wielder and those closest to him were all killed, no one can be sure."

"What if the king gets the Hallow back, and the rumor isn't true? What would happen?"

"I cannot say. Until the White Bear, the Falks ruled this land since the Unification. Before that, they were among the most powerful kings and queens in this realm. The Scepter belonged to them even then."

I dipped my spoon into the stew and soaked in his words. Whoever stole the Hallow put those in Winter's Realm through decades of hard times.

We ate for a while longer in contented silence. I pondered the idea of a missing Hallow, while Roar seemed happy to have time to be quiet. Though I had not been traveling amongst the soldiers, the walls of the sleigh were thin, so we heard their chatter all day long.

When we cleaned our bowls and finished the bread, Galfu appeared. "Anything else, Warden? My lady?"

"Neve?" Roar gazed at me.

"I'm alright." I shook my head. "The soup was delicious. Thank you."

"Anything for the Warden of the West and his betrothed." Galfu cleaned the table.

Roar reached a hand across the wood. "Would you like to see more of the town?"

"Absolutely." Time to stretch my legs sounded divine.

Roar placed five gold coins on the table and stood. I followed suit, trying not to notice as many eyes trailed us on our way out.

The sun had grown stronger since we'd been in the tavern, though a biting chill still hung in the air. Our guard joined us as puffs of white blossomed from their lips.

I turned to Roar. "Is there a shop where I might buy some fabric? I'd like to make a gown. I can even start in the sleigh." My fingers itched to work with fabrics again.

"You really like to sew? Even after what you've been through?"

"I do. It was my one saving grace in my old life. I'm quite good at creating gowns and suits, too."

He studied me as if trying to work out a puzzle. "I'm sure you are. Perhaps, one day, you can make a garment for me?"

The question hung in the air. More and more, I believed that Roar might want me to stay.

And though he was a handsome lord and that should be completely flattering, I wasn't sure what I thought about that. Staying in Winter's Realm was not smart. It was much too close to the Blood Kingdom, *particularly* the western territory. And if I were to remain here, I'd want it to be for true love.

"I'll start with a gown," I said breezily. "Then you can see if you like my style."

"If Clemencia lets you sew in the sleigh." Roar winked.

Just the thought of more studying made me want to run all the way to Avaldenn. But if I were to survive the court, I needed Clemencia's lessons. Sewing would make them more bearable, at least. Perhaps if I mentioned making a dress for my lady-in-waiting, she'd be more lenient and let me study and sew at once. It was worth a shot.

"I'll convince her."

Roar's emerald eyes twinkled with amusement. "Come, there's a shop down this way."

I burst out of the shop door; my cheeks warm despite the chill in the air. Roar's guard fell in behind us, as professional as ever. "Their silks and chiffons were to die for! You're sure that the order will make it to the sleighs?" I cast a glance back into the store where the workers, two nymph sisters, packaged the many materials Roar had purchased for me. Snow lilies decorated their long, flowing green tresses.

"Your order will make it. They wouldn't want to lose such business." Roar laughed. "I have to admit, seeing you in there was something else. You were as happy as a leprechaun in a coinary."

"I'm used to working with fine materials, but not choosing them to my tastes." I admitted. "I suppose I got a little excited by the prospect."

"What will you work with first?" he asked.

"The amethyst silk. I'd like to make an evening gown for myself. For a long time, I've had a design in mind that I simply adore."

His eyebrows rose.

"What?" I chuckled.

"Amethyst would look perfect on you." His gaze went to my eyes, brushing by the scar on my temple. I occasionally caught him staring at the crescent marking I'd had for as long as I could remember. Perhaps he wondered why I wasn't applying Althea's balm there, or covering it with cosmetics, but I just couldn't seem to let go of that part of my past. The scar might be ugly to some, but it represented a time when I'd had a real family, a place in this world.

"Thank you," I said, and was about to suggest stopping into a shop to our right when a satyr appeared before us.

"Pardon m'lord! M'lady!" The satyr picked at a patch

over the elbow of his faded yellow jacket, clearly nervous to have approached the Warden of the West.

Roar laid a soft hand on my shoulder, as if to say that he regretted the interruption, though when he turned to the satyr, he was attentive. "Hello there."

"Pardon me bargin' in." The satyr gave a shallow bow. "But a few in town were wondering if your lordship wouldn't mind blessing our Drassil?"

Roar leaned back. "That's not—"

"You're not a royal, but you're close enough, ain't ye, m'lord? Our tree ain't doin' so good." The satyr hung his head.

"What about your High Staret? Can't he do it?" Roar asked.

"Died twelve turns back and no one has taken 'is place. There ain't a soul in this town that can do the blessing. And I reckon that no one else is brave enough to ask you, but the tree won't last much longer, m'lord."

I didn't know what they were talking about but recognized Roar's uncomfortable shifting from foot to foot. I slipped my hand into his.

The satyr noticed and his eyes softened. "The Drassil might spruce up just by seeing your beauty, m'lady."

Roar gave a defeated sigh. "Fine. Can you lead the way?"

The satyr nodded vehemently. "I'll take you right to it, I will!" He bustled down the street.

Once we'd put a few paces between us, I leaned close to Roar. "What's all this about?"

"The Drassil trees are sacred in the kingdom. Most of

the cities where the Sacred Eight reside have them, even Guldtown."

"Oh," I said. I hadn't seen the tree, but then there was much of Guldtown that I hadn't seen.

"It's said that parts of the souls of our ancestors, the Faetia, reside in the trees and that they're all connected," Roar continued. "They also interact with the winter magic."

We followed the satyr, and for the first time, I realized that many fae trailed along with us and our guard. Had they been there the whole time? I'd been so lost in thought that I had not noticed.

I had little time to wonder, though, because we rounded the corner and the Drassil came into view, stealing my every thought.

The Drassil was unlike any tree I'd ever seen, with its glimmering bark and purple leaves, or what remained of them, anyway.

"Stunning," I breathed when we reached the tree, which stood alone in the center of the snowy town square. Word must have spread that Warden Roar headed that way because fae had already congregated here too.

I squinted taking in the tree more closely, watching the leaves sway and flutter, though at that moment there was no wind. "The leaves almost seem to dance."

"It's the magic," Roar said. "But he's right, this one is dying. There are so few leaves now. A blessing takes some of my own power and puts it in the tree. It might extend its life for a while, which we all need."

If I had to guess, I'd say that the tree had lost half its leaves. In its full glory, it must have been remarkable.

"M'lord, if you please?" the satyr prompted, hope brimming in his eyes.

For a moment, Roar appeared stuck, but then he approached the tree. I hung back, basking in the magic rolling off the tree. It might be bad off, but the power seemed undeniable, vibrating me to my core. It made me more reverent. As everyone around me bowed their heads, I realized I wasn't the only one.

I dipped my chin too but kept Roar in sight. Once he reached the tree, he placed both hands on it and closed his eyes.

The air around the tree glittered, making my heart thump harder. Though I could see Roar speaking, I stood too far away to hear his words. All the while, magic circled the air around the tree, glittering on the bark and making the purple leaves dance on a phantom wind.

Murmurs arose from the onlookers. Though most kept their heads down, a few, like me, were peeking. In the center of it all stood Roar, performing magic to help the kingdom.

The ritual ended as abruptly as it began. The moment Roar removed his hands from the trunk, the magic disappeared. I exhaled as the air stilled and returned to normal.

He walked back to me, eyes downcast and tension in his shoulders. Only when he stood right in front of me did he look up, and I swallowed. Tears filled his eyes.

"Did it hurt?" I took his hand in a now familiar gesture.

"It's tiring but it didn't physically hurt. Knowing that the realm is in danger hurts, though." He squeezed my hand.

I swallowed and cast a glance at the tree. The leaves no longer danced, but they looked more enlivened. Inviting. My fingers itched to grace the bark. "Can I touch it?"

Roar blinked at me. "What?"

"The Drassil, I'd like to touch it. Is it against the rules?"

Roar shook his head. "The tree is for all. Go on."

I approached the tree with reverence. All the other fae had dispersed, and I was glad for it. I didn't want a bunch of onlookers.

That feeling only intensified when I stood before the majestic tree and tilted my head to look up. From this vantage, it didn't seem so barren of leaves. I placed my hand on the bark.

A jolt ran through me. I gasped and nearly pulled my hand back, but something wouldn't allow it. *The Drassil* wouldn't allow it.

Warmth from the tree flowed into me, and in my heart, a stirring began. I swallowed, wondering if this had been a huge mistake. Was the tree trying to harm me? I waited. My skin prickled, and my heart thrummed faster. I squirmed, uncomfortable with the sensation.

Then, phantom whispers filled my ears.

I jerked back, hand still on the bark because I couldn't move it, all I could do was listen, but make out nothing.

The sound of whispers was a roar in my ears, and I knew they had to be the Faetia. A din of those long passed. It was the only thing that made sense, and yet, I swallowed, unease growing inside me.

Before I called out for help, however, the whispers stopped, the heat left me, and a faint violet light glowed under my hand where it touched the bark.

What in the stars?

I pulled my hand away and glanced down at my palm. There was no light, and I remained unharmed. I blinked, unable to believe what I'd just seen.

Had the same thing happened to Roar? I hadn't seen it, but I'd been a distance away, and he probably wouldn't mention it because he'd know what to expect.

Or maybe I'd just imagined it?

Yes, that had to be it. Perhaps I really had felt the tree's power, and my imagination had run away with it. After all, I desperately wanted to feel something, wanted to *experience magic*.

"Are you alright?" Roar called out from behind me.

I turned and tried to appear natural. "Yes. I'm done."

"Wonderful. We should return to the sleighs. We've spent enough time here."

We walked away from the square, but before we left, I stole another glance back at the Drassil, and I swore its branches waved goodbye.

CHAPTER 19

"We're slowing," I said excitedly as I leaned closer to my frosted window.

For the first time in eight days of traveling, Clemencia had been nodding off in the carriage. Of course, I hadn't tried to keep her awake, instead I took full advantage of the moments when I could just relax and sew, but my announcement woke her right up. She started and pulled aside her curtain, squinting into the blinding white snow. "You're right. But why? We're still in the middle of nowhere."

My fingers stopped working on the silk dress, and carefully, I stuffed it into the lined basket that kept it safe. "I don't really care where we are, as long as we stop. I'm dying to get out of here."

Even with my new project and a million things to learn, I was starting to go mad sitting in the sleigh. In all my life, I'd never been so sedentary. It didn't suit me, though, I did not complain about it to anyone other than Clemencia.

As anxious as sitting around made me, I was also one of the lucky ones. The soldiers and the majority of servants riding with us had it much harder. They traveled against the wicked wind and heavy snows that let up for only brief periods. Even the few servants riding the other sleighs were less fortunate as their conveyances were smaller and more cramped.

Still, lucky or not, I wanted to stretch my legs and my aching wings.

It had been five days since Warden Roar first gave me a flying lesson, and we'd continued with lessons—one a night at the various inns we stayed at. As a result, I felt quite sore but also more capable with my wings. The way they twisted and stretched was far more fluid than before, giving me heart. Soon, I hoped I'd truly fly for the first time.

Once the sleigh came to a complete stop, I pulled my heavy cloak over my shoulders and the fur along the edges tickled my face. I'd barely tied the laces when the door opened.

Roar poked his head inside. "The horses need water and another rest." He pushed his red locks back as the wind blew them about. "Trudging through the snow is tiring them more than we'd planned."

"The poor things." Clemencia pursed her lips and shook her head. "They'll need a basket of apples apiece once we reach Frostveil Castle."

"They will," Roar agreed. "Since we have some time, how about another flying lesson, Neve?"

"Sure!" I scrambled out of the sleigh.

"Shall I come for moral support?" My lady-in-waiting kept her tone level, not wanting to intrude, but I detected the hope there. Clearly, she wished for something novel to do too.

"Of course," I replied, and Clemencia smiled as she fell in line behind us.

Roar told a soldier where we were going and that we did not wish for an escort. He knew it helped me concentrate if I wasn't in view of the dozens of fae. He and Clemencia were fine but more fae than them, and I became nervous.

The snow proved dense and deep as we trudged through it. When we reached a spot with a small clearing between trees, Roar waved a hand. Wind sprang to life, sweeping snow to the sides of the clearing so that we didn't have snow up to our thighs.

"Best I can do with so much of it and after riding for hours." He shrugged. "At least it's not coming down at the moment."

"A blessing from the stars," Clemencia agreed.

"Whenever you're ready, Neve." Roar gestured to me.

I stretched out my wings and beat them. Almost immediately, a breeze caught my wings, and a thrill ran through me. Instinctively, I lifted onto my tiptoes.

"Harder," Roar urged. "Today—"

Another gust of wind, saturated with glittering snow

and frost, caught me. I gasped as my wings beat harder, and I rose.

It had finally happened. I was really and truly flying!

"My lady!" Clemencia clapped her hands. "Go higher!"

"Yes!" Roar came closer. "I'll catch you if you fall."

I knew he would. He had many times and tossed me into the air so I could try and catch myself even more. But for the first time, I felt certain I wouldn't need him there. I felt strong, *confident*—like a real faerie for the first time in my life.

If only I had my magic. That's the only thing that would make this better.

I pushed those thoughts away before they took root and spoiled my win. I might not have my magic yet, but that day would come once the potion I'd been given worked its way out of my system. And on that day, I'd finally know the powers inside me. For now, though, I'd savor this moment.

I looked down. My feet hung level with the top of Roar's head, and if I extended my hand overhead, I could almost touch a tree branch. I urged myself higher, trying to touch it.

My wings strained, but in an act of solidarity, the wind gusted again. I surged up and my fingers brushed the barren branch.

"You did it!" Clemencia called out.

I beamed down at them and started to stretch myself further and maneuver to the right when a figure in the woods caught my attention. The figure wasn't faerie, or

anyone who could have traveled with us, but a tiny creature with a sack over its back. I watched the person
running like he was being chased by a vampire. When a
wild boar dashed up to it and the creature hopped on it
and sprinted away from the road, I gasped.

A goblin tribe was lurking about in these woods, and
I'd bet that it had already robbed us.

"Neve? Are you alright?" Roar asked, still below me,
his arms now extended in case I lost control or grew too
weak. "I've got you."

"A goblin was just over there." I pointed. "He
mounted a boar and . . . Well, he's already gone, but there
might be more."

"Blazing moon," Roar swore. "And no one sounded
the alarm. Come down. We need to get back and tell
them."

"How did no one see it?" I fluttered toward the
ground slowly, with as much control as I could manage.
As badly as I wanted to soar over to our escort and tell
them what I'd seen, I didn't trust myself to do so and not
run into a tree. My wings might be able to support my
weight now, but they still weren't too skilled at navigation.
That would be the next step in my training, I supposed.

"Goblins are very sneaky, my lady," Clemencia
explained. Sometimes I thought she couldn't help but be
the one with the answers. Roar had chosen well when he
assigned her as my tutor. "Particularly those of the
Eriking and Trasgu tribes. The latter have even robbed a
leprechaun coinary, if you can imagine."

I couldn't. I'd read of leprechauns, and in all the tales,

robbing one seemed impossible. It explained why they made the best coinmasters in all of Isila.

"Redcaps aren't stealthy," Roar added, "because they don't want to be. They savor the fear in their opponents' faces when they see the Redcap tribe coming."

Finally, I touched down and repressed a shudder at the idea of a small army of squish-faced goblins with blood-soaked caps on their heads.

"But I suppose that if you saw a boar, it's the Eriking tribe." Roar took my hand as we rushed from the clearing.

"I'll bet they're the same ones that barkeep told us about," I said, pushing a branch out of the way as I ran. As it swung, my nostrils filled with the delicious scent of pine.

Roar shot me a sidelong look. "I still can't believe they've come this far from the deep woods and mountain ranges."

Since we'd first heard of the goblin raids, Roar's insistence that the goblin tribes would remain far away from the Queen's Road had made me put the thieves from my mind. Now, however, it was obvious that he'd been wrong, and the barkeep had been right to warn us.

As we neared the line of horses and the sleighs it was clear that no one in our escort had noticed. Roar swore again, his voice catching the attention of the closest knights.

"Eriking goblins are near! If they're still amongst our troop, find them and stop them from taking food, weapons, or gold."

The soldiers went from resting to dogged action—sweeping up and down the line and peering into the forest along the road. Roar's frustration was warranted. We'd packed enough food for the trip, plus a few extra days if the snowstorms intensified, which had been a good call seeing as we were behind schedule. Aside from food, many of the weapons Roar's soldiers traveled with were new and expensive, and the king would expect the soldiers he ordered to arrive in Avaldenn armed. As for the gold, I hadn't seen any, but Roar told me that we would need a lot of coin in the capital, and he'd packed appropriately. Unsure of what to do, I looked at Clemencia.

"We need to stay out of the way," she said. "Come back to the sleigh."

I sighed. No part of me wanted to be confined again so soon, but if it made things easier for the soldiers searching for goblins, then I'd do so.

We made our way back up the line to our own little prison. On the way, I kept a keen eye out for goblins and saw not a single one. Perhaps I'd seen the only one? That seemed unlikely, but what did I know of goblin tribes raiding.

When I reached the sleigh, I paused. The door was cracked open an inch. Had Clemencia forgotten to close it?

No—of course not. My lady-in-waiting was meticulous in every matter. And no one, save for Warden Roar, the servants who carried our trunks in and out of inns, and our driver, who was nowhere in sight, had so much as touched our sleigh since the journey began.

I turned to Clemencia. "A goblin might be in the sleigh."

She sucked in a breath. "We should get a soldier. Until help comes, let them take what they will. We should not risk ourselves—"

The moment she mentioned stealing, my fingers closed into fists. I'd left my project, the amethyst gown I'd been working on, in the sleigh. It was the first dress I'd made for me, just as *I liked*. I'd chance staking a vampire before I allowed some goblin to take that from me.

I stormed over to the door, stopping only when I realized I had no weapon. Luckily, on his seat, the driver had left a bone-handled knife stuck in his apple, alongside a wedge of cheese. I jumped, pulled the blade from the fruit, all the while ignoring Clemencia's hissings that I *'must stop this at once'* and returned to the door.

Inhaling, I swung the door all the way open before I could think of stopping and found a small creature with pointed ears and green skin rummaging through Clemencia's trunk. I reared back slightly as the reek of unwashed feet and raw meat hit me. Stars, he smelled so bad that even Clemencia's perfume, which lingered in the sleigh's interior, couldn't cover it up. I recovered quickly, however, once I saw that he'd tossed my half-completed gown carelessly over his shoulder.

I pointed the knife at him. "Get your hands off that dress!"

The goblin's head popped up, eyes wide with shock, but he recovered, spinning and baring his teeth in a vicious snarl. A blade appeared in his spindly fingers, and he brandished it at me. "Let me out, and I won't cut up your pretty face."

"Leave the silk," I said.

The goblin looked down and laughed. "I think not! Material this fine? My mate and my daughter will have dresses made of it!"

I leapt into the sleigh with my knife outstretched and slashed.

The goblin shrieked. He had not anticipated a lady to actually attack, but little did he know, I was not a real lady. I slashed again, closer to his face, and this time, his blade flew from his hand, sticking into the side of the sleigh.

"Give it to me." I gestured to the silk.

The goblin swallowed. Behind me, Clemencia called for help. Surely, the thief heard it too, and as if deciding that cooperating would be in his best interest, he dropped the silk. I should have let him out and allowed the soldiers to take care of the thief but seeing him with my dress made me feral.

I reached out, grabbed him by the front of his shirt, and pulled the goblin closer. "You and your tribe of thieves are finished on the Queen's Road. Swear it, and I'll let you leave with your life."

"There's no food in the woods!" The goblin trembled in my arms.

I reared back. "Why?"

"The cold is driving animals to the villages, the cities. We goblins need to eat too." His eyes stayed wide.

I frowned. "What of the mountains? Dwarves, orcs, ogres, and giants live there. We've not heard of them reaving."

"They will! Mark my words! They will!"

"Lady Neve!" Clemencia's voice sounded closer now. I turned to find her peeking in the sleigh, white faced and wide eyed. "You shouldn't be touching him!"

"I'm fine," I said, just as the goblin jerked back, making a bid for freedom. I held tighter and snarled at the beast. "You've chosen your fate then."

"Here, my lady." A male appeared behind Clemencia. "I'll take the creature."

I checked that the goblin had nothing else on his person before tossing him from the sleigh to the soldier. Manacles clapped around the creature's thin wrists, and the goblin snarled and fought as the soldier led him away.

Alone, Clemencia entered the carriage and took in the area. The goblin had tossed a few items around, mostly gowns, my sewing supplies, and the books, when he'd been searching for treasure. We tidied up, and once we put everything in its place again, we settled in.

"You tried to bargain with it." Clemencia stared at me as she sprayed her perfume to cover up the goblin's stink of raw meat and unwashed feet.

"I did."

"But *why*?"

Because everyone deserved a choice? Did I really believe that? He'd been a thief, and in that instance, he should have been punished. Still, my background, as a person who'd had practically no choices, made me reflexively wish to give people chances.

"I don't know," I lied. "Did you hear that they're stealing because they have no food?"

"Winter takes much. It always does." Her uncomfortable gaze flicked to the window.

I paused. "Are other people hurting?"

"I know nothing of the various tribes or lone fae in the wilds, but I have heard that a few smaller villages are being hit hard." She paused and cleared her throat. "You should know, Lady Neve, that except for leprechauns, no lady of your standing, or even someone from the merchant class like me, would touch a goblin."

"Soldiers do." The one I'd tossed the goblin to had not hesitated.

"The warriors sometimes must do the most unfortunate things for the rest of us."

She seemed to see no problem in what she said. Maybe she had an underlying reason that I was ignorant to? If one came too close to an ogre, it would eat them, so I could understand not touching them. Who in the world would even get close?

But the goblins? They thieved. They fought too, of course, but all fae did that. The goblins weren't cannibals like ogres. Nor were they violent and dim like most trolls and giants. Goblins actually had intelligence.

Perhaps goblin skin carried an illness?

I didn't think so, but instead of pressing the matter, I

merely pulled out my gown and set to work again, content to think in quiet.

CHAPTER 20

R oar opened the sleigh door and, hanging from the foot planks, leaned inside. Behind him, snow-covered evergreen trees flashed by. "I've spotted the castle's spires."

"*Really*?" I pulled back the curtain to peer outside.

For ten long days, we'd been traveling through the forested midlands. Due to all the snow and wind, we had gotten a full day behind schedule, but since we'd left early, it would not affect us negatively at court.

"I wouldn't joke about that." Roar entered the sleigh and shook the snow from his long hair as he took a seat next to me. "Not after the journey we've had."

Outside my window, those traveling with us began to point and become more animated. With my limited view, I couldn't yet see anything of interest, but I did notice the trees growing thinner. My excitement grew, and I remained pinned to the window, desperate for my first glimpse of the capital.

Minutes later, I was rewarded as we exited the forest, and I finally saw the palace towers topped with spires. They were so tall that they dwarfed even the tallest of trees in the surrounding woods.

"Frostveil Castle." Clemencia sighed. "I've heard it's so beautiful."

The Palais Immortael had been breathtaking too, but even from this far away, I could tell the two were very different. The vampire's castle resembled a night and its stars. Whereas this castle looked as white as the snow outside and the tips of the spires and towers gleamed a bright silver in the midday light.

"What are those at the top?" I pointed to the closest spire. "It looks like there's a—bird? But that's far too big to be natural."

"That's because it's a silver statue of a white hawk," Roar answered. "The Falk's symbol."

My eyebrows pinched together. "Oh . . . you'd think they'd take that down."

"Rumor has it the palace has resisted certain changes since the rebellion." Clemencia spoke with the detachment of an academic. "The royals put the word out that they left the hawks up because they're also a symbol of prosperity and power in our kingdom."

Roar snorted. "A likely story."

"Wait." I gaped and looked to my lady-in-waiting. "You mean they actually cannot remove those? Even *with magic*?"

"Just as they can't find entire portions of the palace that are on maps," Clemencia said with a vigorous nod.

"Stars! You're joking!"

"Not in the slightest," my lady-in-waiting peered outside again.

I shook my head. "Well, that's unbelievable."

We fell silent as the line drew closer to the city gates. When I could make out the six soldiers manning the outer walls, Roar stood and went to the door again. "They'll want to see me before letting us in. For you two, it's time to change."

The night before, in a small country inn, we'd spoken of our arrival. I needed to wear an elegant dress, and when we arrived within the castle walls, Roar and I should appear together—as a betrothed couple would.

"I'll give you a few minutes to change." He winked and left the carriage to present himself to the watchfae.

Thankfully, I had gotten better at shimmying in and out of more constraining dresses. With Clemencia's help, I changed into a dress of crimson and gold. Leaping snow leopards were patterned on the sleeves of my dress —yet another nod to House Lisika. Once I finished, Clemencia fixed my hair, and together we performed a quick clean up of the carriage in case someone important peered in when we stopped. We'd just finished when a knock came.

"I'm decent."

Roar opened the door again and entered. "Not decent. Dare I say, more beautiful than ever."

"Thank you." I beamed, and Clemencia grinned in satisfaction as Roar sat close to me.

"You're confident in the family names? At least the

Sacred Eight and the House of Aaberg?" Roar asked as the sleigh moved again.

"I am." Mostly anyway. Beyond the last three generations of the great houses, the names of the family members slipped my mind. But would anyone really question me about that? I doubted it.

"She's done very well," Clemencia vouched for me. "And she's nearly completed her dress while studying."

Roar arched an eyebrow. "Where is it?"

I'd tucked the amethyst gown I'd been working on during the many hours of travel safely away in a lined basket. I hoped to finish it before the ball that opened the Courting Festival. Beneath the gown lay the vial of Warden Roar's blood; my insurance in our agreement, hidden and safe.

"I'll show you when it's done," I assured him. "Then I'm moving right on to Clemencia's new frock."

My lady's cheeks turned pink. Though she had tried to tell me she didn't need a nice dress, I wasn't having any of that. Clemencia and I weren't close in the same way Anna and I had been, but at the moment, my lady-in-waiting was the closest thing I had to a friend. I wanted to make something for her and to see the delight on her face when I presented a gown fit for royalty.

"Very well." Roar peeked out the window. "We're officially in the city."

A shiver ran down my spine, and Roar placed a hand over mine. "You'll do great."

"What if I forget something important and embarrass you?" I asked.

"When in doubt, say little. Shy away from the Aabergs—especially the princes, Rhistel and Vale." His face hardened at the mention of the warrior prince's name. "They will want to speak with you. It is a Courting Festival, after all, but as you are my fiancée that should protect you from their gossip and wandering hands."

I hoped he spoke true.

"Lady Neve, look outside." Clemencia gestured to the window.

I peered through my window, and my heart beat faster. I was not new to cities. For as long as I could remember, Sangrael had been my home and though I despised the vampires within, I loved the energy that a city gave off. However, I *was* new to this flavor of city.

The wintery feel and the warmth exuded by long-house taverns, log inns, and shops that we passed called to me. Fae walked the streets, and some stopped to wave at our procession. Each individual had rosy cheeks from the cold and excitement in their eyes. A few bowed or curt-sied as we passed, and younglings waved wildly.

"They look happy to see us," I commented.

"No one has seen a Courting Festival since the days of the Cruel King," Roar said. "The early days of his reign, at that."

"But that's relatively recent." I rifled through my learned lessons and came up with an approximate date for the beginning of the Cruel King's reign. It was about five hundred turns ago, which for the long-lived fae, was not so long ago.

Roar nodded. "That's true, but the turns since the

rebellion have been relatively uneventful and fae do love a bit of drama. I'm sure most think that King Magnus is prepared to tear apart alliances set by King Falk as best he can. A promise of courtly drama and the fact that the common fae will be allowed to view some festival events, makes this an exciting time for them."

Any change from the normal monotony of daily life had always been welcome in the Blood Court. Well, as long as that change didn't include pain or death.

"Oh! Lady Neve, look away! You—" Clemencia's tone sounded frantic.

Just then, something caught my eye out the window. I pointed at a hulking creature with the characteristic small head of a troll. Or, most likely, a half troll like Althea as he was out and walking in the sunlight. Leaving a brothel. "You have got to be joking me!"

Clemencia groaned, and Roar leaned closer. His pleasant scent of snow and pine filled my nostrils, and I drew in a deeper breath.

"But that brothel sign says they only have faerie whores, and he's so big." I crossed my legs. "At least five times bigger than you, Roar! That's too big!" Horror laced my tone at the thought of that enormous creature and a smaller fae like me being intimate. He'd split me in two!

"He did." Roar did a terrible job of hiding his amusement.

"I told you not to look!" Clemencia wailed. "It's not proper for a lady to see such things."

If only she knew the horrible things I'd seen.

"I've seen brothels before." I frowned. "Though, I have to say, seeing someone *that* large exit one advertised as having only faerie whores is a little disturbing. Do they allow giants inside too?"

"All types of fae do what they have to do to survive." Roar leaned back. "I assure you, the brothels here are well-regulated. No one is forced, and both the brothel masters and the city sex workers make decent coin. If the fae in that establishment couldn't handle the half-breed, he wouldn't have been let in."

"Hmmm, it's still disturbing to think about the size difference," I murmured, though the idea still turned my stomach.

"If you wish to worry about fae being forced, then worry about the royal harem."

I blinked. "Are you serious?"

"As a dwarf working Zuprian steel. King Magnus did away with many of the Cruel King's practices, but he kept his harem. Expanded it, even." Roar lips curled in disgust. "Many attractive fae have no choice when they enter his 'pleasure stables'. Nor do they have a choice when the king gives nobles their time and their bodies."

Already, the Aabergs left a sour taste in my mouth, but the more I heard, the worse things got.

We rode the rest of the way through the city in silence. As the castle neared, I couldn't take my eyes off it. It intrigued me how the palace clung to its past, hiding parts of itself. Had anyone ever stumbled across those hidden places and kept the castle's secret?

My musings quieted as we stopped before the palace

gate. The royal soldiers seemed to have been waiting for us, because they announced Roar's name and raised the gates quickly.

As we glided inside the palace grounds, the soldiers accompanying us fell back, allowing for the lord's sleigh to be on full display. Already, the displays of wealth and power that Roar had assured me would dominate my time at court had begun.

One more peek out the window left me somewhat disappointed. This area looked so plain, like a regular courtyard. Washer fae carried baskets, soldiers patrolled, and a few stable hands escorted horses—nothing out of the ordinary. After the magic of the city, the yard of Frostveil Palace was bland by comparison.

"Wait until we get inside," Roar assured me. "There will be much to see."

I turned. "It's like you can read my mind."

"Oftentimes, you wear your questions on your face. Remember that."

And work to hide them came the unspoken warning. In places like this, knowledge was the best armor.

The sleigh slowed to a stop, and I turned to the warden, my pulse thrumming with excitement.

"You look perfect," he assured me. "If you're ready, I'd like for you to exit first."

"Won't onlookers be waiting to bow to you?"

"They will, but I wish for them to view you first, my lady, my fiancée."

Clemencia sighed and smiled, and I forced my lips to

curl upward. He wanted an entrance. Though I didn't love the spotlight thrust upon me, I'd do as he wished.

I stood, and by the time I'd straightened my dress, a servant waited at the door.

"Are you ready, my lord? My lady?"

"We are." Roar's dark green, confident eyes locked on me.

The door opened and sunlight streamed into the sleigh, along with a strong gale that smelled faintly of salt and fish. Had I been more sensitive to cold, I'd wish for a cloak, but I wasn't. So much nervous energy flooded through me that I felt hot.

I pushed down my silver wings so they were less noticeable. Taking a deep breath, I slipped through the sleigh door, took the servant's hand, descended a step, and finally stopped.

Huddled against the wind, fae watched from all corners of the castle yard, but as my gaze swept the area in the regal fashion Roar had taught me, I took care not to linger too long on any of them. I studied them and moved on and on and on.

At least, I did so until I landed on one fae in particular. He was tall, taller even than Roar with long, black hair he wore pulled back to reveal that the undercut of his long locks was actually shaved. His face was tanned, hinting that he spent time outside, and he wore a jacket and tunic opened just enough at the chest so that tendrils of tattoos peeked out and waved up to graze his thick neck. His midnight black wings only made him look striking, as did the way he studied me, almost like a predator. My heart skipped a beat at his intensity.

And it wasn't just me who seemed affected. Others watched him too, while the male just stood there, as if he owned the entire castle yard.

Stars, he was the most handsome faerie I'd ever seen.

I swallowed, and remembering what appearances I needed to project, I rearranged my features into that of a noble lady who was not so easily impressed. As I did so, the male moved my way. Only then did I even notice the younger faerie of perhaps sixteen turns with dark brown skin and luminous gold eyes trailing the intimidating male. He carried a sword as though worried he might break it.

"My lady, I'm afraid we have not met." The male approached the sleigh quickly, as if on a mission. When he got close enough for me to see his warm brown eyes, he held out a hand and a smile broke over his face, transforming those hard lines into something warmer, someone I could see laughing rather than hunting orcs with their bare hands. "I'm Prince Vale of House Aaberg."

CHAPTER 21

I stiffened. So *this* was Prince Vale Aaberg, second in line for the crown and the warrior who had left Roar's forces to fend for themselves when they'd requested help. The prince who famously feuded with Roar. At least that explained why he'd looked so hardened and entitled before.

Now, however, watching me, he had softened, and the effect was . . . slightly devastating. I found myself unable to move, to do anything but stare at the Warrior Bear. In that moment, he looked warm, not barbaric or like a scheming sort.

Stupid. You don't know him at all, I chided myself just as Roar appeared behind me and his strong hand landed on my shoulder.

"Come to woo my lady, have you, Prince Vale?" Roar asked as his hand slipped downward to grasp my own and he began to assist me down the steps. It took more effort than it ought to have to move, but my feet found the snowy ground, and Roar followed and stood right next to me, straight-backed and proud.

"Not at all." The prince replied, his tone tightening. That easy smile he'd given me was gone, replaced by one that looked almost painful. "Simply introducing myself." He cast me a glance.

"I'm Neve," I said, remembering that he had, in fact, introduced himself and the polite, courtly thing would be to reciprocate—even if I did already hate his beautiful face because of what he'd done to Roar, to so many soldiers.

He waited.

"No great or lesser house," I added. "I'm from a village so small I'm sure you've never heard of it."

"A pleasure to have you in Avaldenn, my lady. You as well, Warden Lisika." The prince nodded.

I gave a small nod, deferring to Roar but instead of replying to the prince he waved a servant over and directed him. "Take our trunks to our rooms. We are engaged and thus require chambers that are side-by-side."

At that, the prince's lips parted in surprise. Would he go straight to his father and tell the king the news— that the lord of the wealthiest territory had gotten engaged?

Roar cleared his throat. "I must get my lady inside, Prince Vale. We've had a long journey, and it is as cold as a mage's touch out here."

"Of course." The prince stepped aside to allow us by.

Following a half step after Roar, I swept through the palace yard for the front doors. Behind us, keeping her distance, Clemencia walked with my basket of fabric and the warden's blood vial, tucked neatly at the bottom of the basket. Silently, I thanked her for gathering that which was most important to me. She always anticipated my needs.

"You did well." Roar gazed at me. "A bit cold, but that doesn't worry me. In fact, I'm pleased." He smirked.

Cold? I had felt more shocked by the prince welcoming us rather than a castle attendant. That and the sheer . . . overwhelming masculinity of the prince. How annoying it was that someone so handsome could be so cruel. Still, Roar didn't seem to mind the idea of me being cold to the prince, so I wasn't going to dwell on it.

"Keep your head up," Roar continued. "We'll talk more privately in our rooms."

I swallowed. For whatever reason, I had not considered that we'd be staying so close to one another. I had never been a prude, but Roar seemed to be a different sort of male from those I was used to being around.

Our relationship was fake, yes, but he flirted and I got the sense he wouldn't mind being in a real relationship. Sometimes, despite my aim to put distance between me and the Blood Court, I wasn't so sure if, given enough time, I'd say no either. We were friends, and he was a handsome, kind fae. Could there be more between us?

I shot him a sidelong glance but did not feel the burning strike of desire I hoped to feel if I ever wed. Attraction, yes. Respect, definitely. Closeness—well that was building. Maybe desire could develop though? I wasn't very well versed in real relationships, just physical ones. But I knew that nobles often had arranged marriages and surely some of those developed into more?

I wondered how many were soulmates? That was what I really wanted, even if I knew that finding my soulmate would be like finding a needle in a sea of loose thread. Still, a fae could hope . . .

The front doors opened at our approach and a wingless faerie appeared and bowed. "Warden Lisika, Frostveil Castle welcomes you."

This faerie wore a royal blue tunic and spotless, crisp white trousers. A wide gold belt wrapped around his thick waist, straining against his bulk. The male turned his attention on me, and I blinked, taking him in. His deep violet eyes looked even more intense than my own. It was the first time that I'd seen another with my eye color.

"I am the Master of Household in Frostveil Palace. You may call me Genji." The faerie's eyes crinkled kindly at the corners.

"Thank you." I inclined my head. "Lady Neve."

"My fiancée," Roar added.

Genji could not hide the surprise that flashed across his face. "Well, we had prepared a suite of rooms for you, my lord. But I suppose your lady would prefer her own suite?"

Roar answered for me. "We wish to have two rooms within a suite. This is my fiancée's first time at court, and she's nervous. Is there a maid's chamber too?"

"Of course. Two, in fact. One beside each master

bedroom, of which, coincidentally, there are also two." Genji cleared his throat. "You brought a maid?"

"A lady-in-waiting to assist my fiancée," Roar replied in a tone that brooked no argument. The king might have decreed that no personal servants were to join the nobles coming to the palace, but according to Roar ladies-in-waiting were an entirely different matter. "Clemencia will stay in the maid's chamber next to my fiancée's room."

My lady-in-waiting inclined her head, though I felt annoyed for her. She was no maid, and really deserved more, but it wouldn't do to argue with Roar. Not here and not now.

"Very well."

I couldn't tell if Genji approved of our choice to share a suite, but when he swept his hand for us to follow, I supposed it didn't matter. People would think what they would about Roar and me. In fae society, couples shared a bed before they were married as often as they did not.

Genji led us through the corridors packed with people, many of them servants, but some dressed like noble lords and ladies too. The latter stared as we walked by, and a few whispered to friends behind their hands. Surely, they recognized Roar and that I wore his colors. Were they upset that the wealthy and handsome Warden of the West had brought a female? Who did they think I was? A love match? Or a courtesan?

Trying not to think too much about it, I took in the castle. The wide hallways unraveled, grand in both size and decor. Whereas the Aabergs had not been able to alter the outside of the palace as much as they probably would have liked to, the inside appeared to have undergone renovations. Royal blue, gold, and white were the dominant hues—Aaberg colors—and one couldn't go more than a hundred paces before coming across some sort of imagery depicting a white bear. They had been etched in the paintings and tapestries lining the white walls and even had been carved into the walls themselves. Just when I thought I'd seen the most impressive depiction of a white bear, we turned a corner and found ourselves face-to-face with one.

I gasped and took a step backward, ducking out of the spacious junction that we'd come across and back into the hallway. In doing so, I ran right into Clemencia, who'd been following us so closely and quietly that I'd forgotten she was there. Roar put a reassuring hand on my shoulder.

"Sorry, Clemencia," I whispered. "That bear shocked me."

"Apologies, Lady Neve." Genji stopped. "I should have warned you. The bear is stuffed and sometimes I forget how lifelike it appears to those who have not seen it before. Quite impressive, no?"

An exhale parted my lips as my heart slowed. He was right that it looked so real. And *massive*. The bear had to weigh at least eight times what Roar weighed, and he was quite tall, muscular, and broad-shouldered for a faerie.

"It's a sight," I admitted, "but isn't it the royal's house animal? Why would they kill it?"

Roar's family put up representations of snow leopards, but I'd not seen the real thing in his castle. Was that common?

"This one died of old age," the Master of Household said. "To hear King Magnus tell it, this bear was one of the oldest of its kind in Isila. But he keeps a living one on site, if you'd like to see it."

I cocked my head. "Does he have a menagerie?"

"Er, of a sort." Genji's lips thinned as if he wished he had not brought it up. "The king's bear is on display, but he's also used to enact the king's justice."

"I don't understand."

Roar answered my question. "If a fae breaks the law, and the king wants a bit of sport, he puts that fae in a pit with the bear to fight to the death. No one has ever beaten the beast."

My insides froze. How barbaric.

"It's said he got the idea from the Cruel King." Roar's hand gripped mine and squeezed. "Near the end of his reign, King Harald had a fondness for trials by combat. He never used a white hawk, of course. But he was rather partial to frost giants and the most vicious of ogres."

By the stars! What was worse? Fighting for one's life against a magical bear or the massive orders of fae with brutish strength?

"I see." My stomach roiled. What had I gotten myself into by trying to trick the king?

"Shall we?" Genji motioned for us to continue, which we did, and as I crossed the interior lobby, I looked upward at the domed glass ceiling.

In the open intersection of busy corridors, the ceiling allowed everyone a glimpse of the blue winter sky. Through the glass, I spied those silver hawks again, resting atop the spires. I wondered if King Magnus had placed the bear here on purpose, so that when the hawks looked down, they saw they were no longer revered in the palace.

Whatever the case, I felt glad when Genji pulled us down a half dozen more white corridors, each filled with nosey fae who acknowledged Roar and stared openly at me.

Finally, Genji stopped before a door. "This suite is yours."

"Who else is staying in this wing?" Roar asked.

The question surprised me, but why, I wasn't sure. He was tactical and six other doors stood in this hall. Clearly, he wanted to know who we might potentially run into in our hallway.

"Warden of the East, Lady Ithamai, and her daughters have the suite at the end. And Lord Riis is staying down this hall with his three eldest boys." Genji dipped his head. "The other families of the Sacred Eight are nearby, but not in your wing."

"Riis," Roar grumbled. "I take it his eldest bastards are here?"

"They are, my lord."

"Why? Doesn't the Lord of Tongues live in Avaldenn? Can't they stay at home?"

Genji swallowed. "He alternates between his castle

and the city, my lord. He owns many thriving businesses here."

Roar snorted, which told me that whatever Lord Riis did for a living, the warden did not approve. "Why they're allowed at the Courting Festival, I'll never understand. But I suppose being the Lord of Tongues earns you different benefits than the rest of us."

Genji looked away.

Pity for the poor fae rose in me. "Thank you for showing us here, Genji."

"Of course, my lady." Genji looked relieved. "I'll take my leave. Soon a maid and manservant will stop by."

"That won't be necessary." Clemencia shook her head. "Not for my lady."

"Nor me. When we require it, I'll pull the servant cord and request a maid to clean," Roar instructed.

The fewer people in our bubble, the better.

"Very well. I shall see you tomorrow." Genji bowed and left us staring at the door to our quarters.

Roar said nothing as he opened the doors to our suite. We stepped into an antechamber, complete with a hearth embellished with a beige fur rug in front of it. Near the hearth a small table for two sat and a navy settee and three off-white armchairs waited in the center of the room, perfect to relax in. I was relieved to find there wasn't a white bear in sight. Rather, the designer of the suite had decorated it with what looked to be historical paintings.

In one such image, a fae with long white hair stood atop a mountain, a scepter gleaming in his hand. In another, a beauty who could only be a princess walked among frozen gardens. The one that caught my eye the most was that of a mermaid flinging herself out of the water as a ship of sailors watched on in awe.

"Not bad." Roar swept from the main room to one of the side rooms. "Two proper bedchambers and servants quarters right next to them. The one by Neve's room will be for you, Clemencia."

"I'd rather we not call them servants quarter," I said, and Roar had the good grace to look chastened.

"It's not a problem," Clemencia assured me.

"But if anyone asks, you're not a maid," I assured her because a lady with her standing in Guldtown would not like to be thought of as such.

Although her shrug told me she didn't care. She did this for her lord. Maybe for me too.

"Our rooms have their own bathing chambers," Roar added. "We have a dining nook, though of course, once the festival begins, we'll dine with the royals and nobles most of the time. For dinners, certainly. Likely lunches too." He smiled and the strain on his face softened. "And there's a small library tucked close to that window. They must have known a bibliophile was coming."

He pointed, and when I saw what I'd missed before, I smiled. The library was nothing compared to the one in Roar's castle, but I couldn't wait to dive in.

"The trunks will arrive soon." Clemencia cleared her throat. "Lady Neve, will you show me where you'd like your things?"

"Oh, you don't have to—"

"Excellent idea, Clemencia," Roar interrupted in a tone that told me a noble lady would expect such actions and it was time for me to start acting more like a noble. "We should all freshen up."

I played along, shuffling into my bedchambers. The spacious chamber had a large bed, its own hearth in the corner, and small seating area in front of it that would be perfect for reading. An armoire and dressing screen dominated the wall opposite the hearth. Next to the armoire was a door leading to a personal toilet and bath. I went and sat on the bed and fell back. The mattress was softer than anything I'd ever slept on, including the bed at the warden's estate.

"Lady Neve?" Clemencia followed me inside. "If you'd rather rest, I can have your trunks wait."

"No, you can have them brought in and . . ." I rose and pointed to the armoire. "Put them over there, yes? Then, put the body creams and powders in the bathroom. Anything else, well, I trust you can figure it out."

"Are you sure?" Clemencia gazed at me, knitting her brows.

Little did Clemencia know I'd spent most of my life owning nothing. Though I found it nice to have dresses and luxury items to beautify myself, I didn't need them. Nor did I really care where they placed my effects. As long as they were in this room, I would make do. "Please just make sure the books are by the bed."

Clemencia chuckled lightly. "You won't have much time for reading, my lady."

"I'll *make* time."

She smiled. "Alright then. If you insist, I'll—"

A knock sounded on the door to the suite, and I stood to go answer it.

"Allow me." Clemencia rushed out of my room. "It's more proper."

But before she could see who was calling, Roar rushed across the seating area and opened the door himself.

A male brownie dressed in House Aaberg colors bowed and held out an envelope. "Lord Lisika, this is for you. From King Magnus."

"I was wondering how soon I'd be hearing from him," Roar replied. "Thank you." He took a letter and shut the door. "The king has already heard of you, Neve. Let's see what he says."

The snapping of a royal blue wax seal captivated the silent room as everyone held their breath. Roar's eyes scanned the paper, the corners of his lips tightening with every second. "I've been called to speak with him right away."

"Should I come?" I shuffled closer to him.

"No. I want to keep you from the king's eyes for as long as possible. You just relax and unpack." Roar flicked his eyes to me. "If you wish to roam, do so, but perhaps have a maid escort you both? Clemencia has not been here either."

"Certainly," I replied as Roar pulled on the jacket he'd been riding in. Unlike me, he'd been on a horse for days, and I assumed he'd rather be in fresh attire, but the king waited for no one.

"I'll see you soon, my love." Roar grinned roguishly before slipping from the room.

Clemencia watched the door wistfully. "You two are perfect."

"Thanks," I said, giving her a small smile. "I'm going to bathe."

The castle had modern plumbing, and everything in my private toilet looked extravagant and lovely. I marveled at the small soaps that smelled of pine and a flower I could not name. With a deep breath to soak in the aromas, I turned on the water to hot. As the copper tub filled, I studied my room in greater depth and had discovered a pretty jewelry box when a knock came at the door. The trunks, no doubt.

Or at least I thought so until a confident feminine voice called out. "Lady Neve, I hope you're decent!"

I startled. That had not been Clemencia's voice. But who then?

The answer arrived as a slight female faerie with pink hair, black shimmering wings, creamy, pale skin that seemed to glow, and bright blue eyes opened the door and walked in. Her deep blue dress looked elaborate, but not so much so that it seemed out of place in the late afternoon. When she met my eyes, she smiled.

"Who are you?" I asked.

The female faerie cocked her head. "The better question is, who are you?"

I frowned. "You said my name." At that moment, Clemencia tiptoed in, and with wide eyes, shook her head.

But I was too distracted by the girl's loud laugh to wonder what Clemencia might think so inappropriate. "Stars, we're going to get along swimmingly. Especially if you use that tone on my king Father. *Please* do it when I'm around. I love seeing his eyes bulge out of his head."

King Father! This could only be one person.

"Princess Saga." I fell into a curtsey. "I'm so sorry for talking out of turn."

"Why?" she pursed her lips as if holding in another laugh. "It's refreshing. No surprise there."

"Pardon?"

She quirked an eyebrow. "You're *new*. No one knows what to think about you. And that is oh so refreshing!"

"Ah, I see." I nodded.

"All the ladies are talking about you, you know," she added and leaned closer conspiratorially.

And I've barely been here ten minutes.

I swallowed. "They must need hobbies."

Princess Saga, thirdborn to King Magnus and Queen Inga, snorted indelicately. "Too true. What about you? Do you have hobbies? And is playing cards among them?"

"I—uh I don't know many games." None really, except for what I'd played with fellow slaves. Something told me the princess would not be playing the same games.

"We must change that."

What in the blazing stars?

"A few of the younger ladies of the Sacred Eight are gathering. We wish for you to join." Saga stepped closer

280

and looped her arm through mine. "Which means you have no choice but to come."

I opened my mouth to protest, but then closed it. The princess pulled me from my room and into the corridors.

There would be no time for rest. I would have to play cards with the most highborn lady fae of the land.

What could go wrong?

CHAPTER 22

The princess managed to pull me halfway down the hall before Clemencia caught up. "But Lady Neve, what about your trunks?"

"I—" I faltered, not sure why she thought I cared about those right now, before realizing Clemencia was grasping for any excuse to allow me to say no to the princess. "Oh, yes! I'm sorry Princess Saga, I must unpack. I'm afraid I can't go."

The princess rolled her eyes. "Pish-posh. You can borrow our servants for that."

I stared at her. "And Clemencia?"

"She can take care of the unpacking too." Saga eyed Clemencia's dress, nicer than a servant would wear. "Ladies-in-waiting aren't allowed in our games. I've even ditched my own Clawsguard for the night because he can't know what we do. But rest assured, Clemencia, I'll take care of Lady Neve. You may return to the Lisika suite."

My lady-in-waiting opened her mouth, but nothing came out. The poor thing was speechless, which didn't surprise me. I felt sure few argued with Princess Saga, and while Roar had wanted Clemencia to stay with me, the Aaberg princess outranked even the Warden of the West.

Bleeding skies. I hoped I could manage without my lady-in-waiting because the princess would not be dissuaded.

"It's fine," I told my lady-in-waiting. "Take care of the unpacking. I'll be back later."

"*Much* later! She'll be dining with us tonight. Do tell the warden!" Princess Saga chuckled, and we set off again.

I threw Clemencia an apologetic look before the princess pulled me onward. We plowed down more hallways and swung around at least a half dozen more corners before she stopped abruptly to stand in front of a tapestry.

"You must tell no one of the place I'm about to show you. It's only for the Sacred Eight ladies that I approve."

"I'm not one, so surely I shouldn't come?" I tossed out my last lame attempt at getting out of whatever would happen.

"We're far too curious about you to let this opportunity pass." She paused. "You might as well say that you'll keep our secret and try to have a little fun."

I sighed. "Fine. I won't breathe a word."

"Good!" She pulled aside a heavy tapestry portraying a scene of Avaldenn, to reveal a wooden door. "Now, come along. They're waiting, and two of the ladies are not known for their patience."

"Wonderful," I muttered as she took out a key with a bear's head on the top and opened the door.

A curving staircase presented itself. Princess Saga wasted no time in pulling me into the hidden chamber, easing the door shut, and storming up the steps two at a time.

"How high up are we going?" I asked after we'd gone at least three flights.

"Around this corner." Saga chirped back excitedly.

Voices filtered down the winding staircase. Another ten steps, and we'd reached the top and found five female faeries in a circular stone room decorated in pink. The princess must have had a heavy hand in the decor.

Princess Saga beamed. "Ladies, allow me to introduce the enigmatic Lady Neve!"

They stared. No one moved. No one spoke. Did they even breathe?

Then, from the statues posing as noblefae ladies, the only one dressed in trousers stepped forward. She wore her black curls loose and wild, and her gray-blue eyes brought to mind volatile churning waters while her sun-kissed skin spoke to much time outside.

"Good to meet you, Lady Neve. I'm Sayyida Virtoris." She fanned blue wings, similar in color to her eyes, so that her curls bounced. "My mother is the Lady of Ships, if you even care."

I curtsied. "A pleasure."

"Hardly a pleasure. Usually, the indomitable Lady of

Ships is nothing but a pain in my arse." Sayyida rolled her eyes.

Unprepared for such snark, I let out a snort and clapped my hands over my mouth. "Excuse me!"

"Ha! So the mystery girl that Warden Roar brought isn't a cold vessel." Sayyida looked me up and down as if reassessing me already. "She must just not have liked your brother, Saga. You know what? I think I'll like you even more for that, Lady Neve."

Prince Vale had mentioned our meeting to his sister? And he, too, had thought me cold, just like Roar. Though the prince was not a friend, nor someone I really cared to know based on his reputation, I wasn't sure how I felt about that.

"Well, you know how Vale is around Lord Roar." Princess Saga shrugged a delicate shoulder.

"My eldest brother would agree." Another female sashayed up. She had golden-brown hair, light brown skin, and luminous honey-colored eyes and wings. If that wasn't enough gold, the tips of her pointed ears wore a cuff of gold that fit them perfectly, and she wore a hunter green dress embroidered with gold thread.

"I'm Baenna Balik, daughter to the Warden of the South," the golden faerie said. "My brother famously despises your betrothed, though I sometimes think my brother is a prize idiot, so I'm finally looking forward to meeting the Warden of the West myself. I'd like to see what all the fuss is about."

I blinked, and another female appeared. She looked like the mirror image of Baenna, but a touch shorter and bustier. Also like Baenna, this fae wore green and gold, but she inverted the colors on her dress. "I'm Eireann Balik. Baenna is my older, and far more talkative, sister."

That explained the resemblance.

"Neve." I dropped the title of lady because they hadn't used it. Plus, in the presence of some of the most powerful ladies of the land, it felt ridiculous. "I'm not from a great house."

"All the better for us. Fae from great houses are such gossips." Sayyida winked and her quick wit eased the nerves roiling my stomach.

The last two faeries approached more slowly, one with a smile as welcoming as the others, and one with a frown on her rosebud lips.

"I'm Marit Armenil." The smiling one with light green wings gestured to my hand. "Your ring is lovely. So sparkly. Might I see it closer?"

"Thank you." I held the ruby aloft so that she could examine it while I took her in more closely.

Marit wore a simple, light gray dress that seemed too plain for a lady of the Sacred Eight and did no favors for her alabaster complexion. She wore no jewelry either. Even Clemencia's traveling dress had been more extravagant, and my lady-in-waiting always wore earrings. Although, Marit had startling bright red hair, so perhaps she felt she carried enough color without seeking it in her attire.

Armenil . . . I mulled it over for a moment before I remembered.

That was the name of the Warden of the North. So,

ladies from the northern and southern territories were present. I supposed I represented the western territory. Did that mean the last fae had come from the East? I turned to the coldest faerie, dressed most elaborately in a green gown more fit for a feast than playing cards. Silver stags danced around the low-cut neckline.

She said nothing; instead, she just studied me. Not knowing what to do, I inclined my head as Marit stepped back, done viewing my ring.

The final female snorted. "Lord Roar used to have better taste."

"Calpurnia!" Princess Saga hissed. "Why must you be so sour?"

"I didn't want to invite an outsider, *cousin*." Calpurnia spat the last word and rustled her lilac wings as if irritated. "Especially not when you chose not to invite Aenesa or the Ithamai sisters so as not to scare this plain mouse off. If Roar's infatuation can't take our company, what is she even doing here?"

"Failing to invite the others is not why you have an icicle up your rear." Sayyida interjected as she swept her dark curls over her shoulder and looked at me. "Calie here has always fancied the Warden of the West and now he's taken, so she's upset."

Oh, stars. This sour lady was a relation of the queen. There was not much resemblance with the princess, Calpurnia being tanned and with dark brown hair and eyes. Come to think of it, wasn't Calpurnia the name of the person Roar had been worried about forcibly matching with? I reached far back into my memory, to the day when he'd told me about the Courting Festival. Yes, I was sure that was her name. I swallowed. Apparently, he had been right to worry.

"If that's the case," Princess Saga started, "then I don't understand why you're always clinging to Aenesa, anyway, Calie. She wants to marry the Warden of the West too. She wasted no time in speaking with my father about it when she arrived."

Somehow, things had gotten worse.

"And as for the Ithamai sisters," Sayyida rolled her eyes, "we're *gambling* tonight, Calie."

I perked up. We'd had no money in Sangrael, but if we had a few spare hours, the blood slaves I lived with sometimes played cards and waged bets with tin pieces that were of no real value. It passed the time and was fun.

"The Warden of the East would be furious to hear if her precious daughters gambled." Sayyida placed a hand over her mouth in mock horror. "She'd probably try to throw us in the dungeons."

"It's not against the law." Calpurnia crossed her arms over her chest.

"In the eastern territory it is." Sayyida looked at me. "Horrible part of the realm. The Warden of the East might as well be called Lady of Laws; she's all justice and law and no fun. Give me the deck of a ship and a rowdy crew over all the land in the east any day. We sailors know how to have fun."

"Speaking of fun," Marit said, "we should get on with the game."

"How about I give Lady Neve a brief tour of the

tower while you ladies set up the table?" Princess Saga looped her arm through mine, which earned her a pointed glare from her cousin. The princess ignored it.

The ladies dispersed. Baenna Balik moved to a drawer and pulled out cards and dice, while the others drifted toward a table large enough for ten.

"Pardon my cousin," Princess Saga said as we approached an arched window. "Calpurnia was never good at meeting new people."

"That's alright, Princess." I didn't mean the words. Calpurnia had been born a noble fae and likely been taught etiquette from a very early age. Clearly, it hadn't sunken in. Still, it wouldn't do to make enemies so early on.

"Please, I'm among friends, so call me Saga. And, no it's not." Saga gave a soft sigh. "But I'm afraid that you being Warden Roar's fiancée comes with a bit of a target on your back. That is, if Father doesn't dissolve your engagement."

I stiffened. "Do you think he'll actually do that?"

Roar seemed certain that while the royal house would *question* our engagement, in the end it would also be enough to protect him from an arranged marriage. I'd been so busy with learning anything and everything of court etiquette and Winter's Realm, and then traveling, that I hadn't put much consideration into the other option. What *would* happen if the king dissolved our union? That would thrust Roar into a life he did not want. And as for me . . .

Would he still honor his half of the contract?

"The king can do whatever he likes." Saga gazed out the window. "But if he's smart, he won't. Your fiancé has the second largest army in Winter's Realm, and more gold than the crown itself. His mines are old, but they seem to have an endless amount of gold in them. Those two factors mean that no one wants House Lisika for an enemy, and Father has already denied the Lisika family what they wanted twice. A third time would be most unwise."

I wanted to ask what the king denied House Lisika but decided it would be better to pretend like I already knew. So I nodded.

Saga gestured outside. "I thought you might like to see a bit more of the capital. We have an amazing view of the Shivering Sea up here too. I find this view so calming."

I followed her suggestion, and my eyes widened.

Before me spread a blue-gray sea shimmering in the late afternoon light. On it, ships sailed, closing in on and departing the bustling city below. One in particular caught my eyes. It was burning and after a moment of confusion, I realized why. Here, in the wicked north, where the ground was so hard and often frozen, bodies were often sent out to sea or down a river in a flaming boat to meet the afterworld.

Had that happened to my family? Where had they gone? Or . . . *stars*, was it possible that someone in my family was still alive? Suddenly, a spike of hope arose. I hadn't thought about it before, but maybe I could find them.

But as soon as I considered that they might be alive, a hard reality set in. My mother had died fleeing Winter's Realm right around the time that the rebellion ended. In all likelihood, my family had perished in the fighting and she was fleeing because we were in trouble. A sense of grief washed through me, and I turned my attention to the city in an effort to keep my composure.

Instantly, my spirits lifted a touch. Though I'd ridden through the city, and gotten quite an eyeful, from on high the city looked so magical. The fae appeared small as pixies, and the snow glinted, adding a charm to everything it fell upon. Smoke from chimneys drifted out to sea in sharp gales.

"It's all so beautiful," I murmured.

"You'll see a lot of the castle while you're here, but sometimes I like to sneak up in this tower to watch the city. It's always so alive." Saga smiled, and I got the idea that, though she was a princess, she'd rather be elsewhere.

"See that?" She leaned closer and pointed. As she did so, our sides touched and something heavy hit my leg.

I glanced down. The princess's dress had oversized, slightly gaping pockets. In one, she carried a small book.

I noticed she had caught me looking and I lifted my gaze. Instead of meeting her eyes though, I focused on her pink hair.

Fae, as a varied magical order, might have all different colors of hair. Dryads and nymphs were often born with tresses of vivid blues and pinks and any other color one might imagine. Faeries, however, were normally born with hair in shades of white, silver, brown, black, red, or blonde.

"I have to ask, Princess, is that your natural color?"

Her eyes twinkled. "I wish, but no. I see a colorist and they magic it pink about every six moons." Her gaze flitted to my hair. "Actually, my natural color is white, like my father's. Yours too, I suppose, though yours is more silver than mine."

"Well, the pink is lovely."

"Thank you." She beamed and turned to face out the window again. "See that island in the distance?"

I squinted in the direction she was looking. "I think so? It looks quite small."

"It's rather large, but it is also very far away," she answered. "That's Sayyida's home."

Mentally pulling up the map Clemencia had shown me time and time again, I located the island where the Lady of Ships and the head of House Virtoris lived.

"It takes forever to get to the island on a ship." Saga sighed, continuing on in her own world. "The winds are atrocious. Not as bad as in the far north, but still strong."

"And then there are the pirates," a voice came from behind. We turned to find Sayyida, a few paces back, waving at us. "Heard you talking about me." She winked.

Saga cleared her throat. "Nothing bad."

"Did you tell her about that time you blessed a ship, and we got overrun by pirates?" Sayyida's tone dipped into a conspiratorial whisper.

"Another day," Saga hissed, though a spark flashed in her eyes that told me whatever happened that day hadn't been all bad. "We cannot talk about that now. My mother was furious, and bringing it up again will . . . Well, people will talk."

"They *always* talk. Anyway, the table is ready." Sayyida met my eyes. "How are you at nuchi, Neve?"

"I haven't played it."

"Huh," Sayyida mused, clearly surprised. "You really must be from a backwater. Everyone in Winter's Realm grew up playing this game. I've even heard that it's played as far south as the Spring Court."

But I wasn't from here and hadn't even been in the Winter Kingdom until a few days ago. "My family did not approve of games." I figured it made a good excuse.

"Ah, like the Warden of the East." Sayyida's full lips pursed as she spoke. "A pity. My Lady Mother is fond of anything that can earn her a bit more coin. Not that she needs it. But that isn't the point, is it?"

A laugh left my throat. Something about Sayyida eased me and amused me in equal measure. "I suppose not."

"Sit here." Saga pulled a chair out, one of three seats in a row.

As the princess took the middle one, I felt put on display. She showed me kindness, placing me next to her, but I wasn't sure I wanted that. Then again, I could not ask others to rearrange themselves.

"Thank you." I sat with a grace that still did not feel natural.

"Should I go over the rules?" Marit, daughter of the

Warden of the North, leaned forward, excitement on her pale face.

"Drink first." Sayyida grabbed a bottle that had been sitting on the table. "Anyone up for a bit of Dragon Fire?"

Marit paled, making her brownish-red freckles stand out more, but the rest, even Calpurnia, appeared intrigued, so Sayyida passed out a few small glasses of the liquor. When one landed in front of me, I leaned back. The drink smelled potent, hot even, though I didn't know a drink could smell like that.

"It's strong." Saga chuckled. "Drink it fast."

I swallowed, uneasy. "Is this common at court?"

As far as alcohol went, I'd had wine and ale, but nothing else. If the fae of this court drank often, then I needed to be aware. Drink loosened lips, and Roar and I had secrets to keep.

"This drink? No." Sayyida shook her head. "I recently returned from a supply run in the Dragon Kingdom. A friend gave me the bottle, and I saved it to share with friends. But plenty of wine will flow during the Courting Festival if you're more partial to that."

"She only brought the Dragon Fire to get us drunk." Saga nudged Sayyida with her shoulder, and the girls shared a warm, private look.

Others noticed too, for everyone else at the table glanced down at their glasses. And when Marit picked up her glass and offered a toast, I knew I wasn't crazy. Something existed between Saga and Sayyida, and whatever it was, no one wanted to speak of it.

"To the Courting Festival." Marit lifted a glass. "May we all find a mate and love."

The others echoed her words, though Saga and Sayyida refrained.

Calpurnia glared at me so hard during the toast that even the burn of the Dragon Fire couldn't melt her stare.

I set the glass down, shuddering. "That was awful."

"*That* was just round one." Sayyida's lips slid up into a mischievous grin. "Marit, deal us out while I pour another round. The rest of you, place your bets."

As the other ladies reached for purses they'd placed on side tables, or in Sayyida's case, wore around her hips, I grew warm. Never had I worried about being poor. As a slave, poverty had always been a fact of life, but now it made me feel inferior. I cleared my throat to announce that I brought no money and should probably leave, but under the table, Saga planted a discreet hand on my forearm.

"As I pulled Neve from her chambers before she could grab a purse, I'm putting in for her," Saga announced. Gold pieces flashed in her fingers. "We'll start with ten gold bears a piece.

"*Ten!*" Calpurnia scoffed.

"You have the coin, Calie." Saga rolled her eyes. "Stop being so cheap."

In response, the Vagle lady scowled and pulled a few more pieces from her purse. As she did so, Saga handed the money over to me. I opened my mouth to protest, but she shook her head.

"It's all in good fun." Her eyes added, *"don't worry about it."*

So, I took the coin. The gold felt cold between my fingers and an image of a bear stamped on each piece stared up at me. One by one, the other ladies pushed their pieces into the center of the table. I followed suit, noting that Eireann added silver pieces to the mix when she came up one gold piece short. Four silvers laid on the table, so I worked out that four silvers made up a gold. On the silvers, a stag danced on two legs. The stag represented House Vagle—Calpurnia's House and that of Queen Inga, too.

Calpurnia threw money on the pile last. She added coppers marked with a claw. I counted sixteen of those. Four silvers to a gold and four coppers to a silver.

Gold bears. Silver stags. Copper claws. Roar had mentioned the prices of things when we walked Guldtown, but as he held lines of credit at most places, I had seen little actual coin in Winter's Realm. I committed what the money looked like to memory in case I needed to speak of monetary issues while at court.

"Drink up, then we start," Sayyida said as another small glass of Dragon Fire landed in front of Saga first and then me.

Recognizing that arguing would be futile, I gripped the drink.

"To new friends." Saga lifted her drink to the center and turned to toast with me.

"To new friends," the ladies chanted, all except Calpurnia, who scowled and shot the drink back.

I brought the glass to my lips, barely tolerating the burn as it went down.

This would be a long afternoon.

CHAPTER 23

As Saga had warned, the afternoon turned into evening. A *very* late evening drenched in Dragon Fire.

I suspected the only thing that saved me from making an utter fool of myself was my sharp fear that I'd slip and spill a secret coupled with the supper brought up by a discreet brownie servant whom Saga claimed to trust. I'd indulged heavily in dinner, determined to soak up the alcohol as best I could, and downed at least five goblets of water too.

Thanks to the meal, by the end of the night I'd sobered a little, and I was certain I hadn't said a single thing to implicate Roar or myself.

Our secret, our agreement, remained safe.

"Despite my troll of a cousin, I hope you had fun tonight!" Saga said as she escorted me back to my room. "I wouldn't have invited Calpurnia because I knew about

Roar, but she overheard me talking to Eireann. Seriously, sorry about that."

"I had fun," I said.

It was true. Despite Calpurnia's icy glares, and Marit's apologetic looks when Sayyida said something off-color, I'd had lots of fun.

"Me too!" Saga sighed. "Good thing too, because this whole festival is going to be atrocious."

"You aren't excited?"

Marit had been, so had Calpurnia, and I got the sense that Baenna felt excited too. Sayyida and Eireann struck me as more standoffish about the Courting Festival. But Saga had been fairly tightlipped about the whole thing.

"I don't like being forced into things."

"That's something we have in common."

She grinned. "You're around this corner."

Had she not said anything, I would have missed the turn. As it was, I took the corner sharply and promptly ran into a wall.

I groaned and stepped back, nose wrinkling, eyes scrunching closed from the pain, even as the most delicious smell of sandalwood and the aroma of a freshly fallen snow filled my nostrils. What was that?

"Vale!" Saga hissed. "What in the afterworld are you doing here skulking about?"

I froze. Oh, no. That hadn't been a wall I'd run into. I opened my eyes, and groaned inwardly when I found the prince frowning down at me. Ugh. Why must someone so horrible smell like a treat?

"I might ask you the same." Prince Vale rubbed his chest. The action pulled his tunic down a little, revealing the tips of two bear claw tattoos.

Heat unfurled in my belly, and my pulse raced, but as quickly as it came, I shook off the reaction. For moon's sake, what was wrong with me? The male looked handsome, of course anyone with eyes could see that. But a million other fae males were handsome too. And Roar had told me this prince had done horrible things. I should despise him.

No, I *did* despise him. He'd just taken me by surprise was all—what with his masculine airs and scent and . . .

Bleeding skies!

I rolled my shoulders back and curtsied. "Prince Vale."

"Oh, don't bother," Saga muttered. "And I asked first, Brother. Why are you in this wing? Are you trying to find Vidar's suite? Because he's two corridors away."

"Again, I could ask you the same thing." Prince Vale's eyes flashed to my face, dipped down to my lips so briefly I thought I might have imagined it, before landing on his sister again. "Why haven't you met with your intended since he arrived?"

Intended? Saga hadn't mentioned that she was betrothed to anyone.

Saga crossed her arms. "If you must know, he was with Lady Virtoris all day. And I was entertaining the ladies of the Sacred Eight."

Prince Vale rolled his eyes but his annoyance broke a

little and a small smile played on his lips. "Entertaining. I see . . . I hope you didn't get into any trouble."

"And you?" Saga pressed, not bothering to answer her brother.

"I—" Again, his dark gaze flashed to me. "I wasn't doing anything important."

Had he been looking to confront Roar about something? Stars, maybe he had already done so? My stomach dipped. That had to be what he was doing in our wing.

"Hmmm." Saga hummed. "Well, you can keep your secrets and clear out. I must get Lady Neve safely to bed."

Prince Vale laughed derisively. "Then you shouldn't be taking her to the Lisika chambers."

My eyes narrowed. "What did you say?"

"He said nothing," Saga interjected.

"Yes, he did," my tone lowered in a warning.

Roar and I hadn't known one another long, but he'd taken me in and promised to see me to safety if I did this one thing for him. It had been more than most people had done for me in life. And most importantly, we were both lying to the king. We were together in this, and I'd defend the Warden of the West against any harm or slander that I could. "Why would you speak about my fiancé like that, Prince Vale?"

If fae could see through another fae, I felt certain that the prince was trying to do so at that moment. His stare was so intense, so penetrating, that goosebumps raised on my arms. I thanked the Fates that my long sleeves hid them.

"I have my reasons, Lady Neve, and I don't have to share them with you." With that, he rounded us and strode down the hallway.

Once he was out of earshot, Saga let out an annoyed huff. "I love my brother, but he can be a beast at times. I'm sorry that he said that about the warden. As you know, they aren't friends, but still, it was uncalled for."

"What happened between them?" I asked, because the hate in Prince Vale's eyes had been hot but that didn't make sense.

I knew Roar's side and understood why he'd be furious with the prince, but what would make the prince despise Roar? The former had betrayed the latter, not the other way around. Had something happened before that? After?

There had to be more.

"As children, the adult lords and weapons masters pitted them against one another in rings and such, so they were never friends," Saga started. "But after they fought in the southlands, it grew worse. From there, their relationship deteriorated. Whenever Roar is at court, the pair of them—Rhistel too, honestly—butt heads. Hating your fiancé is one of the few things my older brothers can agree on, but I could not tell you why they despise him."

"Hmmm."

"We should get you back to your room." Saga spoke softly. "I've been gone for hours, and I'm sure Mother wants to see me. I may not be taking part in the Courting Festival, but she still wants me to be present, beautiful, and charming."

That struck at another question. "So you're betrothed?"

"Since I turned eighteen."

"To whom?"

The princess let out a long breath. "Vidar Virtoris."

My lips parted in surprise. "Sayyida's brother?"

"He's the heir to the Virtoris fleet, the castle, everything. Father wanted a stable alliance with a means of transporting soldiers."

Her tone had soured, and though I was dying to ask why, I didn't. I'd seen the stolen glances between Saga and Sayyida that night and saw how the pair gravitated toward one another. After a few hours with them, I guessed they felt something for each other. In fae culture, people married whomever they liked, but I suspected royal princesses and high ladies played by different rules.

"Come," Saga said, and together we walked to my door.

When we got there, I turned to face her. "I had fun. Thanks for inviting me."

"*Inviting?*"

"Forcing?" I teased.

I might have been out of my element and terrified I'd let something slip, but really most of the night had been wonderful.

Saga laughed. "I'll see you tomorrow."

"See you then."

She left, and I waited until she turned the corner before I opened the door.

Roar and Clemencia sat in the antechamber. The

warden looked tense, and at my entry, my lady-in-waiting leapt up. "I hope everything went well without me!"

"It did, Clemencia. There was nothing you could have done." My assurance seemed to wash over her slowly, lowering her shoulders, softening her face.

Finally, she nodded. "Would you like me to draw you a bath, my lady?"

One look at Roar and I could tell we needed time alone. "Please."

She swept out of the room faster than she usually moved, perhaps sensing the warden's tension too. The moment we were alone, Roar strode over, his jaw set tight. "You smell like *Prince Vale*."

"What?" Of all the things he might have said, I had not been expecting that.

"Why were you with him?" Roar frowned.

"I wasn't—I mean, I was, but only for a few minutes. Princess Saga was bringing me back from a game of nuchi with other ladies of the Sacred Eight. We—"

"I trust you to hold your tongue around them. But why do you reek of Vale?"

Reek? I resisted smelling myself. Surely, Roar's hate for the prince was just shining through. There was no way I could smell so strongly of the prince. "He was rounding a corner at the same time I was, and I slammed right into him. That must be what you smell."

Roar closed the space between us so that we breathed the same air. "He didn't harm you?"

"No . . ." I trailed off, confused.

Would the prince harm me? He'd seemed annoyed to

be run into, and now that I thought about my 'cold' welcome when I'd met the prince, that might have played a part too, but he hadn't seemed violent.

"I'm fine. A little tired from drinking Dragon Fire and socializing, but fine."

Roar's eyes widened. "Dragon Fire? Where did you get that?"

"Lady Sayyida was at the gathering. She had a bottle."

"That seems in keeping with what I know of her." He reached out and tucked a stray lock of hair behind my ears. "Do you need food?"

"We had dinner. I'm fine."

He studied my face, as if searching for a lie. As he knew that was a possibility, the potion would work for a couple more weeks at the very least, I supposed I couldn't blame him.

"Nothing of note happened. Well, save that I lost all the money Princess Saga gave me to put in, but that's no surprise. The ladies are sharks at that game." Calpurnia, for all her blustering over a high buy in, had been the best. She'd taken nearly all the coin.

"I suppose I'll have to teach you how to really play, so that doesn't happen again." Finally, he smiled. "I'm glad you're back."

"I am too. It was—"

Roar leaned in and his hand slipped to my cheek, caressing it. I stiffened, not expecting an advance right then and there, and I remained that way as his lips met mine.

They felt soft, full, luscious, and the warden used them well. It was very clear that he had experience in this area. And yet, I didn't loosen, didn't lean closer.

Didn't feel a spark.

The heat I'd sometimes felt around him, that pleasure of being noticed and desired, never seemed to fan into a full flame. It never *caught*. By this point, I didn't think it would. And besides, surely, if we planned to begin something, we should talk about it first?

"Roar," I whispered, pulling away. "I don't think this is a good idea."

His eyes widened. "You don't want to?"

My insides warred. He was handsome, charismatic, kind, and a fae of power. I knew I would be lucky to have a male like him in my life. Anyone would. And yet, this still didn't sit quite right. I'd spent all my life living by others' rules, not allowed to make any decisions, but in this, I could choose. If I wasn't dying to kiss him, to be with him in a romantic sense, then it had to be a no. For now, at least.

I would withhold judgment for later. Emotions could change and grow, after all.

"It's not that," I settled on so as not to hurt him, nor go into my emotions, which I wasn't entirely sure that I understood anyway. "It's just . . . so much else is happening, and I need to stay sharp here. Romance would cloud that."

He took a step back. "I didn't mean to pressure you." The warden looked away, and for a moment the confident ruler of a fae vanished, replaced by a male who looked unsure which way to go. "However, I'll admit I feel things for you, Neve."

I nodded. That much was obvious, as that had been the second time he'd initiated a kiss. "I feel warmly towards you, but . . ."

Roar stared at me, unblinking. "Warmly? That's all? Even though you know I can protect you?" He gripped my hand. "How I can care for you as few others can?"

"Yes." I paused, a little startled by the insistence in his eyes. "I agreed to this so that I'd be safe far from the Blood Court. I don't know—"

"But would it be so bad if you didn't leave Winter's Realm? If you stayed?" Roar gripped my hand tighter, as if trying to squeeze his own thoughts and feelings into me. "You've seen Guldtown and glimpsed a fraction of my army. I'll keep you safe, Neve. Together, you and I, we could be unstoppable. We could change the kingdom for the better."

Unstoppable against *what*? The question flitted through my mind, but, really, it wasn't important. For me, sticking to my beliefs and goals and being true to myself was the most important. Not only did I crave freedom, but I could not give into romantic frivolity when so much was on the line. Not for anything less than true love—or even, if I dared to hope, my soulmate.

Plus, Anna counted on me. Her image filled my mind, breaking my heart. Stars, I missed her. And only I could save her, free her. It wouldn't happen today or tomorrow. It might not happen for many moons, but I'd do it if it was the last thing I ever did.

Gently, I retracted my hand. "I'm sorry, Roar. I can't."

His lips tightened. "Very well. I think I'll take a walk around the grounds."

Without another word, the Warden of the West exited our chambers.

CHAPTER 24

Roar wasn't in our suite when I rose to eat breakfast, or perhaps more aptly, lunch, as it was nearing midday.

Although his absence made me worry that I'd wounded him, a part of me also felt glad to put off any serious conversation between us. Though I hadn't felt drunk, or even tipsy, when I returned to our suite the night before, drinking Dragon Fire had resulted in me tossing and turning all night and given me a pounding headache. Lesson learned. I should have eaten at least twice the amount of dinner I'd inhaled. Or better yet, not allowed Sayyida to pressure me into overindulgence.

"Juice?" Clemencia asked, just above a whisper.

I'd admitted I felt poorly, and while she was acting sweet and spoke softly while I tried to eat, my lady-in-waiting also looked anxious. Our first full day in the capital had come. The Courting Festival would not officially start until tomorrow, but others would expect me to make an appearance around the castle.

Would the warden be with me? I fingered the golden vial of his blood that I'd tucked into the pockets of my lounging trousers. Normally, I didn't carry it around with me—it was blood, and I found that far too reminiscent of something the vampires would have done—but today I'd plucked it from its hiding spot in the bottom of my sewing basket. Perhaps I feared that after denying him, Roar would go back on our deal, but the vial helped to remind me of why he would not.

Crippling pain. No one wanted that.

Plus, he might be upset, but we were still in this together. We'd already lied to the king, a punishable offense, and now we had to see our charade through.

"Yes, please." I nodded to my empty juice glass.

"The more you eat, the better off you'll be." With a warm smile, Clemencia filled the glass and nudged my plate, which I'd been picking at since it arrived.

Taking her advice, I continued to eat slowly, and with each bite, I did indeed feel a little better. I'd managed to eat most of the food on my plate before someone knocked.

"Oh, stars." I groaned. "If it's Princess Saga, or worse, Lady Sayyida, *do not* let them in."

Clemencia shot me a look that plainly said she would do no such thing. As it turned out, my worry proved unfounded. At the door stood a servant bearing a letter. "For Lord Lisika and Lady Neve."

"Thank you." Clemencia shut the door. She turned

and looked around, as if expecting to see Roar materialize.

"I'll take it." I reached for the message.

Clemencia furrowed her eyebrows. "Are you sure?" I didn't take offense to Clemencia's question. In matters pertaining to court, I always deferred to Roar. But he wasn't here, and I wanted to know what the letter said.

"The messenger said my name too."

"Of course." She handed the missive to me.

I opened it, scanned the first line. "There's a tourney today! Very soon, in fact." My eyes traveled down the page and when I hit a certain name, my mouth fell open. "And guess who entered?"

Clemencia swallowed. "Lord Lisika?"

"In archery and swords.And it starts quite soon, so that has to be where he's at now." The question of where he'd been all night remained a mystery, but not one I cared about at the moment.

I stood and braced myself for a wave of nausea. Thankfully, it was far weaker than I'd anticipated. Good, that gave me hope for the day. "I need to dress."

My lady-in-waiting watched me carefully. "My lady? Is it wise to go?"

"What do you mean?"

"Shouldn't you rest? The opening ball is tomorrow. Isn't that more important than a tourney?"

"Oh, no. If Roar has gone and entered himself into this tournament, I want to be there to watch."

I wanted to make sure Roar didn't get hurt. The roster had been filled with other names, but one commanded more of my attention than the others: Prince Vale.

I also had a hunch Roar had entered to fight the prince and that my denial of him last night had something to do with it. Perhaps, if I found Roar before the swordplay portion, I might talk him out of this madness before he went up against the fae known as the Warrior Bear.

I retreated to my room and threw off my lounging robe. In the mirror, I caught sight of my body and stopped short. My curves had become far more pronounced than when I'd arrived in Winter's Realm. I smiled, loving how my body could take on the softness it always should have had. All the rich meals had done me some good. And that wasn't the only thing that made me happy.

Day by day, with the help of one of Althea's balms, the older scars on my arms and hands faded. I could barely see them anymore, and no longer worried that others would fixate on them. However, the markings on my wings still gave me pause. Those had had less time to heal and wouldn't disappear for many days, or even weeks. However, the ladies I'd played nuchi with hadn't seemed to notice, or if they had, they did not care, which I took as a good sign.

I dressed mindfully in a crimson gown and a heavy gold cloak that would keep the winds gusting off the Shivering Sea at bay. More importantly, it would shout to all that Roar and I were together. Though I'd never been to a tourney, people filled them, so it seemed as good a place as any to make sure the kingdom knew about Roar and me. At present, he might feel rejected, but I had no intention of going back on my promise to the warden.

"Is this appropriate?" I asked my lady-in-waiting, who had to dress for the event while I did and therefore hadn't been able to help me.

"You look splendid, my lady."

I patted down my skirt, nerves coming on at the prospect of being out among so many people who would surely have questions about me. These weren't just townspeople, either, but fae with great connections and influence. "Then, let's go. We'll ask someone to show us the way."

We left our suite and searched for someone to ask for directions. Shockingly, though, this part of the palace echoed with silence. People had either gone to the tourney already or perhaps the Courting Festival preparations were underway.

We made it all the way to the wide open junction of corridors that houses the terrifying stuffed bear when someone called my name. I stopped and turned to find Lady Sayyida heading my way. She appeared bright eyed, not at all affected by the Dragon's Fire, and wore a white fur cloak and a dark blue dress. The dress was lovely, lined with sparkling white beads around the neckline, but Sayyida kept tugging at the skirt.

"Lady Virtoris," I said as she approached and curtsied.

"Sassa's Blade! Stop that!" Sayyida pulled me up. "You too, whoever you are."

Clemencia began muttering unintelligible apologies, one of which included calling Sayyida a most honorable lady.

I cracked a grin at the affronted look on Sayyida's face. "I only meant to honor your house. You all were so kind to include me last night, even though I'm not of your status."

Sayyida rolled her eyes. "We like you. Or most of us do, anyway. That's all that matters." She looked at my lady-in-waiting. "And who are you?"

"This is Lady Clemencia." I smiled. "She's my lady-in-waiting from Guldtown."

"Lady-in-waiting?" Sayyida looked Clemencia up and down. "If Neve hasn't ditched you, then you must not be too bad. I lose my ladies every chance I can get. They're so insufferable."

I couldn't help but laugh.

"Well, it's true! They're always trying to push me into the most uncomfortable outfits, as if I don't have duties to attend to that require more than sitting prettily. Or worse, they want to find my brother and flirt. Blech! What a bunch of idiots." Belatedly, Sayyida nodded to Clemencia. "Nice to meet you. Anyway, are you two going to the tourney?"

"We are," I said. "You wouldn't happen to know where to go?"

"Of course I do. Would you like to come with me?"

"Absolutely." Better than having to ask a stranger who may or may not want to pry about me and Roar.

"Let's go then. I'm a bit late. I had to oversee my fleet

this morning and unload barrels of wine at the port, and then change into *this*." She gestured to the dress she wore with a wrinkled nose.

"My mother says I have to be more appropriately dressed for the courting events. I'd much rather wear trousers to throw the king off pairing me, but today Mother insisted." She huffed out a breath. "The Courting Festival hasn't even started, and she's already being so overbearing. You'd think I was still a child."

"Well, you look wonderful." I hoped it softened her frustration. I enjoyed wearing fancy dresses but understood being forced to do things you didn't want to do.

"Thanks. Let's run along to the ring, shall we?"

My heart raced as we sped through the palace. I earned many looks of interest, hinting that the fae we passed might have heard about me. Sayyida garnered even more glances of interest, and one male actually dropped the loaf of bread he carried and fell into a deep bow, proclaiming the Lady Virtoris to be 'lovelier than ever'.

Sayyida thanked the fae, calling him Jarl Salizier. When we got out of earshot, she rolled her eyes. "He tried to court me last year, and thank the Fates, I scared him off with a few particularly bawdy sea shanties. If he thinks a dress means I've gone soft, he has another think coming."

I mulled that over for a moment. "Is it common for great families on this side of the kingdom to marry into smaller lord or ladyships?"

Sayyida shrugged. "It's done. Particularly if the lower house is very wealthy or has a lot of land."

Reaching the end of a hallway, she opened a door, and a brisk wind slapped us all in the face. Behind me, Clemencia let out a gasp.

The day felt clearer and colder than the day we'd arrived. With the abrasive wind, I flinched, but the moment the gale died down, I smiled. Cold and sunny was perfect.

Sayyida led us onto a curved path. Other fae walked in front of us, each dressed for the weather and looking excited. After about five minutes, we reached a tall circular building made of stone, and Sayyida veered off the common path.

"We'll go this way," Sayyida said. "To the private boxes."

Relieved that she'd found me, I followed as she waved to a palace guard dressed in a royal blue uniform and a gold cloak. The guard opened a door and ushered us in without so much as blinking. Only up close did I notice the white claw on his breast. That symbol identified him as a Clawsguard soldier, one dedicated to the royal house. We would be near the royal family then.

"The steps are narrow. Watch yourself," Sayyida said as we climbed.

When we reached the floor her box was on, she passed one door before stopping at the one in the middle. A serpent riding an enormous wave had been carved into the wood.

She gestured down the steps we'd just climbed. "Usually, you'd be in the Warden Roar's box, but as he's in the tourney, it might be best that you stay with me. Unless you don't want to?"

"I want to stay with you," I blurted and immediately felt a little clingy.

The high lady didn't seem to mind, though. She pushed open the door. "Perfect. Allow me to invite you to the Virtoris's box at the Aaberg Ring."

We stepped inside a box that could easily fit ten fae. Gray-blue velvet, the color of House Virtoris, covered the seats made of dark wood and polished to a high shine.

Below, to the sides, and above us, crowds of fae watched as archery contestants practiced in the ring, but in our box, we stood separated from the masses. Mostly, anyway. Other elaborate boxes surrounded us, above and below. I peered up and saw people I did not recognize. They were all dressed well, although their boxes seemed to be standardized with royal blue covered seats.

"The most important jarls are just above," Sayyida explained. "To each of our sides are for the Sacred Eight; the boxes for House Qiren and House Riis."

I glanced left, then right, recognizing the banners I'd been quizzed on during the journey. Qiren's banner had a burnt orange fox in a field of white. The seats glowed burnt orange as well. While the Riis banner showed a black spiderweb on a field of red to match the red seats. So lesser houses did not get to show their colors in the Ring, only the Sacred Eight.

As for fae, the Qiren box sat empty, but the Riis box held a lone person. His long, dark red hair flew in the wind, reminding me a bit of Roar, though this male was far tanner and larger. He might have even been larger than the lumberjack, Frode, who was still the largest faerie I'd seen. I was still taking in the mountain of a fae, when he turned.

I sucked in a breath. His deep brown eyes penetrated me in a way that made me shiver. Like I knew him or something. Then he lifted his hand and pressed his hand to his heart. I didn't know what that meant, but I waved back and, unable to take his intensity any longer, looked downward.

"I noticed many events on the letter I received. Which is your favorite?" I asked as we took our seats, and I searched for Roar in the crowd of archers warming up.

"Sword fighting. Though I like jousts too." Sayyida turned to me. "Warden Roar famously favors the bow. Have you seen him shoot?"

"I have." I recalled how cleanly he'd shot the orc that tried to steal me away. "Is that the royal box?" I gestured down, trying to keep the subject off Roar and me. The fewer lies I told, the better.

"The one with the white bear banner is. The Aaberg's box is closest to the action, alongside the queen's family, House Vagle. As the Aabergs and Vagles both hold seats in the midlands, they've always been quite close." Sayyida wrinkled her nose. "It's an honor to be closer to the ring, but I prefer it up here, less stink of innards that spill during swordplay."

My stomach rolled, and I pointed to the line of four

boxes between our level and that of the royals and House Vagle. "That must be the level that the wardens are on?"

Though I asked, I already knew. Since Warden Roar wasn't present, no one was in his box, but his banner featuring a golden snow leopard on a red field flew in the wind. As I studied the other boxes, I also found Baenna and Eireann Balik, whom I'd met last night, with their family, and the red-haired Marit Armenil in the box dedicated to the great house of the North.

"Exactly." Sayyida nodded in response to my question. "Officially, all the Sacred Eight are equal, and the crown rules us all, but . . . " She gestured downward, to the level of the wardens and their proximity to the royals. "As you can see, there's an unspoken hierarchy. Or at the very least, favoritism."

I mulled that over. The Virtoris family seemed very important to the crown. From everything Clemencia had told me, they provided ships for trade, and if a sea battle befell the kingdom, House Virtoris would command the first wave of the armada. Then again, Roar had the largest army after the crown, and he didn't feel close to the king. I pondered that as I studied the other boxes below and caught when Princess Saga pulled a book from a pocket inside her cloak.

My eyebrows knitted together. "Is she journaling?"

Sayyida looked up from her dress, which she fidgeted with, and laughed. "Saga? She's always writing in one of her journals."

I recalled the book I'd seen in her pocket, and

Clemencia telling me that the princess was a writer. "She didn't last night."

"She was trying not to scare you away, but she had it on her, believe me. The *Book of Fae is* always with her."

I scoffed. "Her journal is called the *Book of Fae*? That sounds—"

"Pompous," Sayyida cut in with a laugh. "I've told her, but Saga thinks it fits. She writes all that she wants about fae at court in that book. As you can imagine, many wish to get their hands on that book or a journal she's already filled out and hidden away, but they're all locked up tight."

"Yes, I can imagine." A book written by a royal princess telling of what went on in court? Who she favored? Maybe even who the king or queen favored? Who they hated? That was valuable information, indeed.

I wondered if Saga had written about me, and if so, what?

"Have you seen it?" I asked.

Sayyida shook her head. "No, and I don't think I ever will. Saga is private about that book." She paused. "She writes her visions in it too."

"She's a seer?"

Being a seer was a rare ability in the fae. Some witches in the human world and mages in Isila possessed the ability too, but from what I'd learned, it was never commonplace, no matter what magical order one belonged to.

"She only came into her power in her late teens, and

seeing comes and goes as it pleases, so yes, she is a seer, but with very little practice."

Another question rested on the tip of my tongue when the door behind us opened, and Sayyida and I turned. She rose.

"Mother! Brother! Where are Njal and Amine?"

I swallowed and stood to hurriedly curtsey to the High Lady Fayeth Virtoris and Sayyida's brother. Had she not welcomed them as she did, I still would have guessed they were her blood.

Sayyida had the High Lady's long dark curls and glittering blue-gray eyes. Her brother also looked much like his mother, with the high lady's light brown skin and a long, lean frame, though he wore his hair shorter, in a cropped fashion I found rather unusual. He appeared to be around thirty, which meant he could be that age, or, as fae aging slowed after thirty, far older.

"Your little brother begged off. He's in the library, and your sister wasn't feeling well." The Lady of Ships shifted to examine me and Clemencia. "And who are these ladies?"

"Lady Neve." Sayyida gestured to me. "Warden Roar's fiancée. And her lady-in-waiting Clemencia."

"Ah, you're the one that has the king in a tizzy." Lady Virtoris inclined her head. She did not bother introducing herself, correctly assuming I already knew her. "Good for you."

"Mother, words such as those are unwise in the current political climate," the male said before he locked eyes with me. "I'm Vidar Virtoris, Sayyida's older brother."

"Neve." I curtsied again. So this was Saga's intended mate. "No great house. I'm commonborn."

Vidar's smile lit up his handsome face. "We're happy to host you, Lady Neve. Would you like a goblet of wine?"

"Oh, no, thank you." My stomach rioted at the mention of alcohol. "I don't need anything."

Sayyida let out a bawdy laugh. "I think I gave her too much Dragon Fire last night!"

"Sayyida," her mother warned. "You must learn to *behave*."

"Says the mother who had salt-blooded *sailors* watch me in the crib damp with spindrift!" Sayyida snorted and turned back to face the field where the warm-ups had now finished, and new archers took to the field.

"I don't see Roar down there," I said. "Why isn't he allowed to practice?"

"I'm sure he did so before we got here. The competitors go in rounds, including when they warm up," Sayyida explained. "Otherwise, someone will get shot. This will be round one of the preliminaries."

"Do they actually all compete?" There had to be fifty archers on the field. This part of the tourney would take all day.

Vidar moved to sit next to his sister. "They do, but the rounds weed out the worst quickly. They get three shots and the best archers are the only ones to move forward to the finals."

The Lady Virtoris took her place on her son's other side, closest to the box that House Riis called their own. Immediately, she began to chat with the older male fae.

He wasn't the only one in House Riis's box any longer, but among the dozen watching from this privileged vantage. Three had the intimidating male's red hair and broad shoulders, his sons most likely. Lady Virtoris had leaned over to speak to the older male and the pair had a familiarity about them that hinted they might be equals.

Was that fae Lord Leyv Riis, Lord of Tongues? I wanted to crane my head around and ask Clemencia, but no doubt she had not whispered the name in my ear for a reason. I'd ask later.

Below, a knight pointed archers to a line where they stood about ten paces apart. Targets loomed in front of the line. I squinted. The archers each held three arrows in their quivers.

The tournament began without preamble. The organizers called for the archers to pull and loose and the competitors in round one let their arrow fly three times.

Two dwarf judges descended and pointed to only two from the line-up. The rest left the field. They were out.

"Brutal," I whispered.

"I wish they were more cutthroat so we could move on already!" Sayyida said. "The final rounds take long enough, and I'd like to get to the *swords*." Her eyes gleamed, and I suspected Sayyida had imagined herself in a tourney like this many times.

In fact, why didn't she compete? I didn't know

Sayyida that well, but she appeared strong, and I suspected she liked a bit of sport.

"Do you fight with swords?" I asked.

"Whenever I can," Sayyida replied, her eyes lighting up.

"Then why not enter the tourney?"

Vidar looked taken aback by the questions. His sister, however, threw up a hand.

"You know what?" Sayyida's look of exasperation was unmistakable. "I've asked the same thing many times. All anyone tells me is that highborn ladies from the great houses may not enter these tourneys. Even if they beat their male counterparts at archery or swords or any weapon imaginable, since they were old enough to train." Sayyida smirked at Vidar, a self-satisfied cat. Her brother rolled his eyes but didn't argue.

It made no sense. I could see a female on the field competing to be chosen among the finalists. Why could females rule houses and hold the highest titles in the land, but not compete?

As if to prove my point, the second heat of archers finished, and the judges ran into the ring. This time, the judges chose only one fae as a finalist: a female faerie.

The dwarves rushed the second round of archers off the field and the third preliminary heat marched in from where they waited inside the ring. Prince Vale and Roar were a part of this round, and though Roar's red hair gleamed in the sunlight, demanding attention by its sheer brilliance of color alone, I couldn't help but study the prince; the way he walked, the way he smiled and laughed with other archers.

Others seemed to congregate around the prince, to talk and joke with him if their smiles were any indication. Roar, on the other hand, walked with space between himself and others. And when the archers took to the line, the warden kept his face down while the prince continued to talk animatedly to the fae next to him, telling a story probably.

I wondered what it was about, and why so many fae seemed drawn to Prince Vale. Clearly, they did not know how he'd abandoned soldiers to orcs all those turns ago.

As if he could sense my eyes on him, the prince turned from where he stood in the lineup and his gaze traveled up, up, up. We locked eyes. I swallowed.

Among all the people in the ring, had he felt me staring at him?

No, I had to be imagining things. Over a hundred fae stood between the prince and me. He had to be staring at someone else.

But when he scowled, and shot a furious glance at Roar, it felt like he'd slapped me. Oh yes, he'd been watching *me*. Had Roar said something about last night? It wouldn't surprise me.

"Lady Neve, what in all the nine kingdoms did you do to piss the prince off?" Sayyida leaned closer.

"He wasn't looking at me," I denied hurriedly.

"There aren't that many people in our box," Sayyida teased. "It was so obvious."

Stars. If that had been obvious to Sayyida, it was

probably obvious to others too. Or perhaps others were busy socializing and watching the tournament to notice the prince? Needing to check, I let my gaze dip to the other boxes and my stomach immediately plummeted.

Down in the Vagle box, Lady Calpurnia scowled up at me. Another young female with blonde curls down to her butt stood beside Lady Calpurnia. I didn't know the other fae's name but judging by the golden scales supporting seated snow lions that had been artfully balanced atop her bun, she seemed to be a daughter of the Warden of the East. Their house animal was a snow lion and, just last night, Sayyida had mentioned Lady Ithamai was obsessed with the law. Could that faerie be the friend Lady Calpurnia had mentioned last night?

"I—I'm not sure what I did," I said belatedly.

Sayyida didn't press, and as the third round of archers began to compete for a coveted spot in the final rounds, I breathed more freely.

The first arrows flew, and I had to fight to remain in my seat as Roar hit a dead bullseye.

When the second round soared, my lord sank his arrow into the ring next to the center one. His third, once again, landed perfectly.

I exhaled and studied the others' targets. I'd been so focused on Roar while he shot that my attention had not strayed. Only one other fae had come close to matching the Warden of the West's skill—Prince Vale, of course. He, like Roar, sank two bullseyes.

Still, my heart thudded hard until the dwarf judges made their call. They chose three more archers to go on to be finalists: Prince Vale, Warden Roar, and a female dwarf whose name I could not hear from our box.

"Were you worried?" Sayyida asked.

"What?" I jerked a little when she spoke.

"The whole time your shoulders were tense. Were you worried?"

"Oh, yes. I want my fiancé to do well."

"I said he favors the bow, but that was putting it mildly. Really, he's one of the most skilled archers in the kingdom." Sayyida threw a lazy wave. "There was no doubt he'd be in the finals."

"Do they go straight into the last round?" I asked.

"They'll need to rearrange a bit. But yes, they—"

The door to the Virtoris box opened, and everyone turned. A rush followed in which everyone, save for me, stood. My ears told me that even those in the Riis box had gotten to their feet. A person of importance had entered, and as I took the male in, I knew who.

I swallowed and rose to stand and face the other Aaberg prince, Crown Prince Rhistel. He and his brother were not identical, Rhistel being paler as if he rarely saw the sun and more lithely built. Still, he looked so much like Prince Vale that I had no question about the heir's identity. And even if I had a single doubt, his blue tunic with an ivory bear over the right breast would have eliminated those questions.

"Wondrous day for a tourney, isn't it?" Prince Rhistel's voice came out smooth and strong.

Lady Virtoris sashayed forward. "Prince Rhistel. What brings you to my family box?"

"My lord father wishes to speak with Lady Neve." The heir to the throne looked past the Head of House Virtoris to me.

His eyes glinted dark brown, bottomless and full of cunning. I shrank back, sensing if anyone could discover the secret I hid, it might be this fae.

But as the prince held out a long-fingered hand. I blinked, noting that it was gloved and not in fabric I would have thought was well suited to winter. The fabric appeared thin, almost see-through and shimmered like moonlight. I'd never seen such a material.

"Lady Neve, please join me?" the prince asked, ripping me from my questions.

Knowing it would do no good to say no, I nodded and walked toward him. Once close enough, I curtsied, breathing in the distinct scents of parchment and wine as I rose. The prince smelled as though he'd been drinking in a library. "And my lady-in-waiting?"

"We have a spot for her." He smiled, perhaps thinking that it would soften me toward him.

But the curl of his lips had the opposite effect, spiking my heart rate ever higher, and as I took the heir's offered hand, I steeled myself for the performance of a lifetime.

CHAPTER 25

Prince Rhistel didn't speak as we left the Virtoris box, nor as we descended the stairs connecting the noble houses' personal boxes. Only when we reached the first floor, the royal floor, did he finally turn. "I had wondered what you'd look like."

I blinked. "Excuse me?"

"When Warden Roar met with my father, I wondered what commoner would be dazzling enough to convince a fae of a great house to give up a valuable alliance. More than that, really, what female would be valuable enough to irritate a king's plans?" His eyes dipped to my feet and dragged back upward, lingering on my breasts too long for my liking.

I shuddered. Stars, I wanted to tell him to keep his lecherous eyes to himself, but Roar and I needed to please the royal family, to remain engaged—until a time came to undo this charade in the privacy of Roar's castle.

So, instead of slapping the prince across the face as I

335

yearned to do, I held back and waited until his eyes once again met mine. They were the same dark brown as his brother's but with no intriguing spark, only coldness. Winter's heir, indeed.

"I see the appeal now." His lips pulled up into a sly grin.

I didn't reply, which only made Crown Prince Rhistel smile harder. "Tell me, what does your family do?"

"Mother is long gone from this world and Father, too, recently journeyed to the afterworld. He was a fisherfae."

I thanked the moon that the potion Lord Aldéric had shoved down my throat at regular intervals still pulsed through me strongly. As much as I wished to know what magic I possessed, the ability to lie was as precious as gold. More so even.

"Hmm, perhaps I should take to the villages for a mate?" he said, eyes dipping to my breasts again. "I've been missing out on great beauty."

I inclined my head, hoping he'd take that as a thank you. He did, and the prince turned to open the door to the royal box. "Come, I will introduce you to the king."

Not my father. Not my lord father. The king.

Even the heir must act within the bounds of etiquette around King Magnus. I would do well to remember that.

We entered the box, and the difference of a few floors astounded me. The field was so close that I could smell the dirt and hear the voices of the dwarf judges as they determined the order in which the finalists should compete.

At our entrance, everyone had turned expectantly.

Saga gave me a smile, melting my unease slightly before it could creep all the way over me and freeze me from the inside out. I was thankful for the princess, as no one else's gaze felt warm or welcoming.

Courtiers stared at me as Prince Rhistel had, though in a far less suggestive manner. The king and queen studied me too, an interesting specimen elevated to their level.

While the king was not unattractive, Saga had clearly inherited her delicate beauty from her mother. Though the queen had dark brown hair, much like her sons', she shared many more features with her daughter. Both had luminous, creamy skin, full pink lips, and perfectly symmetrical features. But the princess's eyes were all her father's—ice blue, just like his wings. Truth be told, the king looked as if he'd been carved from a glacier, he was so pale, so cold looking with skin that looked hard to the touch and long white hair. A son of winter, indeed.

I tore my eyes from the king, to take in the Vagle box. Even there, people stared my way and, of course, Calpurnia scowled. I was beginning to wonder if her face could make any other expression.

At Calpurnia's side, a pale blonde female about my age watched me with hard eyes. Two older males joined them in their examination, both in green cloaks that bore a silver stag on the back. Vagles. One had to be Calpurnia's grandfather, the queen's father and Lord of Coin. Courtiers sat there too, but I paid them little mind. In my scheme they were unimportant.

Out of the many fae in both boxes, only the royal

guards took no notice of me. They had been trained to seek threats, and they clearly did not deem me one. That, at least, was a boon.

"We'll go this way. Your lady-in-waiting may stay back here." The prince pointed to the back row, to the luscious velvet, royal blue seats, and he glided down the steps toward his family.

Clemencia seemed upset, but I smiled at her, trying to exude confidence that I did not feel at our separation. "As he said."

She took a seat while I followed the prince. When we stood before the king and queen, I curtsied with trembling knees. "My king. My queen. Princess Saga."

I did not rise but waited as Roar and Clemencia had instructed me to do when meeting the royals for the first time. It took a long time until a feminine voice spoke. "Warden Roar did not overstate your beauty, Lady Neve. Please, rise."

When I straightened, the queen studied me with that same, unwavering intensity. By all the sacred stars in the sky, this faerie made me shiver. Though not as much as her mate, whose icy gaze lifted goosebumps on my arms.

"Indeed, he did not," the king said. "Though I still take issue that he entered an engagement without my knowing or blessing. And before the Courting Festival at that. One might consider his actions *defiant*."

"If you wish to break them up, Father, I'd like to get to know the lady." Prince Rhistel spoke lightly, as if jesting.

The king glared at his son. "You will wed no fisher-fae's daughter."

"Who said anything about marriage?" the heir smirked, a viper's smile.

"The final archery rounds are about to start," Saga interrupted. "Perhaps we should sit? I'd hate to keep Vale waiting for a chance for a title." The princess grinned. "Not to mention, I'd like Lady Neve to myself. We've already made fast friends."

Prince Rhistel snorted, but the king and queen agreed and shifted to watch the archers. I didn't fail to notice how King Magnus's face softened to Saga in a way that his son, or even his queen, did not elicit. Once I was no longer under their intense scrutiny, a weight lifted off my shoulders.

"Here." Saga gestured to a seat with a dark blue glass goblet filled with red wine. "Lady Neve, please, sit by me. Would you like a goblet of wine?"

I declined the wine but sat with her at the far end of the royal line. No one took the seat to my right, but the Vagle box was not far away and filled with female voices speaking in low tones. About me, no doubt.

When the first finalist took his shots, three times just as in the preliminary rounds, Princess Saga leaned closer and whispered to me. "Happy to have you here, though I must apologize for my family. And for the merchant behind us. My mother loves his jewel house but blazing moon, does he stink!"

I sniffed the air and gagged. It was a testimonial to

how distracted I'd been that I had not smelled the stench of onion mixed with wine before. How in the nine kingdoms were those sitting closer to the merchant tolerating him?

"No apologies needed. Your mother seems to be a delight."

Saga laughed dryly. "She can be but take care. She is not a born Aaberg, but House Vagle was once royal in the midlands. Ice runs thick through her veins too, all the Vagle veins, in fact." Saga looked over at me. "As you can see by my cousin, who still has not let go of the fact that Warden Roar is no longer an eligible lord."

I turned. Calpurnia stared at me; her expression quietly furious. Calculating even. I shuddered.

"Who's with her? An Ithamai?" The female wore the colors of the house that ruled the easternlands—a dark purple dress with white beading on the bodice. I was pretty sure because of the snow lion headdress balanced on her bun, but it was best to be positive when talking about one's potential enemies.

"Adila Ithamai," Saga confirmed. "One of the daughters of the Warden of the East, who is above us."

"Adila is friends with Calpurnia?"

"Best friends." Saga nodded. "Calie was a ward of the Ithamai's for a half a year."

"Well, Adila doesn't seem to like me much either."

The princess laughed dryly. "Adila is . . . *difficult*. And just so you know, her older sister, Hadia, is much more so. The entire family has a sense of how things should be.

When those expectations are not met, they become displeased. And I hate to say it, but both sisters have been vying for Lord Roar's attention since they were old enough to want a marriage. To win the west and create an alliance with the east would have been an excellent achievement, so for them, you are a true issue."

I swallowed thickly. The end of the Courting Festival and my return to Guldtown could not come fast enough.

Try as I might to turn to the field and take in the final archery rounds, I continued to feel Calpurnia staring at me, judging me, hating me. Stars, I despised being the subject of ire when I'd done nothing to earn it.

Archer after archer took to the field. Most were skilled and their arrows hit near the center, if not within the middle circle. Though so far, no one in the finals had struck the absolute center, a black dot in the small expanse of the middle circle. I had no idea how the judges would decide the winner with such a tight competition.

When Prince Vale stepped forward for his final three shots, long black hair unbound and flying in the wind, murmurs arose, most of them feminine in pitch. I understood the excitement. Though what Roar had told me of the prince made me dislike him, the hairs on my arms still rose at the sight of him. The fae looked too delicious for words, and I found that quite annoying.

He positioned his feet, pulled an arrow from his quiver, and nocked it. Muscles bulged in his arms, and I swallowed, suddenly parched. After a moment of silence in the arena, the prince let his arrow fly.

A *thwack* resonated through Aaberg Ring, and suddenly, cheers erupted.

The Warrior Bear had shot a bullseye, perfectly in the center.

My eyes widened. That didn't bode well for Roar.

When Prince Vale released his second arrow, it sank right next to the first. He smiled, likely thinking the last contestant in the finals, Roar, could never beat that, before turning to wave and smile and even blowing a couple of kisses at the crowd.

Fae roared, making me snort lightly. Clearly, they loved their prince. How little they really knew about him.

At my side, Saga groaned. "Stars, why is he such a show-off? Sometimes I think he's worse than Rhistel."

I smothered a laugh and, consequently, was still smiling when Prince Vale turned to the royal box.

He froze, dropped the arrow in his hand, and, yet again, locked eyes with me. My heart thundered in my chest.

Though I could not see them, I felt the courtiers behind me stiffen. Out of the corner of my eye, Prince Rhistel leaned forward, gloved hands clasped around his knee. Did he hear my heartbeat? I tried to rearrange my features into nonchalance, but I was not sure that I managed. Rhistel remained so still and the tension in the air thickened to the point where I could barely draw breath.

The spell broke when the Warrior Prince stopped looking at me as though I were an ogre in the royal box, picked up the arrow, and nocked it. Faster than before, he let the arrow fly.

I exhaled when it hit off-center.

The crowd groaned, and some of the heady tension in the box dissipated, finally allowing me to relax. The judges noted Prince Vale's arrow positions, dismissed him, and called in the last contestant—Roar.

All the while, I continued to look straight forward, no longer at the Warrior Bear lingering on the dirt field. Definitely not at Prince Rhistel, who I felt still watched me. Not at the king or queen either, lest they be watching me too. Not even at the amiable Princess Saga, who hadn't made a fuss about what had happened, but she didn't need to.

Her hand had strayed to her pocket, where I assumed her Book of Fae waited. Surely, she was dying to record what had happened, that her brother seemed affected by me though I could not say why. Nor why my heart still beat irregularly just thinking of him taking me in.

At long last, Roar took to the center of the arena, causing a titter among the female fae that rivaled the one Prince Vale had received. The warden wasn't a prince, but he *was* a high lord and that was the next best thing. Plus, many common fae didn't know that Roar had arrived at court with a fiancée. A fact that the warden sought to address, apparently, as he turned to face the boxes. At first, his gaze drifted up to his box. When he did not find me, it dropped a level, until his eyes found mine. They widened almost imperceptibly. I doubted he expected to find me seated with the king and queen and their family.

But Roar made the most of the moment by bowing and blowing a kiss. "To my fiancée, the lovely Lady Neve."

Unfortunately, that only brought more stares, and I felt my cheeks go hot. Perhaps it had been an utter mistake to come here. I ought to have stayed hidden away in our suite.

I sagged in relief when Roar turned his back on us and set up at the line. He positioned his feet and body and pulled his first arrow.

He loosed, and the arrow flew. It sunk into the middle circle.

Fae held their breaths as his second flew. It did the same as the first.

I leaned forward, knowing that the third would be the one that mattered. The one that won it all. It flew and sank into the target with a *thwack*.

It landed dead center.

Fae thundered, and Roar beamed. Pride for him rose in my chest. He might not truly be mine, but we shared feelings for each other—attraction, warmth, and friendship, or so I hoped we still did after last night. Still, no matter how he felt about me, I wanted him to succeed.

The judges conferred for only a moment before they approached the king's box. King Magnus rose and descended a few steps to hear the dwarves' ruling. He nodded at their missive and then walked the rest of the way into the Ring where a dais had been hurriedly placed by two scrappy-looking satyr younglings. Once front and center, the king held up his hands. The arena silenced.

"The archery portion of our tourney is complete," King Magnus proclaimed. "Might the following competitors come forth? Prince Vale Aaberg, Warden Roar Lisika, and Edwing Yarla."

The prince, the warden, and the female faerie, Edwing, stepped forward. Of the archers, only Edwing appeared happy to be in the lineup.

"Stars and Fates, Vale and the warden need to calm down." Saga sipped her wine. Behind me, I heard a servant filling more glasses. "They're like two wolvea in puberty."

I couldn't agree more. A tension that was surely felt all throughout the Ring vibrated between Roar and Prince Vale, stiffening their shoulders, feathering muscles in their jaws. Worst of all, both of their gazes kept flickering to me.

As far as I was concerned, only Roar had a reason to be upset. Roar had disliked that Prince Vale's scent was on me, even if it had been an accident that we'd run into one another. I felt very sure Roar had said something to the prince before the tourney, which had only made things worse.

What a mess.

"Third place goes to Edwing Yarla!" King Magnus beamed a winning smile though I noted it did not reach his ice-blue eyes, while the judges walked forward to hand the faerie a trophy arrow made of copper.

"The judges tell me that second place was close," the

king continued and again, the crowd quieted, waiting for his word.

Would it be prince or warden? Anyone who watched would have seen Roar best the prince, but perhaps the judges took the other rounds into account? And of course there was always the option of favoritism . . . I didn't like to think that would happen, but The Warrior Bear *was* a prince. Was he pampered and entitled as well as vile enough to leave his people to fight on their own?

"However our esteemed judges determined one fae showed more prowess than the other, so second place goes to . . ." A pause rang through the arena. "Prince Vale of House Aaberg!"

The prince bowed and stepped forward to receive his trophy arrow of silver.

Behind him, Roar smirked, and when Prince Vale rejoined the lineup, the warden shot the prince a smug look.

"That leaves only one fae as the winner." King Magnus held out a meaty hand. "Warden Roar Lisika takes the archery portion of today's tourney!"

The crowd went wild, and Roar spun on his heel, waving at the common fae, in a smart move. The more he endeared himself to the commoners, the less likely the king would be to deny Roar's engagement.

When my fiancé turned back to the royal box, one dwarf ran up, carrying a golden arrow. He handed it over, but before Roar took hold, a scream from the other side of the arena rang out.

When I located where it came from, I gasped. A male

faerie soared into the arena, a black cloak fluttering behind him, bow at the ready, and an arrow aimed at the king.

Then, many things happened all at once: the arrow flew and Roar leapt toward the king at the same time as Prince Vale spun to take on the attacker. From the arena, two more faeries leapt into the sky, each pointing arrows at the royal box.

I sat there, frozen in place, horrified. When the first arrow plunged into Roar's right shoulder, I screamed.

Chaos broke out as fae began running and the other two arrows flew. They struck, but not their targets. Instead, two courtiers in the royal box fell, blood gurgling from their mouths. A goblet of wine flew past my head only to shatter on the stone wall that separated the box from the field. Blue glass scattered across the floor, and wine ran at my feet, red like Roar's blood.

At my side, a guard grabbed Saga by the arm. She dropped her goblet, and another glass shattered on the ground as her guard pulled her to the side to safety. Fae around me ran, fleeing. Coming out of my shock, I stood to follow when the merchant reeking of onion tripped out of his seat directly above mine and fell forward.

He was far larger than me, and his weight threw me forward too. The fae flung me into the half stone wall that separated the royal box from the arena, his weight threatening to crush me, squeezing the air from my lungs. I groaned as, beneath the pressure, my ankle twisted unnaturally.

When the weight of the other fae lifted, I slouched

into the wall, finally able to get a full breath. One would think that he'd help me to stand, but no. The merchant didn't even yell an apology over his shoulder before he ran off, leaving me alone in the box.

I swallowed down the pain and fear and looked up and over the banister in time to find soldiers swarming the field. They'd already captured the first archer, though the second two still soared through the air, shooting at the soldiers.

As though the culprit could feel me watching, they twisted to find me staring and pulled back an arrow.

I yelped and dropped to the ground. Glass from the goblets of wine that had shattered dug into my hands and shins, where my dress had hiked up. I swore, but pressed down harder into the floor, trembling and trying to ignore the glass cutting me up, the wine soaking my dress.

And when an arrow hit the chair right behind where I'd been kneeling, I was glad I'd taken every precaution. Had I been a second slower, the arrow would have gone through my skull. Breath coming fast and thin, I got on my hands and knees and tried to crawl, tried to escape the box like everyone else had. But before I made it halfway to the steps, a figure landed in front of me.

"What in the name of Sassa's bloody blade were you thinking?"

I knew that voice. Chancing a glance, I looked up to find Prince Vale standing there, his face bloodied and streaked with dirt and fury blazing in his eyes. My mouth opened and closed, but no words came out.

"What are you doing here?" he growled again.

"Y-your family invited me to their box."

"No. Why didn't you *run*?"

My heart rate kicked up. "I—I don't know. I wasn't fast enough."

"Stand up."

"But there's a shooter!"

"Not anymore, there's not."

I stared at him. "Are you certain? Because he nearly just took my head off." I gestured to the arrow in the chair. I might have lived most days of my life being prey for vampires but being shot at had unlocked a new level of terror.

Prince Vale spared it a glance, and his jaw tightened. "I saw to it that he'll never shoot another arrow again. The soldiers have wrested everything under control. Can you stand?"

I pressed myself up, wincing as the glass cut deeper into my hands. Once on my feet, a twinge in my ankle made me cringe, but I said nothing as the prince looked me over, and his hardened expression faded to concern.

"You're bleeding." His eyes burned as I took two steps closer. "And limping. Tell me who did this to you."

The demand, his heated words, took me by surprise. And how was it that his eyes seemed to blaze even hotter than just seconds before?

"I—no one."

His jaw tightened, and though I owed the smelly merchant nothing, in that moment I feared for him.

"At least not on purpose," I amended. "A courtier ran into me by accident and my ankle twisted." I placed my elbow on the banister for support as I held up my hands to calm him, the prince who looked ready to bash someone's face in. "And I fell on smashed goblets."

"Who fell on you?"

"I don't know his name," I huffed back as pain shot from my ankle up my leg. "But I'm positive that they didn't mean to."

Prince Vale didn't look so sure. "Come with me."

"What about Roar?" I looked into the arena. "Where is he?"

"Soldiers pulled him out of the arena right away." He gestured, presumably in the direction they'd gone. "They're taking him to the healers."

"I need to go to him."

"Of course." The prince waved for me to follow, but the moment I took one more step, my knees buckled.

A hiss left my lips, and I caught myself on the stone balcony, pushing the glass deeper into my hands. I cried out in pain.

"Lady Neve!"

"It's my ankle. I—" I tried to take a step and again, my ankle couldn't hold my weight. Before I could try again, he caught me and scooped me into his arms.

My heart thudded. We were close, much too close. Roar had been upset when I ran into Prince Vale and now, we stood even closer. Burning moon, if Roar were to see . . .

"Let me down," I demanded.

"So you can fall again? I think not." His eyes dropped to my bloodied hands, awkwardly held against my fluttering stomach. "You'll get to the healers faster this way. To the warden." It looked like he hated saying that, but those words did the trick.

Roar might rage that I smelled like the prince again, but I'd get to the warden faster, just as a dutiful fiancée would aspire to do. As a friend would too.

"Take me to him," I said, and we took off.

CHAPTER 26

With me in his arms, Prince Vale raced like the wind out of the Aaberg Ring.

"Out of the way!" Prince Vale boomed, carving a path through the crowds desperate to hide in the city and the soldiers trying to direct fae to safety.

"Lady Neve! Wait! My lady, please!"

I jerked and craned my neck around the prince's impressive bulk to find Clemencia fighting against the waves of fae; her face frantic. I pointed. "That's my lady-in-waiting! Stop!"

"Are you sure?" Prince Vale didn't show the slightest interest in slowing, let alone stopping. "You're still bleeding everywhere."

"I'm not going to die, and I need to let her know where I'm going, or she'll worry."

He huffed, but slowed to a stop and waited as Clemencia dashed our way, tears shining in her eyes. "My lady, I'm so sorry. I tried to stay with you, but a soldier pushed me out of the royal box!"

"Which is what they're supposed to do to keep the people safe." Prince Vale's eyes narrowed. "Clearly, they failed on some accounts."

"True, but *I'm* to stay with my lady." Clemencia swallowed, taking in my wounds. "What happened to you?"

"It's nothing," I said, to which the other two shared unconvinced glances. "Prince Vale is taking me to the healers, and I'll need new clothes once they bandage me. Go to my room and get some?"

Clemencia inclined her head. "I'll meet you there."

"Thanks, Clem." The nickname flew out of my mouth before I even realized and though Clemencia's eyes widened as if she felt taken aback, she nodded and darted to the palace.

"Now we can go," I said.

"Oh, *can we*, now? Thank you ever so much for the command." Prince Vale sounded somewhat disgruntled but wasted no time in racing toward the palace and through an inconspicuous side door.

I looked around and realized I'd never been in this part of the palace before. However, I knew when we neared the healing wing because the scent of herbs filled the air. When we arrived, the prince kicked open the door and rushed inside.

The area resembled Althea's healing room, though with dozens of fae rushing around, rather than one serene half-troll. One fae wearing the white chains of a Master Healer stopped for the prince. "My prince, are you hurt?"

Prince Vale gestured at me. "No, but Lady Neve is. See to her."

The healer's eyebrows shot up as she took in my wounds. "Just your hands?"

"My legs too." I tried to peer beyond the healer. "Is Warden Roar here?"

"Her ankle is twisted too," the prince said, clearly not caring at all where the Warden of the West was at the moment.

"The warden is unconscious and being seen to. He's in expert hands, so do not interrupt. Now, let me look you over." The healer studied my hands and legs for a few seconds and shook her head. "There are far more dire cases we must see to first. We'll check on her when we can. Until then, the lady can lie over there." She pointed to a bed at the far end of the room.

"This is absurd," the prince retorted. "She's bleeding everywhere."

"And others have holes in their bellies." The Master Healer narrowed her eyes. "So, I respectfully request that you do not tell me how to do my job, my prince." With that, she left and began working once again.

Prince Vale seethed but took me to the bed and laid me down. I thought for sure that since I was safe, he'd leave. Instead, he turned to a small chest and opened it.

"What in the stars are you doing?" I shifted into a more comfortable position.

"Removing the glass from your hands and legs."

I blinked. "Are you capable of that?"

He turned, dark, serious eyes penetrating me. "I'm a warrior."

"*And?*"

"Do you think we have many healers, if *any* at all, standing by when our army fights orc tribes? When we defend villages from giants? Or when we—"

"I get it," I interrupted. "You can pull glass out of my hand."

"Of course I bleeding well can." He turned back around and removed several instruments from the drawer and sprayed a clean cloth with a solution that smelled of vinegar. When he faced me once more, the prince nodded. "Your hands."

I offered them, and he wiped the damp rag across my palms. I sucked in a breath as the glass shifted but said nothing. He was trying to be gentle, and I would not complain.

Once he cleaned as much of the blood off as possible, Prince Vale began to extract the glass shards. I hadn't been aware of just how many had cut into me, but it seemed like I'd absorbed all the glass from both goblets that had shattered. The prince's calloused fingers had to have pulled at least a dozen from each palm and placed each in a shallow metal bowl. With each extraction, I bled anew, and he needed to wipe up the blood to continue.

Finally, neither of us saw any more glass in my hands. He stood and grabbed a new towel as a young healer rushed over.

"Prince Vale?" the short, hairy brownie asked. "What are you doing?"

The prince squared his shoulders. "The Master Healer on duty wouldn't help Lady Neve, so I did."

The brownie paled. "I'm sure she didn't mean—"

"It doesn't matter what she meant. I took care of it." He waved his hand to dismiss the healer. "Carry on with what you were doing. When you can spare someone, show them here. Actually, if there is only one Master Healer here at present, go get more. My family pays four of them, do they not? And it seems as though you could use the help." He looked at me and sighed. "And Lady Neve has a twisted ankle, and that needs to be set properly by a master, not with a soldier's splint."

"Very well, my prince." The brownie bowed before running off.

I let out a soft exhale. "He's going to be worried for the rest of the day about the state of his job."

"They're doing their jobs, though, it's truly not good enough. I'll be speaking to Father about it later. Time to move on to your legs." He paused, as if only realizing what this meant, and cleared his throat. "Could you . . . lift your skirt?"

If I had not seen his cheeks turn red, I wouldn't have believed that Prince Vale ever blushed. I stared at him until he cleared his throat again, more loudly the second time.

"Oh, yes. Sorry." I blinked myself back to reality and pulled my skirt up to bare my shins, not at all shy about it. After all, I'd grown up bathing in common bathhouses, often where male guards checked on us. I did not flaunt my body around males, but I wasn't unaccustomed to others seeing it. Plus, I merely showed my *shins*. Of all my body parts, they did not rate as one of the most alluring.

"Very good." He didn't meet my eyes as he got to work, pulling out shards. Ping after ping of glass into the bowl, told me at least a dozen more shards had launched themselves into my shins.

"What happened to your wings?" Prince Vale asked.

The question took me by surprise. "Nothing. No arrow hit them."

"Not today, but in the past. They're scarred, just like your hands and arms."

At that, my fingers curled into soft fists that I brought to my sides.

He noticed the movements, his eyes flicking up and back away. "I apologize if it's a sensitive subject. But I'm a soldier and notice such things. Something happened." He kept working as he spoke, making conversation. A weird topic, though perhaps not for a warrior. I supposed they compared scars often.

"As a youngling, I fell into a patch of brambles."

"Hmm, the markings don't really look like that. And the ones on your wings look newer."

"I misspoke. The brambles only hurt my hands and arms. My wings were . . . attacked by orcs." My voice lowered as I did my best to sound pitiable.

It seemed to work. He stopped extracting glass and his dark brown eyes met mine. "I'm sorry. Your village was attacked?"

"My father and I were attacked while traveling," I corrected, sticking to the tale Roar and I had spun across the Western territory of Winter's Realm. "He died saving me."

"I'm so sorry, my lady."

"Thank you. It truly was awful."

He swallowed. "Yes, I'm sure. I've seen the aftermath of orc attacks, tried to stop them many times." He closed his eyes briefly, and I wondered if he was reliving horrors that he'd witnessed. When he opened them again, he didn't meet my gaze, just reached for a rag, cleaned up more blood.

"One of the castle's Master Healers developed a balm for scars. It's the best I've ever seen. Has even erased some of my oldest scars from when I was a youngling. And, unlike most balms, is sensitive enough to use on wings. When we're done here, I can ask if they have some to spare?"

My lips parted. That was unexpected. I wasn't sure what to say. Would it actually be better than the elixir Althea had given me? I supposed there was a chance. Althea was no master and the tissue of the wing had been too sensitive for Althea's balm.

"It's just," the prince said when I didn't answer, "I know that scars can trigger memories."

Of course he'd know about that. Even if he had left Roar to his own devices that one time, Prince Vale was known far and wide as the Warrior Bear. He had to have seen a few things that haunted him.

"I'd appreciate that," I said finally. "Thank you."

He smiled, which softened his entire face. "The least I can do."

I didn't know how to reply to that, so I just remained quiet as he worked, and more glass pinged into the bowl.

"Can you fly or did the attack alter your wings irrevocably?" He broke the silence. I wondered if he was uncomfortable with the quiet.

"It did." I sighed. "I can do it, though I'm not very good anymore."

"Which explains why you were crawling from the royal box and did not soar away." His lips downturned. "I often feel bad for fae without wings. They are much more defenseless than those with them."

I couldn't argue with that. For most of my life, my wings had been rendered as useless as my magic, and I had been one of the fae he pitied.

I was about to ask about one of his soldierly exploits, if only to get the topic off of me, when he stopped and made eye contact. "I see more, but they're higher up."

Nonplussed, I lifted my skirt a touch more.

His eyes widened. "Lady Neve."

"What?"

He cleared his throat, cheeks going red again. I almost laughed at the sight but held it back. He appeared much too mortified . . . and worried. "I can barely see it, but there's a large piece of glass between your thighs."

"No, there isn't." I shifted to sit up. "Where?"

Hesitantly, he pressed a hand to my skirt, which I only then realized wasn't just bloody but torn. Through the rip, glass glinted, a large shard, just as he'd said.

"*How* did I not feel that?"

"Soldiers can block out pain when they need to. Especially when it's life or death. You must have done the same." Prince Vale shook his head. "A Master Healer will have to close it up. Unlike the more shallow cuts, it needs magical help. But it will need to come out quickly to avoid infection, and I need to bandage it." He stared at the wound, cheeks turning red. "I can start the job. But how to extract and bandage it quickly? I'll have to lift your thigh too . . ."

Luckily, at that moment, Clemencia arrived, her arms laden with dresses. "I wasn't sure what you would find more comfortable, so I brought four." She eyed my bare legs, and her lips pursed. "What's happening?"

"I have a large shard of glass stuck in my inner thigh." I was still shocked I hadn't felt it because now that I'd become aware of the glass, it had started to burn. "Prince Vale is trying to figure out how to remove it and bandage it."

"I'll help." She laid the gowns across a chair.

"Are you sure?" I'd known Clemencia for almost two weeks. Never had she mentioned she had even basic healing skills.

Clemencia met my gaze with a firm nod. "You're my lady. What do I need to do?"

Prince Vale straightened and rolled his shoulders back. Apparently, Clemencia's presence had pulled him from his embarrassment over seeing a lady's bare thigh. He looked ready for action.

"I'll lift her leg and pull out the shard," the prince said. "Before I pull it out, though, we'll place a wrap beneath her leg, and when the blood pours, tie it up. Can you manage?"

"Certainly." My lady-in-waiting rolled up her sleeves with a determined expression on her face.

I was impressed. Not just by the fortitude of my lady-in-waiting, but by how the prince acted. His gruff demeanor from the night before was nowhere in sight. He seemed so different from the faeries I'd run into in the hallways. Also the person Roar had told me about.

I did not have long to wonder at this, however, for the pair got to work. First, Clemencia washed my legs and Prince Vale swept in after her, extracting the smaller bits of glass higher up. There were fewer shards than in my hands, so that didn't take long. Once they finished, the prince applied a tourniquet in preparation for extracting the larger piece and pointed to the bandage roll. My lady-in-waiting set to cutting off a length as Prince Vale moved around my leg. "I'm going to lift it now. Apologies for the proximity." His wings tightened and flexed behind him, and his jaw ticked. The prince looked so uncomfortable, and yet, for a moment, something else flashed in his eyes that I couldn't pinpoint.

"It will be fine." I waved off his concern.

He reached beneath my thigh and lifted my leg enough to allow Clemencia to slide the bandage beneath. At the prince's touch, my skin burned. He gripped me so tightly the callouses on his fingers and palms pressed into me, making me extra aware of our closeness. I swallowed.

"Are you alright?" Prince Vale caught my gaze.

"I am."

"Good. I'm going to pull the shard out now. There will be blood."

"You should look away, my lady," Clemencia whispered.

"I want to see." It was my body, and for so long, I hadn't had a choice over what happened to me. I'd watched Prince Vale extract every other shard of glass, and I'd do the same for the final one.

The prince studied me, approval flashed in his eyes, and he reached down and pulled.

Pain shot through me, and blood gushed. I hissed and jolted, but the prince held my leg tightly, pressing his chest against my outer thigh to still me. Clemencia proved quick and skilled as she wrapped the bandage around my leg and tied it up.

Once the bandage had been set, he lowered my leg, released me, and studied the binding. "Well done. It seems to contain the blood, so the shard didn't go as deep as I thought. Thank the stars, and thank you for your help, Clem."

"It's Clemencia," she corrected him.

"Apologies. Lady Neve called you Clem."

For a moment, my lady's eyes darted to me. A hint of a smile flitted across her lips. "She did, but we do not know one another like I know her, my prince. For now, Clemencia will do."

He seemed nonplussed by this, no doubt used to boundaries with his staff, but my heart swelled. The nickname had slipped out, but I'd thought it a few times and wondered if Clemencia would care. Maybe she considered us friends.

"Your Highness?" Clemencia ventured.

"Yes?"

"I was wondering, what will happen to the attackers?" My lady-in-waiting watched him expectantly.

Prince Vale stayed silent for a moment before he answered. "My father will decide their fates, but I can tell you they are in the dungeons now."

"Were they rebels?" Clemencia pressed. "Anti-monarchists?"

"I suspect both," he replied with a twist of his lips. "They were aiming for my father, not Warden Roar. Although I am certain they were not upset to hit him as the warden is an important figure."

It was the first time that Prince Vale spoke about Roar in an even remotely positive way. To be fair, he did not seem to relish it, but spoke it more like an unfortunate fact.

Another Master Healer arrived—not the first faerie who had denied me care, but a fae race that I couldn't quite place.

"There's an ankle to heal?" The healer's tone sounded lyrical.

Prince Vale pointed at me. "Lady Neve, Warden Roar's fiancée."

"Oh, dear." The healer looked at me with wide eyes. "You'll be happy to know that your fiancé is still asleep but healing nicely. We're performing layered enchantments on him now."

"Wonderful," I said with a soft exhale.

She approached and laid a hand on my ankle. Her touch felt rough, like tree bark, and her race of fae became clear; she was a dryad. It surprised me as her skin didn't *look* like bark, nor was her hair a vivid shade of pink, blue, or green, which seemed to be common with her kind.

"It's quite swollen, but nothing that I cannot fix. Do you mind?" The dryad gazed up at me.

I shook my head. "Do whatever you must."

She began to work, and immediately, relief flooded me. Minute by minute, the swelling lessened until the healer leaned back. "Your sprain is all good. Whatever swelling remains will be gone by the morning. Do try to stay off of it, though."

"I will. Thank you."

"Can you seal deeper wounds too?" the prince asked. He'd been quiet, standing behind the healer the entire time, watching. "She has one on her inner thigh. It—"

"How would you know the state of my fiancée's thigh, Prince Vale?" A sharp voice cut Prince Vale off, and suddenly Roar was speeding over, knocking over a cart and slamming into a small fae as he went. He appeared dazed, stumbling slightly, possibly because he was still under the influence of healing spells or potions, but also red-faced and furious.

I swallowed thickly. "Roar! Please be still! You're hurt!"

"Why does he know about your thigh, my love?" Roar growled territorially.

"He helped me get here. I couldn't walk, and you weren't around."

"Because I'd *been shot*!"

"Of course." I held up my hand. "I wasn't saying that you weren't there for me because you didn't want to be. I meant—"

"I wasn't there for you, but *he* was?" Roar reached us and leaned against my bed to thrust a finger at the prince. "Is that how it is, my love?"

"Seems that way," Prince Vale answered, unable to hide the smugness in his tone.

"It also seems that out of all the royal guards and the soldiers in the arena, I was the one to save the king from an arrow," Roar retorted. "Shouldn't that have been you? The famed Warrior Bear?"

The prince's jaw worked from side to side, and though it would only cause more trouble, I desperately wanted to speak up for him, to tell Roar he was acting ridiculous.

But I had no need, for at that moment, Prince Vale stormed out of the healing sanctuary.

CHAPTER 27

Eventually, both the warden and I returned to the Lisika suite. Once we were alone, I tried to talk to him, to make him see sense, but Roar would hear none of it. Instead, he stormed into his room, slamming the door behind him. Sighing, I too retreated to my room to wash up and consider how to better broach the subject of Prince Vale.

I, as much as anyone, knew people in power were not always kind, and the story Roar had told me of the prince was absolutely infuriating. And yet, the prince's recent actions had softened me toward him a touch. He was more than just a pretty face now, but a fuller person, and a bit of a mystery.

After I washed the lingering smell of healing potions and vinegar from my skin, I checked my cuts. Between the potions and balms the healer had applied topically and my own accelerated healing abilities, most of the

ASHLEY MCLEO

smaller cuts were already healed. The larger ones would probably be fine by tomorrow.

Finally clean and cared for, I slipped on a simple crimson shift dress that closed high at the neck with a gold brooch and asked Clemencia for privacy. Once she was in her room, I approached the warden, who had decided to read in the antechamber area as though nothing at all had happened.

Like me, he had cleaned and dressed in finery, though beneath his tunic, he still wore bandages just in case his wound opened and began bleeding again. The Master Healer had assured us that this probably would not happen, that they'd layered many enchantments onto the warden and pumped him with healing potions, but as he was a very important figure in the kingdom, they were playing it safe. Roar was to wear the bandage until right before the ball.

Though I studied him, and he must have felt my gaze, Roar didn't look up from the book he pretended to read, not even as I stood right in front of him. After a full minute of the warden ignoring me, I sighed. "Roar, this is absurd."

"Is it?" Roar's eyes lingered on the page. Not a single muscle moved to accept me. "You seem to be a magnet for the one faerie I despise the most. That's absurd to you?"

My throat tightened. "No, but I never seek Prince Vale. The first time was a pure coincidence. I turned a corner and ran into him. How can you be mad about that? The second—"

Roar hurled the book across the room, where it slammed into a wall, making me jump. "In this world, there are *no* coincidences. Among the Sacred Eight, *everything* is calculated, Neve. Why can't you see that?"

I could see the calculations, the scheming. I hadn't been here long, but it became plain to me that the highest-ranking fae played a different sort of game, the game of houses. And they played for only one prize: power.

However, that didn't fit with my time with Prince Vale. It was common knowledge that he and Roar did not get on, and yet, the prince had helped me. He'd stayed with me in the healers' sanctuary and did what he could to ensure my cuts didn't become infected. If the prince had been playing the game of houses, he'd have left his rival's fiancée to suffer while healers attended to others.

I sat next to Roar. "I understand why you dislike him, and I don't like him for what he did to you and your soldiers." I let out a long exhale. "But I *am* glad he helped me to the sanctuary. Did you know I didn't even feel the glass in my inner thigh? Imagine if it would have dislodged while I walked? Or if while I walked, I caused it to work its way deeper into me and something more serious happened? The entire kingdom fled the Ring, Roar. What else was I to do?"

At that, his face softened. "Stars, Neve . . . Of course you're right. You could do nothing."

For a moment, silence hung between us. I'd done my part—extended a rowan branch. It was his turn to try and mend this splinter between us. And if there was one thing growing up among vampires had taught me, it was that silence could be as powerful as words.

He released a long sigh. "I never would have forgiven myself if I made a calculated risk on my life that saved the king, and you suffered for it." He stood and hooked his finger beneath my chin. "Are you well, now?"

My shoulders loosened. "I am. A Master Healer fixed my ankle, and they doused me in potions and such before I left. I'll be fine by tomorrow."

"My first thought after the arrow pierced my shoulder was of you." His emerald eyes sparkled, and he seemed to look deeper inside me, as if he wished to touch my soul with his.

I grew warmer—uncomfortable. Was he going to try to kiss me again?

Warden Roar was charming, attractive, and kind. He had a temper to be certain, but no one was perfect. And shockingly, at least for me, he'd admitted to having feelings for me.

So why did this feel . . . off? Even if I'd wanted him in the same way that he wanted me, I wasn't sure it would be right. Roar simply kept too much to himself, and while I trusted him in our deal, I didn't really know him. Not deep down.

And most importantly, why did he keep trying to be closer when I'd set the boundary at being friends?

Physical limits were part of our deal. While I could excuse the first advance, even the second due to circumstances, any more and . . . I wasn't so sure what he was trying to do.

Roar, seeing that he'd lost me, frowned.

I leaned back, looked away. "Today was trying."

He straightened and a short silence stretched between us. "Yes."

A knock at the door spared us another uncomfortable word. I looked at Roar, who shrugged. Seeing as Clemencia had made herself scarce at my bidding, I answered it and found a fae with antlers, deer-like legs, and cloven feet holding out a letter.

"For the Warden of the West and his betrothed." He bowed shallowly, mindful of his antlers.

"Thank you." I took the letter and examined the parchment as I shut the door. The paper was fine and thick, more so than the invitation to the tourney had been. When I turned it over, a royal blue seal with a bear stamped in the wax stared back at me. "This is from the royal house."

"Well, what are you waiting for? Open it." Roar eyed it with interest.

Somewhat surprised that he didn't want to do so, I did as he asked and read the contents. "The king wishes to see us as soon as possible. The same messenger will wait at the end of the hall to escort us when we're ready."

Roar gestured to my dress. "Are you comfortable presenting in that?"

"I am."

"Then, we'll go now."

I set the letter down, poked my head into Clemencia's room, and told her we'd be back soon. As instructed, the messenger waited for us at the end of the hall. He bowed again when we approached.

"Right this way, my lord, my lady." As the messenger walked, his cloven feet struck the diamond patterned floor, so that his steps echoed through the castle.

Roar and I simply remained silent and followed. Again, someone led me through parts of the palace I had not seen. From the outside, Frostveil Castle loomed over Avaldenn, impressive and vast and as sparking white as snow. Inside, it unfolded larger by the day. How much bigger would it be if the royals could access the parts of the palace that used magic to evade them?

After about ten minutes, the messenger turned right and led us to the end of a hallway, where a set of gold double doors imprinted with snowflakes stood. Two armed soldiers framed the doors, though they did not acknowledge us. They were Clawsguards, beholden only to the royal family.

"The king waits for Warden Roar and Lady Neve," the messenger said to the guards, who didn't even blink. Just when I thought we'd have to ask someone else to let us in, however, one gripped the doorhandles.

The messenger clasped his hands together. "I will remain here to escort you back."

"Thank you," Roar said, as the door opened to reveal a semi-sheer navy curtain.

Confusion set in but dispelled almost right away as sounds of feminine laughter rang out, mixed with lower tones of moaning and gasps. My cheeks warmed. It was well-known that the king had a harem, and it seemed we would be welcomed inside that den of sin.

"I'm with you." Roar reached out a hand.

"By the stars, why did he bring us here?"

The warden shrugged. "He's the king."

"But why would someone want to come here?" My skin crawled. "Doesn't he think it odd? Invasive?"

"Many of the lords in Avaldenn frequent the harem at the king's invitation."

"Have *you*?"

"No. I try to avoid the city as much as I can." Roar sighed. "Let's see what he wants."

No one denied King Magnus, certainly not a couple trying to win his favor and blessing, so I straightened my shoulders and approached the curtain. Before we had even pushed past the curtain, the doors shut, sealing us inside.

The scent of jasmine overwhelmed me as a warm humidity I was not used to hugged my skin. I swallowed as, step by step, the room unveiled itself, each sight invoking a new emotion, not all of them unpleasant. Attractive females and a few males lounged and laughed on velvet cushions, and that brought a sliver of happiness. The scenery, a sort of indoor oasis complete with a pool surrounded by gorgeous flowers explained the humidity and was pleasing to the eye, though the whole thing felt distinctly off in Frostveil Castle. I imagined such a scene would look more natural in the Summer Court.

But then I spotted the displays of copulation and other acts that no one, save for the participants, should be privy to and the illusion of paradise was shattered. I looked away, mortified for the fae, both female and male, some costumed, some bare as the day they were born, some being treated viciously, and all of them being used by others—lords of the kingdom, judging by their dress.

I enjoyed sex, but this? It made me uncomfortable and furious. It was wrong.

When the king, surrounded by female fae of all races and various stages of dress, called for our attention, I had to push my emotions to the side. I needed to remain sharp and think of us, our futures, *our lives*.

"Majesty." Roar approached the king first and knelt.

I came next, standing slightly behind the warden, and curtsied. The act felt preposterous in a place of such depravity. "Your Majesty."

"Yes, yes. Rise." When the king spoke, the reek of wine washed over me. Stars, how much had he downed since the tourney?

We stood together.

"You called, my king?" Roar met King Magnus in the eye, even when a female fae with scaled arms sat in his lap and pressed her lips to the king's jaw, trailing kisses upward. Another of her race stood behind him, rubbing his shoulders. The other two fae, both faeries, lounged at his sides, breasts bare and bodies clad in outfits that covered practically nothing.

"Leave me, my lovelies. I wish to speak with the warden and his lady alone."

Pouting, the scaled fae slipped off the king's lap. The

other three slinked off with more grace, leaving us alone with the king.

He didn't even straighten, just clapped two hands together, as if this was a normal meeting. "I wish to thank you for your service today, Lord Roar. For taking that arrow meant for me."

Roar inclined his head. "Any loyal servant would, my king."

"The attackers have been in the dungeons since the attack. They're rebel forces, and one admitted to targeting me and my family." King Magnus cleared his throat. "You've done your kingdom and your king a great service. I always acknowledge those who have served me well."

Roar shifted. Had the circumstances been different, he might have questioned such a claim. He felt slighted by the king, the fae who expected House Lisika to provide soldiers whenever the crown wished and taxed Roar's people the same as the rest of the kingdom, despite their sacrifices. The king had not even visited the West since Roar's parents perished; a slight known by all in the kingdom.

"I know how to repay you." The king's eyes, a startling icy shade of blue that held none of the warmth Saga's did, shifted to me. "I will not stand in the way of your betrothal. I will not arrange a different engagement for you, as I intended to do. You and Lady Neve may wed and even announce your intent before the Crown and the Grand Staret of Avaldenn at the opening of the Courting Festival. An honor, as you know, Warden."

I'd met High Staret Celi, but I hadn't realized that the

royal house gave the leading staret of Avaldenn an *extra special* title. I suspected that made him the leaders of all holy fae.

For the first time since we'd arrived, Roar smiled. "Thank you, my king."

"However . . ." King Magnus held up his hand, calloused and red, cracked from the cold. "You will remain for the duration of the Courting Festival."

"But why, my king?" Roar frowned. "If we have your blessing, there is no reason to be here."

Or get me out of the Winter's Realm.

"The Courting Festival is not only to make matches but to bring together the lords and ladies of the land. Your fiancée will do well to remain here. As will you." The king rose, stretched, strutted to a nearby table, and poured himself a glass of wine.

As he poured, I shot Roar a glance. Could we fight it? Was it worth it?

Roar shook his head, and I frowned. Fine. I wouldn't press. Not now, anyway. It grew late, and even if we could leave, we wouldn't do so tonight. Roar's troops and the few servants he'd brought to attend us on the return journey west were scattered throughout Avaldenn, probably already tucked in their beds.

But I still had questions.

"My king?" I asked.

King Magnus turned, his eyes wide, as if he hadn't expected me to speak at all. "Yes, Lady Neve?"

"I was wondering, what will you do with the rebels? And, excuse my ignorance, in my village we did not hear of such things, but what were they rebelling against?"

For a moment, the king's face soured, but he sipped his wine as if it softened the frustration my words brought him. He shook his head. "The bleeding rebels. They call me a usurper and wish to see me ousted."

"Preposterous." Roar shook his head. "I was but six turns when the rebellion began, but I recalled my father mentioning the atrocities of the late Cruel King many times. You saved Winter's Realm, my king."

King Magnus looked him over, as if considering Roar's words. "Your father was a good lord. Pity the Fates took him from us too soon."

"May the stars protect his soul," Roar replied.

Hearing the sadness in his tone, I took his hand.

The king eyed the gesture. "They believe another Falk is out there, a bastard no doubt. The Cruel King had many. They would see that lowborn ilk on the throne." He returned to his seat and plopped down without grace. "As for what to do with the rebels, I have a plan. I will reveal it tomorrow."

His tone sounded ominous, and though I'd asked about the rebels, I was no longer sure that I wanted to learn of their fate. So, I merely inclined my head as if I agreed, as if I wasn't dying to leave. Anything to get us out of here faster.

A peal of laughter caught the king's attention, and he grinned lecherously. "I am wanted. Lord Roar, Lady Neve, join me and my queen for breakfast tomorrow." The king rose.

"We will, my king. Thank you. I'll escort my lady back to our chambers now." With Roar still clutching my hand, we turned to go.

"I didn't say that you could *go*, Warden. You stay. My messenger will show your lady fiancée back."

My mouth dropped open. Was he serious?

"My king, I—"

"You will be wed soon and wish that I had given you this chance. Plus, my concubines enjoy a hero!" Magnus clapped Roar on the back and though the warden stood as a tall fae, the king looked bear-like in proportions. "As your monarch, I insist."

My jaw tightened. Even though Roar and I were not really together, the king's command rankled. How dare the king push a female on a fae who was engaged! One who was not even interested! Did he have no honor?

"Very well, my king. But might I have a moment with my lady?" Roar's gaze beseeched the king, and though the king did not appear impressed, he nodded. "Come to the falls. I have a nymph you should meet." With that, King Magnus left.

Roar turned to me. "I'm sorry. I—"

"You did nothing," I cut him off, my gaze veering to the concubines again and my stomach rolling. "Though I can't say I'm impressed with your monarch. This place is disgusting."

"*Our* monarch," Roar whispered. "Be careful with your words. You never know who is listening."

He was right, of course. Places such as this one had spiders everywhere.

"I'll leave as soon as I can." He clutched my hand. "I don't want to be here. Even if we've had troubling times, I'd rather be with you."

My heart swelled. Our friendship might be rocky at the moment, but we endured this together, and I needed this partnership to work.

"If not tonight, I'll see you in the morn." I leaned in and kissed him on the cheek.

"Warden! Come!" the king bellowed.

"Appease him," I said. "I'll see you later."

Roar sighed and joined the king, prepared to do whatever it took to make King Magnus happy. Whatever it took for us to leave sooner rather than later.

CHAPTER 28

As promised, my escort waited outside the harem door, and when I exited alone, he looked at me expectantly.

"My Lord Roar will not be joining me."

The guards flanking the door to the harem's wing remained stoney, but the messenger's doe eyes widened for a moment before he caught himself and inclined his head. "Does my lady wish to return to her chambers?"

"I do."

We left, and with every step we took, my anger grew. And not just for my situation with Roar.

Brothels, at least, had contracts with their whores, but Roar had told me the king's concubines had no say in what happened to them or who they bedded. In that, they were like the blood slaves—especially the ones owned by masters who did, in fact, use them sexually.

The unjust issue continued to distract me as I followed the messenger through the palace. It distracted me so much that I didn't hear footsteps coming our way until Calpurnia Vagle, Adila Ithamai, and another short, curvy faerie rounded the corner. I swallowed, but there was no hiding. We were only a couple dozen of paces apart and the trio spotted me instantly. As usual, Calpurnia scowled as she looked me over.

"Lady Vagle, Ladies Ithamai." My escort bowed, and I noted his use of plural in reference to the Ithamai House. "Good evening."

"One that is about to get much better." Calpurnia sneered at us. "Leave."

The escort reared back slightly. "Me, my lady?"

"Are you deaf? Of course I mean you." Calpurnia narrowed her eyes at him.

He stiffened. "But I am to see Lady Neve to her chambers."

"We'll help her." Adila's voice sounded soft and sweet, but I caught the hard glint in her eyes. "I'd like to get to know Lady Neve." She nodded to me as if she meant it. "I'm Adila Ithamai."

I acted like Saga had not already told me this and curtsied. "A pleasure, my lady."

"And I'm Hadia Ithamai." The plumper of the sisters nodded. "Now, *you* really should leave." She glared at my escort.

He tossed me an apologetic glance and left me to the direwolves. The moment we stood alone; my heart began to race.

"So, Neve, how did you like the tourney today?"

Calpurnia placed her hands on her hips. "Probably quite a big to do for someone from your background?"

"It was eventful."

Calpurnia nodded, as if she weren't a snake planning to strike. "Particularly when the warden you stole took an arrow for our sweet king."

I wanted to say that their king was anything but sweet. Instead, I managed a smile. "Roar was quite brave. He—"

"Use his title you undeserving creature," Hadia hissed. At her side, her fists formed tight balls. "Warden Roar should be with a lady of the Sacred Eight. One who understands decorum. And one with no hideous scars marring her body."

Fury built inside me. I didn't love my scars, but I'd earned each one by living through a difficult time. What had Hadia ever done? Sit in a castle and be waited upon?

"I can't help that you think that, but *Roar* does not."

Hadia bristled, but her sister swept in before she could lay into me again.

"He's infatuated." Adila snorted, with a loose twirl of her hand. "Once he's done enjoying you, he'll discard you. We can only hope it will be before the Courting Festival is over so that the king will not worry about upsetting the entire west and set a *proper* match."

Calpurnia's lips flattened. It stunned me, according to Princess Saga, all three faeries wanted Roar as a husband, and yet they hated *me*. Why did they not despise one another?

Oh, that's right, because I'm the one that doesn't belong. I'm just the common fae taking their lord.

"Where did you come from, anyway?" Calpurnia asked. "There's not much this way, except . . ." She trailed off and her eyes widened. "The king's harem lives in this wing."

My stomach flipped. "How would you know?"

Calpurnia snorted. "I live at the palace for weeks on end."

"Why were you there? Whoring for the king too?" Adila took a step closer.

"We should tell the warden!" Hadia beamed.

I would not admit that both Roar and I had seen the harem, or that Roar remained there.

"Do what you will." I lifted my chin. "I'll be going to my rooms now." I wove around them, in the direction that the messenger had gone.

"We didn't say that you could leave," Calpurnia snarled. "You might have entranced a warden and Saga might have indulged you, but I will do no such thing. I'm a lady fae of a great house, and you are a commoner. You will wait until I release you."

I most certainly wouldn't, and as I did not turn and acknowledge her, I trusted the trio would get the hint.

I did not, however, expect to be bowled over by a wave of air magic. I gasped and fell to the floor, my hands catching me before my face hit.

"How dare you!" Calpurnia shrieked and another stream of power slammed into me, the wind so powerful it flattened me to the ground. "How dare you ignore your betters!"

"Let me!" Adila's soft voice cooed, malicious and conniving. A moment later, a bed of air lifted me and left my feet dangling well above the ground.

"Let me down," I growled, furious, embarrassed, and worried. Unlike these ladies, I had no magic to draw upon.

Adila shrugged. "If you wish."

I dropped, and only a clumsy fluttering of my wings prevented me from collapsing. The girls laughed.

"Did you see that? Can you even fly properly?" Hadia scoffed. "Or are you an idiot?"

"Better an idiot than a highborn lady looked over by a commoner, don't you think?" I regretted the words the moment I said them. The ladies' faces grew stoney, and magic built in the air. So I did the only thing I could do; I spun and ran.

"Get her!" Calpurnia shrieked. "I'm going to tear up that pretty face!"

Footsteps followed, slamming against the stone ground, and magic shot by me. One blast of air came so close that my hair flew around my face. I pushed my legs, willing them to go faster. Within seconds, the sounds of the ladies following me dimmed.

"*Fly!*" Adila screamed. "We have to catch her!"

Bleeding skies, they might be slow runners, but I would bet they weren't slow fliers. I cast a wild glance around, looking for a place to hide. Heavy tapestries lined both sides of the wall, from floor to ceiling. Would they do?

As the ladies' voices got closer, I realized it was my only shot. I could not outrun someone in flight, nor could I fly well enough yet to beat those who'd been flying all their lives. Quickly, I dashed to the wall and slid behind the tapestry, willing myself to become as small as possible, pressing my back into the wall.

Then, my hand brushed metal. I gasped. A door? Had I stumbled on a hidden tower like the one Saga had shown me?

The voices sounded far enough away, and I didn't know where the door led, but figured it would make a better hiding spot than this. Slowly, I twisted the handle and pulled open the door. A faint flash of light nearly blinded me. I stopped, and the skin on my arms prickled. Had they seen that?

"This way!" Calpurnia screamed.

I sucked in a breath. Whatever that light and the sensation had been, whatever they might do to me, I had to risk it. I pushed the door and slid through.

Once on the other side, I closed the door and pressed my back to the wood.

My chest heaved, but I forced myself to quiet my breath and to listen for the highborn ladies.

Had they turned around?

No. They had been so determined to hurt me. But I kept listening, and no sounds filtered through the wall. I pressed off, sure the trio would have passed the area. I would be safe for now.

Exhaling, I looked around. I wasn't in a stairwell, like the one Saga had shown me that led up to her secret tower, but rather a wide corridor. One that smelled stale, as if they had not cleaned it in a long time.

I cocked my head. From what I'd seen, the servants kept Frostveil Palace immaculate.

As I didn't want to poke my head back into the hallway yet, I strolled down the corridor, trying to pinpoint where I was in the palace.

The further I got, the more confused I became.

As in the other hallways, portraits and tapestries lined the walls, but these did not show white bears or the fae of the royal family.

Rather, faeries dressed in exquisite violet gowns and doublets stared back at me, landscapes of places I'd not been, and most peculiar of all, a painting of two faeries flying with white hawks.

My hand flew to cover my mouth. Had I stumbled into a part of the palace hidden magically from the Aabergs? But how did I get here? Chills dashed down my spine.

Was I the first person in two decades to see this place?

Unable to help myself, I continued exploring. A violet silk dress stood on display in a case. Below it, a plaque stating that it was Sassa Falk's coronation dress. Another display held a steel dagger crafted by a dwarf king in the mountains and gifted to an early Falk king. Dust covered every surface, hinting that no one had been back here in a long time. This had to be part of the palace that the royals could not access, and the castle had shown it to me.

Did it show it to me out of goodwill? Or perhaps it had taken pity on me?

I found the idea that the palace had a personality, a will of its own that it exhibited, odd, but no matter. When pitted against stronger and vengeful fae like Calpurnia and her gang, I'd take a little pity and protection. Some fae might believe me weak for thinking that, but they probably had magic to defend themselves. And I was not too proud. At least not most of the time.

Continuing on, I marveled at the art, all the blatant Falk imagery. One image showed the late King Harald, his wife, Revna, and their many children sitting for a formal portrait. The king stood next to his wife, who was the only one sitting. King Harald looked much like King Magnus, with long white hair and bright blue eyes. Considering that King Harald was King Magnus's uncle, that did not surprise me. I shifted to the queen. Stars, she was stunning. With long black hair, violet eyes, and a jawline that could cut diamonds, the queen commanded the portrait.

Four males, three of them adults and the other around thirteen turns of age surrounded their parents. In her arms, the queen held two infants swaddled in violet blankets. The infants' faces gave no clue as to their sex.

The Falk brood had been large indeed. Happy looking too, I thought as I took in the smiles and the mischievous expression of the younger boy.

Stars, King Magnus would have a fit if he knew all this was back here.

I had moved on to examine a painting of a battle, one

titled Sassa's Revenge, when a sound filtered through the hallway. I stilled, listened.

Is that . . . singing?

I stiffened. Had I been wrong and someone else lingered in this area? A male, judging by the voice.

Taking greater care to keep my footsteps soft, I followed the sound. The closer it got, the curiouser I became. How could someone know of this and keep it a secret? Was it the rebels?

While I should have been terrified by that notion, I was actually far too curious to stop. After a few minutes of searching, I reached a point where the person singing sounded so close; it was like they stood beside me. But they weren't there.

Spinning on my heel, I took in the area again. No fae hung around this hallway, but two doors stood on opposite sides of me. I veered to the right, opened the first one. A study or den of some sort revealed itself to be empty. Pivoting, I went to the other door and opened it to find myself in a smaller hallway. Or maybe a long entryway?

I glanced left and right and saw no fae, but to the left were other doors. One was slightly ajar, revealing a bathroom.

The singing was so close, and I thought to the right, where the short hallway seemed to open into a room. Perhaps they were just around the corner? I shut the door behind me and began to investigate, stopping only when the hallway funneled me into a room.

A bedroom.

In which Prince Vale stood, shirt off, polishing his long sword.

I couldn't even appreciate the beautiful sight, for my heart rate spiked as realization of where I was set in. The room the prince stood in was relatively clean, with clothing tossed over a chair, but not a speck of dust in sight. The door I'd taken somehow funneled me into the prince's private suite.

Blood thrumming in my ears, I backed quickly into the entry hall again, determined to make it back to the hidden part of the castle to escape. But that plan came crashing down when I tripped over my own feet, fell flat on my arse, making a racket that no one could fail to hear.

"Who's there?" Metal clanged. Footsteps sounded and stopped. "Lady Neve? What are you doing in my chambers?"

"I—I got lost." I picked myself up off the floor and did my best to keep the color creeping up my neck at bay.

"How did you get past my guard unannounced?" Prince Vale frowned and glanced at the door at the end of his entry hall. That must be the door to the main part of the palace, where his guard would stand.

I swallowed. How would someone like me have gotten by a guard? I could pretend like his guard had announced me, but the prince hadn't heard because of the singing. Would that work? Or did I show him the door?

Quickly enough, I concluded I had to show him. Roar and I had just earned the king's blessing, but that could be taken away in an instant. Especially if they thought me a spy. Or worse, a rebel. I would be better off taking my chances with Prince Vale and telling the truth.

"Over here. There's a door." I went back to where I'd exited into the short entry hallway leading to his room. When I reached the spot, I pressed my hand against the wall. As there was no handle, I thought that it would swing inward. It did not.

The prince narrowed his eyes. "Do you take me for a fool, Lady Neve?"

"No! There's a hidden hallway behind here and tons of rooms! I promise. I—" It hit me then that the reason I could not locate the door was because Vale Aaberg was not a Falk. Certainly, his father carried bastard Falk blood, but King Magnus had also killed his entire biological family. King Magnus and his children were not Falk in the ways that mattered. The palace would not protect him, like it did me—a nobody.

"*A hidden door*," he murmured, and his eyes lit up. "To the long closed off part of the palace?"

Of course, he would know that the palace had concealed portions of itself off to his family. If Clemencia knew, then it wasn't a secret.

"But why would it allow you back there?" he demanded, a new tone in his voice. It took me a moment to register it as excitement.

"I can't say. I was in need of refuge and found a door." I swallowed, hoping that he'd believe me.

It was almost laughable, really. This time I was actually telling the truth, whereas I'd been lying through my teeth, and no one had outwardly questioned me.

He studied me with interest and as the seconds passed, any hope I had left withered.

"Warden Roar would be very irate to find you here," the prince finally said with a frown. "Shall I have someone show you back to your room?"

My mouth fell open. He wasn't going to press? Why? In his position, I surely would. I—I stopped my thoughts before I could get into more trouble and closed my mouth.

The better question was why was I just standing around questioning this mercy?

"I know the way!" I lied and nodded frantically, not about to add another person to the web of lies I'd spun tonight. I'd figure it out even if I had to walk every hallway unescorted. "Goodnight!"

Before he said another word, I turned and dashed down the entryway, passing the toilet room, and the other rooms, one that appeared to be a personal study and another room filled with swords.

When I got to the door leading into the main hall, I pulled it open and shut it quickly behind me. When I turned, I found a Clawsguard with skin as pale as the moon staring at me in horror.

"How did you get in there?" the guard asked, hand gravitating to his sword, violet eyes wide.

"I–uh." By the stars, I'd been so relieved to be dismissed by the prince that I hadn't even worried about the guard at his door.

I was still fumbling for a lie when a voice boomed from inside the prince's room.

"Let her go, Sir Qildor."

"Ah, yes, my prince." The guard stepped aside, looking like he wanted to do anything but follow orders.

Taking the grace I'd been shown, I scurried back to my room.

CHAPTER 29

Worry struck me the moment I woke up the next day.

Would Prince Vale mention I'd been in his suite? And who would he tell? Or would the guard spread a rumor? Fates, what would I say if Roar confronted me? Or even the king?

Why had the prince even let me go?

I rose, hoping answers might come faster in the bath. The sprinkling of snow lily petals in the water made the room smell floral, much like Clemencia's signature perfume. As I slipped into the copper clawfoot tub, I sighed, but still answers did not come.

My mockery of peace proved short-lived, however, as Clemencia knocked and entered before I could say a word. She held a tin in her hand, and she lingered on the edge of the room. "Good morning, Lady Neve. I hope your audience with the king went well?"

Another thing I felt uncertain if I should mention. My secrets began to pile up, stifling me from the inside.

"Did you hear Lord Roar return last night?" I answered her with a question of my own.

"He arrived minutes before sunrise. That the king wished to entertain him is a good sign." She beamed.

I swallowed. In Avaldenn, most everyone knew about the harem and the king's practice of bringing others into that lurid space. What would stop the king from talking about it when he saw nothing wrong with his actions? That settled my decision on one matter. She wouldn't like it, but my lady-in-waiting should know the truth of this, at least.

"Clem, we went to the king's harem." I met her gaze firmly with my own.

Her eyes went wide. "Pardon me?"

"The king invited us to his harem."

She remained quiet, as if unsure of what to say, but from how her face paled, I could guess at how I'd struck her.

"It was very uncomfortable," I said sinking deeper into the tub.

"I can imagine so." She came closer and set the tin down and began to pull out lotions and cosmetics, probably for something to do to distract from the news. "I—I am sorry you had to witness that. It is no place for a lady."

"It's no place for *anyone*. And Roar didn't want to stay. The king commanded him to do so." My hand trailed over the water, leaving ripples in its wake. "A brothel, where they are paid and have signed contracts protecting their rights is one thing. But if they are unwilling, that is . . . barbaric."

Clemencia kept her voice low. "Their children are well cared for. And the king's favorites are too."

A pittance. "And the rest? There were over fifty fae in there last night. He's disgusting."

"Lady Neve, it is unwise to speak such words."

"Even to you?" I turned and looked up at her.

Clemencia remained silent for a moment before replying. "I will say nothing. You're my lady."

"And friend, I hope." I smiled. "Tell me the truth. Do you mind that I called you Clem? You told the prince that it was fine, but I want to make sure. If you do mind, I won't do so again."

"I rather enjoyed it. My friends growing up called me that. Though, I'll admit, it took me by surprise. Most ladies are not so familiar with their help."

"I wasn't born a lady," I replied. "And you're not really the help, more like a helper. One I couldn't do without."

She walked that line here, but in Guldtown she lived as a wealthy merchant's daughter.

"Thank you, my lady." She plucked the mystery tin off the counter. "This was waiting outside the door, in a hamper to welcome the start of the Courting Festival. It says it's for you, though not who it is from."

Drying my hands on a towel, I took the tin and opened the attached note.

This is the balm I told you about. Use it liberally on your skin and wings.

This had to be the balm that one of the castle's Master Healers created, and the note had to be from Prince Vale . . .

He'd not mentioned my intrusion into his room. Would he ever? What did he think about it?

I looked at Clemencia. "Did Roar see this note?"

"It came after he returned and retired. Lean back, my lady." She held up a glass jar of shampoo, and when I leaned back, she began washing my hair.

"And there was no other note?" I asked as her fingers massaged my scalp.

"None. Is everything alright?"

I set the balm on a little table beside the tub. I wasn't sure how to answer that, but I certainly wouldn't involve Clem in whatever was happening between the prince and me. "Yes. It's a balm for scars. Can we apply it before I get dressed?"

I'd need her help to reach parts of my wings.

"Of course," she replied, not an ounce of suspicion in her voice. "Would you like to wear your hair in braids today? That way, your hair will be curled for the ball tonight."

The ball. Just those words instilled mild panic.

The ball officially opened the Courting Festival. After the event, there would be gatherings day and night, many more balls, smaller socials, and other events in which I'd have to play my part perfectly. Was I ready for all this? So far, my time at Frostveil Castle had been filled with highs and lows, and aside from the younger ladies of the Sacred Eight, I had not met many fae. That would all change tonight.

"That sounds wonderful," I murmured as Clem rinsed the shampoo. "We're supposed to be meeting the king and queen for breakfast. Do you know anything about that?"

"There was a card announcing the breakfast in the hamper. We have time." Her tone assured me that she'd take care of getting me there.

That brought me relief, and I closed my eyes, sinking deeper into the steaming bath. I wasn't looking forward to dining with the king and queen, but for now, Clem had things in hand. Stars bless her.

"If only you'd been there when I ran into Calpurnia and her friends last night." The words flew out of my mouth before I could stop them.

Clemencia had been reaching for a jar of conditioner, but my words made her freeze in place. "Why's that, my lady?"

Blazing stars. One moment of trust, of relief, and I lost composure. I needed to be more careful, even around Clemencia.

"I was coming back from the harem with an escort and ran into Calpurnia Vagle and the Ithamai sisters. They harassed me, chased me." I drew in a deep breath. "They're displeased that Warden Roar is already engaged."

"I had wondered." Clemencia scooped out the conditioner and resumed massaging my scalp.

My eyes widened. "You did?"

"High Lady Ithamai has made it *very* clear that she wishes to unite east and west by marriage. She has been speaking with the warden for many turns, visiting merchant families too, if they have enough influence. And Lady Calpurnia . . . Well, that would be a good alliance for her house."

"The queen was a Vagle, and she has vast power," I murmured. "So how would allying her house with Roar via Calpurnia be to their advantage?"

"Warden Roar controls many gold mines. The crown has always been envious of the Lisika wealth and the seemingly endless gold that comes from his mines. A connection would benefit the Vagles and, hence, the Aabergs."

"I see."

"My lady?"

"Yes?"

Clemencia let out a soft breath. "You need to take care around them. Those ladies are powerful. I have not seen most of them use magic, but I've heard tales of many Sacred Eight abilities. And then there's the power of reputation. Theirs weighs so heavily; it's enough to crush most fae."

"I'm aware," I huffed. "Painfully so, as a weak fae of common birth, I need to take care."

"I will help you," she affirmed. "That's what friends do."

"Thank you, Clem." My throat tightened as I thought of Anna. She'd been stouthearted too, the best of friends.

Not had been. She is my dearest friend.

I'd save Anna if it was the last thing I did. This arrangement between Roar and me would secure my safe travel south, where I could find us a home. Then, I'd hire someone to extract Anna from the Blood Court.

I tried not to ruminate on the vast quantities of coin one would need for such a dangerous mission because it didn't matter. I'd do anything, pay *anything*, to get her out. And Roar would get me started with a heavy purse.

The sound of broken glass and a burst of swearing interrupted my thoughts. I sat up straighter and cast a glance at Clemencia. "The warden is awake. I need to speak with him."

Clemencia finished with my hair as I scrubbed my skin. Once done, she presented me with a towel as fluffy and white as the faintly flurrying snow outside. Another wrapped my hair, and I dressed in a simple but elegant dress, the color of dark red wine from the Summer Isles. Here, nearly all my gowns came in various shades of red or gold. I didn't mind, though I preferred shades of blues and purples, but appearances were important at court. They signified power, and that was the name of the game of houses.

Once ready, Clem disappeared to her room, and I entered the suite's antechamber. Roar sat in a chair, one foot rested on the opposite knee and a hand over his eyes. The glass he'd broken remained on the ground, and as no stain covered the floor, I assumed he'd been trying to drink water.

"Are you well?" I kept my voice soft, so as not to startle him.

He groaned and opened his bloodshot eyes. "Not at all. The king kept me there all night, drinking and . . ." He trailed off.

"I understand." A true fiancée might have been upset, and perhaps I should have pretended, but what was the point? "You didn't want to stay."

"I didn't. Though I'll admit, I wish that my frolicking around in a harem all night long affected you a touch more." He sighed and looked away, still hurt that I'd spurned him.

I frowned. It almost felt like he was trying to make me feel sorry for him, but I did not take the bait and instead decided to pivot the conversation. "Why does the king think his actions were appropriate?"

"I really can't say. As a bastard-born Falk, one would think he was averse to siring bastards and, by extension, having a harem, but he is not." Roar shook his head. "King Magnus is a fae of mystery."

The fact that Magnus had a harem made me think his wife was removed from him. Though they'd made no such appearances at the tourney.

"Did you sleep well?" Roar asked, clearly keen to get off the subject of the harem and on to something more innocuous.

I crossed my arms. "Not really. Something else happened last night."

"Oh?" Roar leaned forward.

I told him about Calpurnia and the Ithamai sisters. With each word, his face grew more stoney. I finished my tale by cutting it short, saying I outran them and hid behind a tapestry.

"That is outrageous," he condemned.

"It is. More importantly, how do we react to this? Do you think they'd believe that I'd keep this to myself?"

Roar stood, got a second glass of water, stepping over the broken one on his way. "Some ladies are trained to keep their woes inside. Not all, of course. Particularly not if the female is more powerful than her mate."

"Like Lady Virtoris?" I hadn't even heard of the Lord Virtoris, but as Sayyida's mother held the title of Lady of Ships, it stood to reason that whether her husband lived or not, she was the more powerful fae. In this kingdom, magical power dictated which heir inherited a title from their parents. And if the title holder was female, they did not change their name when they married.

"Exactly." He sipped from his glass. "I believe our best course of action is not to make waves."

"You do?"

"Last night, the king made it quite clear he wanted us to remain to build ties. Perhaps if you were not new to this world, he would have released us, but that is not the case. Hence, we endure. I will pretend like you did not tell me this, as if you are merely a weak common fae too scared to tell her betrothed of more powerful fae's misdoings."

I hated that, but at the same time, I understood. We had to go about this with intelligence. Perhaps, if we socialized enough, the king would change his mind and release us before the end of the Courting Festival. By the moon, I hoped so. I did not want to be here weeks longer.

Of course, playing nicely would likely be easier said than done.

CHAPTER 30

Roar and I strolled down the castle corridors, hand in hand, our chins held high. Though I'd have loved to have her with me for support, Clemencia had not been invited to breakfast with the king and queen, so she remained in our quarters, preparing for the ball.

Along the way, I noted the twists and turns we took. I was determined not get into a situation like I had last night, frantic and running and not sure where to go. Too much had been left to chance then and counting on the castle's goodwill seemed foolish.

But I'm still counting on Prince Vale's . . . the intrusive thought arose, and I banished it quickly. Roar could never know of that, and it would not do for me to linger on the thought. The prince held all the power, but he'd been merciful last night. Though I didn't know why that was, I had to hope he'd continue to be so.

When we reached the busy intersection of corridors

where the massive white bear stood, I tried not to look at it. Though I'd seen it a handful of times, it continued to make me uncomfortable.

"Are you well?" Roar squeezed my hand.

"Enough. I had a difficult time sleeping last night."

A truth, though not for the reasons he'd assume. How very fae of me.

"Just remember that I'll be with you. And the king won't overstep with his wife present." He glanced at me and gave a firm nod.

"Of course," I said softly, agreeably. Since arriving in Avaldenn, we'd had enough strife between us and I wanted to smooth that over.

We entered another hallway, this one more crowded. I took in the tapestries lining the walls. How different they looked from those I saw last night in the hidden part of the castle. White bears were everywhere, and now that I had seen all the royal family, I recognized their portraits. Some, however, stood out. An older female fae stared out from one portrait. She looked at the viewer with a sad smile.

"Who is that?" I nodded at the portrait.

"King Magnus's mother. Kilyn Aaberg."

The one the Falk prince, the Cruel King's brother, had gotten with child.

"What house was she from? If I recall correctly, her husband was more powerful in magic and rank. So, she took his name?"

"Correct. He's an Aaberg by bloodline, and she hails from a smaller branch of House Qiren."

I tucked away that information, still struck by the female's sad expression. Why would King Magnus want to portray that image of his mother? Why not pick something happier?

We continued until I spotted two armed soldiers standing in the hall before a doorway. They wore the gold cloaks of the Clawsguard, our indication that we'd arrived.

"Smiles on," Roar said.

We beamed as we strolled past the guards and thank the stars I was a decent actor, for when I saw the guests, dread gripped me.

This was no private breakfast with the royal family, but a gathering of many. Far too many.

"All the Sacred Eight are here," Roar whispered. "The king didn't mention this."

I searched the room that smelled of fresh bread and fruit desperate to find a friendly face. Thankfully, it didn't take long.

Princess Saga spoke with the Balik family, all dressed in their house colors of dark green, gold, and black. The Armenils of the far north were present too—most of whom were identifiable by their gray attire and bright red hair. Seeing Marit, Saga, and the Balik sisters smile at me made my breath come easier. At least until I saw Calpurnia.

Her gang had grown since last night. The Ithamai's joined her, but so had another female. The new fae had inky black skin, hair as shiny as a raven's wing, and piercing green eyes that looked furious to see my hand tucked in Roar's hand.

"Who is that with Lady Calpurnia and the sisters?" I nodded toward her.

"Aenesa Qiren." Roar flicked his gaze to her and back to me.

Aenesa, firstborn daughter of the Lady of Silks, Head of House Qiren, Clemencia's instruction during our lessons flitted through my mind. Their family seat was in Traliska, the place where I'd touched the Drassil tree.

"Warden Lisika, Lady Neve, welcome." Queen Inga appeared with a warm expression on her face. She looked immaculate with her dark brown hair pulled back and a crown of sapphires on her head. I admired the stitching on the royal blue gown. A true master had created it, though I felt certain I could have done even better.

My fingers itched to work the silk I'd bought during our journey east. Since arriving in Avaldenn, I'd had little time, and there would be none tonight either. Perhaps I could steal time before the ball? I only needed to apply a few last-minute touches to the gown.

"My queen." Roar bowed, and I curtsied. "Thank you for hosting this event."

"I'm pleased you could make it. As you can see, my lord husband will not be joining. He's unwell."

"A pity." Roar shook his head.

I did not feel that way but inclined my head as if her philandering husband having a hangover was the worst thing I could think of.

"I hear he granted you two betrothal rights." The

queen spoke lightly. "A very suitable prize for saving his life."

Roar nodded. "We agree."

"The noble houses of all courts are becoming more diverse," the queen said. "It is a surprise, but a welcome one. We need a bit of shaking up."

"How do you mean?" I asked.

"The Prince of the Spring Court took a fire witch from the human world to wife," the queen twirled a finger at the novelty. "It is as rare as your situation—a high lord marrying a commoner."

I had nothing to say to that. How could such a thing be true? Commoners existed everywhere, but fire witches from the human world did not. I knew some witches lived as slaves at the Blood Court but had heard no mention of witches here.

"Will you announce your intent here, before the Grand Staret at the Tower of the Living and the Dead? Or do you prefer your own High Staret in Guldtown?" the queen asked.

"Nothing would make me happier to declare my engagement to the holiest of fae." Roar replied.

I was about to add that I was pleased to do so too when the oddest thing happened. A pressure built in my head. Even more shocking, the sensation flitted. It traveled from temple to crown to the base of my skull, pressing inward.

Then it vanished. The release came so abruptly that I gasped. I hadn't realized how much it hurt or how tight my jaw had become.

"Lady Neve? Are you well?" The queen kept her tone soft.

Narrowed blue eyes watched me. Moons. I acted strangely and caught Queen Inga's notice. We couldn't have that.

"Apologies," I murmured. "Since the attack, I've been feeling off."

"My son told me of your injuries. I'm so happy he was there to help." Queen Inga swept her hand out in front of her. "But I've kept you too long, and I must make the rounds before we sit. Please, enjoy the breakfast."

"Lady Neve!" an excited feminine voice called out the moment the queen left us. In the same heartbeat, another female called out, "Lord Roar, a moment?"

I sought the one calling my fiancé first and frowned. Aenesa walked our way with a smile on her blood-red lips, and her eyelashes fluttering madly. I refrained from rolling my eyes. Barely.

"Lady Aenesa," Roar said, bowing his head. "How are you?"

"Marvelous. I wish to speak with you about a cart of textiles sent to a merchant in your territory."

"I—" Roar looked at me.

But I caught Princess Saga bounding my way, so I placed an assuring hand on his shoulder. "I'll be fine. The princess wishes to speak."

"Very well." Roar kissed my cheek, which made Aenesa scowl. "Have a pleasant time catching up."

I wanted to laugh out loud. I'd known the princess for a day. What did we need to catch up on?

Nonetheless, Saga approached, took my arm, and we were off. Once we stood a distance away from Roar, she stopped. "Vale told me about your injuries. I'm so sorry that my Clawsguard didn't help you."

"It wasn't his job."

"Still, I'm thankful that my brother was there. To lose you after we just met would be so painful."

It was an odd idea that I'd be friends with a princess, but I could tell she meant her words. I found that I, too, would hate to never see her again.

"All is well." I placed a hand on hers and squeezed. "You weren't injured, were you?"

Saga shook her head. "Not a scratch."

"I'm pleased to hear that." A pause followed, in which neither of us knew what to say. Finally, I settled on a safe bet. "Where's Sayyida? I see her brother, but not our friend or her intimidating mother."

"Vidar is here on my account. I used you as an excuse to escape him and his talk of rigging and other ship matters." She rolled her eyes, clearly not at all interested in the life of a sailor. "Sayyida and her mother, Lady Virtoris, are at the city docks."

"Are they leaving?"

"Oh, Sayyida wishes." Saga laughed. "But no. A shipment arrived from the Summer Court and Lady Virtoris went to accept the goods because they're coming to the palace for the festival. And then a second diplomatic ship arrived, and it's custom that one of the Sacred Eight or the royal family receives it. As they were already there, Sayyida and her mother volunteered." She snorted. "Or I should say that Sayyida volunteered her mother to stay longer to greet the ship, so that she didn't have to come here. Say will do anything to avoid wearing a gown."

I chuckled. "Must be sheer torture to do so two days in a row."

The princess's eyes sparkled. "You already know her so well."

We took a turn around the room, chatting like old friends.

"So, I heard you keep a diary?" I asked when the conversation fell into a lull.

"Sayyida told you?"

"She did."

"She's such a gossip."

"It sounds like *you* might be the gossip," I teased. "Your book details the court?"

Something in her eyes became shielded, and she pulled me to the side of the room, as far away from others as possible. "It does. There are dark things happening here, Neve." She leaned closer and her tone softened to a whisper. "I heard about last night. You, Calpurnia, and the Ithamai sisters. Be careful around them."

I was shocked. Since I'd gotten here, she'd acted so light, so happy, that I assumed Saga didn't know. Now, I thought that there was little the princess did not hear about. "I will."

"Good." She smiled, a small affair. "I—"

"What are you two doing, hiding over here?" a masculine voice cut through, one I recognized. One that made me freeze in place. Was this when Prince Vale would mention last night?

"Brother!" Saga cried out. "Good of you to actually leave training and come to breakfast."

"It appears I arrived too soon." The prince came up to us and grinned as he pulled his sister into a sweet side-hug. The scent of cold and sweat and sandalwood rolled off him in waves, sending a delicious shiver down my spine. "I wish that we were already eating."

"Oh, stop." Saga beamed up at him and punched him playfully in the chest. "It is good for you to socialize with more people than Sir Caelo and those of your *cabal*." She hissed the last word, as though it were a secret.

They broke apart, and the prince eyed me warily.

"She doesn't gossip. Apparently, that's all me and Sayyida," Saga said with a flourish of her hand that made me snigger. "Vale has a little group of friends called the cabal. They fancy themselves real fae of history and current events."

"Oh?" I asked, somewhat surprised. I'd only ever heard of Prince Vale described as a warrior. "And what do you do regarding those events?"

"Not much, and only my sister calls us that" the prince said with a shrug that looked a touch forced.

"Well that's because you have no imagination!" Saga snorted. "Every group needs a name!"

"Anyway," the prince took his sister in with amusement, "after talking to Caelo, I don't need to socialize at all, dear sister. He talks enough for everyone in this room and fills my cup for listening." Prince Vale caught my eye again. "Moving on to more important matters . . . Lady Neve, how are your injuries?"

I waited, but he said nothing else about me winding up in his quarters, so I nodded. "Thank you."

His eyes flickered to my wings, which tightened beneath his gaze. Was he seeing if the balm he sent already worked? Should I mention it? Where was Roar?

"Oh, stars!" Saga craned her neck around her muscular brother. "Please, excuse me. Mother is calling."

My heart stuttered. I felt safer with her by my side, but before I could stop the princess—as if that were possible—she flitted off to the queen. Prince Vale and I stood alone. Immediately, the air warmed. I swallowed and glanced away.

"So . . ." He started, seemingly at a loss too. "Are you enjoying your time at the palace?"

"I am." No need to go into the bullying, the harem, and the attack. Or remind him of how I'd shown up in his room. But I did want to thank him for the balm. I found Roar in the crowd, made sure he was far away.

"I got your balm. And put it on my wings. Thank you for sending it."

"I said I would."

"Well, yes, but people do not always do as they say."

"True." Prince Vale inhaled and cast a glance around. "Listen, Lady Neve. About last night."

I swallowed. It appeared I would not be avoiding this conversation. "Perhaps we should . . .?" I trailed off. Do what exactly? Leave the room? Moons, that would cause so much gossip and infuriate Roar.

"I'll be brief," he said quickly. "Last night, after you left, I went to look at the palace blueprints."

"You . . . what?" That had not been what I was expecting.

"I just couldn't let it go." He paused. "It took a while to figure out because my wing has been remodeled, but wouldn't you know, I found that when Frostveil was originally built, there would have been another hallway leading to the area where my chambers are now. In fact, a door would have been right where you said it was."

"Ah, really?"

"Really." He paused and studied me thoughtfully. "You are quite the mystery, Lady Neve. Parts of the palace that have remained stoutly closed to everyone, opened for you. For refuge, so you claimed." The prince's eyebrows drew together. "Might I ask why you felt unsafe?"

I wasn't sure telling him the truth was wise. If anything, it might earn me more ire from the ladies who despised me. Again, I wasn't sure what to say.

Before I could decide how to reply, Crown Prince Rhistel appeared at my side, making me jump.

"What have we here?" The heir smiled, snake-like. "Didn't mean to surprise you, Lady Neve."

I cleared my throat. A distraction was welcome, though I wished it wasn't him. "I simply didn't hear you."

Standing next to one another, I was even more struck by the differences in the twins. Prince Rhistel was pale and less muscular, probably due to spending less time outside fighting battles. He still wore his gloves today, hinting that he might be delicate, whereas the younger Aaberg brother was muscular and tanned in a way that spoke of hours riding a horse or fighting battles.

"I have been known to have a light step. Light touch too." Prince Rhistel stared at me and licked his lips in a way that made me shudder. Thankfully, he didn't linger and turned to Prince Vale. "Brother, Warden Roar seems to be upset that you're talking to his fiancée."

My pulse jumped, and I twisted to see Roar, still in conversation with Aenesa and now the queen and Saga. The warden's eyes flickered to meet mine, and in them I spotted barely suppressed anger. Queen Inga's presence was probably the only thing that kept him from storming over.

"So," the heir continued, "why not make it the both of us?"

I turned. My eyebrows knitted together to find his sly gaze locked on me. "What do you mean?"

"Vale and I have little in common, but irritating the Warden of the West might as well be a family sport." Prince Rhistel grinned, as if he thought I'd be fine with his words. His gloved hand rose and he traced my collarbone softly. "Speaking with you seems to send the warden's blood boiling. I wonder what kissing you would do?"

I gasped and took a step back.

"Go away." Prince Vale's voice tightened.

"And why would I?" His brother waved off his comment. "I have not gotten to speak much with the lady that threw the court into chaos. Though from our short time together I can see why so many are interested in her." He leered at me.

"I threw nothing into chaos," I hissed.

"You don't think so?" The heir smirked at me in a way that made my blood heat.

"I've done nothing except arrive at court and attend events." I kept my gaze on him firm and hard.

And attend a secret card game and find a hidden hallway. But Prince Rhistel did not need to know either of those.

"You've also tempted my brother," Rhistel said. "That intrigues me. Do you know we've shared a whore a time or two? One was even a fisherman's daughter. So familiar . . ."

I stiffened, and at the heir's side, Prince Vale did the same. "What did you say?"

"My dear brother here has been acting quite erratic since you arrived. Perhaps because you are Warden Roar's, and he has a feud with the warden, not that I blame you, Brother. Nor do I disagree that she'd be worth a tumble. She's quite pretty. Though I wouldn't want to own her."

My fists clenched. "No one *owns* me."

Prince Rhistel laughed. "Unless you have more power than the warden, you belong to him in every way that matters. Come to think of it, you're just a glorified whore, aren't you, *Lady* Neve?"

I opened my mouth to argue when Prince Vale did the unthinkable: he punched his brother in the face.

CHAPTER 31

I darted back three paces, unable to believe what I'd just seen. But as Prince Rhistel wound up to punch his brother back, I knew one thing for certain. That wouldn't end well.

I was proven right when Prince Vale caught his brother's punch seconds before it would have landed on his nose. "Nice try, soft hands."

The heir snarled, blood dripping from his nose. "She's that enticing to you, is she? *A commoner is enchanting you!* Bleeding skies, Vale." The word rang out in the otherwise deadly silent room and Prince Rhistel spat at his twin. The spittle marred Prince Vale's doublet and the Warrior Bear's eyes flashed with danger. "Father will—"

"My princes!" A tall, broad-shouldered faerie rushed forward and stuck himself between the two.

It took a moment before I recognized the copper-haired fae from his box, Lord Riis, the Lord of Tongues. Though the princes continued to egg one another on,

Prince Rhistel going as far as to lunge at Prince Vale, Lord Riis was as large as the younger Aaberg twin and seemed as strong as a dragon. He held them apart long enough for two soldiers to increase the distance between the twins.

"My princes, that is unbecoming behavior." Lord Riis said as the princes glared at him. Though most would have cowered beneath those glares, Lord Riis looked unperturbed and almost fatherly in his disappointment. Had he put himself between the brothers before? What right did he have? No one else had made a move to break them up.

"It certainly is." Queen Inga's imperious tone cut through the otherwise silent room as she swept over. "Thank you, Leyv, for stopping my sons from continuing to make utter fools of themselves." Her eyes narrowed in fury. "I can't imagine what they were thinking, sullying the Aaberg name in such a manner."

Fully grown fae males shrank before their mother, and everyone else, save for Lord Riis, seemed to do so too. The back of my neck tingled. Queen Inga was formidable, but I got the sense I was missing something about her.

And as Prince Rhistel's back curled inward, and Prince Vale's eyes wrenched shut as though he had the worst of headaches, I felt even more certain that I was correct.

What was the queen doing to them?

"I see." She nodded a moment later. "How crude. I suggest that you two clean up. We wouldn't want to get blood on the floors." Inga glared at her eldest son and the blood dripping off his angular face.

Before anyone could utter another word, the princes stormed toward the doors, neither bothering to look at the other. The moment they left the room, Queen Inga turned to me.

"Apologies for my sons' behavior. What Rhistel said to you was uncalled for, and Vale must learn to harness his temper. If you wish to take your breakfast in your chambers, I would understand."

I looked about, searching for Roar, and found him at the far side of the room. His jaw tightened as he balled his fists at his sides. Aside from him, many others watched and whispered. Bleeding skies, I didn't want to endure the gossip—I wasn't ready to.

"I think I'd like that." I curtsied.

Queen Inga inclined her head, and I left. I expected Roar to join me, to demand an explanation, but instead, Princess Saga appeared at my side. "Walk with me."

"What of Warden Roar?" I gazed at him over my shoulder.

"I wish for your company." The princess then raised her voice. "The warden can meet you in your chambers when we're done."

Fae hearing left me no doubt that Roar had heard her, and as Saga outranked him, he would not argue. Not here, anyway. His household, meaning me, had already caused enough of a scene. So, Saga and I left the breakfast hall, and she walked me down the corridor. As we distanced ourselves from the other fae, the blood drops on the patterned ground did not go unnoticed. Prince Rhistel had gone this way.

"I overheard what Rhistel said from where I stood. I apologize for both of my brothers," Saga said after a moment.

"That's not something you should have to do."

"Yes, well, you'll probably get an apology from Vale later for making a scene, but don't count on one from Rhistel. He is far too proud, so consider mine as a replacement for his." She frowned. "Thankfully, Lord Riis was nearby to stop them before it got too ugly."

"I'm surprised he did." Lord Riis might be a lord, one of the Sacred Eight even, but the princes outranked him.

"He and mother grew up together in the midlands, and so he's always been close to our family," Saga explained. "We see him as an uncle and growing up he even insisted that we called him by his given name. Not during official functions of course, but when he'd stop by the palace and such." She sighed. "Unfortunately, this is not the first time he's stopped one of their fights, though this is the most public one."

I recalled from my lessons that House Riis was the newest great house of the Sacred Eight, raised to replace House Aaberg when they ascended to royals. Not that the raising of a new house was completely necessary. Clemencia had taught me that along with House Falk, the previous royal family, there had been another family exterminated by the White Bear's Rebellion. House Skau, birth family of Queen Revna, had been completely obliterated. But House Skau had never been replaced and as a result nine sacred houses became eight.

But Lord Riis *had* been raised and he was the only fae to have been given the honor. He must have done something very noble in the eyes of King Magnus to be so elevated. That was a question to mull over another day.

"Do your brothers fight often?"

A sigh gusted out of the princess. "My brothers had a falling out eight turns ago. Actually, it was soon after Vale quarreled fiercely with your fiancé. Their brotherly relationship has never recovered, and any little thing can set one or the other off. Vale, more so. He has a hotter temper that Rhistel loves to instigate."

I didn't care for Rhistel, but the idea that they often fought made me sad. They were brothers, *twins*. Surely, they should enjoy a strong bond throughout their lives?

"What happened between them?" I asked.

"I don't know." Her lips pressed together. "Mother knows, but she won't tell anyone. Even my father."

"They confided in only her?"

Saga stopped; her ice-blue eyes that so resembled her father's had gone wide. "Oh, you sweet thing."

I rolled my shoulders back, annoyed at being spoken to like a child. "There's no need for that."

Saga shook her head. "No, I mean that it really is sweet. My mother is infamous for her powers. She probably finds you quite charming for not knowing."

"How would she know that I'm ignorant?"

She let out an unamused laugh. "Mother has mind magic. She's one of the strongest fae with such a power in all of Isila. If she wishes to know something about some-one, all she needs to do is get close to them. Touch them, preferably. Then she can read all their secrets."

I gaped as that odd sensation of my head constricting came rushing back. "When she uses it, does it feel like your skull is being squeezed?"

"That's usually when she's not touching you and does not know you. The more familiar she is with you, the easier she can slip into your mind." Saga rolled her eyes. "Try keeping secrets from a mother like that. It's *impossible*, even with the elixir the White Tower developed. I take it religiously, and even so, Mother can slip into my mind if she truly wishes. As you saw with my brothers, if she's angry, she isn't always graceful about entering. If she forces her way in, it can hurt."

I had so many questions but most of them fell away at one fact: The queen's power was sort of like a vampire's compulsion. Vampires could take information from people's heads and make a person do something. My skin prickled with unease. Could the queen do the latter?

"Saga, can your mother force others to do things with her mind?" I asked, feeling sick.

"What! No!"

She sounded so distraught that my eyebrows pinched together. "Why do you say it like that?"

"Yes, it's just . . . do you not know that the power to influence others like you're suggesting is illegal?" Saga glanced behind us. "It's called whispering, and a fae can be put to death for using that magic."

I hadn't known. Fae had such varied powers, and

often more than one that they were strong in. It was diffi-cult to keep up.

"I've never heard of that. How does it work?"

The princess looked away.

Something more was afoot.

"Saga, I'm sorry that I made you uncomfortable. I don't mean to."

She sighed. "I know you don't. You're truehearted and naïve to the point that you don't know about my family. I should be pleased but . . ." She chewed on her bottom lip, as if struggling to speak.

"Please don't speak of whispering and my mother in the same sentence. Mother is already a bit of an outcast, for a queen." The princess swallowed. "Her magic is so well known that she walks a fine line, and very few are willing to get close to her. She doesn't even have ladies-in-waiting for that reason. I don't want her hurt."

"I won't speak a word," I assured her. "I promise that I didn't know."

And really, the horror of whispering aside, having Queen Inga be able to read my mind was bad enough. A fresh wave of dread rolled through me. Why wouldn't Roar have told me about this? It seemed a rather large thing to omit. I needed to speak with him. "Saga, I'm not feeling well. Do you mind if I return to my chambers so that I might rest for tonight?"

Saga nodded, her shoulders relaxing finally. "Of course. But first, I was wondering, do you wish to get ready for the ball with me? Sayyida and Marit will be there. It's a tradition that we have, and we'd love for you to join."

That took me by surprise and warmed my heart too. The tension in my body faded.

"It sounds marvelous, but I should talk to my lord before I commit." Roar and I might have to go over last-minute details before the ball.

"Very well. Do you need my help to find your room?"

"No, thank you." I'd paid attention on the way here, determined to learn my way around the palace so I'd always be able to escape if anyone chased me again.

We parted, and I rushed through the hallways, hoping that the queen had excused Roar too, and he had already arrived in our chambers. Then he'd be able to reassure me.

When I reached our wing, I increased my pace and barreled into our room, chest heaving. Just as I'd wished, he was present, pacing the middle of the sitting area. Clemencia was there too, watching him, her eyebrows drawn together with worry.

"Clem, can you give us a moment?" I asked.

Right away, she rose and left the room.

"What happened?" Roar gritted out the moment my bedroom door closed, leaving us with privacy.

"I'll tell you, but first, you must answer my question." I met his gaze firmly.

Roar snorted. "Must I?"

"The queen tried to get into my head." I'd expected his face to pale, for him to take a seat and despair, for him to worry as I did.

Instead, he shrugged. "She isn't supposed to use that power on the families of the Sacred Eight, her own children aside, of course. However, I suppose you do not qualify yet. It is a good thing that I have dosed your wine against her power on many occasions."

My heart skipped a beat. "Excuse me?"

Roar glared at me. "You really expected me to let you loose at court without taking precautions? The queen has the strongest mind magic in the kingdom. Of course she would be interested in you, and though you can presently lie, you cannot hide your thoughts from her. Not without the potion I gave you."

"You could have asked me. In fact, you *should* have." My fists balled up tightly.

Others had controlled me all my life. I did not intend for that to happen again. Roar knew that, so why had he acted like the vampires who'd fed me potions to stifle my magic?

Actually, he was worse. The vampires made no qualms about what they'd done to me. They told me to my face, made me tip the potion back myself. The warden, the male I'd partnered with to trick a king, a court, a kingdom, hid his actions from me.

My throat tightened. "I need space."

Roar shrugged, nonplussed. "I was only doing what was best for you."

"That you believe you know what is better for me more than I do speaks volumes," I snapped. "You should have told me. Had I known about the queen, I would have done whatever was necessary to protect myself, to protect *us*, but you never gave me that choice."

I twisted to face Clem's room. "Clemencia! I need you!" With that, I spun before Roar could reply and stormed into my room.

Clemencia entered a second later, wringing her hands. "My lady? What can I do?"

"Pack up a spare gown and whatever else I'll need for the ball." I grabbed my basket with the amethyst gown inside, nearly done. "I hope to wear this, but if I don't have time, I want a backup."

She dropped her hands but didn't move. "Why do they need to be packed?"

"We're leaving."

Clemencia's lips parted. "To where?"

"Princess Saga has invited me to get ready for the ball with her. I'm hoping that she wouldn't mind if I came early to keep her company."

Clemencia cleared her throat nervously but readied the trunk. Once she prepared it, we each picked up a side, and when I stormed out of my room to find Roar still on the blue settee, seemingly unbothered, I got mad all over again.

"I'm leaving."

"What?" He leapt to his feet. "You can't, we . . ." He trailed off, his gaze sliding to Clemencia. I knew what he'd been about to say. He wished to remind me of our deal.

"The princess has invited me to get ready for the ball with her. That's where I'll be."

Roar was stunned into momentary silence. "Very well. I will come to her chambers to escort you to the ball. Please, wait there for me?"

I read the words he wasn't saying.

Please, do not storm into the ball and make a fool of me. Or undo all that we have achieved.

I exhaled. "Very well. I'll wait."

It wouldn't do anything to renege on our deal or hurt our futures. I simply did not want to see Roar for a few hours. To make that quite clear, I turned my back on him and left our chambers, determined to forget about the warden until tonight, when we would need to convince an entire kingdom that we were madly in love.

Hours later, I sat in a vast bedroom decorated in tones of pink—Saga's quarters, of course—tapping my foot.

The start of the ball was upon us, and with each passing minute, my nerves grew. So much so that I didn't hesitate when Sayyida suggested I have another glass of wine.

Clemencia, however, stopped my friend's pour before the goblet filled all the way. "I don't want to spill on her dress."

Sayyida shrugged. "Whatever you say."

She did not seem to be the same girl that pushed Dragon Fire on us the night we played cards. No, since she got back from port and joined us in the princess's rooms, Sayyida had been tense.

Had I not met Sayyida before, I'd assume it was because balls were horrible affairs, but I knew that was not to be the case. Sayyida simply despised being made up, shoved into a gown, and being forced to make small talk with everyone who wanted to kiss her highborn rear —her own words, not mine.

I was of a different mind.

Though nerves roiled inside me, the idea of a ball, of dressing up and celebrating, still intrigued me. I'd never imagined I'd be able to do it before. For the first time, I was about to live a night that I'd dreamed of, and my lady-in-waiting had made certain I looked the part. She had dressed me up beautifully with painted lips, a gold shimmer across my eyelids, and a subtle shade of rouge to bring color to my fair cheeks.

Best of all, I worked on my dress in the hours that Saga and I had been together. I'd finally finished the amethyst gown. I could wear my own creation.

My hands slid down the silk, admiring the gold lace I'd applied at the bottom and along the neckline. Though it wasn't in Roar's house colors, the gold paid homage to the Lisika House and the purple hue made me happy. Even Sayyida had been impressed when I told her how little time it had taken. Marit Armenil and Princess Saga seemed completely taken with the piece fit for a lady.

"I should have you make something for me," Marit said from where she perched on Saga's dusky pink blanket. "Would you?"

"I could start on it while we're here," I replied.

Marit was sweet, and I'd love to make her something

434

to complement her red hair and fair complexion. I either made her a gown at court, or it would never happen. That would break my heart, like I'd let down a true friend.

My heart clenched. Though I'd only been in Avaldenn a short time, I already considered these ladies to be friends, especially Saga and Sayyida, who had taken every effort to include me. But others, like Marit and the Balik sisters, had been friendly too. If I had been a normal fae, if I didn't have to flee south, I could see our relationships growing.

"Whenever you have the time," Marit assured me, "I would love a creation by the one and only Lady Neve."

My cheeks warmed. "And you shall have one. Are you opposed to green?"

"I love it!" Marit exclaimed. "Our house wears so much gray and black, but I adore a bit of color." She beamed at me, and I made a note to have someone go into the city and bring me back bolts of emerald fabric.

"Now that that is settled." Saga approached me. Her maid servant had finished her makeup and the pink-haired princess looked stunning in a gown of royal blue and gold trimmed with white fur. "Might I have a moment, Neve?"

"Of course." I stood and placed my wine on the side table to follow Saga across the room.

She stopped before a vanity. "I have something for you. The moment I saw your dress, I thought of it." She opened a wooden box inlaid with a gold moon surrounded by stars and pulled out a circular item covered in amethyst gems.

My breath caught in my throat. "It's lovely, Saga." I paused. "But what is it?"

The circular, silver piece looked slightly smaller than the size of my palm. On the circle, gems shone, and a rod of silver ran through the center, bisecting it and extending on each side. This was not a necklace, bracelet, or ring. I'd never seen a piece of jewelry like this.

"It's for your hair." She twirled it between her fingers, and the amethyst gems caught the dying sunlight coming in through the windows. The snow had let up, and the day had been cold and crisp. I examined the piece closer and saw that the gems formed snowflakes. How very fitting.

"I can put it in, if you like?" Saga asked.

"Please." I turned, presenting my long silvery-white hair, curled to perfection thanks to Clem.

"I'll pull back a few pieces from the front and weave it through the circlet, if that's alright?" Saga asked, already working her magic.

"Do whatever you think looks best." I tried not to sound like I was about to burst into tears, which I definitely was. Though, when I caught Marit and Sayyida watching us from across the princess's chambers, I realized it didn't matter. They smiled warmly, plainly reading my emotions. Clemencia looked even worse. Her hand was gripped to her chest, and a soppy expression crossed her face.

Blazing stars, I'm getting too soft.

"Here we are," Saga announced a moment later. "Have a look?" She plucked a gold-plated mirror from her vanity and handed it to me.

Using the larger vanity mirror, I positioned the hand mirror so that I could see the back of my head. I smiled. Saga had pulled back wisps of my hair from the front and woven them through the circle of snowflakes, which made my hair half up and half down. Curls cascaded from the accessory, and the gems gleamed against my white hair.

"I love it. Thank you, Saga." I gave her back the smaller mirror. "I'll return it to you tomorrow."

Saga shook her head. "Oh, no. I wish for you to keep it."

My lips parted. "I—it's too much. I can't."

"Yes, you can. I've only worn it once, and Mother gave it to me when I was a small youngling." Saga placed a hand on my shoulder. "Take it, use it, my friend."

Stars alive! I would cry and ruin the makeup Clemencia had helped me artfully apply. I swallowed and pushed back the tears threatening to leak from my eyes.

"Thank you." I sniffed. "I'm so glad that I met you."

"And I'm so glad that you'll soon be one of the Sacred Eight." Saga grinned. "It gives us a chance to come see you more easily."

My stomach rolled. I hated lying about this. "Both the warden and I would love that."

"I'm not so sure about Roar wanting us there," Sayyida spoke up. "But we'll take your welcome. You can show us around the western territory!"

I nodded, as if I would like nothing better. It wasn't

too difficult. If this were really my life, I would enjoy having these ladies visit and the Balik sisters too. Sadness threatened to overwhelm me, so when a knock came at the door, I felt relieved.

Saga's maid rushed to open the door. She fell into a deep curtsey. "Lord Lisika."

"I've come to escort my fiancée to the ball." Roar's voice came from the door. "Is she ready?"

"I am," I said when the servant glanced at me while keeping the door mostly closed so that the lord could not peek in and spy on the ladies. "I'll be right there." The maid relayed the message to Roar. While she did so, I turned to Saga. "See you there?"

"We're about to leave. I only need to put on my neck-lace and crown." She gestured to a table where her crown and other jewelry lay. "I'll find you and we can all dance!"

"Perfect." I smiled.

I did not know what sorts of dances a group of females might do—Clemencia had only instructed me in couples dances, but my new friends would teach me. The idea made my heart soar, and the smile remained on my face as I went to the door and found Roar on the other side.

Then, remembering what he'd done, how he'd slipped a potion into my drink, my smile fell.

"Hi." I shut the door behind me, tense from wings to toe to head.

"Neve," Roar whispered. "We need to talk." He offered his arm, and I took it, albeit stiffly. Roar led me away from Saga's chambers. When we came a fair distance from the princess's door, he turned to me. "I owe you an apology."

"Yes, you do," I said the words with confidence, when in reality, Roar's words struck me.

I hadn't expected him to say that so quickly, if ever. Warden Roar was kind but proud, and he had an agenda just like I did. If we continued to succeed in this farce, he would justify his actions as something he needed to do for us to succeed.

"I apologize, Neve. I should have told you about the potion and that I wished for you to take it."

I nodded, saying nothing.

"And of course, I should have given you a real chance to say no," he added.

An exhale parted my painted lips. "Thank you for saying that. Given my past, choice is important to me."

"I realized that after you left." His hand dropped and gripped my own. "You're simply so different from anyone I've ever met, and yet you play this part so well. Sometimes I forget you're not of this realm. That you are not the Lady Neve everyone else sees." His emerald gaze locked with my eyes, searching.

I'd felt this from him before, as though he was trying to lure me in. When we first met, it had affected me more. Back then just the idea of being lavished upon by a fae of power, one who was undeniably attractive and powerful, had stunned me. Since coming here, however, I felt less attraction to Warden Roar. He was still a good fae, a friend, but I sometimes felt that he tried to force feelings between us. And I knew for certain that while he could not lie, that did not mean he told me everything that I deemed I needed to know. He hid things, even things that had to do directly with me. Now, I felt we were bound only by a contract.

I looked away. "Thank you, Roar. We should get going, I think?"

"Of course." He released my hand and offered me his arm once again. "It is time for the show of our lives, my lady."

CHAPTER 32

As we neared the throne room, the site of tonight's ball, more fae than I'd ever seen in one place streamed through the halls. Lords and ladies had come from all over the kingdom for the Courting Festival and as tonight marked the opening night, they all wanted to be present. To stun.

And stun they did.

I'd been around much finery the last few days, and crafted elaborate gowns and suits for noble vampires in the past, but nothing could have prepared me for seeing so much of it in one place. Nor for being a part of the spectacle.

Furs, feathers, and beads adorned each gown, cape, and headdress. Jewel tones appeared to be the most popular, which I found surprising. In daily life, most fae of this court did not usually dress so colorfully, favoring muted tones that suited a winter palette. Of course, there were exceptions, like the princess, who seemed to love anything pink. Bell sleeves and voluminous skirts lined with fur also appeared to be in fashion. I made a note of that for when I made Marit's dress.

My head was still spinning from all the finery when we came to a stop at the threshold of the throne room to find it full of fae.

I cast Roar a confused glance, but guards on either side of us lifted horns to their lips and blew.

Ah, right, as a member of the Sacred Eight, Roar would be announced as he entered the ball.

Adhering to the custom, the fae in the room stopped whatever they were doing. The music ceased to play, and everyone turned. Already, there had to be at least three hundred fae in attendance, and the ball had only just begun.

I swallowed. Trying to keep my heart from racing, I glanced up at the ceiling

Jewel tones in every shade imaginable spanned the floor, but above our heads only two dominant colors existed: the royal blue and gold of House Aaberg.

Enchanted snowflakes in gold floated among the rafters, and flying blue candles provided an ethereal glow. Along the stark white walls hung banners representing the greater houses of the kingdom. The snow leopard of House Lisika, the ice spider and the web of House Riis, and all the others of the Sacred Eight were grouped together. The white bear of House Aaberg stood out as the largest of all the banners. Where there were no banners, windows made of stained glass depicted scenes of fae fighting valiantly, praising the stars, and studying tomes.

The guard to my left cleared his throat. "Warden of the West, High Lord Roar Lisika and his betrothed, the Lady Neve."

Fae fell into bows or curtsies, the depth of which depended on their rank relative to Roar's own. In a sea of fae, that made finding the royal family and the Sacred Eight members easy. They inclined their heads, or in the case of the princes, the queen and the king, they did nothing.

"Come, my love." Roar gazed at me, and we swept into the room.

The crowd parted as we cut through the center and approached the high-backed thrones, to pay our respects.

Only when we stood at the base of the dais leading up to the thrones did Roar stop. King Magnus and Queen Inga lounged on grand thrones of gold, with blue cushions on the seat and back. At the top of each great chair, a circle of snowflakes haloed the royals.

The princes sat on either side of their parents in smaller thrones, also blue and gold. Saga's throne was the only one to remain empty.

My eyes drifted to the Warrior Bear first. He stared at me too, but I looked away almost as quickly as I'd sought him out. Taking care, I avoided Prince Rhistel too. Instead, I focused on the king, who seemed to have recovered from the celebrations of last night, and the queen. Of them all, Queen Inga's stare was the most intense. Did she wonder why she could not break into my mind before? Or did she know Roar must have protected me?

"My king, we thank you for throwing the opening ball to the Courting Festival. And for sharing your roof with us. My lady fiancée and I have enjoyed our time here." Roar bowed.

I curtsied, but otherwise, remained silent.

When we straightened again, the king lifted a welcoming hand. "You are always welcome under my roof, Warden Lisika. You and your lovely fiancée, who I hope in the turns to come will bear you many sons and daughters."

Murmurs rippled through the crowd. Surely people had put money down that the king would break up our engagement. Well, now they'd just lost a bit of coin. I exhaled a long breath filled with tension.

"Thank you, my king," Roar replied. "I hope for a large family, too."

King Magnus grinned lecherously, and I tried not to think of last night when I'd seen that same look on his face in the harem. "Go forth, and enjoy your night, Warden Roar, Lady Neve. May all the other fae lords and ladies find matches as well suited as yours."

I twisted, and because I had let down my guard a touch, I caught sight of Prince Vale once more. He was still watching me, but now he was leaning forward, as if about to jump from his throne.

Heat flushed my body. When it came to the Warrior Bear, I could not deny that my body wanted him, but my mind was confused.

Roar slipped his arm through mine, bringing me back to the moment. "Come, my love. Let us celebrate."

We turned away from the thrones, the first test of the night done.

"Be prepared," Roar whispered. "Now that the king has approved our betrothal, others will want to know you. The females will wish to speak with you, and the males to dance."

"Dance?" I'd practiced enough to be confident with a handful of dances, but I wasn't sure I wanted to dance with unknown fae. "Why with them?"

"I'm a warden. They will wonder how a commoner came to be engaged to a titled male, and dancing assures them privacy. And in such a scenario, it would be poor form for you to deny them. Or for me to stop you from being introduced to society. The night will be a long one."

Already, a dozen fae approached us. One by one, they offered congratulations.

At first, most spoke only to Roar, though, as he predicted, a few ladies reached out to me. They introduced themselves as the wives of jarls, which explained their eagerness. Jarls were important to their home locales, but high lords and wardens held greater influence over the entire kingdom. The lesser lords and ladies wished for Roar and me to remember them. Little did they know that all this effort would be wasted on me.

And yet, I played my part, weaving a web of lies and smiling with each one. The attention felt so all-consuming I didn't even notice someone coming up behind me until he stood there, so close that I could reach out and touch him.

"Lady Neve." Prince Vale's voice cut through me, quieting the others around us, even Warden Roar. "Might I have a dance?"

I turned and my breath left me. His chest filled out his royal blue tunic in a way that screamed of a strong fae beneath. The v-neckline revealed a hint of ink, and I had to pry my eyes away to stop from staring. His long dark hair had been pulled back into a thick plait, revealing the shaved portion of his head beneath.

With effort, I tore my eyes away from the prince and looked at Roar.

Would he be furious if I accepted the dance? Even when he'd said that it would be poor form to deny dances with others?

To my surprise, Roar nodded with a smug expression on his face. It had to be all pretense and seemed to take all that Roar had to see protocol done.

I turned back to Prince Vale, my body drawn to him and my mind wondering why he'd approached me. Was it as Saga said and he wished to apologize for his outburst at the breakfast?

"One dance, my prince." I would try not to prolong Roar's pain for any longer than necessary.

Prince Vale held out his hand. I took it. Those callouses I'd felt when he pulled the glass from my skin were still there, rough against my hands. I found them reassuring. It made me think Prince Vale worked as much as his people did. I suspected that his twin's gloved hands would be smoother than mine.

As the prince led me on to the dance floor, I once again became engrossed in everything around me: the prince and the many types of fae present—dryads, faeries, nymphs, brownies, and even a fae I thought could be a selkie. Though I'd grown more accustomed to seeing fae around me, rather than vampires or humans, I still found it astounding at how diverse the fae order was.

"Were you taught the latest dances?" the prince asked as we stopped near the center of the dance floor. His hand landed on my waist as the other took my right hand. I touched his shoulder, putting us into position.

"I was," I replied. "Were you?"

A smile grew on his face at my jest, and the music picked up in a new song. We moved with the tide of fae, the prince leading me in a circle. "When I was younger, I was given lessons more often than I liked."

"If you don't like dancing, what would you rather be doing?" The question flew out of my mouth before I could stop it.

"Riding into battle, defending villages, towns, or smaller cities—some jarls have no armies. If I'm at home, I'd rather be sparring with my friend, Sir Caelo, or enjoying the beaches. Sometimes, I like to frequent taverns too." He paused. "And I never said I didn't like dancing, just the lessons. When one has an interesting and beautiful partner, dancing can be quite fun."

I blushed as dark eyes stared down at me.

"And you?" the prince asked, mercifully breaking the silence. "What do you like to do?"

The question struck me as so innocent, so normal, that I laughed. Nothing about my life had ever been normal.

"What's so funny?"

I scoffed. "Do you actually care? Or are you just using me to anger Roar right now? Or something else?" I hoped it would give the prince a chance to give up this farce and either interrogate or apologize, whichever he really wished to do.

Prince Vale nodded. "I do care."

I took in his expression, which looked genuine, and a touch hurt from my questioning. Another thing I'd gotten wrong about him, apparently. I felt bad, so I answered with the truth. "I like to sew. Creating gowns is a hobby of mine."

He glanced down. "Did you make yours?"

"I did."

"It's lovely. The prettiest dress at the ball."

"I—I'm sure you'll say that to all the ladies you dance with."

"I won't."

At that moment, his wings unfurled and, for a second, my heart stopped. Then, as the black wings wrapped around him and me, I remembered it was an optional part of the dance. Of course, the prince, who I had to admit had an impressive wingspan, would not fail to show them off.

"I didn't mean to startle you," he breathed.

"I know." I looked up at him and found myself unable to stop. The music played, beat by beat, and as we stared into each other's eyes, a shiver ran down my spine. Around us, the air warmed, electrified. His lips looked so soft.

The music changed its tune, and the prince's wings retracted. Lights blazed down on us, as did a hundred eyes.

I inhaled and looked away. Stars, I'd wanted to kiss him! What an idiot. It would not do to gain the king's blessing to marry the warden and then moon over the prince's lips.

"Lady Neve." The prince's voice came out slightly strangled. "I apologize for my actions earlier today. It was unbecoming of me."

I nodded, furrowing my eyebrows. "Why did you punch him?"

He swallowed. "My brother and I have a difficult relationship. And I found his claim that you beguiled me to be . . . too forward."

Prince Rhistel had not used the word beguiled. Nor had Prince Vale said that his brother was incorrect. I stiffened.

"It shocked me, to be certain." I tried to keep my mind from racing into questions I would never ask. "But . . . you've been understanding of me." I gave him a meaningful look. He nodded, catching my meaning, but he did not move to speak. "So I accept your apology."

"If I got blood on your dress, let me know. I'll have it cleaned for you."

"You didn't." It had been close, but I'd backed up enough to avoid any spatter.

At that moment, the song ended. Prince Vale stopped and bowed. I curtsied.

"I'm parched." The prince held out his hand. "Would you like to join me for a wine?"

I took it. "I would."

My quick agreement startled me, but I'd spotted Roar speaking with Lady Virtoris. They stayed deep in conversation, and I found that, while I enjoyed Sayyida's company immensely, I did not want to go speak with her mother. Surely, she'd wonder what happened to me in the royal box, and I'd have to bring up that Prince Vale saved me. Roar had been so good natured about the dance, but no need to remind him of the prince gripping my leg in the healers' wing.

At the thought, warmth pooled in my belly, but I pushed it aside as the prince led the way off the dance floor. A servant approached quickly, offering wine. The prince took the first gold goblet, handed it to me, and plucked another from the tray. He held his glass aloft.

"To a wondrous Courting Festival." The words sounded flat as they left his lips, but we drank to the toast anyway.

"Is there a highborn lady that you wish to court this festival?" I asked, then realized he might have as little say in the matter as everyone else. "Or one that your father will match you with?"

"Father would wish me betrothed to the lady with the most to offer the crown." He finished his wine in one gulp. "Many fit that description, but in differing ways."

"You don't seem happy about that."

"I wish to find my soulmate."

That stunned me. Not that I found it unreasonable. Rather, it was more romantic than I'd expected from the Warrior Bear. I too had often dreamed of finding my soulmate.

Taking a moment to compose myself, I finished my wine, waved a servant over, and set the glass on the tray. Prince Vale did the same, and when the servant offered more, we declined. I already felt too warm, too loose. I needed to keep my wits about me.

"Ambitious," I said finally. "Fated mates are rare."

Or so I'd heard. Humans didn't have fated mates, and I'd grown up around them. Fae could have them, though with humans all around me, I'd had little real hope of finding mine. Actually, I wouldn't have wanted to have found my mate—not if he were a slave too. I knew that some vampires were fated mates, like King Vladistrica and Queen Narcissa, but the concept seemed very removed from me. A fantasy. One that I would never experience.

"They are rare, but that doesn't mean I don't want to find her." He looked at the ground, as if sheepish to admit he had a bit of a romantic side. "If I'm to marry, I don't want it to be for political ambition or status."

I understood, even though that had never been a genuine issue for me. "Perhaps one day you'll find her. You'll be her prince in shining armor."

As I spoke the words, my heart gave a stutter of hope. Silly thing. That would not happen to me. Whomever I married, if I did, I'd find him after I saved myself.

Prince Vale smiled. "Comes with the title of Warrior Bear, I suppose. Though I often prefer thinking of myself as a shield rather than a sword."

I eyed him curiously. "The moniker gives off an—" From behind, someone ran into me, knocking me off my balance. "Oh!"

Slurred apologies flew, just as I did. Right into Prince Vale's chest.

He caught me, and I stiffened before looking up at him. Our faces were so close, our breath intertwining. Stars, he smelled so good, like sandalwood but also like falling snow on a cold day. And his eyes looked like dark pools, so warm and rich one could get lost in them. They locked on me, and for a moment, a fire blazed in them. A want. I swallowed, wanting too.

Whispers flew all around us, snapping me out of my trance. My cheeks heated as I cleared my throat and straightened. "Apologies, Prince Vale. I—"

"You did nothing." He shook his head. "A drunk jarl who has since disappeared into the crowd is to blame."

"Right."

We stood there, staring at one another. Neither of us knew what to say.

Again, the air seemed to heat, and my heart pounded harder. Stars, I needed to leave, to recompose myself. How to politely do so?

My answer came in the form of the pink-haired

princess. Tonight, Saga wore a tiara, a small circlet of gold mountains decorated with sapphires. But that was not the most inspiring item that she wore. Down the front of her royal blue dress spilled a gold necklace in a geometric pattern that had to have been made by a master craftsfae. It looked stunning and large, covering much of her chest and ending at her navel. Saga looped her arm through mine.

"Brother, I will steal the Lady Neve now, if you don't mind?"

He bowed. "Have a wonderful night, ladies."

Saga beamed and guided me away from her brother.

CHAPTER 33

"What's going on between you two?" Saga hissed the only words that could pull my attention off Prince Vale and focus it entirely on her.

My whole body, even my wings, tensed. "What do you mean?"

Saga laughed, her blue eyes that looked so much like her father's twinkling with mischief. "Don't pretend with me, Neve. We're friends, and I saw that look that passed between you and Vale when you fell into him."

A lump rose in my throat. As much as the idea might entice me, that the prince might actually like me, it would never happen. To his knowledge, I was a commoner. If he learned the truth, he'd be even less interested. A blood slave was not good enough for a prince.

Plus, I was engaged to his enemy. That would surely be a deterrent.

"Neve," Saga whispered. "You can be honest with me."

I cast a glance around. She'd led me to the edge of the room, away from the gossiping groups. As they had all night, fae stole looks in my direction, but they did not approach. Saga kept them away.

An exhale parted my lips, and I turned to my friend, eyes catching on the large necklace again.

"That's lovely," I said, hoping to change the topic.

She snorted. "It's pretty but showy. Mother insisted that I wear it, however. For the ships."

My eyes narrowed. Before I'd taken the cascading design to be geometric, but Saga spoke correctly; they'd been designed to be ships with overly large sails. The queen likely thought that would be appealing to Saga's betrothed, Lord Vidar Virtoris.

"Neve." Saga whispered. "*Talk* to me. We can't count that others will stay away forever. What is happening between you and my brother?"

Of course she wouldn't be deterred. It had been a fool's hope.

"Nothing," I lied.

"Stop. That look between you screamed otherwise."

I spun to look her in the eye, annoyance flaring. "What would you have me say, Saga? That he's the most handsome fae I've ever seen? That something charges the air when we're too near? Well, that might be true, but I cannot say it. I'm a commoner engaged to Warden Roar." I held up my hand. On it gleamed the ruby ring Roar had given me when we stayed in Guldtown.

"Your own father blessed our union!" Though I kept my tone low, it grew tighter with each word.

I considered the princess my friend, but we were new to one another, and she asked too much. Even if Prince Vale and I were attracted to one another, nothing could happen there. I would perform my duties at this festival and return to Guldtown as specified by my contract. From there, Roar would secure my passage south, where I would build a future of my own.

That would be my life. It would not include any lord or prince. No dancing at balls and wanting to kiss someone.

My stomach clenched in revolt, but I fought down the reaction. My body would have to deal with the truth. I did not belong here and needed to leave as soon as possible.

"I—you're right." Saga clapped a hand on my shoulder. "I shouldn't have asked you to say anything. It's too dangerous."

"It is." For a commoner to cross a lord and a king would be insane.

"I'm so sorry. It's just, I like you, and if you were interested in my brother, that is a match I would push for." Saga smiled, and her words made my heart swell. The idea sounded ludicrous but sweet. "Forgive me?"

"Of course." I already had. "I understand others wondering, but your brother wished to apologize to me. And smooth over that . . . situation at breakfast."

"You deserve that." She twisted to look up at the thrones. Her parents still sat there, and Prince Rhistel stood on one of the lower steps of the dais, speaking with an older male fae lord with red hair dressed in gray—Warden of the North, Lord Armenil, I suspected from the coloring that reminded me of Marit.

"If only Rhistel would do the same." Saga rolled her eyes. "I doubt he will even come near you though, after all that."

"That's fine by me."

She snorted. "Most ladies are *dying* for his attention. I like that you aren't."

Prince Rhistel was attractive, in his own way. And of course he held great power. But his personality put me off him.

The conversation took a turn as we observed others and wondered if Saga's father had decided on any matches for the Courting Festival yet. Across the crowded throne room, Roar spoke with other lords. He looked happy, likely relieved that our plan worked. His ease allowed me to relax, too. It felt nice to talk with my friend and enjoy the music.

The peace, however, was short-lived. From the crowds, Lord Riis appeared and strode our way.

"Lord Riis," Saga whispered. "Have you met him? *Really* met him? Not just what happened at breakfast?"

"I saw him while I was in the House Virtoris box during the tourney. He noticed me too, but we didn't speak."

"He will want to speak with you, which is a good idea. You need to create relationships with others. However, take care of what you say." Saga kept her voice low enough that Lord Riis could not hear, despite being only a few paces away. "As I said, I think of him like an uncle, but his loyalty as spymaster is to my father. Mother too, I suppose, but not really in the way his title demands."

I wondered what that meant. Probably that they were still friends, as they had been in childhood.

Whatever the case, Lord Riis approached and bowed to the princess. "Princess Saga, Lady Neve, I hope you are enjoying the ball?"

"We are." Saga replied. "And you, Lord Riis?"

"Splendid. I hope to see all three of my sons engaged by the end of this festival."

"Stars willing, Father will find them good matches." Saga bestowed him with a small smile. "We could use three fun weddings in Avaldenn and House Riis certainly knows how to throw a party."

"Indeed, Princess." Lord Riis turned his attention to me. "I actually had hoped to take a turn around the room with you, Lady Neve. We have not yet had time to meet properly." He smiled, and I found something so familiar about that smile, warm and inviting, that it disarmed me.

"I'd like that, Lord Riis," I said. "Princess, until later?"

"Have a fun night, my friend." Saga leaned forward and, for the first time, kissed me on the cheek. Then she swept away, leaving me alone with the lord gossiper of the kingdom.

I turned to Lord Riis. "Shall we walk?"

"Indeed."

We fell into step with one another, and I cut the lord a

sidelong glance. At this proximity, the freckles on his face became more pronounced, as did the darkness of his eyes, a warm deep brown.

"My son has been quite taken with your lady-in-waiting. He says that she smells like heaven. It's snow lily really, but I suppose that is close enough for him."

The comment shocked me, nearly as much as Lord Riis pinpointing the floral notes in Clemencia's perfume. "It's her signature scent."

"Every lady should have one."

I chuckled. It was exactly what Clem had said, though it sounded more natural coming out of her dainty lips than the mouth of this rather large, muscular, masculine lord. "So I've heard. Which of your sons fancies Clemencia?" I would absolutely be telling my lady-in-waiting this news when I saw her tonight.

The Lord of Tongues pointed to the crowds. "That one there."

I followed his direction and found a red-haired male talking with Prince Vale. The younger Riis looked to be around my age and just like his father, the son was barrel-chested and as tall as Prince Vale, which I'd come to see was rare. Only Lord Riis was taller at court. As I watched the pair, Riis's son began to laugh. The prince followed, clapping the younger faerie on the back and shaking his head as if the young Riis had said something naughty.

My lips quirked up, and I found myself wanting to be in on the joke.

"He admires the prince. It pleases me that they spend time together. Luccan could learn much from Prince

Vale," Lord Riis said, and something in his tone caught me off guard.

I turned to find the lord staring at the pair wistfully. For a moment, I found it odd, but then I remembered that Saga considered Lord Riis an uncle. It seemed as though the lord had a soft spot for Prince Vale too.

"His feats are legendary." I stuck to the safe line.

"Of course, but my eldest has no desire to fight. He admires the prince for other attributes."

"Like?"

"His ability to rouse the common fae to action. To bring people together."

I didn't know Prince Vale well, and I had preconceived notions of him that weren't flattering, but as more fae joined the prince and Luccan, I could tell that though the prince had made comments about not being social in front of me, he did enjoy the company of others. As they enjoyed his company.

"He does seem to cause a stir just being around others."

"Just like I've been hearing that you have caused a stir in court, Lady Neve, more so than just this morning." Lord Riis eyed me sidelong, amusement in the crinkled corners of his eyes. "It is quite refreshing."

"I'm sure you often cause one, my lord, with a title like yours."

He laughed. "I see my reputation precedes me."

"It does." I turned to him, hoping to keep most of the conversation off me. "I wonder . . . what secrets does a Lord of Tongues keep to himself? Is there such a thing? Or do you tell the king everything?"

"I serve House Aaberg." He lifted an eyebrow. "Thus, my king is kept well informed of events in his kingdom. Others too."

"What about *your* secrets, your dreams?"

He stopped and looked me over. "That's rather forward."

Better than him learning of me and catching me in a lie. I'd been careful so far, and skilled at hiding my truth, but this high lord might be able suss me out. In that case, I preferred to turn the tables and focus on him.

"Perhaps, but I'm at a disadvantage." I shrugged. "Many people know who I am and where I come from. I know nothing of you, and you have the most interesting position."

He looked me over, as if sizing me up. "I keep my own secrets. I'd advise you to do the same. Especially at this court."

"And your dreams?" I pressed.

"Those I share only with ghosts."

My breath caught.

He began to walk again. "Please, don't apologize. I've come to terms with how my life has panned out." He glanced up at the thrones the king and queen sat upon, taking in the male who controlled his life.

The king controlled my life, too. For now.

"So do you do anything besides what your duties to the Sacred Eight entail?" I tried to lighten the subject.

When Lord Riis turned back to me, his eyes were wide with amusement. "I own many businesses."

"Of what sort?"

"Brothels, mostly. A few taverns too. And one ridiculously opulent bathhouse in the midlands."

I cringed. This discussion was becoming more inappropriate by the second.

"I expect Lord Roar would not like me discussing my businesses with his intended." He chuckled good-naturedly. "However, I must tell you that some of my earlier ventures in life have made me attuned to female fashions. Not to change the subject, but I couldn't help but notice your hair pin? Where did you come across it?"

"Saga gifted it to me. The princess is quite generous." I still had half a mind to return it. The piece looked too pretty, held too much value, but another part of me didn't want to give it up. Not to mention, Saga probably wouldn't accept it.

"She is, just like her mother," Riis's eyes flickered to my hair. "I wonder if she knew it was a Falk heirloom?"

I barely held in my gasp. If that was true, would I be in trouble? The Falk rulers were hated at court. What if others recognized it?

"How do you know?" My hand fluttered to my hair.

"I was not a lord when King Harald and Queen Revna ruled. Instead, I was a merchant, specializing in rare gems, fine perfumes, and other luxuries. The kinds that were usually only found in other kingdoms"

I looked at him questioningly.

"It was before I expanded my business to include

pleasure houses," he said. "Anyhow, I mostly sold gemstones, most of which I procured from the elves and the dragon realm. Have you ever seen a phoenix opal?"

I shook my head. "I have not."

"They form near the volcanoes in the dragon kingdom and are a blazing red and white. It's said they are constantly destroyed and remade from their own ashes, though they are not really like phoenixes in that way. Just very rare. In any case, I obtained one there, and Queen Revna heard of it. She ordered me to court, and I had a private audience with her to show her the jewel. She wore that very same pin that's in your hair now. I complimented her on it. Apparently, it is quite old."

"I—do you think I should take it off?" My hand went to the pin.

"What do you mean?"

"It's from them. Isn't that dangerous?"

Lord Riis laughed. "I wouldn't worry about that. Queen Inga took many of Queen Revna's jewels for herself. No one could blame her as the jewels were spectacular, and some were known to be healing stones, a passion of the old queen's."

I cocked my head. I wasn't so familiar with healing stones, but I was sure that only healers could use them. "Was Queen Revna a healer?"

"Before she married the king, yes. And a very powerful one at that. So, you see, it would have been foolish to destroy such treasures. Queen Inga knew that and she gifted some to her daughter, too. After all, it is a crime to carry the Falk name, not to own ancient, beautiful pieces."

I frowned. "Are you certain?"

"I am. And if anyone questions you, please, blame me. I will endure it."

My eyebrows arched. "If you wish."

"I do. Now, tell me, are you feeling up for another dance?"

I hadn't been expecting that question, hadn't even been paying attention to the dance floor. Turning toward it, I saw that the dancing had become livelier. Fae were working up an appetite for the feast that would be served later.

"I don't know the one they're doing right now." I watched the dancers. Two lines of fae spun and exchanged partners with exuberance. It looked like fun, and I even spotted Sayyida on the dance floor, grinning at a young lord as she spun, so it must have been. But it also looked as though it would be very easy for me to knock someone out. "It looks a touch dangerous for someone who doesn't know the steps."

"The next one, then. I—" He trailed off, his gaze sweeping to the great door where guests entered. "Fates alive. That can't be who I think it is."

I turned to learn what had stolen his attention so thoroughly, and my skin turned to ice.

In the doorway, two figures stood. One dressed in red and black, as menacing as the angel of death. The other, a person I loved more than anyone else.

CHAPTER 34

S urely, I hallucinated.

What else could explain Prince Gervais Laurent and Anna standing at the threshold of the Courting Festival Ball, looking down on the fae, waiting to be noticed?

I almost convinced myself that was what was happening, when the king called for the music to stop and for the dancing to cease. Only when no one spoke or moved did King Magnus stand. "My Lady of Ships informed me that a Laurent ship entered our harbor this morn. Identify yourself, my lord."

My mind raced back to that very morning when Saga had mentioned Sayyida had gone to the docks to welcome diplomats from another court. I wanted to slap myself for being so stupid.

Had I possessed even an inkling that it had been this prince who'd arrived, I would have been halfway to the southlands by now.

The vampire of my nightmares stepped forward and bowed. "I am Prince Gervais Laurent, and this is my consort for the evening, Anna."

My heart thudded when he mentioned my friend's name.

"I'm afraid my ship took on water and your harbor was the closest to port. I hoped to settle here for the night, if you'll allow it, King Magnus." The prince gave a blindingly dazzling smile. "My crew, of course, will remain on the ship."

"Of course. Dreadful luck. Please, approach." The king invited the prince with a wave of his hand and a returning smile on his face. Diplomacy was at hand and the masks were up. "We must speak."

Blazing moon! That meant the vampire would get closer.

I drew in a sharp breath filled with blades of air that cut my throat and lungs to pieces. The silk of my dress, though loose enough minutes before, grew uncomfortably tighter. I gasped, reaching for the ties at the back as air became more difficult to come by.

"What's wrong? Lady Neve?" Lord Riis leaned closer. "Are you quite alright?"

I shook my head. "I—no, I'm not. I need air."

Oh stars, but *how*? The vampire who'd promised to purchase me, who wanted to tame the so called *wildcat fae*, blocked my exit. It didn't help that at this ball, I was an attraction. Where I went, eyes followed. I feared if I took one step in Gervais's direction, I'd garner attention from other fae. Then he'd surely spot me.

"Follow me," Lord Riis said. "We'll seek a quiet place."

I dared not glance at the vampire, even though the draw of seeing Anna again was great. As Lord Riis led me to a small door not far away, I realized that must be where the smell of food wafted from. Sure enough, he opened a door, and the aromas of bread and meat grew stronger.

Fae servants scurried about a beverage staging area, bowing and apologizing for doing their jobs. Lord Riis waved them off as we descended a wide staircase lined with paintings. I tried to focus on the art, not my thundering heart or the rushing of blood in my ears, but only one caught my attention enough to truly distract me. It showed an orc battle, and in it the monstrous breed of fae sacked a town. I swallowed as my eyes latched on to one biting into the neck of a youngling.

Not helping.

At the bottom of the steps, we found ourselves in the palace kitchen. Or one of them. This one appeared somewhat small to serve an entire palace that housed hundreds of fae. Obviously, it was here for events. A support kitchen of sorts.

The high lord maneuvered me to the back of the kitchen, where a few chairs sat, dilapidated and dusty. As he did so, an elderly servant rushed up to offer another— one with a cushion. I started to wave the servant off when I noticed he wasn't fae at all.

Rather, he was a human.

I stared at him, and my throat constricted. I'd heard

stories of fae courts that enslaved humans, but since I'd been here, I hadn't seen one and hadn't wanted to either. It reminded me too much of my old life, and that the Winter Court was not all that different from where I ran from.

This man looked thin and dirty and old, worn down. I felt certain that he did not work here because he wanted to. Why would any human stay in this realm, always relegated to being second-class?

The seconds passed as I stared, and the man's face reddened, but I didn't know what to say, what to do. When an old woman, also human, came up and took the man by the arm, I was almost relieved. That was until she looked at me.

Her face fell.

"You," she whispered, and her trembling hand went to her right temple.

"Do I know you?" I asked softly.

In response, the woman turned away from me. "Set the chair down."

The man complied, and the pair turned and before I could ask again, the pair scurried off.

What in the stars had just happened?

"Lady Neve, please sit," Lord Riis said softly.

I didn't sit, but I did turn my attention to the lord next to me. "They're slaves?"

"Pardon me?" Lord Riis's eyebrows pulled together.

"The humans." Annoyed, I gestured the way they'd gone. It wasn't like he could fail to see them. "They're slaves, aren't they?"

"Uh, yes." He shook his head. "Lady Neve? Can you breathe more freely?"

Not really. My breath still came in thin streams, and my entire body burned with fear.

"You really should sit down." Lord Riis gestured to a chair when I didn't answer.

"Where are the slaves from?" My mind latched on to this, likely because handling the issue of the vampire proved impossible.

"Many are born here. To slave parents."

"But not all?" Anna had also been born a slave. But Yvette and Simon and so many others in the Vampire Court had arrived here from the human realm.

"No. Not all. I—"

"What are you doing with her, Riis?" A sharp tone cut the Lord of Tongues off, and my eyes snapped up to find Prince Vale racing down the stairs, his face set like stone.

"What are you doing here?" I backed up so quickly I stumbled and nearly hit the ground before Lord Riis caught me.

"Riis!" Prince Vale barked. "Take your hands off of her."

"She's weak, my prince." Lord Riis sounded confused too. Maybe more so than me. "Would you rather I place her on the ground?"

"Of course not."

Powerful hands took me over. Prince Vale's hands.

What in the stars?

"What happened to you? I saw you run out of the ballroom and . . . " The prince trailed off, perhaps for the first time hearing how crazy he sounded. It bordered on territorial.

"Shouldn't you be with your father and the," my voice cracked, "vampire?"

"Are you fearful of him?" Prince Vale growled, dark brown eyes blazing. "That would explain what I saw."

Behind the prince, Lord Riis cleared his throat. "If the lady is amenable, I will leave you in Prince Vale's hands?"

I found it sweet of him to check. As if Lord Riis had any control over the prince of the realm. But did I mind? The answer came quickly.

No, I didn't.

Prince Vale had startled me, and I still wasn't sure why he rushed after me, but now that he had come here, I felt better. Safer.

"Or shall I retrieve Lord Roar?" Lord Riis added when I did not reply.

"No." I shook my head.

Having Roar come down here, when I was with the prince, would be a disaster. I'd rather the warden not learn anything about what happened.

"I'm feeling a chill," I said and gave a little shudder. "I wish to return to my chambers for the evening. Would the king mind?"

King Magnus had already blessed my union with Roar. I'd endured hundreds of fae watching my every move. I'd even celebrated. What more could the king want from a common fae when he had a vampire prince to entertain?

"I'll escort you to your suite and tell him you fell ill," Prince Vale said confidently.

Lord Riis took a few steps back, clearly assuming he was no longer needed, and that I was fine. "Very well. I will return to the event. Rest well, Lady Neve." He bowed and left.

Once alone, the prince looked down at me, still in his arms, like a damsel in distress. "Would you like to walk? Can you?"

I nodded.

He set me on my feet, and I did not so much as wobble. I gave the prince a watery smile. "I really can see myself to my chambers."

"Fates, no you won't." Prince Vale shot me a look with determination in his eyes. "I'll take you and make sure you don't fall again."

That look of his told me that I had no way out of this, but I would try nonetheless. "Why do you care? What are you doing down here, Prince Vale?"

He scoffed. "Should I not care? You're—under my family's roof. You're a fae of Winter's Realm, and you seem terrified." He paused. "Neve, what happened? Was it the vampire? Or did one of the ladies of the Sacred Eight say something to you out there? Saga told me that a few have been unkind to you. Or was Lord Riis saying something untoward?"

The ladies of the Sacred Eight? Lord Riis? Ha! Compared to a vampire prince, the young ladies of the Sacred Eight were but frost beetles. But I couldn't tell Prince Vale the truth. I was a common fae from a backwater village in the west, not an escaped blood slave who had killed a vampire.

I swallowed deeply. "They did nothing. The event simply wore me out."

He studied me. "I see."

His tone made it plain that he did not believe a word I'd said. Too bad. I would give him nothing more. And as much as I wished to question him about the humans, for now, I felt a burning need to get out of the kitchen. I needed to get to safety and think clearly. Besides, what could I do for them? I hated that they were down there, but I hadn't even been able to help my best friend.

"Will you take me to my chambers? I wish to lie down." I paused as my stomach roiled. "But I don't wish to make a scene. Might we avoid the throne room?"

The prince nodded. "Certainly. Going that way would only extend the journey to your wing anyhow."

As he led the way out of the kitchen and into a dark hallway, I thanked the moon for the alternate route. I hadn't even considered such a thing.

It soon became apparent that neither of us knew what to say to the other as we walked. Briefly, I wondered what he'd say if I told him the truth. He'd mentioned wanting to be a shield, a protector, more than a sword. Would he do so for a fae that was not actually one of his subjects? Someone who had been the property of a powerful, cruel family? Was that asking too much?

I couldn't risk finding out, so I remained silent as we traveled the empty corridors. We neared my wing, and my breath came easier. Only once I stood in front of my door did I feel safe.

I could hide in the suite. Prince Gervais wouldn't know I stayed in the palace. It wasn't like he'd come here for me—that was such a vain idea, brought on by terror rather than logic. His ship had taken on water, and he'd be here for a night, maybe a day.

That wasn't so long to stay in one's room. Roar could make excuses for me.

"Thank you, Prince Vale." I looked up at him. "I appreciate your concern."

He looked me over and inched closer. "Are you certain you're alright? Is your lady-in-waiting inside?"

"She is," I lied. Clemencia had been told to mingle and have fun at the ball. This had been her one night off, and I hoped she enjoyed it.

"Why do I feel that you're being untruthful?" His dark brows knitted together.

The intensity with which he studied me threatened to steal my breath. It was like he was trying to peer inside me, to figure me out, perhaps even see to my soul. Stars, no matter how much I enjoyed looking at the prince, no matter how much he intrigued me too, I couldn't have that.

"I cannot say, my prince." My hand found the door-knob as I felt desperate to leave. "I shall see you tomorrow."

With that, I let myself into my room, hoping to find Roar inside so that we could discuss this new development. But he wasn't there.

Had the warden even noticed my absence? Perhaps, if he had, he would cover for me. If that turned out to be the case, he'd be back soon. As the only person who knew the truth of my situation, it would be cruel to leave me alone for long.

Trying to keep my mind off the vampire prince and my best friend, I undressed, changing into a night shift. I had no intention of leaving this chamber, so I might as well be comfortable.

I washed the makeup from my face and took down my hair, admiring the pin that Saga had gifted me once more. I put it in a box when the door to the suite opened, and I rushed from my bath.

But instead of Roar walking into the room, Clemencia appeared, her eyes wide. "My lady! Lord Riis told me you were ill, and I rushed here as fast as I could. What can I do to help?"

Blasted stars. It wasn't that I did not want to see Clem. Rather, I found it sweet that she ran here on her first night off since meeting me. Still, I had wished to speak with Roar first.

"I'm already better. Being around too many fae had my head spinning." I forced a smile. "I nearly fainted."

She gasped. "Did you hurt yourself?"

"I'm fine. I promise." I paused. "Did you notice if Warden Roar was still at the ball when you left?"

"I looked for him, but I didn't find him in the crowd." Clemencia shrugged. "He might have retreated to a private room with the king and that vampire lord. The king pulled aside the three other wardens, so I did not think it odd."

Drat. If that was true, then who knew when I'd be seeing Roar? Perhaps not until the morning. It would be difficult to sleep tonight, knowing that a vampire lurked in the castle with Anna. My heart squeezed.

Fates, I wished to go to her now, to hug her and pull her away from that monster, and to hide her.

I sighed, and Clemencia rushed forward, probably worried that I'd faint again.

"Truly, I am fine." I tried to calm her down. "I might go to bed."

"Very well. I will wait out here in case you need anything."

"You don't have to, Clem."

At the nickname, her cheeks turned a sweet pink. "I know that you and the warden gave me the night off, but if something happened to you, I'd never be able to forgive myself. And after the fun I had, nothing can top it."

The fun? I arched an eyebrow. "Did you dance with someone handsome?"

The pink of her cheeks deepened to red. "I—I did."

I leaned forward. "What's his name?"

"Luccan."

"Oh! I spoke with Lord Riis! That's one of his sons, isn't he? He's quite handsome too." I didn't add that the lord had told me his son was quite taken with Clem. Better to hear what she thought first.

"He is one of Lord Riis's *bastard* sons." At the word bastard, her brightness dimmed.

That was right, Riis's sons weren't legitimate because the Lord of Tongues was unmarried. While Roar had previously expressed distaste with such a birth status, I didn't care. And I didn't like that such an opinion stole my friend's joy.

I met her eyes gently. "Was he kind to you?"

The smile returned to her face. "He was. He said he loved my perfume. Even nicer, he was an excellent dancer."

"His kindness and how he treats you is all that matters."

It might be a lie. I wasn't sure if Clemencia's father would appreciate such a match for his daughter, but he wasn't here. And really, who was trying to match her, anyway? No one at court. She attended the festival to help me and deserved some fun. For tonight, Luccan's status mattered nothing.

"Tell me about him as I prepare for bed." I looped my arm through hers, hoping the story would keep my mind off the vampire in the palace.

CHAPTER 35

I woke in bed to the sounds of joyously shrieking younglings and the sun warming my face. Yawning, I rose and rubbed the sleep from my eyes.

What time had I finally fallen asleep? Last I recalled, I was still waiting for Roar at the hour of the aura owl, when the moon hung high in the sky.

For a moment, I wondered why he didn't knock and wake me when he returned to our suite, but then I figured he knew I would be terrified by the appearance of Prince Gervais. Roar had likely tried to be kind and save me the horror of dealing with the vampire until the morning.

I slipped from the bed and wrapped a robe around my shoulders as I shuffled to the window and cracked it open. Judging by the position of the sun, it was late morning. Events for the Courting Festival would begin soon. Not that I planned to attend. I'd already decided to play sick until the vampire left court.

I swept from my room to find Clemencia sitting on

the settee and staring at the door to the suite, her back unnaturally straight.

"Clem? Is something wrong?" I asked when she didn't notice my approach.

She twisted, and I drew back. Clemencia was never anything short of put together, but today dark circles ringed her eyes, and she appeared pale. Slowly, she stood. "My lady, I don't mean to startle you, but Warden Roar did not return last night."

I stopped walking and pivoted to see Roar's bedchamber door open a hand's width. When he was in his room, he was in the habit of closing the door behind him, and no sounds came from within either.

"Are you sure?" I asked, searching for an explanation. "Maybe he came back and left already? It's rather late for waking."

She swallowed. "I've been awake all night."

"But why?"

"You were so distraught; I couldn't sleep thinking of you waking up in fear." Her teeth sank into her bottom lip. "Would you like me to light the hearth? It's colder than usual this morning."

My throat tightened. "I'm fine, but if you want a fire, please do. I wish you would have rested."

She ignored my comment as her attention once again swept to the front door. "I worry about Lord Roar."

I nodded. Roar must have celebrated too hard—after all, the king had announced us as matched. Not only was it a personal triumph for the both of us, but perhaps other lord and ladies had wished to drink and be merry with him? Would they really still be out though when they'd be expected at events today?

Clemencia gazed at me. "Would you like tea, my lady? I suspect that other lords and ladies ate together already, but I could go to the kitchens and request for breakfast to be sent."

At the mention of food, my stomach rumbled. "That would be welcome. Perhaps a broth? I'm not feeling so well."

Her forehead crinkled. "Still?"

"Yes. I'm afraid that I might miss the events of the day. Have they sent an itinerary to tell what the king has in mind for activities?"

She pointed to a letter on the table that I had not even noticed. As she prepared to walk to the kitchen, I picked up the letter and opened it. It did indeed include an itinerary for the day, which began with a promenade along the shoreline, followed by a tea. At the end of the itinerary, I found that the rebel fae who had attacked during the tourney would face off with a magical white bear and a feast would follow. I wrinkled my nose, happy to miss what would be a gruesome event, when someone knocked at the door.

The skin on my arms prickled. I didn't wait for Clemencia to answer the door, but did so myself, hoping to find Roar.

Instead, two palace guards, each with white claws on the breasts of their blue uniforms, stood there.

"Lady Neve," the Clawsguard on the right spoke, "the king has requested your presence."

Nothing in the soldier's face looked soft or welcoming.

"I—I'm ill." I fought to control my breathing.

His eyes stayed firmly on me. "It's a command, my lady. We are not to return without you. Get dressed. We will wait."

I swallowed. "Does this have to do with the warden? Is he injured?"

"We cannot say, my lady. We were told to bring you to the king right away. Do hurry. We would not wish for you to be seen in a robe."

"I'll be right back." I shut the door behind me and exhaled a shaky breath. I did not know why the king would want to see me, but the last time I'd been called to an audience with King Magnus, it had been less than delightful.

And why would he want me and not Roar?

"My lady? What did they want?" Clemencia poked her head into the room.

"The king wishes to see me."

Her eyebrows knitted together, but she nodded, as if ready for anything. "I'll go with you."

"That would be welcome," I said. "I need to change."

"Perhaps the red silk with the—"

"No. I'll wear something simple. I don't need help either." I required a moment alone to stifle my trembling arms. Something wasn't right, but I had no option except to go to the king.

Maybe he'll have answers.

In my room, I slipped from the robe and pulled on a simple dress of red. My hair held a bit of last night's curl, and I'd had the foresight to remove my makeup last night, so while I did not look my best, at the very least no powders smudged my face. I was presentable, if underwhelming in appearance. Considering I was playing ill, that could work to my benefit.

The moment I left my room, Clemencia opened her mouth, probably to tell me I should put on rouge or something to bring life into my face. I shook my head. "The king wants me there in a hurry."

Before she could protest, I opened the door to find the soldiers waiting. "I'm ready. Come Clemencia. We—"

"Only you." The armed fae who had spoken before grunted. "The king wishes only to speak with you."

"But I'm her lady-in-waiting." Clemencia appeared at my side in an instant, looking indignant.

"And our orders come from the king. Come with us, Lady Neve." The soldier guided me from the room, and when I turned back to catch Clem's eyes, she looked like they'd slapped her.

"I'll see you soon." I tried to sound reassuring, even though my belly ached with dread.

"I'll—have breakfast waiting on your return." Clemencia spoke so softly I almost didn't hear her.

The members of the Clawsguard led me through the palace. Now that I'd been here for a few days, things had begun to look more familiar. At least they did until the soldiers took a turn, and I found myself in the most opulent corridor I'd seen yet.

As in the rest of the palace, the tapestries hung on the white walls, though they were thicker than before, and the brocading on their edges looked finer. At least three bore images of King Magnus in the midst of harrowing and heroic deeds.

When we reached a set of double doors guarded by Clawsguard soldiers, I knew we'd arrived. Without my escorts saying a word, the fae at the door knocked and opened the king's door. A high, feminine giggle seeped out.

"Should I be here?" I asked with a swallow.

Having seen the king's harem already, I recognized he was not a shy fae. I might be walking into anything.

"Your king commanded you," the Clawsguard that had told me to come with them replied.

"And he is ready for you," the one at the door said. "Enter."

I took a step forward, steeling myself. My eyes landed on bare breasts and the king, blessedly still clothed, fondling them. I cleared my throat and forced my eyes to take in the rest of the vast room.

The single chamber spanned the size of Roar's entire suite, roomy indeed. Diamonds in shades of white and off-white patterned the marble floor. A fireplace dominated the wall across from the king's bed, spanning from floor to ceiling, and two white bears with claws extended were carved into each side of the hearth. Arched windows featured the Shivering Sea glittering in the day's sunlight. At the moment, judging by the waves and the motionless tops of the trees, the temperamental winds were down. If I wasn't playing ill and worrying about Roar, I'd have looked forward to the promenade on the itinerary.

The king gestured to me. "Lady Neve! Please, approach!"

I did so, stopping a few paces away as the king motioned for the female to lie on the bed. I was thankful she slipped beneath the gold brocade covers, especially when I recognized her. She was not a harem fae at all, but a daughter of a jarl who had spoken with Roar last night.

"As I have many matters to attend to today," he eyed the bed, "I will make this quick. Your lord was seen fleeing Avaldenn in the small hours."

I stiffened. "Pardon me, my king? I thought you said that Lord Roar has fled the city?"

"I did. He left alone and on horseback. Three of my men spoke to him in the stables, and the city gate confirmed seeing him ride down the Queen's Road. A bell later they claimed that three soldiers wearing the snow leopard on their breast followed to the west." The king frowned. "The idiots didn't even try to stop any of them."

"But—why?" With each second, I grew colder.

What had happened that would make Roar leave? And if he'd called for soldiers to follow, which it seemed like he had, why wouldn't he tell me—*take me*? We had a deal, and if he was in danger, I would be too.

"I hoped that you might answer that question." King Magnus studied me, his expression fierce. "I blessed your union. I told you to remain in the capital for the duration of the Courting Festival . . . and then the Warden of the West leaves?" He shook his head. "Not only do his actions make me look a fool, but they are also treason."

"It can't be!"

The king glared at me. "As is speaking to your king in such a manner."

Bleeding stars.

Magnus paced his vast chambers. "My lady, you know nothing of why your fiancé left?"

"Nothing," I admitted. "Perhaps something went wrong in Guldtown?"

"I would have been informed."

I wracked my brain but could not think of a single reason for Roar to leave the city as he did. After all, he had no family to worry about. And he'd surely guess that the king would deem his actions as treason. What in the stars had he been thinking? And he couldn't even have stopped by our rooms before leaving?

No, this made no sense. Roar was hiding something, just like when he'd hidden that he'd been dosing me with potions.

Anger rose in me at the position I'd been put in. "I-I don't know, my king."

"The Lisikas have always been a self-interested family." He stopped and turned to me. "That being said, I cannot abide by my lords disrespecting my commands. Lord Roar has committed treason, which puts you in a precarious situation."

The hairs on my arms rose, but I said nothing; I just waited.

"However, I am a merciful king." A small smile grew on his face. "So I will not blame you, a powerless fae in the face of a warden who swept you off your feet."

I curtsied. "Thank you, my king. I—"

"Henceforth," he interjected, "your union with Lord Roar is dissolved."

Straightening, I weighed how that might affect me. Roar had messed up, and he could hardly blame me for his actions. *I'd* kept to our contract. My shoulders released a touch. "Might I leave Avaldenn then, my king? Return to my village?"

The king shook his head. "No."

The soft sense of relief vanished. "But . . . why not?"

"Too many noble lords have seen you with Warden Roar. They expressed curiosity as to how a common fae female intrigued an eligible bachelor from the wealthiest house in the realm. One of the most powerful, too." He frowned at that admission, as though Roar's success made his own house appear weak. "You've piqued their interest. And mine. I might even keep you for myself." His gaze dropped and raked up my body in a way that made me shudder.

So now that Roar left, the other fae lords would want to claim me. Or the king might toss me in his harem. I'd have no say on the matter.

And to make things worse, I'd have to continue attending the Courting Festival events. Prince Gervais might see me.

No. I needed to buy myself time and escape as soon as possible. Clearing my throat, I bowed my head. "My king, I don't deserve such consideration."

"The warden has put you in a unique situation. Why would you not wish to seize it?"

Indeed, he had. Once I found the Warden of the West, I would be questioning Roar thoroughly. But first, I needed to make my excuses and get out of here.

"I'm not sure if you've heard that I'm feeling ill? Might I have a day to rest before joining in on the festivities once again?" I kept my tone deferential, though inside my emotions warred.

The king stared at me as if I'd asked him to pull down the moon. Then, shocking me stiff, a laugh burst out of him. "You truly are something, Lady Neve. A commoner lifted by a warden is now asking for a king to make an exception for her?"

"Majesty, I ask humbly." Each word stuck in my throat. All my life I'd had to ask for every little thing, and now that I was the most free I'd ever been, I did not want to do so any longer.

Soon, I reminded myself. *Soon, I will flee again and find Roar and demand that he make good on his promise. And when I'm free, I won't have to bargain ever again.*

"You have the day. Tonight, you will join the lords and ladies of the land as the rebels we caught meet their doom. Then, I'll see you at the feast after."

Stars, I'd hoped to avoid the trial. The bloodbath. But I couldn't deny the king, especially when he believed he had indulged me.

"Thank you, my king." I curtsied. "I shall rest until then."

Magnus twisted to the bed. "You're dismissed."

I turned and exhaled. When I reached the door and

opened it, the same Clawsguards who brought me to the king's chambers waited outside.

"I'm going to return to my suite," I said.

The soldier shrugged. "As you wish."

I blinked at him. "You aren't to escort me?"

"My orders were to bring you here. Now I wait for the king's next request."

"Fine." It wasn't so much that I wanted their help. I could find the way back on my own. However, I did want a barrier around me should I encounter other fae lords and ladies. Or Gervais.

Any moment spent outside the Lisika suite put me at risk, so I strode down the corridor with all my senses on alert. Step by step, however, my worries slowly eased. Though midday had come, the castle seemed less bustling than usual. In fact, I'd never seen it so quiet. Perhaps I could get back to the suite with no issue.

I had made it all the way to the domed chamber with the massive stuffed white bear and felt quite positive about how I'd avoided any interaction when my luck ran out. I froze, terror gripping me.

Prince Gervais Laurent leaned against a wall; his arms crossed over his chest as though he'd been waiting for someone.

Me. My mind supplied the thought, though it made no logical sense.

I might have been anywhere in Isila—frozen to death in the mountains, most like. And yet, here he stood, smirking as if he'd known I'd be here all along.

The vampire pushed off the wall and stalked toward

me. More fae walked here, mostly servants but a few lesser lords and ladies. I hoped none of them cleared out, hoped they'd be a sort of flimsy shield that would keep the vampire in check.

"Wildcat," the vampire prince crowed, approaching with the preternatural grace only his kind possessed. "I was hoping I'd run into you here."

"How?" I choked out.

"You had to go somewhere, didn't you? And seeing as you made it past the city gates, I realized you were far more determined and resourceful than most of your kind." He glared but kept a distance from me that would be appropriate for a lord and lady in polite conversation. "We found no fae remains in the woods and, as you know, we can search quite fast."

I didn't reply, largely because I was trying not to visibly shake. Fae still milled about, my only saving grace.

"Your trajectory led straight to this kingdom, and it didn't take long for me to find someone who'd seen you. A lumberjack slighted by this duplicitous lord. He willingly gave up information on a bedraggled fae female."

Frode. That son of a harpy! Then, the other part of what he'd said struck me. Given what I'd just learned of Roar's escape, it struck a chord with me.

"Why do you call Lord Roar duplicitous?"

Prince Gervais blinked, appeared shocked, and then a slow smile spread across his face. "You really don't know the fae you're engaged to very well at all, do you?"

"I . . ."

I trailed off because the answer was no. I'd thought I

494

knew a little about Roar. I'd thought that even if he wanted more from me, we could weather the storm of court and come out as friends. But he'd left me here, high and dry. And I could find no excuse for that.

It turned out that I didn't know him at all.

"He's a powerful fae," I shot back, grasping for something to say. Something to protect myself with. "You'd do best to leave me alone."

"Is he?" Prince Gervais looked amused. "True power doesn't flee."

Bleeding skies, I hated that vampire. To make sure he knew it, I scowled.

Gervais chuckled, clearly enjoying my torment. "I'll admit, he might not be the power you believe him to be, but he *is* a good actor, good at hiding his deeds. But because I like games, I'll give you a hint. The Lisika's mines have given gold for centuries, but isn't that odd? One would think that they'd need to diversify. Or find other valuable *investments*. Can you think of nothing as valuable as gold, wildcat?"

I swallowed and opened my mouth to reply, to demand that he stop these stupid games and tell me what he knew, when none other than Queen Inga waltzed into the foyer. My eyes latched on to her, and my heart began fluttering wildly. If I could only get her attention, perhaps I'd be safe.

"Before you run to hide behind her royal skirts," Prince Gervais tone dipped dangerously as he leaned even closer, so close that I could smell the tang of blood on his lips, "understand this, wildcat. If you flee the castle, your friend dies. And if you think I will leave this frigid kingdom before I have you in my grasp, you are seriously mistaken."

"Have you hurt her?" I rasped, forgetting all about Roar.

"I've taken what is mine, but her blood is a mere snack and I'm ready for a meal." He eyed my jugular, leaving no doubt as to what he meant. "Think on that, and on how you might save her life."

With that, Prince Gervais walked past me, leaving me trembling in his wake.

CHAPTER 36

By the grace of the Fates, I made it back to the Lisika suite where I promptly collapsed onto the settee. Tears I'd been holding back made a fast appearance, and by the time Clemencia returned from the kitchen with a breakfast basket in hand, I was a sniffling, snotty, teary mess.

"My lady! What happened?" She set the basket down and approached on light, fast feet. "Is it something to do with the warden? Is he injured?"

Of course, she would think that I cried over my missing fiancé.

What could I say to her? I couldn't tell her the truth, or at least, not all of it. That would be dangerous, and if by some slim chance Clemencia stayed loyal to me, it still put her at risk.

My oldest and dearest friend was already in danger. Clemencia could not suffer the same fate.

"My lady Neve?" Clemencia perched next to me. "Please, tell me."

The lump in my throat grew until I swallowed it down. I took a deep breath and forced the tears to stop.

"Roar left last night, Clem." Her mouth fell open, and I rushed on to avoid questions that might trip up my story. "I don't know why and neither does the king, but he took offense to it and dissolved our union."

"Not your betrothal," my lady-in-waiting whispered as her own eyes filled with tears. "But that's cruel! You two are so in love."

I looked away as another sob burst out of me. Though I was glad Roar and I had been convincing, the better I got to know Clem, the more I hated lying to her.

"Are we to return to the west?"

"The king wishes for me to continue in the Courting Festival."

My lady-in-waiting stilled. "I mean no offense, my lady Neve, but that is quite odd. You are an elevated lady, not one of blood. Why would the king want such a thing?"

"Noble fae have taken an interest in me." I huffed out a breath and wiped another stray tear from my cheek. "And the king said I might become a part of his harem."

Shock rippled across her delicate features. "He would not . . ." She trailed off, possibly recalling all the tales of what the king had done before. By comparison, taking an unwilling common fae into his harem was nothing.

"We must not let him!" The resolve in her tone stunned me.

"Clem, he's *the king*. We have no power over him."
What in all the nine kingdoms did she expect me to do, us
to do? The only person who could get us out of this–and
even that was a *huge maybe*–was Roar.

And after what Roar had done and speaking with
Gervais, I wasn't sure I trusted the Warden of the West
anymore.

Clemencia stared at me for a moment, stood, and ran
into her bedroom. I watched her door, puzzled, until she
emerged a minute later with a vial in her hand. "I should
have thought of this earlier. It's a calming potion. Althea
gave me a few before we left Guldtown. Just in case the
festival got to be too much."

I took the vial, downed it, and thanked Clemencia.
Immediately, a sense of ease washed over me, calming my
racing heart a touch.

She sat back down. "My lady, I know you're
distraught, but there *are* fae the king might listen to. One
of whom likes you." Clemencia gripped my hand. "You
must call Princess Saga. She can plead with her father on
your behalf. At the very least, you will not become a part
of the king's harem, though . . ."

She closed her eyes and shook her head, unable to
finish her sentence. She didn't need to. Clem must have
thought it atrocious that I might be married to another
noble when I was so very in love with Roar.

I inhaled, considering her idea. In truth, it seemed like
a good one. "You're right. Clem, can you send a
messenger to bring the princess here? I would go to her,
but . . ." I placed a hand on my stomach, feigning illness.

"Of course! The princess will understand, I'm sure!" She leapt up and left the room.

The moment she left, I set to cleaning myself up. Saga may or may not be able to do something, but I didn't need her to see me like this. Something about the princess instilled strength in me, and though I was in a bad place, I wanted to meet Saga on a more level field.

I washed my face and applied makeup. As Saga still had not arrived, I went to the basket in which I kept the vial of Roar's blood. I pulled it out, hands trembling as I did so.

Should I drink it? The idea disgusted me. Though I would be within my rights by our contract, a part of me wanted to believe that Roar left for a good reason. But what could that reason be?

Then, holding my vial, another thought struck. If Roar hadn't been back to our room since he went to the ball, perhaps he'd left his vial containing my blood. I hadn't seen it since the day we'd made our deal.

I rushed from my room into Roar's chambers to find the space immaculate. Where would he hide it? Going with my first guess, I opened the bedside tables. Nothing. A sweep of the drawers in the bathroom proved equally fruitless. A sense of frenzy built inside me and I searched faster, beneath the mattress, under the bed and rug, even feeling the hemlines of the thick curtains. After that, I was sweating and still empty-handed.

I huffed and, determined to leave no stone unturned, took a step back, scanning the room again. That time my gaze landed on the bedside table. A book lay there.

Roar once told me he and his brother hid messages in books. *Would he . . .*

I strode to the table again and snatched up the book, opened it carefully and turned the pages. Near the end, a gasp ripped out of me.

There it was, a small cut out in the pages. And inside it, the vial of my blood gleamed. I wasn't sure what made me do so, but I took the vial out, shoved it in my pocket and replaced the book before returning to my room, hands trembling.

So whatever state Roar had left in, he hadn't dared return for the vial of my blood. Had he expected me to look for it? If so, why? What was his motive?

I let out a groan of frustration. None of this made sense.

And what about what Gervais had said? Gold was the currency of all the nine kingdoms, the one thing that could buy power and safety. What was more valuable? Precious jewels perhaps?

A knock came at my door, and Clem poked her head inside. "The princess is here, my lady."

"Thank you." I swept over to meet Saga, who already waited in the sitting area. "Saga, thank you so much for coming."

"Of course!" Saga beamed. That morning, her pink hair looked more vibrant than normal. Or perhaps it only looked that way because I felt so low. "Your lady-in-waiting made it seem quite urgent. And you disappeared so quickly last night that I wondered about you. Are you well?"

"A little off, but that is not what I want to talk about. Please have a seat."

We settled into a pair of chairs. Clemencia made herself scarce in her room. I appreciated that Clem always recognized when I needed privacy.

"Is it your stomach?" Saga asked, sympathy crossing her delicate features. "That's what I heard."

"Who told you?"

"Vale, of course."

"Oh . . ."

She shifted in her seat and tucked her ankles beneath her. "He was upset when he returned to the ball. So much so that Father told him to leave."

"Are you serious?" I was certain that having two sons to marry off was a big deal to the king. It gave him a way in to maintain power over every lord and lady in residence.

"He did. Many ladies were upset." Saga shrugged as if she didn't care at all. "They had Rhistel to flirt with, though."

I laughed dryly. "Because they're so comparable."

The princess's eyebrows rose. "They're not, but most of the ladies would take either. And now I have to ask, again, what happened between you and Vale?"

At his name, my heart fluttered, betraying how much the prince affected me, even if I tried to ignore it. Even if I didn't understand it. A pretty face was not enough for me, but my body didn't care about my standards.

"I'm sure I don't know what you mean."

Saga rolled her eyes. "Neve, I admitted that he looked

upset when he came back. Actually, *furious* might be a better word to describe my brother last night. Something happened to you, and Vale could not get over it. That means that you're important to him, Neve." She swallowed. "Does Warden Roar know?"

We had arrived at the crux of the matter.

I cleared my throat. "My Lord Roar doesn't know. Nor am I sure if he is my lord any longer. He left last night."

"Left?" She blinked. "You mean left the castle to stay in the city?"

"He left *Avaldenn*. As far as anyone knows, he's gone for good, Saga, and your father has dissolved our union, leaving me unprotected. King Magnus wished to keep me in the Courting Festival—or as part of his harem— neither of which I want."

With each word, the princess's face grew paler, stonier.

I stared at her desperately. "And I want to leave. Please, Saga, we're new friends, but is there a way you can make that happen?"

"I—I don't know what to say." Saga stood and, like the king had in his chambers, paced the room. "My father is not always kind. But he really said he'd place you in his harem?"

"He did."

"He'd leave you no choice." Her fists tightened and for a moment she stared at the window, as if composing herself, before turning back to me. "That is my lot in life, and I cannot abide for you to join me. Not when you were betrothed by your own will, and now you can't even say where Warden Roar is."

I refrained from noting that the king was currently playing at making hundreds of matches. Surely, some had to be unwilling.

"Since he left willingly, I don't know where Warden Roar and I are now," I said. "But I can't abide by the options given to me either. Especially not when I need to find my fiancé and speak with him."

"You deserve an explanation." Saga exhaled. "So, my answer is yes. I will help you escape here, but we will need one more person to make this happen."

"Who?"

"Vale."

My stomach tightened. Roar swore the Warrior Bear Prince was a horrible fae. And while I could not reconcile the story Roar told with what I knew of the prince, would the Warrior Bear really help? I was Roar's fiancée, or more accurately, ex-fiancée, and going against his lord father's word. He already held one secret for me, but would this be too much?

I scrubbed a hand over the back of my neck. "Saga, you love your brother, but are you sure that's a good idea? What about your father? Doesn't your brother report to him?"

"You don't know Vale like I do," Saga replied. "He might be a soldier and act somewhat brutish at times, but he is a fae who knows right from wrong. Plus, he has connections that we will need to call upon to get you out of here."

"I see." Did I have a choice? If Saga couldn't orchestrate an escape alone, and I couldn't either, I needed to trust in her ideas. "But please, can we keep this to us three?"

"And whomever Vale chooses to help." Saga took my hand. "Whether it is protectors to travel with you from the city, or someone to sail a boat, you cannot do this alone."

A thought struck. "I can't. You're right. Which reminds me, Clemencia needs to come with me. And one other."

Saga gave me a long look. "I understand taking your lady-in-waiting. Otherwise, she will be questioned, perhaps even cruelly, after you leave. But who is the other?"

"Prince Gervais has a human consort named Anna. She must come too."

Saga reared back. "But—*why?*"

"I can't tell you why." I found I wasn't worried about admitting that. The calming draught must have well and truly kicked in. "But do you think Prince Vale can make that happen?"

For a moment, she said nothing, just stared. When she spoke, it came in a low voice. "We'll do our best, Neve. I'll relay this information to my brother. He will be the decider. Does that suit you?"

"It will have to." I rose and made to curtsey, but Saga stopped me by wrapping her arms around me in a hug.

My chest tightened, knowing I was lucky to have her

as a friend and that if I made it out of here alive, I'd miss her forever.

"You will be at the trial by bear, right?" Saga asked as we pulled apart.

"And the feast. Your father told me I must attend."

"I will be there too, standing with you." Saga squeezed my shoulder. "Now, I must go see my brother. Rest and prepare until tonight, Neve."

CHAPTER 37

The hours passed, and my nerves grew. From my window, I watched fae enjoying the late afternoon, but I stayed safe inside, trying to piece out what had happened last night and, more importantly, what was to come. The vials of blood, both mine and Roar's, seemed to burn a hole in the pocket of my dress. I would not part with them again. Not after what had happened.

Recently, a message from Saga had arrived saying I would have an escort to the trial. Would it be Prince Vale?

I got ready at the specified hour, dressed in attire suitable for the trial and the feast after, with a glamorous twist. Though the hairpin Princess Saga had gifted me looked much fancier than my dress, it also comforted me. I'd wanted to wear it, so I did.

When the knock came at the door, I rushed to answer. Clemencia, however, beat me there, and when she opened the door, I cocked my head.

A tall faerie dressed in the uniform of the Clawsguard stood there. He had dark black skin and the most brilliant blue eyes and matching wings. I was certain that I'd never seen him before, as this male was the type anyone would notice in a crowd. Handsome, strong, and as his face split into a wide smile, I suspected he was kind as well.

"Lady Neve, I'm Sir Caelo." He inclined his head as I approached. "Part of Prince Vale's Clawsguard. Are you ready?"

"Let me grab my cloak. Clem, get yours too." I whirled and reached for my sage-green fur-lined cloak I'd set over the back of a chair. Clemencia disappeared into her room and returned with a pretty wool cloak embellished with snowflakes.

Sir Caelo ushered us from our rooms and down the hall. Fae stared and shook their heads, hinting that word of Roar's departure had already spread far and wide, but with a Clawsguard at my side, they did not approach me. I thanked the stars for the knight's presence.

We reached the part of the palace where we would have needed to turn left to go to the tourney grounds, but Caelo went right instead, and I stumbled.

"Pardon." I righted myself. "Aren't we going to the tourney grounds?"

"I'm afraid that the Pit is much less luxurious. Though, of course, you'll be in the best seat." Unease flashed across his face. "Not that that means much in the Pit."

"I see," I said, though I really did not.

Once the knight turned and continued to lead us

through the halls, I caught Clemencia's eyes. She shrugged.

I supposed I'd learn soon enough, so I followed Sir Caelo's path.

"Brace yourselves, ladies." The knight approached a door to the side of a hallway. "The winds coming in off the Shivering Sea have picked up. I swear, they're colder than a mage's touch."

He opened the door, and right away, the wind whipped inside, stealing my breath. Once I'd pulled the cloak tighter around me, and I could breathe again, I peered out. Mounds of blinding, white, glittering snow on either side of a manicured path stared back at us, but there wasn't a soul in sight.

"Is this event not well attended?" I thought back to when we went to the tourney, many fae flooded the walkway.

Sir Caelo nodded. "It is. Everyone invited to the Courting Festival is already at the Pit. Some common fae from Avaldenn, too. The prince was specific about how he wanted this timed."

"Can you share more?"

He eyed me carefully. "Afraid not."

If I didn't trust Princess Saga, I wouldn't have taken another step. But I did trust her.

And despite all of Roar's stories against Prince Vale, I trusted him, too. The memory of his hand on my leg as he pulled out pieces of glass with care and precision pressed on me. How he'd delivered the balm to me and how he had not turned me in after I'd ended up in his

513

rooms.

And Roar is clearly not the most trustworthy. He dosed me with potion without my knowing. And now he's left . . . Perhaps I've had everything all wrong.

That idea terrified me, but I'd had many hours to consider such a thing. Roar had left. We'd had a deal, and he'd broken it and put me at risk. Whereas I'd believed us equals before, thought I trusted the warden with my life, now, I felt unsure about where we stood.

Sounds of a crowd met our ears. I looked about but found no structure large enough to contain the number of fae I'd seen at the ball, let alone them plus common fae from the city. "Where is—oh!"

Sir Caelo took a sharp turn on a snow berm lined path and the Pit came into view, silencing me. Hundreds of fae filled the gaping hole in the ground, all looking down into the center of the Pit.

Our escort marched up to the edge of the Pit, and from a few steps down, soldiers saluted him by pounding fists to their chests. He descended the steep wooden steps but did not salute back. Either Sir Caelo had not noticed them, or his rank made it inappropriate for him to salute back. Clemencia clasped my hand, and we trailed behind him, walking deeper into the inverted stadium.

Dirt covered the bottom of the Pit rather than snow like the outside, hinting that an invisible overhead shield protected the Pit. As I felt no wind, when before it had been whipping over the grounds, I was sure I was right.

No white bear prowled the center yet. Instead, jesters played at using magic. At the bottom, still high above the floor of the Pit and out of range of a white bear's claws, sat the royal family, apart from the rest.

We headed straight for them. My stomach fluttered, and I watched the jesters to quell my nerves, until we reached the lowest level, and Sir Caelo stopped. "My lady Neve, Lady Clemencia, here you are."

We took a few more steps and joined him to stop before the king, queen, the winter princes, Princess Saga and, of course, Prince Gervais. The royals sat in a partitioned area made clear by soldiers who surrounded them. From above, other fae could see the royals.

They'd see, too, that I joined them. Why? What were Saga and Prince Vale thinking?

"Thank you, Sir Caelo."

He bowed and waited for us to enter the box. I did and came face-to-face with King Magnus.

Between the king and his queen perched Prince Gervais in a position of honor. Hiding my revulsion at both the fae king and the vampire, I smiled and curtsied. "My king. My queen. Prince Laurent."

"You're looking well, Lady Neve." King Magnus eyed me. "So pleased that you could join us at the invitation of my son, though I do wonder at the late arrival." His eyebrows rose, plastering a judgmental expression on his face.

"Apologies," I said. "I could not find my cloak."

The king didn't look convinced, but it didn't matter because at that moment Prince Vale stood and came over to me. He inclined his head, and I curtsied again. All the while, the vampire studied me, silent as the grave and deadly as a snake in the grass.

"My lady." The Warrior Bear took my hand. "I have saved you a seat next to me. Your lady may take up a place with Saga's lady-in-waiting." He gestured behind the first row where the royals sat in cushioned wood chairs, luxurious only when compared to the bench seating the other fae used.

"Thank you," I replied as confidently as I could. Showing fear in front of the king or the vampire was suicidal.

Prince Vale led me to the end of his family's line and placed me between him and Saga. I caught the princess's eye, and she winked.

Once I settled in, a bell tolled outside. At that note, the king stood and snapped his fingers.

The jesters reacted, rushing into the bowels of the Pit where we could not see them. I imagined the rooms to be dark and dank subterranean areas, behind a metal gate for protection, waiting for the white bear to be released from its cage, just like the rest of us. What terror they must feel.

Prince Vale leaned closer. He wore fighting leathers, and the scent wafted off him and mixed with a more seductive aroma of sandalwood. A chill dashed down my spine. I no longer felt immersed in what happened below.

"You look wonderful, Lady Neve," he whispered.

"Thank you." My eyes met his and asked another question. *What are we doing?*

He smiled broadly. "Did you wear that color for me? It's one of my favorites."

"I—wha—"

Saga's sharp elbow found my side, jabbing in. I winced and twisted to find the princess glaring at me.

"Play along," she hissed, just loud enough for me to hear over the excited murmurs of the crowd.

I turned back to the prince. "I didn't know green was your favorite color, but I'm glad it pleases you, my prince."

He grinned; the sight so lovely that I swore it stopped my heart. "I like hearing that." Then, he reached out and took my hand, pulling it closer and placing it on his upper thigh.

Eyeing my hand's position, I swallowed. I wasn't sure what we played at, and while I found Prince Vale attractive, this behavior came off as strange and far too forward. Anyone might see.

Actually, that wasn't a theoretical idea. People could see, and they *were* looking.

Prince Gervais leaned forward ever so slightly and trained his gaze on me. The king also stole glances, and Prince Rhistel, somehow the most innocuous of the threatening lineup, stared at his twin, mouth ajar. I squirmed and glanced around. Common fae watched openly too and whispered behind hands.

Why is he doing this?

I wished I had been privy to their planning session, but I had not, so I sat there, wracking my brain to figure out their motive.

As far as other fae knew, my fiancé had left court, and now the Warrior Bear was acting very familiar.

A sharp breath sunk into my lungs. Was he trying to convince others that Roar left because Prince Vale had an interest in me? Everyone knew that they did not like one another. Were rivals even. Was this supposed to look like a conquest for the prince?

But how would this get me out of Avaldenn?

My questions fell away as an announcer soared into the center of the Pit and glittering white magic flew from his hands. "Today we witness a trial of rebels! A trial by the white bear!"

I gasped at the show of magic, but the cheering of the crowd swallowed the sound. Though I was living in the land of the fae, and most had at least a base level of magic, fae did not use their powers often. For now, that suited me, as I had no magic to show off. I wondered what mine would do when I could wield it. Would I be strong or weak? What color would it be?

I didn't know, but as the announcer's magic swirled through the air and zoomed at a second gate at the base of the Pit, I lost all thought. His power hit the gate, and it burst open. Four fae, their wings torn off, raced out, chased by soldiers with spears on fire.

"Their wings," I whispered.

"Father deems it appropriate that they can never fly again. Even if they win." Prince Vale spoke just as softly in response.

A muscle feathered in his defined jaw. I didn't think the prince agreed with his father on this course, and I had to wonder if anyone ever won against a white bear. Though I was not about to ask. The king sat too close and might overhear.

Besides, at that moment, the announcer's magic soared toward the wall closest to me. I could not see a gate beneath where we sat, but the metal shuddered violently, and the next thing I knew, a great white bear surged from the bowels of the Pit.

Fae screamed, and my hands flew to my mouth. I'd never seen a living white bear before, but I'd read about them. On all fours the creature stood as tall as a large horse, and it had to weigh at least three times as much. The stuffed version in the palace looked tiny by comparison. "It's enormous." I gasped at the sight.

Prince Vale twisted to face me. "It was born from the largest of its kind."

"Has it ever been free?"

"Free?"

"In the wild?"

The question appeared to strike him as odd, but after a moment's hesitation, he shook his head. "It was bred and raised in captivity. It was the first white bear born after my father took the throne. The most savage of its line. My father is quite fond of it."

That this bear remained alive and that the king used it for trials against those who committed crimes meant that it had never lost.

As the bear charged the fae, I pitied the defenseless rebels. Not only had their wings been torn from their backs, but not one of them used magic. I suspected they could no longer do so. Without wings or weapons, how could they fight in this so-called trial?

The white bear neared his first victim, and roared. I sucked in a breath as a blast of ice burst from the beast's maw. Mere heartbeats later, the ice formed points and tore into the fae. The rebel dropped to the dirt, screaming in pain, but the bear silenced him by tearing into his throat.

"One rebel found guilty by the stars!" the announcer, still flying above the bear, shouted. "What will come of the others' fates?"

I felt ill. As if we didn't all know. This was no fair trial.

Nor did it seem that it was much of a contest for the bear. He killed one female dwarf, and then another male fae in quick order. With each kill, the king grew more rambunctious, pleased with the beast that was the symbol of his house.

"It will be over soon." Prince Vale leaned closer, shifted his hand to clasp mine, and squeezed as the bear flung a barrage of magic at the final fae. The male leapt out of the way just in time.

That move enraged the beast as much as it did the king, now roaring with displeasure along with his subjects. The bear charged as more icicles flung ahead of it in an unavoidable spray.

One impaled the fae's chest, then two, three, and four. The fae staggered, and the bear closed in. With a giant swipe of its claws, the fae's guts flew from his body. And yet, somehow, the fae still twisted, tried to run. Bloody teeth bared in a macabre smile, the bear followed, as if ecstatic to continue the hunt.

"Oh stars," I moaned. "I can't wat—"

Prince Vale took my chin in his hand and turned my face so that we stared at one another. I started, but he shook his head, "Don't look at them. Just look at me. Only at me."

The king bellowed at the general depravity in the pit, the crowd clamored for more blood, but I did as the prince said. I stared at him, relieved to have a focus, something to do rather than listen to the screams below.

"Watch me," he whispered. "It's almost over. I promise."

Finally, the bloodthirsty cries of the fae in the pit died and with their last breaths, I exhaled. The farce of a trial ended, the last rebel died, and no one had anything more to cheer about.

"It's over," he whispered and squeezed my hand.

We broke apart, and I stared at my hands, head full of questions. What was he doing? How did this fit into his plan?

I got no answers, but rather more questions as he leaned closer and dropped a soft kiss on my cheek. "My lady, the feast awaits."

My cheeks flamed, but I nodded, willing to go along with anything if it got me out of this barbaric place, away from his cruel father.

Together we stood, and I became acutely aware that, once again, we had the attention of most of the fae in the

Pit, as well as that of the king, the queen, Prince Rhistel, and Prince Gervais.

The vampire's eyes narrowed. A small predatory smile curled his lips, like a cat stalking a mouse. Vampires loved the chase, a challenge. Was this plan enticing him more? Or would he tell the king who I was?

No. Telling Magnus would be too easy. Plus, he'd have to admit that a slave escaped and killed his brother's child. A vampire's pride would not allow for that.

This could go only two ways. Prince Gervais would either want me to come to him and beg for mercy that I would never get, or the vampire would hunt me.

As for the king, his expression turned stony. By inviting me here and laying a claim to me, his son had done things he did not like. The fury on his face looked so intense I averted my gaze, looking right into the pit.

My stomach dropped. Innards were strewn about the dirt and the bear feasted on the corpses of the rebels. Stars, it was horrible.

And if whatever Prince Vale and Saga had planned did not work, and they caught me trying to escape, then soon, it might be my broken corpse down there.

CHAPTER 38

How anyone could want to eat after watching the massacre in the pit was a mystery. And yet, the jarls, great lords and ladies, and royals alike, filed toward the grand dining hall. Few looked as upset as I felt inside.

We were among the first to arrive, and the prince swept me through the narrow, rectangular room to the head table. The expanse of wood was long enough to seat twelve and elevated above the other hundred or so fae who would be dining with us. He gestured to two seats at the end.

"Your cloak?" A servant appeared beside us.

I sloughed it off and handed it to the male. Another servant, this one a brownie, pulled out the last chair for me. The prince took the one next to me, far from the center of the long table.

His rightful place would be by his brother, the heir,

but I was thankful that Prince Vale didn't take it. The thought of sitting next to Prince Rhistel made me shudder. I wondered, though, aside from the Aabergs, who would claim the other five seats?

"They won't make you move?" I asked the prince, mindful of Sir Caelo taking his place to stand behind us. They had not spoken as we walked here, but something in the way the knight and the prince took in their surroundings told me they were waiting for an attack.

"I'll say I'm giving up my seat for the Laurent prince. It's a great courtesy to sit close to my parents, and no one can deny it."

"Right." I swallowed. "Are you ever going to tell *me* anything?"

The prince laughed. "I apologize for the secrecy. I need others to believe I'm seducing you. It is not uncommon for highborn males to stake a strong claim on a female if they desire her. Saga and I thought it would look better for you if you were pulled along, rather than scheming to ensnare a prince after your engagement was dissolved."

"Seduce me?" I scoffed and brought a coquettish hand to my chest. "Are you that much of a strumpet?" His eyebrows rose, taking the jest in stride with an amused twitch of his lips. "Or is it really just because you and Roar don't get along?"

"If you must know, there's a rumor that he stole a faerie lady I was interested in once." Prince Vale shrugged. "It wasn't true, but most people believe it. And they know the warden and I despise one another. They'll see this as me getting revenge." His eyes locked with mine. "I can't say I mind. Spending time in your company is a pleasant sort of revenge."

My cheeks warmed, and while I wanted to ask more, to learn how we'd leave the castle and I'd flee, I did not, for at that moment, the other royals and their entourage entered the dining hall.

Everyone stood as the Aabergs filed in. Calpurnia Vagle, Prince Gervais, Lord Riis, and three other fae accompanied them and talked amongst themselves as if they hadn't witnessed horrific murders. Though I still felt a little queasy, I realized it would behoove me to act as unaffected as the rest.

I rolled my shoulders back. "Who's the high lady by Calpurnia?"

"Nalaea Qiren, Lady of Silks," Prince Vale replied.

I cringed. I should have known from her silky ebony skin and long raven-wing curls that I'd seen on only one other fae, that she would be Aenesa's mother. I found it bad enough that Calpurnia would sit at the head table. If Aenesa had told her mother anything about me, Lady Qiren might not like me either.

"The elder fae is my grandsire, Lord of Coin, Airen Vagle." The prince nodded to the oldest male, who I'd seen before at the tourney. "The other is my uncle, Captain Eirwen Vagle. Calpurnia's father."

So, Lady Qiren was the only non-family member.

"Why is the Lady of Silks invited to sit at the head

table?" I asked quickly. They neared, and soon I'd have to keep these sorts of questions in and play along with Prince Vale's plan.

"Her alliance with my parents is strong. She's trying to bargain for her daughter's betrothal." He swallowed thickly.

I wondered if that would be Aenesa or a sibling? I did not get to ask, however, because just then the royal family arrived at the table.

"Son." King Magnus kept his tone tight as he glared at me. "I allowed her to sit with us in the Pit, but is this the place for her?"

"She's my guest, and I'm happy to give my place to Prince Gervais." Prince Vale gestured back to the vampire and others joining the royal family. "After all, Lady Neve is now an unaccompanied female at court. Is there a problem with me helping her to feel more comfortable, Father?"

The king scowled at me. "Fine. She can stay tonight, and be your plaything, but do not get too comfortable among us, Lady Neve."

So he was fine with pairing me off with a noble lord if that pairing benefited him, and definitely fine with me being a part of his harem, but the king was not happy to see me with his son. Not as anything other than a faerie to sleep with anyway. My fingers itched to toss the king a vulgar gesture, but I held back.

Instead, I smiled placidly and placed my hand atop Prince Vale's. The prince's fingers twitched. He had not expected me to take the lead, but he recovered and lifted my hand to his lips to kiss it.

"I thank you for your family's graciousness." Determined to play up the ruse, I threw the prince a simpering look that sent whispers washing through the dining hall. If Prince Vale wanted me to act seduced, then so be it; I'd act my wings off.

The king stormed to his seat, followed by the queen, Prince Gervais, Prince Rhistel, and Princess Saga. Only the princess appeared disinclined to hurl me from the high table. In fact, she seemed to be trying not to laugh.

But then Calpurnia glared at me. As she strolled by me behind her father and grandsire, she whispered, *'whore'*.

I swallowed. Surely others thought it, too, but what did it matter? I only played along with this charade to escape the kingdom. Soon enough, I'd leave, and the opinions of these fae would not matter.

Still, I felt all too glad when Calpurnia sat at the far end of the table. There would be no speaking with her tonight. That left only Lady Qiren to drop into the seat between Lord Riis and Prince Vale. The Lady of Silk's bright green eyes took me in with interest. Stars this woman was not only stunning, but she radiated an aura of confidence that made her slightly terrifying. I wondered if Calpurnia might not be a better option to spar with conversationally. This female appeared far too shrewd.

"Lady Neve, we have not met." Lady Qiren inclined her head.

Had we been standing; I would have curtsied because she was of a higher rank. Instead, I bent my head too, and maintained the position for longer than she. "Good evening, Lady Qiren. I'm pleased to make your acquaintance."

"Deepest sympathies for your broken betrothal." She paused. "Though you seem to be losing no time in finding another suitor. Do all females move so fast in the villages?"

I cleared my throat. If that was how she wanted to play, I'd rise to the occasion. I opened my mouth to reply, but the prince shifted his large body between us so that I could barely see Lady Qiren.

"Lady Neve is my guest. Such talk is not welcome at this table, Lady Qiren. Is that understood?"

The high lady blinked. The look of astonishment lasted but a second before she mastered herself once more and rolled her shoulders back. "My prince, while you always seem in excellent conduct, this," she waved her hand in my direction, "commoner, is beneath you."

"You called her Lady Neve a mere moment ago. As did I, a prince. Surely, those words mean something?" Prince Vale kept his tone smooth and polite as he spoke to her, and he smiled pleasantly at her.

"Only because Lord Roar insisted upon it." She hissed, and I couldn't miss the derision in her tone. "He raised her well above her station, and now he has left her! Why do you think that is, my prince? Do you believe being seen with this fae is in your best interests when my own daughters would make suitable mates?"

For a moment, Prince Vale did not speak. Though his back faced me, and I could not see his face, the hard set of his shoulders hinted at his frustrations. On her other side, Lord Riis looked taken aback as well.

Lady Qiren had garnered all the eyes on this side of the table. I supposed that while I was mortified, I should just be happy that the king and queen and Prince Rhistel remained occupied with the vampire, and that other lords and ladies in the hall sat too far away to hear.

"While your daughters are lovely and any lord would be lucky to rule with them at his side," the prince spoke softly, "my father is arranging matches during this Courting Festival."

"He would listen to you. You are a respected warrior, the Sword of Winter, and the strongest Aaberg heir. And yet, you choose her?" Lady Qiren shot up from her seat. "This is a slap in the face to the noble ladies your family forced to come here." Without so much as another glance at Prince Vale, the highborn lady marched off.

"Where is she going?" The king twisted our way.

I shrank back. Food had not even arrived, and the king had already pinned his ire on me.

"Lady Qiren needed to speak with her daughter, Aenesa," Lord Riis came to the rescue.

"Ah, very well." King Magnus glared at me once more but servants brought the first course, and the queen took that moment to claim her husband's attention.

While servants gave the rest of us meat and vegetables with a side of a flakey sort of bread that I'd never had, the vampire prince drank a goblet of blood.

I hadn't thought about Anna in hours, but now I found myself pleased she wasn't here, serving as the vampire's meal.

"Rebel blood." Lord Riis leaned closer to Prince Vale and me.

"Pardon me, my lord?" I asked.

"You're watching the vampire drink. Surely wondering who would have supplied his meal. The rebels did. They were drained of a few cups each before they fought, which normally would not be necessary. However, with a vampire in residence, the king thought it prudent."

My stomach twisted, but I tried to remind myself that this would be good for the plan. As bad as I felt for the rebels, if Anna wasn't part of the prince's meal, she would have a lot more energy. She would need it when we ran.

Prince Vale leaned over and took my hand, kissing me on the cheek. At his touch, butterflies erupted in my stomach.

"We will not speak of the rebels, Lord Riis," the prince said. "The trial troubled Lady Neve's heart."

"I suppose that most fae from the country are not used to seeing justice being served." Lord Riis waved a hand in dismissal.

The meal progressed, and the conversation drifted to more mundane affairs: the price of fae wine coming in from the Summer Court, the damage to the roads that the recent storms had wrought, and the score of a recent game that had taken place in the stadium. All the while, Prince Vale caressed my arm or bestowed me devastatingly handsome smiles. Many fae noticed, the royals included, and the king reddened as he downed goblet after goblet of wine.

Something that I'd been denying had awoken that night of the ball and sitting in front of the most influential fae in the kingdom, my skin felt like it was on fire. The prince put on a show for others, but stars alive, I couldn't help that his charms were working on me.

The courses passed, and I played along. I was just giving him an easy smile as I called for my second goblet of wine.

The servant approached, and as she poured, I took in the room below us. Many fae still watched me, though less obviously than before, Lady Qiren among them. She'd chosen to sit near her daughter, Aenesa, and two other females. Her other daughters, I assumed. All four ladies glowered my way, hating me, I was sure.

I sighed. Though Aenesa preferred Lord Roar, that really did not matter. Her mother wished for her to attach herself to a prince, and now I stood in the way. Where the highborn ladies were concerned, I could not win.

And when Prince Vale shifted his hand up to my shoulder and rubbed it, the ladies scowled harder. I turned away, facing him.

"Are you well?" he asked. "Did you change your mind about dessert? I can request the cake for you." I wasn't sure if it was part of the show, but his eyes dipped to my cleavage and held there for a beat longer than was polite.

My mouth dried up at the thought of him cupping

my curves, and I swallowed, trying to wet my tongue. "I'm fine. I . . ."

I trailed off, catching something behind the prince.

The vampire stared at me intently, and my stomach churned as he leaned closer to the king and whispered something in his ear, always maintaining eye contact with me. The king twisted, saw his son's hand on me, and frowned. He'd done that many times over the course of the meal, but this time it was harder, crueler. Just like when the vampire threw me a wink.

When the king stood, I swallowed. Prince Gervais had planted something in King Magnus's mind, and I felt certain I would be on the receiving end of whatever it was.

"Silence!" Magnus bellowed, belligerent from the many glasses of wine he'd indulged in.

The chamber quieted, and all eyes fell upon the king. At his side, Prince Gervais looked delighted. Dread swelled inside me as the king crooked a finger at me. "Come here, the mysterious Lady Neve."

I scooted my chair back, but Prince Vale stopped me. "Father, what are you—"

Magnus shook his head. "Do not question your king, Prince Vale. I wish to speak with the lady."

"It's fine," I whispered.

I had no power of foresight like Saga, though I didn't need such magic to recognize that he would humiliate me.

But I could handle it. I'd undergone far worse as a slave and would soon be gone. These fae could do nothing to hurt me that I had not already experienced. And if a little verbal humiliation threw the king off my trail for even an hour longer, it would be worth it.

So, I approached the king, who placed a soft hand on my shoulder as his son had done. I fought the urge to recoil and, in doing so, caught the queen's eye. Hesitation swam in her lovely features.

"Not all of you may have heard, but hear it now, from your king. Lord Roar has committed treason!" The king raised his voice to shout across the entire room. "And his union with Lady Neve has been severed by royal decree. Many of you have asked about the enigmatic lady since then, and as your ruler, I wish for you to know what you are getting."

Know what they are getting? What—oh!

Magnus's magic lit up around him, as cold and white as the snow outside. The bottom of my gown sliced off, leaving my calves and part of my thighs bare. That would have been bad enough, but I also began to levitate in a vortex of snowflakes. He put me on display like a whore to be bought.

Tears filled my eyes, but I refused to shed them, refused to give the king anything he wanted. As my heart thrummed, I grew warm, my skin tingling as I raged over the injustice.

Some fae in the crowd gasped and pointed. Some looked away, but most appeared not to be able to. Many laughed, and males viewed me lecherously.

"Now we see why Lord Roar would take in a commoner, don't we, my lords and ladies? She is well-formed, is she not?" The king's lips split into a wide smile. "Perhaps the top shall go now?"

I swallowed, and the heat inside me spread, running from my core down my arms. I blinked when I caught sight of a faint silver-violet light around my fingers. But it vanished so fast I had surely imagined it.

The king approached me and his vortex created an opening for him and his finger tipped with his magic as he touched my breast, readying to rip open my neckline and expose me. "She is quite bountiful, isn't sh—"

"Stop this at once!" Two powerful arms gripped me from behind and ripped me from the vortex. Prince Vale pulled me to his chest. I gasped and hid my face, embarrassed and furious all at once. They would not see me cry. Not here. Not ever.

"You dare speak to me that way?" The King of Winter rounded on his son, his eyes flashing with fury. Magic sparked behind him, terrifying in its might and potential, but his son did not flinch.

Prince Vale glared his father down. "This is no way to treat a lady."

"She is no true lady." King Magnus spat out the words like venom. "We extended a courtesy to Warden Roar, and now he does not even want her."

The Warrior Bear shifted me behind his bulk and got closer to his father, close enough to stand chest to chest and whisper. "I said *enough*."

"You forget your place, son."

"That does not change the fact that if you touch her again, Father, it will be the last time you have hands."

I stifled a gasp. The prince had spoken so softly that I was sure only those closest, those at the head table had heard. But still . . . to threaten the king. Father or not, it was madness.

For a moment, the king stared at his son, fury blazing in those ice-blue eyes. After what felt like an age, his mouth opened and a hard, almost manic cold laugh burst out. Nothing about the sound or the forced smile settled my nerves.

The king's chin lifted. "You wish for your toy to remain unharmed while you play with her? Fine then, take her away, Vale. Do what you will with her. But tomorrow, and from that day forward, she is *mine* to command."

My throat tightened at the many implications those words held. Had the king just referred to his harem? Or did he intend for my public mortification to continue? Or did he want to use me as a bargaining chip?

From the way some jarls in the crowd salivated, I suspected my value had risen dramatically. Not only had I 'captivated' a warden, but a prince stood up to the king for me. And the king himself . . .

I shuddered as King Magnus's attention shifted back to me. He licked his lips. No matter if the king sold me off to a lord for a favor or soldiers or an act of powerful magic, I was certain he intended to see what all the fuss was about first.

Only leaving could save me.

"Let's go," I whispered. "*Please.*"

Prince Vale had been stiff, his fists clenched as he

faced off with his father. At my word, however, the prince turned. His eyes widened as he took in my trembling shoulders.

Without warning, he lifted me in his arms like a fae would on their wedding night and marched out of the great hall with a hundred eyes drilling holes in our backs.

CHAPTER 39

S ir Caelo had the good sense to follow Prince Vale from the feast.

"You know your father." Sir Caelo broke the tense silence shrouding our trio only when we reached the prince's suite. He opened the door for us as I was still in the prince's arms. "The feast is far from over, and your actions have likely elongated it well into the night. Gossip will run through the court like dragon fire."

"Let them talk and distract themselves," Prince Vale replied. "All the better for us."

"Same plan?"

"We'll start at the next changing." Prince Vale took a step into his suite.

"That's mere minutes away."

"Yes. And until then, you'll remain here."

"Of course. I've got you, brother."

The door shut behind the prince and me. Once it was just us, he strode to his bed and softly set me down. I allowed myself to sink into the mattress stuffed to bursting with feathers as the prince poured a goblet of wine. He downed it, poured two more, and offered me one.

I took it, still trembling from the humiliation I'd endured at the king's hands and the anger that was beginning to rise within me, and drank half of the glass. The wine helped ease my nerves a touch.

"Thank you," I croaked, finding my voice. "You didn't have to do that, but I appreciate it more than you know."

It hadn't been the first time someone had humiliated me in public, but it *had* been the most frightening, which said a lot. Vampires were terrifying creatures, and yet something in the way that King Magnus watched me— like a predator about to rip out the throat of his prey— made my heart hammer.

"I did have to." Prince Vale's jaw tightened. "My father has mistreated females under his protection before. I've always hated it."

A haunted look flashed in his eyes. His father had a harem, but were those the only females he used and abused?

"We need to talk." He took another swig of wine. "You're hiding something, and before I put myself at even greater risk to help you, I need to hear what."

That, of all things, had not been what I'd expected him to say.

"What do you mean?" I needed to narrow down what the prince was suspicious of.

"Who are you, Neve? The vampire watched you closely at the trial. At dinner too, and I suspect he egged my father on to hurt you, not that the king needs much to act out." Prince Vale snorted. "Why would a vampire prince be so interested in a fae female? A commoner at that?"

"Don't they love fae blood?" I asked, feigning like I didn't know that fact intimately.

The prince studied me like a puzzle to solve. "Yes, but as Lord Riis mentioned, Gervais is well fed with the blood of our prisoners. He could also ask for a living fae if he wished. As he is a royal guest, Father would have to oblige."

"Perhaps that was his intent?"

"Prince Gervais knows the law of other lands. He'd be given a whore who would be paid. Or drink from a drained living prisoner who would not earn coin. There is no in between unless someone offers themselves to him. And he looked at you like you had wronged him."

I swallowed. "You're imagining things."

He set his glass down and crossed his arms over his muscular chest. "And then there's the matter that you wish for me to save his human? Why would you want that?"

He had me there. What could I say about wanting to free Anna?

The prince, perhaps seeing that I was trying to come up with an excuse, continued. "And of course, let's not forget that you somehow got into my chambers by a hidden door. No, Neve. Things are not adding up. If you don't come clean with me about who you are, I—I cannot help you tonight."

I sucked in a breath. "But you promised already."

"I did, and I always keep my promises, but there's a first time for everything."

A scowl overtook my lips as I glared at him. The prince, however, did not back down. He merely stared back, waiting with patient brown eyes.

If I told him the truth, Prince Vale would be within his rights to return me to the Blood Court. It would be easily enough done, depositing me into Prince Gervais's care.

But would he? I wanted to think not. This fae had pulled me from the stadium and cared for my injuries by himself. He'd punched his brother for calling me a whore. He'd stood up to the king—for me.

Prince Vale told me he wanted to protect others and had already shown that he'd put himself in danger to do so. And yet, I hesitated.

Did I dare let another person in on my secret?

Did I have a choice?

If Prince Vale didn't help me escape, I wouldn't get far. And saving Anna and Clemencia, too, would be impossible.

Of course, I could still lie, but something in the prince's hardened gaze hinted he would not be fooled so easily.

I licked my dry lips. "If I tell you, do you promise to help me still? You can't go back on our plan?"

"If you tell me the truth." He stood and walked to a

desk on the far side of the room. "I have a ring that will tell me if you are. I'd like you to wear it."

"I—why do you have that?"

He arched an eyebrow. "My family is royal, Lady Neve. We do not only deal with fae. Dragons, vampire, wolvea, and mages are all more than capable of outright lying—not just twisting the truth or omitting things like our kind can." He paused. "And for all I know, you're half fae. Maybe your other half actually gives you the ability to lie?"

He was wrong, but not far off. "I didn't see one on Prince Gervais."

Of course, I had not known to look, but I felt certain the vampire would not permit wearing one. He would take it as an affront.

"His ship was taking on water, a story confirmed by Lady Virtoris. Nothing about his story is odd, except that he seems infatuated with you." The prince held out the ring.

A pregnant pause passed between us, in which I considered all the angles. But again, I saw no options other than telling the truth or flat out lying. With the ring around my finger, I would be discovered. But if I didn't wear it, Prince Vale would have doubts, and doubts meant a chance he would not help me.

I had to take the risk.

Accepting the ring with a steady hand, I slipped it on my finger and looked up at Prince Vale. "As for how I got into your chambers, I told you there was a door, even showed it to you."

"And I believe that. The blueprints and your story line up, though I'm still stuck on why the castle allowed you into a place it has denied so many? Can you answer that?"

"I really don't know." I shrugged. "I assume the castle was being nice, protecting me from Calpurnia and her gang. That's honestly the best I can figure."

His eyes drifted to the ring, which did nothing. What would it do if I lied? Zap me? I wished I'd asked, but did it matter? I had no intention of finding out.

"Alright then." Prince Vale nodded. "The other matters? Why does the vampire prince watch you so? And why must you rescue his human?"

My heart began to race. My truth could change everything.

"I've already promised," Prince Vale whispered, his face softening.

I wrangled my courage. "You're correct in thinking that the prince knows me. And that's because I'm not who I've said I am. I'm no commonborn fae."

"You're highborn? But that makes even less sense. Why pretend to be lower born?"

"I'm not that either." I cleared my throat. "I've only been in this kingdom for a couple of weeks. Before that, I lived in the Vampire Court and was once a blood slave."

He stiffened, but he said nothing, so I plowed onward, fighting back the stinging in my eyes as tears formed there.

"The human that Prince Gervais has brought to court

is my best friend, Anna." At her name, two tears streamed down my cheeks.

I had no idea what the vampire was doing to her and that terrified me, but deep down, I cried for more than that. Saying my story to someone, not having to pretend after weeks of lying and deceit and playacting, felt cathartic.

At least, for me, anyway. Prince Vale's mouth hung open as he came to sit next to me. To his credit, he let me cry for a few moments before he asked another question. "You were a blood slave to the Laurent family?"

I held my head in my hands for a moment before I finally looked at him and answered. "No. Well, sort of. My master was a Laurent, but not a core royal. I didn't live at the palace or ever go there. I only ever met Prince Gervais right before I left the kingdom."

His hand found my back, and he began to rub it in small, gentle, comforting circles. "Then why would Prince Gervais have a claim on you? Does he love you?"

I snorted out a half laugh. "Rather, the opposite. He hates me. I killed one of his brother's children."

His hand stilled. "Blazing stars! How did you kill a vampire?" He paused. "Not that you don't look strong, but they're quite difficult to defeat."

I waved off his concern that I was offended and met his eyes. They were so soft, so sympathetic.

"I didn't actually set out to do so. I acted in defense of another blood slave. And then Gervais threatened to buy me. He has an evil reputation for mistreating his slaves and then killing them in horrific manners, so I escaped into Winter's Realm. Here, I found a safe harbor. For a while."

"In Lord Roar's territory, right next to the vampire kingdom." he said. "It makes much more sense now why no one could find anything about your father."

I stiffened. We'd been here for mere days. "People checked? *Already*? How could information even get back to the palace so fast?"

"My father requested that Lord Riis work on it, and he has a vast network of spies who can pass information on faster than you'd imagine. Word arrived from a handful of his spiders—that's what he calls them—the morning after Roar left. So far, Lord Riis has come up with nothing on you. I had wondered if that was why he'd shown interest in you at the ball. If he was searching for something then."

I pursed my lips. "He didn't ask about any of that. Though, because the vampires gave us potions to dim our powers, it also dims other parts of being a fae. Like the inability to lie. I can do so, as you've realized—at least until that potion wears off."

I shivered at the idea of losing my protection but there were plus sides too, like finally learning about my powers. At the notion, a flash of a memory came rushing back. When the king had been humiliating me, for the briefest of moments, I'd thought I'd seen my magic. It had wreathed my hand, a silvery-purple light . . .

I shut the thought down before it could take hold. That was impossible. The potion the vampires gave me should last two weeks longer, and as much as I might want magic now, this was no time for daydreaming.

"I'm familiar with it." The prince's eyes looked me over, as if I were a puzzle he still tried to figure out. "What sort of magic, or magics, do you possess?"

"I have no idea." I sucked in a deep breath. "For as long as I can remember, I've taken the same potion every moon cycle. And the vampires mangled my wings to keep me from flying away, which is the true reason why I have scars. The warden helped with those . . ."

Roar's title tasted sour on my tongue. He'd helped me, yes, but he'd also left me here in a dangerous predicament without an explanation. As far as I could tell, he'd betrayed me. And yet, I could not find it in me to drink his blood. A small sliver inside me hoped that I was wrong about him, even when all signs pointed to the opposite.

"They're healing well," Prince Vale offered. "You've been using the balm I sent?"

"I have. Clemencia helps with application." A small smile pulled at my lips. "So, what else do you want to know?"

I'd already told him the most important bits. If he requested more, I'd divulge. I'd do anything to leave this kingdom.

"There's so much I wish to ask, but you've given me the truth of what I wanted to know most." He exhaled a long breath. "I feel bad asking for more, though there is one thing I noticed."

I nodded. "Go on."

"The day you arrived, you didn't wear a cloak, though it was freezing, and the winds were atrocious that day. You said you were born in the Vampire Court, but where are your parents from?"

"I was told my mother was from this kingdom, though I know nothing of my father." I shrugged. "I'm rarely truly cold."

He balked. "So, you feel nothing until it is dire?"

"No. I can *feel* when it is cold, but cold doesn't affect me as it does others. I'm able to endure it for longer. The quirk helped when I was a blood slave. We didn't get the thickest of bedding, clothing, and we received just enough food to remain healthy so vampires could drain us, and we'd stay alive."

At that, his face shadowed over. "Then you are likely from this kingdom. As a subject, my family should have protected you."

"Even if I'm of tribal blood?"

There wasn't much known about the few fae who lived nomadic lifestyles. They lived in the mountains, the traditional home to the giants, ogres, orcs, and dwarves. Perhaps most importantly, none of those groups claimed the crown as their leaders either.

"Save for malicious races of fae, orcs chief among them." He scowled at the thought of his greatest nemeses. "Fae should help other fae. So, yes. I would fight to keep a tribal member from the fate you've endured. I would be your protector, should you want one."

Before he'd said he wished to be a shield. I'd believed

him then, and now, even more so. He might look like a brooding brute, stacked with muscle and not much else, but I'd seen behind that façade. I'd seen his eyes darken when he spoke of orc attacks. I'd seen him relate to the archers he went up against in the tourney and other fae at the ball. Since coming here, though it hadn't been a long time, I'd seen different shades to the fae before me.

"I would be glad for your help." I wiped a tear from my eye. "Now, do you see why I must escape? And why I must take Anna and Clemencia with me?"

"It's clear to me." He stood. "One moment."

I watched, stunned, as Prince Vale left the room and walked down the short corridor to the door that separated his apartments from the rest of the palace. A faint *snick* of the door opening and indistinguishable whispers between the prince and Sir Caelo met my ears.

When the door shut and footsteps came my way once more, I tried to appear as though I hadn't been doing my best to eavesdrop.

"The changing of the guard is soon. Caelo will get Anna first. She's staying in a room separate from the vampire prince, so it will not be so hard to extract her. He'll retrieve Clemencia as well." Prince Vale came to stand in front of me. "The moment they are in the stables, we move."

I gasped and leapt up, gripping him in a hug so tight that he let out a soft '*oph*'. More tears leaked from my eyes. It seemed that they simply wouldn't stop tonight.

"Thank you so much! I cannot tell you how much this

ASHLEY MCLEO

means. I—" I pulled away and only then realized how close we stood, how I could count all his eyelashes. Or how, if I reached up, I could caress the stubble on his fine jaw. As if my hand had a mind of its own, it did just that, and in the prince's eyes, something sparked.

I let go and took a step back, letting my hands fall to my sides even though they burned to touch him again. "That was inappropriate. I'm so sorry, but Anna . . . This is my best chance to save her and—"

"You needn't apologize for wanting to save those you love," he murmured, though the words reverberated in the room. "What you're doing, what you've been through, and who you are—Lady Neve, it's astonishing. I only wish I had gotten to know the real you earlier."

"I do too," I breathed, shocked by how much I'd meant it.

Roar and I had made a deal to propagate a story, but he'd broken our arrangement and my trust. Prince Vale, on the other hand, had been someone I felt inclined to despise from the start, but that had been on Roar's judgment, and I no longer agreed with the warden.

He was someone worth knowing, a fae you wanted on your side, a male who, if I had the time, I would want to know more intimately.

At the thought, my breath deepened. My rising and falling bosom did not fail to draw the prince's eyes, and he swallowed.

Desire flared in his gaze, igniting my own. I felt it too, had for a while. We had been drawn to one another, and

552

after all the emotions of the day, that attraction hit a peak. A raging band of orcs would be easier to ignore.

And do I want to ignore it? No . . . I do not.

So, I closed the space between us again. My hands found Prince Vale's hard chest, snaked up around his neck. Would that I could wrap my hands in his hair, but he stood too tall.

"Lady Neve," his words came out raspy. "We——"

"Kiss me. Please."

Despite the lust written across his face, I expected a denial or for him to pull back. So, when the prince leaned in and brushed his lips to mine, I gasped as my eyelids fluttered closed.

The sound undid him as much as it did me. Prince Vale wove his hands into my hair, pulling me closer, tasting me, exploring me, devouring me. He gripped my waist, lifted me, and my legs acted of their own accord, wrapping around him.

A low growl left the prince's mouth as he broke our kiss, shifted his lips to my neck, and nibbled at my ear. His black wings curled around me, a protective, almost territorial gesture that brought to mind our dance. My heart thrummed as I tilted my head back, eyes fluttering open to take in the ornate ceiling with a wonder that only boosted the fire ravaging my blood.

Skies alive, I might explode at any moment. What sort of magic was this?

My other lovers had all been human, and they'd given me pleasure, but nothing like this kiss. Prince Vale clung to me, held me like a precious thing, and as if his only job was to pleasure me. His lips trailed down to the crook of my neck, a sensitive spot, and my legs became weak, loosening around him. I slumped into his hard chest and a soft whine escaped my lips.

The prince must have read something into the ecstasy, for he moved, and in three powerful strides lowered me on the bed. I clutched the silk sheets, relished how cool they felt, but as he pulled back ever so slightly, I released them and gripped him by the shirt instead. "Come here."

"Caelo will alert us soon," he said, but didn't move away.

"Then we should make every moment count." I pulled him on top of me.

None of this had been planned or foreseen, but now that I'd had a taste of pleasure, a relief from the fear that had gripped me for far too long, I did not let go. I did not think Prince Vale minded so much, either. Since we'd met, there had been a certain energy between us. A warming of the air. A draw to the other.

As I would leave soon, a short dalliance, a few kisses, could hurt no one. I would consider this a hard-won prize for my time at court.

When we broke away the next time, he exhaled a long breath. "You are unexpected."

"Not in a bad way, I hope?" I smirked.

He snorted, and his one free hand rounding my hip and exploring there. "Stars, my lady. Why must the Fates test me so cruelly?"

"That, I can't answer." With a rasp, I dragged a soft

finger down his chest. "But you might be able to answer me this?"

"Anything." In that moment, the strongest warrior in all of Winter's Realm looked ready to hand me the world.

"Why in all the nine kingdoms have you stopped kissing me?"

CHAPTER 40

Passion surged through me, hotter and hotter with each kiss, each touch of Prince Vale's hand on my face, each caress of my body.

As we took our pleasure at each other's lips, time seemed to lose meaning so when a faint tapping at the window caused the prince to stop, to look up and over.

When I followed his gaze, I yelped.

A raven stared inside with vibrant blue eyes. It lifted a talon and waved, to which Prince Vale laughed.

"Um, what is *that*?" I asked, head swiveling from the prince to the raven and back again.

"Caelo's signal." He sighed and looked down at me. "Though it's the last thing I want to do, we need to get weapons and leave."

"Is that *Sir Caelo*?" I asked. Some fae could shift into animal forms, though I had yet to meet one with that power.

"No, he can only inhabit animals. He prefers birds."

That felt like more of an elven magic. Fae had many varied powers, and while elves were technically a race of fae—though they insisted on being thought of as an order unto their own—they usually dealt with animals. Faeries might shift, but elves could have other animals do their bidding, a magic not usually found in my kind. Perhaps Sir Caelo wasn't full faerie?

"Oh," I murmured, keeping my questions in as he rose from the bed, and I straightened the front of my dress which had gone askew with all the kissing. Only then did I realize my poor choice of attire. "I wish I'd worn trousers."

One corner of his luscious lips curled upward. "My sister set some aside for you. They're in my bathing chambers, down the hall."

"Saga is a lot smaller than me." Where I had round hips and breasts, Saga had a sleeker body.

"I'm sure she chose well." The prince seemed completely unconcerned, which showed a great deal of trust. Clearly, he'd never had to force his breasts or hips into a dress that was too small. "Try them. I'll get our weapons."

I walked down the hall, sensing the prince's eyes on me with each step. A thrill ran through me, but I forced myself not to turn. As I neared the section of the wall where the hidden hallway opened to, I stopped and pressed my hand to the wall.

The wall didn't shimmer. No door appeared. In fact,

nothing at all happened. Deflated, I continued down the short corridor until I found the bathing chamber.

Folded trousers, a tunic, an undershirt, a fur-lined cloak with a hood, and boots rested on a small bench. I shifted my dress off and, hoping to the stars they'd fit, shimmied into the pants.

To my relief and surprise, they worked. Saga had come through, bless the princess.

Another pang of sadness hit me. I'd miss Prince Vale, and the simmering potential and desire that had just ignited between us, but Saga had been a true friend. I'd miss her dearly.

Once ready, I retrieved the blood vials from my dress pocket and tucked them into those of my pants. Having what I needed, I folded my dress and laid it on the bench. Prince Vale would know what to do with it. From my time at the Winter Court, I kept only the pretty hair pin Saga had given me. Not only did I find it beautiful, but it did a nice job of holding my masses of hair back. One last parting gift.

When I opened the door, the prince stood there, holding stakes in one hand and a dagger in another. He held them out. "The stakes are ash wood—the only wood that can kill a royal vampire."

"Why two?"

"Backups are always necessary."

I swallowed, hoping I didn't need one stake, let alone two, but took them all the same. The moment Prince Gervais learned that I'd fled, he'd be tempted to hunt me. I wasn't sure if he'd do so right away—it would blow his cover and cause strife between courts—but he'd come, eventually. To be armed was only wise.

"Thank you."

"I have holsters too, on the bed. You can choose the most comfortable."

I smiled at him as we walked deeper into his chambers, impressed by how well he'd considered the various aspects of this escape. Then again, he was a soldier of high regard. Tactical aspects were surely well within his repertoire.

Quickly, I chose two stake holsters, which wrapped around my thighs, and a sheath for the dagger. He cinched them tight, and I tried to ignore how my skin burned at his touch.

"Do they feel secure?" He assessed the weapons.

"They're not going anywhere." I shifted the dagger on my hip so that it didn't hit a stake. "I think I'm ready."

He looked into my eyes and heat sizzled between us again. The temptation to kiss him one more time overwhelmed me, but I forced it down as he glanced away.

"Let's go then." He grabbed my hand and pulled me, not toward the door, but away from it.

I looked back, confused. "Where are we going?"

"I am going out the door, so I have an alibi. *You* are going out the window."

I froze. "I don't think I can."

I'd flown, but not for long and not well enough to be sure my wings would handle the three-story drop. Or the winds that so often blew off the Shivering Sea.

His attention strayed to my wings; eyes wary. "They move naturally. Do they not work?"

"They do, but I just learned to fly and have had little practice. They're not very strong. What if I drop?" I paused. "And aren't there watchers at the walls? Or windows? Or *somewhere*?"

"Caelo chose his timing to accommodate that. The guard all over the castle is currently changing. We only have a few more minutes to capitalize upon it." He flung open the floor-to-ceiling windows, letting in a biting wind. The prince turned to me with his arms opened wide. "Deviating is dangerous. I need you to take a good look. To truly assess the situation and your abilities."

I did as he requested, leaning out the window as far as I dared.

"Do you see that building just beyond the next tower?" He pointed. "The one with the torches on each corner?"

I followed his finger to where a building that was unconnected to the rest of the palace stood. Hitching posts dotted the area outside the structure. "I do."

"That's the stables, where you need to land, near the back if you can." The prince's eyes met mine. "It's not so far. Do you think it's manageable?"

I gauged the distance, my stomach rolling as I did so. We stood many floors up, and tonight the winds howled. My last flying lesson had been on my journey here, in the woods where the air stayed still and quiet and it didn't matter if I fell because I wasn't going to break a leg. Or die.

"Are there *any* alternatives?" I asked softly.

Prince Vale didn't answer right away, but the moment the sigh left his mouth, I already knew the answer.

"Not really. I have to be seen leaving this room without you. That way, others will believe that you escaped without aid." He turned me so that we faced one another. "I haven't seen you fly and don't know the pain that you lived with or your healing, but Neve, I believe that you can do this. From what you told me, you've been through more difficult things."

I swallowed as the depths of his dark brown eyes threatened to swallow me whole. I wanted to prove him right, to show that I had a hand in my escape—*my life*.

"I guess I don't have much of a choice anyway." I looked out the window again. "So straight to the stables?"

"Going up and over. That tower will keep you out of sight. Once you've cleared it, begin to lower slowly. There are few windows in that part of the palace, so you're covered."

"How can you be sure?" I asked.

"I've done my fair share of sneaking out and taking to the city with Caelo." A mischievous smile crossed the prince's face.

"What if I can't make it that far?"

"If you have to land faster and run there, that's better than falling. But definitely aim to clear the closest tower. And pull up your cloak over your head. Your hair color isn't unusual in Avaldenn, but it will catch the moon's light."

I did as he said, covering my silver-white hair with a nod. "I can do it."

"Wait until I leave the room." Shockingly, he wrapped his large arms around me. "May the stars bless you."

"And you," I replied. He released me, and had started to cross his room when I blurted out, "Prince Vale?"

He turned.

"Thank you, again. For everything."

"You're a fae of Winter's Realm," he replied. "Of my people. And you need a shield. I'm happy to be one."

I watched him retreat down the short hallway that led from his room, heard the water in the bath chambers turn on and what sounded like marbles hitting the floor. I cocked my head, but the next thing I knew, Prince Vale opened the door to his suite and told the soldier on guard to keep watch.

"She's bathing?" the guard asked, clearly confused by the sound of running water.

"Things got messy in there." The prince spoke in the way of males talking about sexual conquests. I snorted, suddenly understanding why he'd spilled whatever it was that he'd spilled—yet another fae twist of the truth. "She needs a moment, and I wish for an ale. My men are supposed to be at the Warmsnap. Figured that's as good a place as any to find one."

The soldier at his door let out a booming laugh. "Well done, my prince."

"No one goes in or out," Prince Vale said.

"Of course not."

The door shut, and knowing this was my moment, I

turned to the open window. The expanse of air I'd have to conquer looked much darker than when the prince stood with me, giving me strength.

But he was no longer present. I had to do this myself.

I inhaled and stepped closer to the opening, fanning my wings out as I did so. Though I hadn't practiced with them in days, they felt good, stronger.

Were they good enough to withstand the wind? To keep me from dropping to the snow and ice? To save me?

"Time to see," I whispered to myself, and began to beat my wings. It didn't take much for the wind to catch beneath them, nor for me to lift from the floor. It took considerably more willpower to push myself forward, to take to the open air.

But I closed my eyes, and did it, and suddenly, I was flying amidst the wicked winds of the winter kingdom, my heart thundering so hard I would not be surprised if those at the feast heard it.

Glittering snow from the rooftops whipped around me, and I held my breath as I soared up and over the closest tower. Among the gold roof, frost shimmered in the starlight. The silver hawk, remnants of the Falk line, glared down at me from atop the spire, its metallic wings spread. Something in me welled up at the sight of the bird of prey. To fly away to true freedom, I needed to be strong and fierce like those hawks.

Below, lights of the sprawling palace glimmered. Sir Caelo had said the feast would go well into the night. Was he correct? Were the nobles and the royal family still mingling, the king still exerting power over his subjects and forcing matches? I hoped so. Anything that would keep others occupied bought me time, and I would need every moment.

Already, my wings ached, and they seemed more sensitive than usual to the cold winds buffeting them. Probably because I felt terrified, and everything just felt *more*. Still, I focused only on moving forward, on passing the tower.

Once I'd succeeded in that, I dared to look down. Prince Vale had been correct that this side of the castle had few windows. I suspected because it looked out on to the area where deliveries would be made, not the pretty picture of the sea.

The torches lining the stables flickered in the dark, not so far away, I chanted to myself as I pushed forward against the biting wind.

I'd covered most of the distance to the stables, and my heart began to slow, when the wind kicked up. It pushed me closer to the castle wall where, on the other side, fae strolled or slept or gossiped. I fought to stay on course while also attracting as little attention as I could, but I overcorrected.

One wing spasmed hard, exhausted, and I dropped like a stone in the river. I swallowed a squeal rising in my throat as I fought to master my wings again, to be strong.

Through sheer force of will, I regained control of my wing and caught the air again, saving me seconds before I would have slammed into the icy dirt of the yard.

I exhaled, wiped the sweat from my brow and, with control, landed properly. When my feet touched the ground a stone's throw away from the stables, I had to force myself not to drop to my knees and kiss it.

"In here." Prince Vale whispered from where he stood hidden in the doorway of the stables, nearly scaring the piss out of me. I recovered quickly, however, and when he opened one of the large doors for me, I ran over. Inside, the musty smell of horses and hay grew stronger.

"You made it." He grinned proudly.

I supposed I had, though I didn't allow pride to bloom in me. If anything, that trial only reminded me that this was step one in what would be a rigorous and deadly journey.

"This way." He led me deeper into the stables, around a corner where three people waited with horses behind them.

"Anna!" I cried out.

"Lower your voices!" the prince hissed as I ran past him to my best friend in all the world.

We collided together, arms wrapping around one another and squeezing. Anna's face squished into the crook of my neck, which suddenly became wet.

"Anna, no tears," I whispered. "We're together now, and we're going to start anew."

"I'm so relieved to see you alive." She wiped her face but didn't dare loosen her grip on me. "Neve, Prince Gervais is *furious* with you. I can't even repeat the things he told me he'd do to you. They're too horrible."

"That's why we must run." I pulled away and looked her in the eye. "You look healthy."

"He drank from me, but rarely. I'm not to his taste."

She nodded to me. "Aside from the labor of finding you, he was quite happy to stop here and have his fill of fae."

Behind Anna, a shift caught my eye, and I peered past my friend to find Clemencia wringing her hands. My stomach pitted. I wanted to save her, had to do it, but I'd forgotten that Clemencia remained in the dark about what was happening.

"How much does she know?" I whispered to Anna, trusting she'd understand.

"Almost nothing. She was here when I arrived, and I don't think Sir Caelo told her anything. I didn't tell her about your past and how we know each other either, so she's anxious and confused. I think she is only here because Sir Caelo told her she's in great danger."

And she was. I felt so relieved that Clemencia had gone along with what Sir Caelo said, that she hadn't fought it.

I swallowed deeply. "I need to speak with her."

"Quickly." Prince Vale spoke from behind me. "We need to move."

I approached Clemencia, pulled together as ever, and still smelling of perfumed snow lilies, despite the late hour. Relief flooded her face as I laid a hand on her shoulder.

Her voice stayed calm. "Lady Neve, they told me I was in trouble. Is this because of Lord Roar's disappearance?"

"Clem." My voice cracked on her name. "This is a lot, and we don't have much time. We need to leave. To *flee*. There are things about my past that you don't know, and they put you in danger. Can you trust me that I have your safety in mind, and I'll tell you everything once we're safe?"

A pregnant pause followed before she gave a slight nod. "I trust you."

"Then, line up, ladies." Sir Caelo cleared his throat. The knight did not wear his golden cloak. In fact, he appeared more like a merchant—albeit a very muscular, armed one. A good disguise indeed.

"You'll each need facial glamours," Sir Caelo said. "Rough ones are all that we have time for, but it will get you out of the gates."

I looked at Prince Vale, who nodded. "My friend is a highly skilled glamourist. Far better than me."

The knight snorted. "If you trust Vale to glamour you, you'll end up with two noses."

"I'm not *that* bad," the prince muttered as we lined up.

"You're not that good either." Sir Caelo shot back and began working on Anna.

My best friend transformed from a black-haired human with slanted, dark eyes to a fae with elongated ears, brown hair, and round blue eyes. The way she moved would be the only risk of giving her away; clubbed foot aside, which she'd do her best to hide with her cloak, humans always lacked the grace of faeries. Sir Caelo pulled a wine bottle from one of the sidesaddles and splashed wine on the hem of her pants. He instructed her to act tipsy to counteract any trouble her foot gave her.

Clemencia, also dark-haired and brown-eyed, became

a blonde with yellow wings. The knight also tweaked her nose shape to make it larger. Though he claimed he'd done it in a rush, I found it quite convincing.

Finally, the Clawsguard knight stood before me. His magic swirled in his hands, ready to do the work, but before he could start, the prince spoke up. "Leave her eyes."

Sir Caelo glanced at his friend, and it seemed like an unspoken conversation passed between them before he nodded and began working. The sensation felt unlike anything I'd ever experienced, tingly and light, like warm water washing over me. In no time at all, Caelo clapped his hands together. "You're done. The glamours were a rush job, so they'll wear off by first light."

I turned to Anna. "How do I look?"

"Not like yourself." Her eyes widened. "You have red hair and so many freckles! I'd never recognize you."

I laughed. "If you're saying that, it's a good sign."

"Caelo, do yourself." Prince Vale's voice had taken on a new level of tension.

The knight nodded and pulled a small square mirror from one of the horse's saddlebags. Magic flowed from him as he worked. He'd clearly done this before and knew exactly what to tweak on his face because he worked faster than he had with us. His blue eyes became violet, his dark skin lightened a touch, and his hair grew longer and turned silver.

I turned to face Prince Vale. "What about you?"

"I need to remain looking like myself. In case the worst happens."

"I've already sent a messenger to get the lads, changing the time of your meeting. See you by the Warmsnap Tavern," Sir Caelo said, and the prince took a horse and left. "Saddle up, ladies. Neve takes the black mare. Her saddlebags have gold. The rest carry food and small weapons."

I went to the horse set aside for me and then froze. Could Anna ride? When I turned to ask, though, my worries fell away.

Sir Caelo had hoisted her onto a horse and showed her how to maneuver the beast. "I'll ride with you through the city and past the gate, but I won't be traveling through the woods. You have until then to get the feel of riding."

"I will." Determination laced Anna's voice.

I exhaled. Anna was smart and when she set her mind to it, little could stop her. After a tutorial, she'd be fine to ride at a moderate pace. They had everything under control. I simply needed to do my part.

Keeping that in mind, I mounted the horse. I found it easier this time, a reassuring thought. Even better, Clem looked like a natural on her horse. More confident this would actually work, I arranged my cloak, so it covered the stakes strapped to my thighs. They needed to be handy, but if anyone saw them, it would raise questions.

"Follow me, ladies." Sir Caelo gazed at all of us once more. "Don't speak unless you must."

We did as he said, guiding the horses through the castle grounds. With each step, I couldn't help but look around. Everything seemed normal. No noble lords and ladies milled around the yard. I hoped Prince Vale was right, and they still gossiped about us at the feast.

As we neared the main gate, I assessed the situation. Only two fae guards manned it—light security. But then again, the king had made a statement today by feeding rebels to his white bear. Anyone who wished ill on those in the palace would think twice about acting again

Ahead of me, Sir Caelo raised a hand to the guards. "Evening."

"Going somewhere at this late hour?" the guard on the right asked. The question seemed nonchalant, but everyone saw the truth behind it—a demand of what we were up to.

"I've worked up quite an appetite." Sir Caelo chuckled. "Heading to the Warmsnap now."

"Ah, the lords and ladies left you nothing from their feast, did they?" the guard gestured to the palace, where the feast was being held.

"Their appetites are always voracious."

I marveled at the way he insinuated that we planned to go to the Warmsnap to eat, but we wouldn't be stopping in, no matter how hungry anyone was. I noted this fae method of twisting the truth. One day, when my magic returned, I'd likely have to use it.

"Fill your bellies then." The guard opened the gates.

I exhaled as we plodded into the greater city. Aside from when we arrived, it was my first time in Avaldenn proper.

Despite the late hour, or perhaps because of it, many fae walked the streets. Some hawked wares, some watched their younglings play, and some strolled with lovers. One pair of lovers made my skin tingle and the kisses I'd shared with Prince Vale flashed through my mind. Perhaps in another life that could have been us.

"Two copper claws, and I'll give ye the best night of your life!" A whore called out and caught my eye with a saucy wink, deteriorating any thoughts of romance.

I looked away, which only made the whore cackle something about what a sweet, pure thing I must be.

Sir Caelo turned, and I guided my horse in the same direction. We rode down a few more streets, all of them filled with life that I could watch openly—another difference from Sangrael. There, had I been stupid enough to walk the streets after dark, I never would have observed the vampires. They would have taken it as an invitation for a snack.

Here, I existed among my kind. Even if I didn't belong in this kingdom and planned to leave, I found comfort in that.

I had begun to salivate over a food stall serving a fried cheese dish when Sir Caelo held out a hand and guided us to the side of the snow-covered cobblestones. Across the street, a sign proclaimed that we stood in front of the Warmsnap Tavern. A spider crawled over the words, making me shiver. Usually, a tavern brought to mind a business more rundown than this one. The Warmsnap appeared well maintained, clean, and sleeker than most taverns I'd seen.

"He should be out here already," Sir Caelo muttered. "Where in the bleeding—"

The door to the Warmsnap opened, and Prince Vale stepped out with none other than Lord Riis.

"They knew I had a prize in my bed," the prince spoke loudly, so that others would hear. "Wish that I hadn't left for nothing."

Forgetting that the knight had disguised me, I hid my face beneath the cloak, a reaction that did not go unnoticed by Lord Riis. Though I could only see a part of his face, I knew he studied me from across the street. After a moment, the king's spymaster seemed to move on.

"Perhaps they're too deep into their cups elsewhere." The Lord of Tongues turned back to the prince. "A bit of advice, my prince?"

"Yes?"

"Do try to stay out of trouble with the fair Lady Neve."

"I'll do my best." Prince Vale's tone sounded strained, as if he really had been upset by some slight of his friends.

Lord Riis disappeared back into the tavern, allowing my breath to come freely again before more worries crashed down around me.

Why was Lord Riis here and no longer at the feast? Was it actually over and the prince had been wrong?

Fear that Prince Gervais would have returned to his room and checked on Anna filled me. If he found her gone, would he suspect I was behind it?

My face still averted, I heard Prince Vale untying his horse, mounting, and then whispering to Sir Caelo.

The knight nodded, and the pair began to ride, the

prince in front as Sir Caelo waved for us to follow. We fell in line again, this time with Clem at the back. Only when we were far from the tavern and they had turned down an empty road did Sir Caelo twist to face me. "We must hurry and get you beyond the gates and down a forest trail."

Then we'd be on our own. I gripped the reins. I hadn't allowed myself to think so far, but that would be the natural conclusion. Neither male could go with us. They'd already given so much, risked too much.

Our pace hastened, and soon the streets became wide enough for six horses to travel abreast, indicating these roads were traveled more often than those deeper in the city. In the distance, the city wall rose above the tops of buildings, the torches lighting them up in the night.

I exhaled. We had almost arrived; now, we rode only a few streets away. Rolling my shoulders back, I prepared for the journey of a lifetime. As soon as we got out of Avaldenn, Anna, Clem, and I would take to the woods and—

A scream ripped through the night.

I stiffened and scanned up ahead, past Anna, Sir Caelo, and Prince Vale, where dark figures sprinted to clear the area.

What in the stars? What did they see?

As if in answer, a cloaked person with their hood pulled up, prowled around a corner, another fae in his arms.

I swallowed. The person moved with a feline grace that the hairs on my arms rose and when he effortlessly hurled the fae in his arms against a wall, ice ran through my veins. The discarded fae didn't move. Didn't groan. Was that person . . . dead?

Before I could inquire, the cloaked figure stopped and turned our way. He smiled and pulled down his hood to reveal cold, hard eyes and gleaming red fangs.

CHAPTER 41

"I see that Lady Neve didn't please you, Prince Vale. But is she so bad that you need to fling her from your city?" Prince Gervais raised his voice. "Or might I take her off your hands—much like you've taken my human off mine? We can call it a repayment for your thievery."

So much for the glamours. The prince smelled Anna and me.

"He can't use me to repay you. He doesn't own me," I spat. "I'm not something to be bartered or sold, you monster."

The vampire barked out a laugh. It resonated off the buildings lining the wide street, echoing through the dark night. "You're right. Technically, *I own you*, though I have yet to act on my rights."

My blood froze in my veins. "No you don't."

"You, my wildcat, were the property of Lord Aldéric

577

who, after your disappearance, sold you to me at a reduced rate. Better he get something than nothing, right?" Gervais licked his lips, his gaze darting to the others for a moment before he smirked. "As the prince does not look surprised, I deduce that you told him about who you are? Mere filth. Shocking that he wanted to keep you after that."

I snarled. "I'm not filth. I'm fre—"

"*You* are nothing but property. *My property*, and I intend to do with you what I wish." He stalked closer, and my horse, perhaps sensing danger, trotted backward.

Taking up the rear of our line, Clemencia gasped as my horse butted into hers and caused it to trot backward quickly too. The steed sensed the predator coming our way. It wanted an escape.

I couldn't blame the horse for its self-preservation instincts, but I knew we had no true escape. Or I didn't, anyway. Somehow, despite our best efforts, the Laurent prince had known I'd be fleeing Frostveil Palace tonight.

He must have eyes everywhere, watching, waiting, reporting.

Of course he did. I'd dishonored his family. I'd escaped their cage of power. And by vampire law, now belonged to him. He wouldn't stop hunting me, not tonight. Not ever.

The only way out is to kill this vampire.

I pulled my feet from the stirrups and, since the horse was still trying to back up, I fluttered my wings. I rose, and my horse, now free from my attempts to restrain it, turned and bolted. Clemencia's horse followed mine. She tossed a terrified look back at me as she tried to win control back and lost. I was glad her horse didn't obey. At least she'd be safe. For now.

Prince Vale's eyes widened as my feet touched down on cobblestones, and I stepped toward the vampire. "Stop where you are."

The Warrior Bear dismounted too, and Sir Caelo followed his prince's lead. Before I took five steps, both males placed their hulking forms between me and the vampire as they pulled out their broadswords.

"Anna," I hissed as I darted up to her. "Run. Take the horse and run."

"I'm not leaving you." She struggled to dismount.

My heart sank, but I didn't repeat myself because I'd do the same thing. I'd left my friend once, and I'd never do so again. To ask her to leave me would be the height of hypocrisy.

"Prince Gervais," the Warrior Bear's voice boomed down the dark street. "Let us come to an agreement. By the laws of your kingdom, I'll pay Neve's purchase price if you promise not to harm her."

My fists clenched. "No! No one will buy me ever again!"

"Too right." The vampire chuckled. "I'll be your last master and the last eyes you see as I drink the life from you." He struck, zipping forward in a blur of vampiric speed.

My breath stilled in my lungs, but to my shock, Prince Vale stood his ground, ready for the strike.

Air magic pulsed from him, slamming the vampire in

the chest. The force sent Gervais soaring backward, a roar ripping from his throat as he collided with barrels. The scent of ale filled the streets as the liquid inside the barrels leaked onto the cobblestones. The vampire, not losing a moment, hurtled forward again, right for Prince Vale.

Before the vampire attacked the prince, however, Sir Caelo swiped his broadsword for Prince Gervais's neck. The bloodsucker jerked backward and danced around the faeries with unnerving grace. Suddenly, nothing stood between me, Anna, and him.

"Fly away!" Prince Vale roared.

I grabbed my friend tightly and beat my wings, hoping they were strong enough to hold us both. To my surprise, we rose, but we didn't make it far off the ground before Prince Gervais reached us. He leapt and gripped Anna's feet, which dangled below mine and ripped her from my grasp.

"Anna!" I screamed as she hit the ground. The vampire slammed her thin body into the stones and sank his fangs into her neck. "No!"

My wings gave out as my friend thrashed against the vampire and her blood pooled stark red against the snow covering the streets. I plummeted.

Somewhere in the street, a roar sounded. Prince Vale's, I thought, though I wasn't certain. I could only focus on Anna below, fighting for her life.

I had to help her, to save her. She was in this mess because of me.

Unthinkingly, my hand dipped to a stake strapped to

my leg, but hidden from view by my long, heavy cloak. I clutched it as I fell.

Before I could use the weapon, Prince Vale and Sir Caelo appeared, glinting blades swiping. They aimed to decapitate Gervais, and although royal vampires were difficult to kill, even they could not withstand that.

The vampire tore himself from Anna's neck and shot down the street, so fast that even to fae sight, he appeared like a blur, and I fell next to Anna. The stake dropped from my hand, and I cupped her cheek. "Anna, are you alive? Please say you're alive."

She wheezed, and my chest tightened.

Behind us, swords clashed. The vampire had pulled his, probably thinking his job would be so much easier if Prince Vale and Sir Caelo just died.

"We need to get out of here."

The bite wound stared back at me, ragged and horrible. Thankfully, vampire venom had a natural clotting effect that mitigated the flow somewhat—enough to where she wasn't already dead. But if we didn't get help, she would be soon. Quickly, I ripped off a part of my shirt and bound it as tightly as I dared around her neck, hoping it would buy her time.

"We need to find somewhere to hide, Anna."

Where, I had no clue. She needed a healer. The castle had many, but it was too far away. Anna would never make it, not on foot. I eyed the remaining horses. Could I get Anna over one and ride her back to the castle?

Stars, what would happen then? I'd have lost my

chance to flee, but that didn't matter now. Not when my friend lost blood. Not when I might lose *her*.

"Anna, I'm going to pick you up and take you to the horse. We're going to find a healer at the castle. We—"

"W–w-ood-s." Anna forced the word out and placed a trembling hand over mine.

She wasn't thinking clearly. The moment we left the city, she'd only have me and I would be unable to heal or help her.

"We can't," I retorted. "I'll lose you, and then I'll die. I—"

"You're going to die anyway, you worthless piece of slave trash."

I twisted around fast, and my heart stopped. Prince Gervais had landed blows to both Prince Vale and Sir Caelo, filling the air with the tang of blood. Both faeries staggered to their feet, but the vampire was already closing in.

My eyes darted to the stake I'd dropped before my hand did. Prince Gervais caught the motion, and he blurred to it, kicked it down the street. "No more of that. No more fighting your fate. I've waited long enough for you."

His hand shot out, wrapped around my neck, and he lifted me so that we were eye-to-eye. My legs kicked as it became harder to breathe. "Pity it had to end this way. I do love a wildcat. We might have had fun."

He bared his fangs. This was my last chance. Prince Vale and Sir Caelo remained too far away to be of help. I had only one chance, but if the prince saw me move too early, my chance would evaporate. I waited until the moment he sunk his fangs into my skin, slowly, deliberately, so I'd feel every bit of the pain. I waited until he pulled his first drink and moaned with delight in getting to feast on my blood.

My hand shot down to my other holster. The second stake was still there, ready and waiting. I gripped it tightly, fighting through the shooting pains of my neck and ripped it up. I struck below Prince Gervais's left rib and pushed the stake into his heart.

Fangs tore from my neck, and I screamed as the vampire released me. I fell right on top of Anna, who let out a gurgling whine of pain.

I rolled, hoping I hadn't done more damage to her, all the while grabbing at my neck to staunch the flow. I came to a stop just in time to witness Prince Vale relieve the vampire's head from his neck.

Blood spurted out, covering my face, my chest, and Prince Vale's legs. The vampire's head rolled away as the rest of his body slumped on the ground. But I didn't get to focus on the vampire for long because the next moment, Prince Vale stood in front of me, covered in blood with a wicked cut on his face.

"Let me see the wound."

Slowly, I lifted my fingers from the bite marks.

He exhaled. "A relatively clean exit. Here."

The prince knelt and wiped vampire blood off me and rubbed it on my neck, then wiped again and brought his hand to my lips. "I have no cup, so you have to lick it.

You need to ingest the blood. Between his blood and your healing abilities, it will seal your wounds quickly. The stars granted you luck that he didn't tear an artery, or even that much skin, on his way out."

Disgusted, but knowing he was right because I could already feel the vampire blood working topically, I licked his hand until there was no blood on it. The magic in the vampire's blood worked with my own and the skin of my neck grew hot as it healed rapidly.

"The skin is sealed," Prince Vale said and exhaled. "Those bastards are nasty, but their blood certainly is good for something."

"Thank you," I rasped, aware of how lucky I was to not only have vampire blood at my disposal, but powerful Laurent blood. All vampire blood could heal, but the royals' blood was the most potent.

"You'd already killed him. I just wanted to pay him back." Prince Vale had murder in his eyes. "That son of a harpy deserves to die ten more times for what he's done."

"Agreed. But I feel fine, and I can talk." Each word was coming out stronger and easier, so I must actually be fine. Or as fine as one could be given the circumstances.

"You look well enough." He pivoted to Anna. "However, even if she ingests some vampire blood, we need to get her to a real healer. She's human and doesn't have our rapid healing. I know of a discreet one close by."

I nodded, thankful that, at the very least, we wouldn't have to return to the castle, but when I took Anna in this time, my breath stilled. Her eyes had closed, and her chest fluttered up and down with shallow breaths. She was deteriorating by the second. Why had I wasted precious seconds allowing Prince Vale to examine me? My friend was human and far more fragile.

"Anna," I whispered. "Stay with us. We're taking you to a healer. We—"

Her chest stopped moving.

CHAPTER 42

I ce flew through my veins.

"*Anna!*" Tears streaked down my cheeks, and I flung my torso onto hers, gripping my best friend's body. "You can't leave me. We're going to escape. We're going to be *free*!"

Sobs wracked my body. She deserved so much more. I had failed her, my best friend, so entirely. After all that I'd been through, the dangers I'd faced, it still wasn't enough to get Anna and me to a better life.

I didn't know how long I held her, but the moment a hand landed on my shoulder, I recognized the feel of it.

"Lady Neve." Vale barely spoke above a whisper. "If you still want to escape, we must go."

"I can't leave her here," I said, unable to look at him. "She's all that I have. She's my sister."

Prince Vale didn't respond right away, and in the absence of his voice and my all-encompassing sobs, new sounds hit my ears.

Frantic talking. *Gossiping.*

I lifted my head, and promptly I wished I had not. No one stood in the street, but a few fae watched us from their windows above.

"They've seen everything," a voice that wasn't the prince's, nor Sir Caelo's spoke from behind me. "As did I."

I stiffened. I didn't recognize the fae above, but I knew that voice. Still clinging to Anna, I turned and found Lord Riis walking toward us. Behind him, Clemencia rode, her porcelain cheeks and nose turned red and tears streaking her face. "My Lady Neve! I didn't tell him a thing, but he guessed!"

"He caught us in his web." I glared at the fae lord. "It isn't your fault, Clemencia."

Lord Riis was the king's spy, his Lord of Tongues. Duty bound him to relay what had happened to the king, and when he did, I felt certain King Magnus would do away with the notion of pawning me off to the noble who promised him the most in return. He'd take revenge on me, on how I'd made him look like a fool, how I'd killed a vampire prince in his city, which would cause strife between the kingdoms. After tonight, King Magnus's fury would be so horrible that I'd probably wish to be made a concubine, rather than suffer whatever fate the king threw at me.

The thought overwhelmed me, and unable to handle it, I turned back to Anna. My hand slid from her arm to her face, and I cupped her cheek. The physical sensation of cracking in half pummeled through me. A wail burst from my lips, and my hands fell to her shoulders as I shook her gently.

"There's no bringing back the dead," Prince Vale said close to my ear. "I'm sorry, Neve."

I squeezed my eyes shut. A cold fire of rage, of despair and guilt, lashed through me one after the other, building such a heat inside me that soon it became too painful. Everything inside me was just *too much*. If there were a way to escape my body, I'd do so happily.

I opted for the next best thing. I opened my eyes to seek any distraction I could, only to find the faintest glow coming from my hands. I gasped.

So, I *hadn't* imagined the glow when the king had been humiliating me. But . . . what did it mean?

Acting on instinct, I looked deep inside, searching for something bigger than me.

Almost instantly, the warmth at my core intensified and my skin prickled.

Stars alive! I *had* felt these sensations before—the heat, the prickling, the fast heartbeat—and not just in the grand dining hall. I'd felt it all when I touched the Drassil tree. On that day, the tree had pushed magic into me, and I'd felt *exactly* like this.

But no sacred tree grew in these streets. Only I knelt here. Roar had said Drassil trees housed the Faetia, ancestral fae souls.

I sucked in a breath of frigid air. Was this my magic coming to life? Were the ancestors pushing for me to use it? Maybe the Faetia were telling me that she wasn't all the way gone. That maybe her soul remained, and somehow, I could bring it back?

The idea, far-fetched though it sounded, took hold of me entirely. After all, I had nothing to lose.

I focused on the heat and directed it into Anna, hoping that, on the most basic level, it would warm her. That warmth meant life. I pushed and pushed and pushed until streams of sweat dripped down my face. I pushed until I trembled, until my head pounded with exertion. And then, when I felt as though I couldn't go any longer, I pleaded to the stars to keep me up. To allow me to save Anna.

I never expected what happened next.

Whispers dancing on the wind filled my ears. I blinked as a cacophony of voices came at me, too much to understand. Exactly like at the Drassil tree. Unlike that day, though, I didn't try to retreat.

Help, I pleaded, and hoped it was the right thing to do. *I need her. Need to bring her back. She's everything to me.*

Suddenly, the voices stopped. Panic rose inside me, but before it could take root someone spoke in my head.

You wish to snatch her from the jaws of death?

That voice . . . It sounded so familiar.

Do you, child?

Yes! I replied, terrified that whoever this was, she'd leave if I didn't answer quickly. *I'll do anything.*

Give anything?

I swallowed. I wasn't a fool. Fae were notorious for making tricky and dangerous deals. I could very well be handing over my own life for Anna's. And yet . . .

Anything, I affirmed.

No living being has this power, the female said, this time sounding as if she wished that I'd reconsider. *I ask once more.*

I'll give absolutely anything.

This whispers sounded again, a roar as the female voice melded with others. Burning moon, how many were there?

The moment I asked the question, the whispers stopped.

The price will be paid in due time, the singular, familiar female voice said.

Before I could respond, the heat that I'd been painstakingly pushing into Anna, began to flow out with ease and a brilliant violet-white light flashed. It seeped from my hands into Anna's chest as snow circled around us in a vicious whirlwind, cutting us off from the the sight of the others.

Were those behind the whispers trying to distract me? Or was this the price, being paid already? Would I die in this tunnel of wind and snow as Anna was reborn?

But then I caught the pulse, the widening of the tunnel, the giving of space. It wasn't threatening me. Or Anna. The release of my power, or use of another's magic, or whatever this was between me and the voices, drew the snow, but it wouldn't hurt us.

Exhaling, I shifted my attention back to Anna. Some color had returned to her cheeks. I checked if she was still bleeding. She wasn't. In fact, the gap on her neck had knitted together.

Pushing harder, more heat flared in my core, rushed up my arms, and out my hands.

But would it be enough?

The answer came an instant later when Anna's chest rose ever so slightly. One breath. The second was fuller, larger, more needy. On the third time, she gasped, and her eyes flew open. They locked on me. Around us, the swirling snow fell to the ground.

"Neve." My name came out as a tremble off her tongue and her hand went to her neck. Though I couldn't see it, I suspected that it was now fine. That whatever I'd done had healed her. "What happened?"

I let go of her, and began to tremble violently. I felt as if I'd run here all the way from the Vampire Court.

"You died," Prince Vale whispered to Anna as he came up behind me and lowered to squat. Seeing that I trembled, he slipped a strong hand beneath my arm so that I didn't collapse on top of my friend. "Neve brought you back."

"She did . . . but how?" Anna positioned herself on her elbows, only to moan and lower herself down again a second later.

"I—I don't know." I forced the false words out, forced myself to stop shaking. I wasn't ready to admit to the others what had happened. Not yet, maybe not ever. Not if it made Anna feel guilty that I'd pay a price for her. I'd pay a million lifetimes for my friend.

"I think your soul was still inside you, and I felt it," I lied. "I had to try to bring you back, so I acted on instinct."

"Interesting, though, right now, that's not the most pressing question." Lord Riis's came closer and looked down at us.

"Lady Neve has never used her power. That seems rather pressing to me." Prince Vale gazed at Lord Riis.

Sir Caelo came to stand by his prince's side, sword at the ready. His bright blue eyes narrowed on Lord Riis.

"Although, I suppose you're right that there are other pressing matters," the prince continued. "Like, why are *you* here, Leyv?"

The Lord of Tongues clapped his hands behind him, and in that posture, he appeared disarmed, though a fae of his standing, raw strength, and cunning was surely anything but. Snow dusted his long red mane, standing out in the moonlight, but no more so than his dark brown eyes. Those shone with an intensity that made dread curl in my belly. Whatever Lord Riis prepared to say next, I wasn't sure I'd like it.

"You ran from my tavern rather quickly, Prince Vale," Lord Riis said. "That was enough to pique my interest. Particularly when you were supposed to be locked away with the lady here and had seemed so ready to savor every moment at the feast. Why in all the nine kingdoms would you leave your rooms for *an ale*? No, it was quite unlike you, my prince."

He gestured to me. "But then Lady Clemencia, Neve's own lady-in-waiting, rode by, reeking of her signature snow lily perfume that my son is wholly obsessed with. She was unable to control her steed and clearly very fearful. With another riderless horse right behind her, I knew something was amiss. I managed to get control of her horse and commanded her to lead me here, and it was a good thing I did. You will need help if you all wish to survive this night."

"As will you," Prince Vale spat back. "You're my father's spy. How can I trust you? Why shouldn't I spill your blood and mingle it with the rest shed here?" He continued to steady me, but one hand shifted to his dagger.

Lord Riis's lips quirked up, ever so slightly. "I serve House Aaberg. Are you not part of that house, too, Prince Vale?"

"Obviously. But you have never worked with me."

"You have never *asked*."

Prince Vale didn't reply, which I had to take meant that Lord Riis spoke the truth. The Warrior Bear had never sought the services of the spymaster.

"Fine . . . Leyv, will you help us? Will you be of service to your prince, rather than the king?" Prince Vale asked the treasonous words with hesitation. "Will you keep my secrets?"

"Yes, I will help you." Lord Riis replied solemnly. "For a price, which we can work out later."

A price. Those words . . . I wanted Prince Vale to deny the Lord of Tongues, but before I could interject, the prince nodded.

"Tell me, Leyv, what do you think we must do to survive this?"

"Word will spread quickly that Lady Neve killed the vampire. Too many common fae saw." Lord Riis waved to the windows above, the same ones I'd seen fae peeking out of.

"There is no avoiding the storm her actions will bring down on the court," the high lord continued. "The Laurents will seek vengeance, and your father will be all too happy to comply. Only one thing would stop him from killing her. Or worse. My plan will buy the lady time for a true escape. Perhaps she can strengthen her magic in that time too, so she will not be so defenseless."

"*Tell us* already," Prince Vale commanded.

"You wish to protect her?" the high lord asked.

"I do." Prince Vale answered without hesitation. "I don't wish her harm and will protect her from the events of this night."

"There is only one way to save her life. You must marry Lady Neve and give her every possible protection. That of your name, your sword, and your strength."

I gasped, and the prince released me as if the Lord of Tongue's words had stung him.

The gesture did not go unnoticed by Lord Riis, but he didn't stop. "You must marry her tonight, before the High Staret of Winter's Realm and as many witnesses as you can muster, so that not even your father can deny the union."

"Riis . . . There has to be another way," the prince said.

"No. She is commonborn. Worse, actually, a slave." Lord Riis stared at me, but I barely noticed. I felt too cold inside, too much like this was a dream. "The only thing that can save her is a shield with the power to stand up to the king. You're one of a handful of fae who are strong enough to do so in this kingdom. But will you?"

For a moment, no one spoke, perhaps no one even breathed. My eyes dropped to Anna, and she seemed to have turned to stone. For a moment, I wished I had too.

"Lady Neve, can you stand up?" Prince Vale asked.

I looked him in his eyes, but they gave away nothing. Clearing my throat, I rose on trembling legs and faced him. "This is crazy, Prince Vale, you don't have to. You—"

He pressed a finger to my lips, and without another word, the Prince of Winter's Realm dropped to one knee and stared up at me. "Neve, will you marry me?"

THE NINE KINGDOMS OF ISILA

The Blood Kingdom - vampire
The Elven Kingdom - elves
The Winter Kingdom - fae of various races
The Autumn Kingdom - fae of various races
The Spring Kingdom - fae of various races
The Summer Kingdom - fae of various races
The Wolvea Kingdom - wolvea shifters
The Dragon Kingdom - dragon shifters

*** Each kingdom is colloquially described as a court, though technically, the court is a specific place or places in the larger kingdom.

Some kingdoms have additional names, such as the Winter Kingdom being called Winter's Realm or the Dragon Kingdom being called the Kingdom of Flame.

THE HIGH NOBILITY OF THE KINGDOM OF WINTER

HOUSE AABERG - ROYAL HOUSE
King Magnus Aaberg
Queen Inga Aaberg née Vagle

Children
Prince Rhistel Aaberg
Prince Vale Aaberg
Princess Saga Aaberg

The royal house is not a part of the Sacred Eight.[1] They do rely heavily on the families of the Sacred Eight but the royal house is distinct from all others.

Before the White Bear's Rebellion, House Aaberg was a member of the Sacred Eight. Since the rebellion House Riis took their place as a reward for loyalty to House Aaberg.

❄

THE SACRED EIGHT FAMILIES OF WINTER'S REALM

* Lord Sten Armenil - Warden of the North - Head of House
* Lady Orla Armenil née Balik
Children

* Marit Armenil - female
* Connan Armenil - male
* Rune Armenil - male
* Tiril Armenil - female
* Jorunn Armenil - female
* Raemar Armenil - male

* Lady Vaeri Ithamai - Warden of the East - Head of House
* Lord Tiarsus Itamai née Skau - deceased
Children

* Hadia Ithamai - female
* Adila Ithamai - female

* Lord Tadgh Balik - Warden of the South - Head of House
* Lady Kilyn Balik née Armenil
Children

* Sian Balik - male
* Baenna Balik - female
* Eireann Balik - female
* Saoirse Balik - female
* Fionn Balik - male
* Garbhan Balik - male - deceased

* Carai Balik - female
* Filip Balik - squire to Prince Vale of House Aaberg - male
* Colm Balik - male

* Lord Roar Lisika - Warden of the West - Head of House

Unmarried

No children

* Lord Leyv Riis - Head of House

Unmarried

Children (only the children at court are included)

* Luccan Riis - male
* Arie Riis - male
* Thantrel Riis - non-binary

* Lord Airen Vagle - Lord of Coin - Head of House
* Lady Eliana Vagle - deceased
Children

* Queen Inga - married to King Magnus Aaberg
* Captain of the Royal Guard Eirwen Vagle - Father to Lady Calpurnia Vagle - his wife has passed to the afterworld
* Fival Vagle - acting lord in their family seat in the midlands - male
* Selah Vagle - married to a wealthy Jarl in the midlands - female

* Lady Nalaea Qiren - Lady of Silks - Head of House
* Lord Virion Qiren née Ithamai - deceased
Children
* Aenesa Qiren - female
* Thalia Qiren - female
* Iro Qiren - female

* Lady Fayeth Virtoris - Lady of Ships - Head of House
* Lord Kailu Virtoris née Oridan, from the Summer Court
Children
* Vidar Virtoris - betrothed to Princess Saga of House Aaberg - male
* Sayyida Virtoris - female
* Njal Virtoris - male
* Amine Virtoris - female

Extinct Greater Houses - All members of these noble houses were killed during the White Bear's Rebellion

House Falk
King Harald's royal house
House Skau
Queen Revna's birth house. She married into House Falk and had six children with King Harald.

THE HIGH NOBILITY OF THE KINGDOM OF WINTER

Beneath the Sacred Eight there are hundreds of lesser houses. These are led by jarls of various territories.

---

1. Prior to the White Bear's Rebellion, the Sacred Eight were actually the Sacred Nine, with House Skau being the ninth member, and House Falk being the royal house.

Also by Ashley McLeo

The Winter Court (Crowns of Magic Universe)

A Kingdom of Frost and Malice

A Lord of Snow and Greed

A Hallow of Storm and Ruin

A Crown of Ice and Fury

Coven of Shadows and Secrets (Crowns of Magic Universe)

Seeker of Secrets

Hunted by Darkness

History of Witches

Marked by Fate

Kingdoms of Sin

Bound by Destiny

Standalone Novels

Curse of the Fae Prince (The Spring Court: Crowns of Magic Universe)

Spellcasters Spy Academy Series (Magic of Arcana Universe)

A Legacy Witch: Year One

A Marked Witch: Internship

A Rebel Witch: Year Two

A Crucible Witch: Year Three

The Spellcasters Spy Academy Boxset

The Wonderland Court Series (Magic of Arcana Universe)

Alice the Dagger

Alice the Torch

The Bonegate Series - A Fanged Fae sister series

Hawk Witch

Assassin Witch

Traitor Witch

Illuminator Witch

The Bonegates Series Boxset

The Royal Quest Series

Dragon Prince

Dragon Magic

Dragon Mate

Dragon Betrayal

Dragon Crown

Dragon War

ABOUT THE AUTHOR

Ashley lives in the lush and green Pacific Northwest with her husband, their dog, and the house ghost that sometimes makes appearances in her charming, old home.

When she's not writing fantasy novels she enjoys traveling the world, reading, kicking butt at board games, and frequenting taquerias.

For all the latest releases and updates, subscribe to Ashley's newsletter, The Coven. You can also find her Facebook group, Ashley's Reader Coven.